the light among the shadows

Lily B. Art

Contents

I dedicate this tale to the
Light of my life.

Prologue *Brenda*

"I am a spokesman for Uxaar, the Shadow God!" The intruder's voice pierces the cacophony of the crowd's cries. I've never encountered this man before. The man's brawny build towers high above the two guards beside him. His chaotic red curls, constructed into a bun, face me. Surely, I would have recognized him if I had seen him in the past. His outlandish accent also proves him a foreigner. "On a mission to retrieve Syann, the Goddess of Light! She's been discreetly living among you, but tonight, the stars will reveal her on this very stage, as the prophecy states! Syann is one of the women we display before you!"

My capture, along with that of these other women, quelled the fear that this attack was connected to Syann's prophecy. Athena revealed that the goddess was an eighteen-year-old female among us, and that her true identity would be unveiled tonight. I didn't want to believe her.

My broad eyes scan the crowd, searching for my family, Liam, or even Athena. However, the public rioting obstructs my view. The air storms with the clamor of protests for the women's freedom.

"Brenda!" Liam belts in anguish. He staggers as he cuts through the chaos. His father, Byron, precedes him to the barrier of armed intruders guarding the stage.

The intruder raises his voice, challenging the volume of the crowd. "We've taken every suspect captive, every eighteen-year-old female among you! Momentarily, we will watch as the stars reveal her identity!" Despite the power in his voice, he sounds as if he's reciting a rehearsed speech. His words are spaced out and stiff. Nevertheless, his message is empowering enough to send a shiver down my spine.

Byron is permitted to enter the stage and stomps his way up the steps. "I don't know who you think you are, but you are unwelcome here!" Unafraid, our governor barges toward the redhead, who is easily a foot taller than Byron and armed. If only I could say I was as fearless as Byron. "Not only have you interrupted our cherished festival, but worse, you have also assaulted our dear women! You and your men will leave Seren at once, or there will be hell to pay!"

The redhead hesitates, as if he's contemplating Byron's order. He's trembling and puffing for air, but why? "Get off this stage while you still can, Byron. Uxaar is not a god of mercy," he warns our leader.

"Spare me your absurdities! I'm not budging until you free our daughters and flee far away from here!" Byron demands through gritted teeth.

The intruder fidgets in place, his attention diverted from Byron. Someone else has captured it, yet his wavering eyes fail to meet anyone visible. It's as if he's watching a ghost. Whatever this phantom is, it instills terror in him.

The intruder retreats from Byron, but the guard behind lunges at him. A blade pierces Byron's chest, releasing an oozy red liquid that churns my stomach. I stare in horror, unable to look away. If I stare intently enough, will the atrocities cease? Will I awaken from this nightmare? Beads of sweat cascade down my face, yet my mouth is as dry as a desert.

The redhead's body trembles violently. His wide eyes reflect a deep sense of dread. Is he equally horrified by Byron's lifeless body, slumped over and slain by the sword?

An unruly crowd stands before us. Liam struggles against the guards to reach his father before the townspeople drag him away. My father, as pale as a sheet, stands like a distant statue. The rest of my family must've fled home, like many others are now.

The redhead and his men approach me and the hostages. Are we next in line to die? Hot tears stream down my cheeks as I puff through the cloth swathing my mouth.

"Quiet!" Byron's murderer roars at the crowd, who hushes at once. Pleased, he chuckles as he pivots toward the hostages behind him. "Ladies, I am a spokesman for Uxaar the Shadow God. You may not be able to see him, but I promise he is as present here as I am! He sees all and has been pristinely observing each of you to prepare for your capture. There's no escape! Your options now are allying with Uxaar by the Shadow Incantation or matching your fate with your former, weak leader, Byron Asbury. So, who will be the first competent one to accept Uxaar's offer?"

No response follows.

Byron's assassin carries himself with pride on the stage, which I find much more intimidating than the impressive build of the redhead. I question why he wasn't the primary messenger to begin with, as well as his association with the redhead. Their accents aren't alike.

"No takers?" He clicks his tongue through an amused grin. "Well, then, Uxaar chooses you first, Brenda Fields."

My heart clenches at that name. My name.

"Uxaar has observed you, oh so closely. You're an intelligent, confident, and spirited woman. He has faith you have the intuition to heed my words." He removes the gag around my mouth, to allow me to speak.

"If Uxaar has watched my life closely as you say, he'd know

I'd never follow you!" I spit at his feet. "Especially for killing my future father-in-law, you monster!"

The guard finds my outburst amusing. His arched eyebrow rises as a challenged grin spreads on his narrow face. "Only to make an example, my dear. No one defies Uxaar without consequence. However, Uxaar understands humans withhold the compassion and soul that the Geron lacked. So, I will offer a deal to you, Brenda. If you say the Shadow Incantations, Uxaar will reverse the death of Byron and ensure no harm ensues upon Liam or your family."

"How should I know you have the ability to resurrect Byron?"

"Brenda, you have your heart closed off from the power of magic and have a foolish sense of denial! Do not doubt Uxaar or the power of the Underealm or Secreth, as you disregarded the warnings of Athena. This is no game. You either say the Incantations and Byron lives, or you refuse, and we kill you and all those you hold dear! Starting with her!" His blade points toward my cousin, and the guard behind her grabs her restraints and bears their sword up to her neck.

"No! Brenda, don't!" Sophie belts once her gag falls out of her mouth.

My cousin faces death's doorway. If I don't say the Incantations, we die. If I do say it, I might save Byron, but at what cost? My soul and the lives I'll endanger? All I can think to do is stall for time.

"What would I even say?" If I were to agree to say the Incantations, I'm unfamiliar with the words. I only know that if I say them, I'm selling myself away to a Geron. He would be able to take full control of me.

A different guard hands me a piece of writing carved into a deep purple crystal tablet. The tablet is as coarse and chilling as the murderer himself. Does this crystal possess magical properties? I'm certain these words audibly hiss in the air as I read them.

Set yourself free,
take over me,
Use me to make you higher,
In me have your way,
You get the say,
Do with me as you desire.

"After you recite these words, you will enter a brief meditative out-of-body state. There, you will select which Geron you'll bond with. So, what will be your choice? I've given you more than enough time to decide."

Sentencing myself is one thing, but my family, my loved ones? I can't. If Uxaar is real, Syann must be, too. I'll have to say these Incantations, hoping she'll save me and this town.

"I'll do it! Let her go!"

"Say it first!" the intruder demands. "Then she'll be free!"

I can't bear to listen to Sophie cry anymore. The words of the Incantations spill from my mouth. The more I say, the faster the words expel. Slowing down is impossible. It's as if I'm vomiting uncontrollably.

As the spokesman described, my surroundings are no longer visible. A hazy light surrounds me instead. Within this light is an army of odd creatures. The Geron.

They're not human at all—neither is their appearance amusing, as was Jace's costume at Athena's play. These creatures are *demons.* They have charred bones for armor and two large angular eyes, which are traditionally discolored. The pupils glow white, the sclera is pitch-black, and their irises illuminate unique neon colors. Their lashes are long, white, and made of jagged skin. Their upper lips are large, gray, and sit above a row of fangs that outline their jaws. Two sets of rounded downward horns crown their heads. Their hair burns aflame, and this flame cascades into a great cape. They lack clothing, revealing their jagged rib cages like tree roots intertwined. Instead of entrails, there's nothing but flame inside. This flame extends far below their rib cages, allowing them to levitate instead of walk. Each one says their name simultaneously, yet somehow, I can comprehend each name.

Uxaar's name is striking. His eyes and hair radiate an intense neon blue. His jawline and chin are the most elongated and robust I've ever seen. I must say one of their names, and it won't be his.

Something unexplainable in me tells me to say another's name. The urge is powerful and impossible to ignore, like the need to vomit. "Roe!"

Bright light swallows my surroundings, until it dims away and I'm back on the stage. To my horror, the ghosts the redhead was so scared of now surround me. My eyes are now open to a supernatural realm I couldn't previously envision. The intruders were repeating words that the crowd couldn't hear, being Uxaar's spokesmen as they claimed they were.

Ahead of me is a Geron with scarlet-flame hair and neon-green eyes. Glowing freckles make his cheeks appear like the night sky. This creature, Roe, forces a sensation like no other onto me. He crashes into me, and it stings as if I've face-planted into a lake. Instead of Roe bouncing off, he absorbs into me like I'm a body of water. The violating sensation thrusts a loud whimper from me.

On all fours, I dry heave profusely. The intruders are asking if it worked. The redhead says I'll be subject to the Geron's power once the stars fall.

Far out above the mountains, a bright light appears in the sky. Erupting from the light, smaller, glimmering stars pass through the atmosphere. These shooting stars crash onto the stage one after another, forming a circle of fading light around my body.

The women and the terrorists all lie unconscious in the wreckage. I'm unharmed by the flash of light, but my hands glow as brilliantly as starlight.

A radiant light that hovers over the mountain snags my eye. This star is more luminous than any star I've ever seen.

"Go and free Secreth, Syann," Roe says like a thought in my mind.

1 *Brenda*

Little do I know that my pressing fear about the Festival of the Stars will pale in comparison to the reality that awaits me.

This morning, I overheard Liam asking my parents for their blessing to receive my hand in marriage. Since he has acquired my father's approval, he intends to propose to me under the falling stars.

The shooting stars that will alter life as I know it.

What on earth am I thinking? Any woman in Seren would rightly think I'm daft for doubting accepting his proposal. How could it be more perfect? The most handsome and eligible bachelor in Seren, kneeling before me as the stars race as fast as my heart? Any woman in my position wouldn't hesitate to give the obvious answer—*yes*.

This is the answer I plan to give Liam, regardless of my doubts.

I've regretfully come to terms with the fact that the boy who had captured my heart long ago is gone, and that my childish dreams of reuniting with him are no longer feasible. In the end, Liam offers me exactly what I desire—a family of my own and a partner to share life with. While I may see him more as a friend than a lover, out of all the men in our small town, Seren, there is no one I would rather marry than Liam.

Why risk losing all I hope for, waiting for the one who will never return? No, I'll do everything in my power to avoid ending up alone at all costs.

I go on a walk to clear my mind. Perhaps I can find someone outside my family to confide in about the proposal. My parents can't know that I eavesdropped on their conversation with Liam. I have to play my part, to give everyone the element of anticipation they long for.

The cobble-stone streets are adorned with banners, wreaths, and lanterns, while everyone has dressed in their finest attire for the festival.

I'm no exception. A white silk dress drapes to my ankles. Over it, I wear a green corset adorned with gold embroidery on its cap sleeves. The corset has a skirt of the same color that splits in the front and only extends to knee length. I reserve this corset for special occasions such as festivals and weddings. To complement the dress, I braid my long hair into a half-up, half-down updo. Instead of wearing one of the flower crowns I'm distributing for the festival, I incorporate flowers into my braids.

I approach the town square, an ideal place to lighten my basket of flowers. There, a nearby shout demands attention. "Gather 'round everyone! In five minutes, our performance will begin!"

A wooden stage stands in the square. I've never seen a stage performance at the festivals before. A crowd gathers to listen to a middle-aged woman on the platform. She has a hefty build, dark skin, a wide-swooped nose, lively brown eyes, and coils of black hair tied back with a bandana. This woman, Athena, hosts the horse races at her stables annually. Interestingly, I never cross paths with her except during the festival.

Behind the stage, two tents are set up, and people in costumes surround them. My curiosity lures me closer to the sight. Someone I never expected to see beside the tents, in costume, is Elouise, the town carpenter's granddaughter. He must enjoy spoiling her with fanciful wooden pendants, as one always dangles from the chain around her neck.

Elouise, my friend, is a rare sight. It's been months since we last spoke. Occasionally, I catch a glimpse of her in town. Her older brother, Jace, the carpenter's apprentice, watches her like a hawk. Whenever I invite Elouise to my place, he turns down my invitations for her half the time, if she doesn't first. So, she's only visited my home twice in the three years I've known her. Both times, she appeared uneasy, as if she felt under surveillance. Consequently, I stopped inviting her. Like Athena, she's enigmatic and elusive. Despite this, she was the ideal person to confide in about my fears regarding Liam's proposal.

Elouise notices my approach and enthusiastically embraces me. I return the gesture the best I'm able while holding my basket.

Her floor-length lace gown, as light as her skin, has sleeves that extend to her fingertips. The trimming is gold, matching the costume tiara on her head.

"I've never seen a stage play at a festival before!" I say.

"Yes! We've been working on it for a while now. Oh!" she interjects with a wide smile. "And Jace is playing a part, too. His costume is hilarious! Come see!" Elouise takes my hand and leads me behind the stage, revealing Jace's costume.

She wasn't exaggerating about the humor in it. Blue-and-white face paint outlines his green eyes, while gray paint covers what would be his olive-toned skin. His long-sleeved shirt and cape, extending from his back, match the gray pigment. A brass necklace and bangles embrace his neck and wrists, while a leather belt cinches his waist, securing a long white—skirt? Fluffy fabric hangs to his ankles. It all seems bizarre with his tall and bulky frame. I imagine he's aware of that.

"Oh my—Jace! What have they done to you?" I laugh.

"I can't fathom how I was talked into this." He rolls his eyes.

"Who are you playing?" I'm even more curious when other people in matching costumes exit the tent. The paint color around the eyes varies.

"Uxaar, the Shadow God," Jace replies begrudgingly. His answer confuses me. Elouise tries to clarify, but Athena summons her to the stage.

I make my way to the growing audience and find a seat on the stone wall that hems the square.

The play commences with Athena gracing the stage. Her expansive, gap-toothed smile remains steadfast as she extends a warm welcome and gratitude to the audience for their attendance. "Today, we share with you the tale of truth—the origins of humanity, our town under the stars we know as Seren, and a place that we don't know, Secreth—the realm of Light!"

The curtains part, revealing a painted backdrop of a radiant castle. On center stage stands a long, gold-painted crate. Elouise lies peacefully on the box, as if in a deep sleep. Behind her stands, in the shape of an arc around Elouise, several more people dressed in costumes similar to Jace's. "Long live Syann! Long live the Goddess of Light!" they chant.

"It all began with the power of Light, bringing our universe to be. It was once unrecognizable from the universe we know. No bad thing, evil, death, or pain existed. That was, until the power of Darkness came within the shadow of the Light. It swept through the universe and disrupted the peace. These two powers opposed a war over Earth that ended in a draw. It left a balance between the two powers within this world, known now as the Dusk realm. This balance created our way of life, day and night, warmth and cold, sickness and health, and birth and death. After death, spirits would drift into the Underealm, the realm of Darkness. Until one day, the first-ever spirit crossed into the realm of Light instead, a baby girl who had never committed an act of Darkness. The power of Light enchanted the babe's spirit, choosing her to be its form. She was called Syann, the Goddess of Light!"

Elouise, a portrayal of grace, rises to her feet. "I am Syann, the Goddess of Light. My Light, which preceded me, created a kingdom within the Light realm called Secreth. A secret Earth far out of Darkness's reach. Secreth is a land of no death, evil, or exhaustion, but of peace, immortality, and joy. This is the life I intended for those on Earth to have before the Darkness came. I yearn to allow those beyond my realm to live here, where Darkness won't reach them. With the power of the Altar of Light, I can rid the nature of Darkness that is within them. So, I command the guardians of this land, the great and powerful Geron, to do the undone. To venture beyond the borders of Secreth to the outcasts of the Dusk realm and bring them into Secreth."

Athena recounts how Syann would say the sacred Incantations of Light while a human lay on the Altar of Light, purifying them from Darkness and elevating them to an immortal state akin to hers. Following their cleansing, they were granted the privilege of residing in Secreth. Over time, Secreth became a haven for a substantial population of humans, thanks to the benevolent Geron who facilitated their arrival. Secreth flourished, and a harmonious coexistence endured for centuries.

Elouise bids an audience with the lead guardian, Jace, accompanied by two more Geron actors beside him, and they arrive in Elouise's presence. "Uxaar, Captain of the Geron," Elouise speaks. "I request that you and your league depart beyond the border to bring in more outcast humans."

"With all due respect, my goddess—" Jace replies. "The population of humans in Secreth is already generous. If we persist in fetching more, the creatures of Secreth's kind will fear a takeover of Darkness in our land."

"I haven't heard of such concerns, Uxaar. Our land is at peace and will continue flourishing. Do I not have the power to surpass the Darkness, and to extend our borders? All will be at peace. Now send your league at once."

"It will be done as you commanded, oh goddess Syann." Jace bows his head, turning around to the Geron behind him. "You heard her, fellow Geron! Let us go at once!" Jace exits with the others through a sheet prop, representing a portal. Jace and his league gather in front of a forest backdrop. "My trusted allies. What will become of Secreth if we continue to fetch more humans? Another Earth, rich in Darkness and deceit from human nature? I won't have it!" Jace roars. "The goddess claims to be the incarnation of the power of Light. It can't be. She's a human! And as corrupt as the rest of them. Syann only cares for those beyond our borders when it should be the opposite. Therefore, we must free Secreth of humanity by conquering her!"

"How will we do this?" A Geron actor asks. "Syann is far mightier than us."

"We must prove to her the true hell that humans possess. Syann is the Goddess of Light. She will not be able to withstand the Darkness—Bring me two children! One male and female, and we will expose the secrets of their Darkness within. We will take them outside the borders of Secreth, in a den hidden in the Dawn realm. There I will uncover their mysteries."

"On a hunt for answers, Uxaar manipulated the children through spells, physical harm, and torture. Successfully, Uxaar seized the children's minds with these methods," Athena narrates. "In the process, Uxaar ventured depths no Geron had with their power, traversing the line between Light and Darkness. Parallel to when the pure human spirit passed from Darkness to Light and created Syann, Uxaar crossing the line from Light to Darkness made the Darkness consume Uxaar and their every intention of guarding the Light. Uxaar, with their new title, the Shadow God, had the authority to use the Shadow of the sacred Incantations.

Any human who recited these Incantations became Uxaar's Shadow, giving Uxaar the ability to possess their minds and use their power of destruction through their body. Uxaar granted all the Geron who followed him the ability to have Shadows of their own, as long as a human said the Shadow Incantations on his behalf. Many Geron succeeded, and as expected between the Dark Geron and their Shadows, the Great War broke out in Secreth. Numerous humans within Secreth were deceived into saying the Incantations and joining the Geron's forces, and one-third of the Geron forces joined Uxaar's side. Syann was his target, but with her power and the remaining loyal Geron, she made her way to the altar. There, she expelled the Darkness from Secreth by lying on it."

The wooden altar prop rolls onto the stage at the queue of Athena's words. Elouise lies on it and declares through the ruckus of war occurring on stage, "I release the power of Light from my form! For the good of Secreth! And the unraveling of Darkness!"

Jace and the other Geron performers plummet to the ground, their human counterparts freed. The curtain falls as Athena paces briskly to the center of the stage. "When Syann lay on the altar, she fell into stasis. This way, the power of Light diminished the Darkness from Secreth. The Light sealed the borders of Secreth away so Darkness could never lurk in again, and it exiled the Geron who betrayed Syann to the Underealm for a thousand years. After those years passed, the vile creatures crept into the Dusk and Dawn realm like shadows. Here, they were unnoticed as ghosts. While in the Dawn, the prevailing Light uncovered their presence. Syann knew they would escape in time, so she condemned them as powerless spirits. The only way the Geron could recover their lost power was for a human to recite the Shadow Incantations on their behalf. Then that human would become their vessel of power. So unsaid, the Incantations remained for over a millennium after the war. The humans who bonded to the Dark Geron were also exiled from Secreth, for

Syann was not awake to cleanse them. So, the power of Light guided these humans in the form of a star, which led to our town, Seren. The Light created this town for us until Syann returns and left us with this prophetic message on a stone in this very square."

Elouise enters through the curtains beside Athena and speaks, *"When the Darkness casts its Shadow on Earth, Syann will return in her earliest form through the stars to balance it. For eighteen years, the stars will mask Syann and the Shadow for the balance to remain. Once revealed, the two will wage the final war against Light and Darkness over Earth. In the end, Secreth's gates will open wide, and the Dusk realm will bleed into Night."*

"This prophecy was etched here in the town square for over millennia. During the first shower, the engravings vanished along with everyone's memories of them through the power of Light. This protected Syann's identity from Uxaar and his Shadow when the stars first fell eighteen years ago. As the prophecy stated, Syann would return when the Shadow Incantations were said again. She returned through the falling stars, in her earliest form, a babe. These stars have protected us by disabling the Geron's use of power through their human Shadows until Syann is of age to fight for us. The last of the stars fall tonight! So, we must beware! If Uxaar attacks, do not sell your soul by saying the Incantations! Uxaar is coming with their Shadow with the intent to destroy us all. This I know! I own writings of this history, which have kept the memory alive in me," Athena claims. "According to the contents of the writings, tonight the prophecy will pass!"

Many murmurs rise within the crowd at these bold statements. People rightly question how Athena can recall Syann's prophecy while no one else can, or her assertion that the stars have only fallen eighteen times. Everyone has always claimed that they fall annually, and I've always believed them. Although I'm only eighteen years old, the claims from those I trust that the stars have always fallen are sufficient for me.

Angry explosions of voices challenge her words. The crowd

is right—how could she claim such things? If she had writings, wouldn't other people have them, too? And if they do exist, who's to say they are legitimate?

Seren has always been a haven, a small village in the middle of nowhere. Why would she dare disrupt our peace over controversial lore? Surely no real danger is headed toward us.

"Be aware! Please listen!" Athena begs throughout the commotion. "Syann could be any eighteen-year-old woman among us! She is in disguise! When Syann reveals herself, Uxaar and the Geron will bring the dangers the prophecy told us of. Again, I warn you now to stay strong and observant! Do not recite the Shadow Incantations or give in to the Geron's threats! Instead, prepare yourself for Syann's return and our welcoming to Secreth! Thank you!" Athena vanishes through the curtains, dodging the roaring crowd. It isn't long until a council member of the town scurries onto the stage and instructs people to calm down and go about their business.

I make my way backstage, catching Elouise before she goes into the tent. She turns toward me with a wary glint in her eyes.

"I'm supposed to hand out all these flower crowns before the feast starts. I want to gift these to the cast of the play." I offer her one out of the basket.

The glint in her eyes sparkles as she smiles. "Thank you, Brenda! That's so kind of you! The crowd's reaction wasn't what we were hoping for, so this means a lot to me." Elouise puts a flower crown on her head.

"I think some people just took it a little too seriously."

"And you don't? The story should be taken seriously! Have you never heard Syann's prophecy before?"

"I can't say I have. Even after hearing it, I'm unsure I believe it, to be frank with you. It was offensive to hear Athena suppose I could be a goddess in disguise, but you agree with her? It's a preposterous thought!"

"I believe Syann is here among us. She must be!" Elouise's

tone turns downcast again, as if something is eating her up inside.

"Is something the matter?"

She bites her lip as if to conceal her answer from me, but she nods. "If Syann isn't real, then there's no hope anymore. I need her—I need her to exist!" Her eyes cloud. "If she doesn't—my brother could die."

Perplexed, I furrow my brows. "Jace?"

She sighs heavily. "Brenda, I've been dishonest with you. And I want to start by apologizing."

"Dishonest about what?"

She scans around, as if she's making sure no one is spying, but Jace is walking our way. Elouise freezes until he approaches us.

"Elouise! It's ti—" He catches his tongue. "What's wrong?"

I observe her brother quickly. Jace doesn't seem ill—if anything, quite the opposite. His burly arms and legs implicate his strength, surely from his consistent labor with lumber. The eye contact with his sister casts out alertness and care. Is there something more I'm not seeing?

"Nothing. We need to go home now?" Elouise asks. She seems more drained than her brother is. The defense she displayed in our conversation has diminished into defeat against her older brother. Emotions are taking a toll on her, and thanks to Jace, I won't have a clue why.

"Yes, we can change out of our costumes there, all right? Mum is awaiting us," he says softly, before turning to me. "Brenda, my apologies for the interruption, but we must go. You have my gratitude for watching the play."

"You're welcome." I nod.

I shouldn't be surprised. Jace consistently interrupts our conversations, which is why Elouise and her family are such a riddle to me. Any time I think I'm going to learn something new about her, Jace swoops her away.

Whatever Elouise lied to me about, is Jace in on it?

Is he really *dying?*

I'm not sure, but I have my own problems to deal with. Instead of seeking solace in someone else's opinion about Liam, I should confront the issue head-on.

2 Oren

It's no surprise I couldn't keep my breakfast down again. Should I consider it lunch since it was past noon when I ate it? Since it was my first meal after waking up, it's still breakfast, right? All I know is the familiar foul taste that glazes my tongue. Swishing a mouthful of water to rinse it away is futile.

Sitting in my lap is a bucket of vomit. I've got a bucket solely dedicated for me to vomit in since it's an unpleasantly common occurrence.

Shakily, I extend my free arm to grasp the carved wooden rod resting between my mattress and desk. I pin this crutch to the ground with my left arm and use it to efficiently incline onto my feet. If I rise too quickly, I'm certain I'll black out. The room is already whirling before my eyes. If only closing my eyes could stop the dizziness.

I trudge sluggishly enough through the house for my vision to remain. This effort turns fruitless once I step outside the back door. The afternoon sky is clear and bright, obscuring my vision with spots, like a partly cloudy night displaying the stars. These spots fade, exposing a woman clothed in a blue blouse and black skirt. She launders clothing by the creek with a washboard. Above her are clothes drying on twine hitched between two oak trees.

This woman is my mum. Even without seeing her face, her brunette locks bound in a bun make her identity clear. The only other female in the house is my sister, whose hair is black like mine.

She doesn't notice me hobbling toward her until my cough exposes me. "Oren?" Her closing footsteps shuffle through the green grass. Her eyes, the same color, dart toward my bucket, then spitefully toward me. Her delicate, thin brows furrow, revealing the light wrinkles on her olive skin. The nostrils of her thin, bridged nose flare until the tension in her face dissipates into a dissatisfied sigh. "Are you emptying the bucket again?"

I don't need to hear her tone or see her face to know she's irritated. She's instructed me countless times to ask her or my siblings to take the bucket out for me if I need help. I never listen.

"How often do I tell you to call for someone to help take it out for you?"

I've lost count. Mum knows this, too, so there's no point in answering her question. "I'm s'rry." I attempt to apologize. "Y-y-you weren't inside—I-I-I thought s-some fresh air w-w-would be good."

Her sigh harbors the same guilt I feel. "No, I'm sorry. The laundry doesn't do itself. You were asleep when I last checked on—never mind. I'll make you some tea... Would you like to stay out here? You mentioned needing fresh air."

I nod, signaling her to assist me in sitting against the oak tree. Unfortunately, I'm unable to reciprocate her help with the laundry, as she would refuse my assistance.

Mum rinses out the bucket downstream and trails into the house with it. The sight of her triggers a pang of self-contempt. She shouldn't have to deal with me this way. Even now, she's missing the Festival of the Stars to watch me, likewise with every festival since our family moved here from my grandparents' farm. That was nearly five years ago.

Mum insists she doesn't mind missing the festival, but she always appears grief-stricken when facing me. Her mind is distant, stuck in the horrors of the past and the fate that awaits me. Her sunken eyes and trembling hands constantly expose her fear that her youngest son is on the brink of death. Despite all her efforts to help over the years—from physicians, healers, and medicines from apothecaries—her attempts have proven ineffective against my symptoms. Mum is convinced that she has failed me, and I can sense that pressure crushing her. That mutual guilt stifles talk between us.

She's right to distance herself, as I am with her. It's inevitable in my shape that I'll die prematurely. My mother had already lost my father long ago. I was too young to remember him as an infant when he passed away, and she refuses to speak about it. Instead, she built impenetrable walls that were too high to climb and too strong to break. After numerous failed attempts to ask about my father, I realized that she wouldn't let anyone pass through her defenses. So, I watched as those walls rose higher and higher, accepting that the loss of my father had shattered her heart beyond repair.

Can I blame her? Of course not. Loss has marked me, too. I grieve the life I lived with my grandparents, who I loved immensely. They raised me and were like parents to me. Losing them tossed me into a spiral. I've never been able to see straight since experiencing it. Is it because I'm still spinning, or is it unrelenting dizziness?

Since moving, I've succumbed to my illness and have never entered town. I've accepted towering walls of my own that are an incident away from collapsing on me. My body hurts to live in. My heart aches, my head aches, everything aches. *I don't want to ache anymore.*

I crave peace. Is death the path to achieve permanent oblivion from pain? Death's hand has been persistently reaching out for me, and I've grown tired of resisting it. Would it be easier to take its hand and surrender? Or do I take the example from my family and keep fighting? I'm never certain.

Mum would never resort to cowardice. She endures her suffering, ensuring that my siblings and I are well cared for. If only I could reciprocate her kindness like my siblings do. Instead, I feel like a burden to her. She has always taken care of me, never the other way around. I suppose I would be doing my family a favor if I died, but there's one reason why I'd never willingly offer death my hand. That *reason* is walking through the back door now—my twin sister.

"Oren!" Elouise announces through a bubbly smile. A crown of flowers rests on her braided hair, which pairs nicely with her yellow dress.

Our brother Jace trails right behind Mum. Both my siblings seem surprised by my presence, which is understandable. I seldom venture out of my room, so it's a mutual surprise to see them here. On the festival day, Elouise and Jace are usually out all day. Why would they return so soon?

Jace approaches me, holding a steaming cup of mint tea. "Mum made you this. Be sure to thank her," he whispers with hostility.

"I w-w-will," I stutter defeatedly, not meeting his harsh eyes. However, I have a hard time ignoring the gray paint smudged over his skin. It must have been for the festival play.

Jace has loathed me for as long as I can remember, for reasons out of my control. Initially, he was jealous of my close bond with Elouise, while my siblings are borderline incompatible with each other. Then, when my accident impaired my ability to contribute with the farm, Jace lashed out at me for Grandpa overworking himself to death, and Grandma dying less than a week later. The loss of them hardened Jace, forcing him to assume the role of the man of the house. All his childlike qualities vanished. Sure, Jace is twenty-three now and nowhere near a child, but he never felt like a brother. Instead, he's failing miserably at trying to be the father we never had. Only Grandpa was able to fill that void in my heart.

Jace approaches the creek to wash off the paint. Elouise takes his place in front of me, her full lips curling into a smile. "I missed you!" She kneels at my side, not hesitating to embrace me.

I grin back at her. "I m-m-missed y', too, Elly."

She's my light. I couldn't bear to subject her to more grief than she's already known. I know firsthand how debilitating grief is. It killed Grandma. She refused to eat or leave the house after Grandpa passed, and no one could coax her to smile before she died. Since then, I've never been able to eat well or escape the quarantined lifestyle I've made for myself. If I died, would it be the last straw for Elouise to become like me or Mum? Lost in grief, pondering the ghosts our family has become? Elouise's grief would haunt me in the afterlife, even if it were heaven.

"Are you feeling all right today? I haven't seen you out here in some time."

I shake my head. "D-d-do you really have t-t-to ask?"

She sighs sadly before her smile returns. "Well, tonight could be the night that changes! It's the eighteenth star-fall!"

I know exactly what she's referring to, and I dislike it. My sister is in denial, refusing to believe my illness will kill me. To such an extent, she believes in legends of supernatural powers that could come to my aid. Her best friend, Athena, has indoctrinated Elouise in the legend of a goddess named Syann, who is the whole reason the star shower in Seren supposedly happens. On the eighteenth shower, she is supposed to return, which would be tonight, according to Athena. Grandpa always told me the stars have fallen as long as he could remember. I believe my grandpa over Elouise claiming the star's magic has affected everyone's memories. Elouise is so desperate, thinking there's a chance Syann can heal me. I don't believe it.

It breaks my heart that Elouise seeks answers in the most

unexpected places. She feels obligated to provide me with a remedy, even though I never anticipated such a thing from her. Despite my repeated assurances that it's not her fault, she continues to blame herself for my plight. When we were twelve, she suggested we go climb trees in the apple orchard. Little did she know that I would fall and sustain severe injuries to my left leg and head, which resulted in my limp and stutter.

She'd be better off estranging herself from me as Mum and Jace do, but instead, she has dedicated her free time to searching for solutions for me.

"How was th-th-the play?" I ask her, itching to change the subject off Syann, though I'm failing. The play was about the legend of Syann after all, which Athena wrote. Elouise played the role of Syann in the performance.

"So many people showed up!" Her auburn eyes twinkle delightfully. "You wouldn't guess who was one of them! Brenda came to watch!"

The thought of Brenda pains me, a different kind of throbbing that's beyond my physical ailments. It's somehow worse. She's the subject of conversation with Elouise now and then, but I reminisce about Brenda much more often than that. Every day is exact. I even think of her now because of the flowers crowning my sister's head.

Brenda, the only person in town who makes me regret quarantining myself, was my best friend when I lived in the farm village. We met at the age of eight, when she arrived with Seren's importers. On her first day, she introduced herself and asked to play with me. I showed her around the farm stables, where she especially loved the birds. When she left, I longed to see her again. Soon after, we had numerous adventures on the farmland, many of them on horseback. By the age of twelve, I was in love with her, and I'm confident she returned the feeling. However, I fell ill after my accident, and my family relocated when my grandparents passed away. Amidst all these health issues, I never left the new house or saw her again. Our sudden separation contributed to my depression.

Three years after relocating, Elouise mentioned meeting Brenda in town. A pang of longing stirred within me to inform Brenda I was still alive and I missed her. However, I knew it was best to let her go. My condition would only worry her, the same way it affects my family. Brenda was better off without me, and so was everyone else. Consequently, I made a conscious effort to conceal the truth about my disappearance and the fact that Elouise is my sister. I even told Elouise to ensure that Brenda never discovered her surname, Silvius.

Elouise was unaware of my past friendship with Brenda at the time because I never shared it with her. Elouise always did house chores with Mum during import hour at the farm village. I was concerned if Brenda and Elouise met that Brenda would be more interested in playing with another girl her age. I couldn't bear the thought of losing Brenda as a friend.

Elouise did discover our friendship on her own three years ago. Brenda mentioned me to Elouise, admitting she missed me dearly. If Brenda still longs for me now, it can't compare to how I ache for her. It's agonizing to know Brenda has found a significant other, Liam.

Elouise has told me a great deal about that man. Compared to me, he's the full package—tall, dark, handsome, and the governor's son. She's been smitten with him ever since our move. My sister even jokingly suggested that I should return to Brenda so she can be with Liam. My response to Elouise has always been to be happy for Brenda. It would never have worked out between us. If Brenda has moved on, so should I. It's easier said than done.

"I got you a gift from her!" I had already guessed the gift before Elouise revealed it. It was a flower crown from Brenda's family. Back then, Brenda had taught me how to make them using dandelions from the farmland. She also shared that her family had always made them for the Festival of the Stars. Brenda had a way of making the festival sound like an incredible time. She had always hoped I would attend one day, but I never did. My family used to celebrate the festival on the farmland. After moving, I either watched the shower from my window, the front yard, or not at all. Sometimes, I was too unwell to even get out of bed to watch.

Elouise knows the significance of flower crowns to me. She recounts how after the play, Brenda returned to the backstage and presented a basket of crowns to the cast. I'm incredibly grateful that she brought me one.

"Thanks." I'm beaming, the first time I've smiled today.

"You're welcome, Prince Oren of the Flower People," she jokes, and makes an elegant curtsy.

I chuckle as I notice the pastel shades of cream, pink, yellow, violet, and green woven together seamlessly in the crown. I place it on my head to please Elouise, but tonight, I'll remove it and do what I did with the last flower crown Elouise gave me. I'll press it to preserve it and use it as a bookmark in my journal, ensuring it stays with me forever.

"You fashion it better than Jace does," Elouise says. I chortle.

"It's that horrid costume from the play I had to wear—it threw my style," Jace grumbles as he hangs a shirt to dry.

"If only you had seen his costume, Oren! He wore a skirt!"

"Him seeing this paint on me was enough!" Jace rolls his eyes, redirecting his attention to Mum. "Mum? You still hoped to talk about tonight?"

"Yes. While we're *all* here as a family, we wanted to talk to you, Oren."

My eyebrows furrow as I glance at my mother with unease. They want to talk to me? What would make tonight special? Considering how sick I've been today, I doubt Mum would suggest we all go into town to watch the stars. So, what's the point of a discussion? I lower my head before taking a sip of my tea. "Elouise has been speaking to you about the prophecy of Syann, right?"

You can't be serious?—that's how I should answer. If anyone were to believe these fairy tales, for Elouise it's logical, but Mum? No! I can hardly believe she has faith in legends. I nod, though; if I respond differently, it will only unnecessarily prolong this conversation.

"Then you understand how it's foretold on the eighteenth star-fall that Syann will be revealed, and according to writings, she is powerful. Her powers include healing and life, which you desperately need." The silence persists, as they patiently await my response. I won't! I refuse to endorse this or allow myself to raise my hopes for some unrealistic fairy tale. My hopes are already lifeless—it's a simpler way to live. Why risk everything now? Why would they attempt to shatter my heart more than it already is?

"Since you won't come to the festival," says Jace, arms crossed, "I'm going to seek out Syann tonight and convince her to heal you."

"I doubt she'll even need convincing!" Elouise adds. "Syann sympathizes with the well-being of humanity and will stop at nothing to rescue them from the Darkness. So why not you?"

The better question is, *why me?* If Syann were real, why would she go out of her way to break the curse on her land to help me? One person over the well-being of many? A nobody of a person, lacking any significance outside this house? It's a preposterous thought!

"It's not guaranteed, Oren," Mum remarks, which is the first thing said throughout this whole conversation that has made any sense to me. "But we want to put in the effort for you. We wish for you to have a good, fulfilling life."

I share that sentiment. It's a comforting notion that they still care, but their thoughts and hopes won't heal me; neither will Syann. A fulfilling and meaningful life simply isn't in the cards for me.

"What do you think, O?" Elouise asks.

I hesitantly answer, "I-I appreciate y' c-caring but mum's r-r-right, there's no-no guarant-t-tee."

"Even then, we're going to try."

I glance at Elouise, then toward my cup. My mind is made up—I'm not giving this even a speckle of hope.

***

Once my siblings return to the festival, I withdraw to my room. I take the flower crown from my head, picturing Brenda Fields in it. She wears this crown above her wild curls, which are the color of wheat shining in the sun. Her eyes are somehow the same color, which always fascinated me. I miss her more than words: her bright smile, her boisterous laugh, and her endless tales of her life back home. To think, she's out there!

What if Syann really exists and she does heal me? What if I could go out and see Brenda again?

My smile wanes as I reject the thought. It's hope that will lead to heartache, that I can't afford.

On the edge of my desk lies my journal. I reach for it and open it where my charcoal stick sits inside. The page is blank, so I begin to list my thoughts individually. Once I'm finished, I rest the flower crown inside, pressing it flat against the secret words.

The Light among the Shadows

3 *Brenda*

After the Festival feast, Liam and I decide to go for a stroll before dark. Walks have always been a favorite activity of ours. Unlike at the play, I bring my blue parrot, Stella, along. She may be small and only has one wing, but she has a lot of spunk. She usually has a lot to say when we talk. I've had Stella since I was twelve—she was a gift from my childhood best friend, who rescued her. I dare say Stella has taken care of me just as much as I've taken care of her. She's the best listener I know, besides the one who gave her to me. After the play, once I returned home, Stella listened attentively to all my concerns about Liam when Elouise couldn't.

"Are we headed anywhere in particular?" I ask Liam.

"Oh, Brenda, always yearning to know the plan from the start." He grins.

"I don't enjoy being blindsided. You know that."

"I do know that and admire it. Which is why I thought you could lead us to a good place to watch the stars tonight."

"It's tradition that I watch them in the square with my family, but I know a different place—a field on the outskirts of town where my family picks our flowers. I've always imagined it would be wonderful to watch the stars while lying in the beds of flowers."

"Outside town, you say?"

"Not too far."

"That sounds wonderful. Clear views are quite so. No buildings, no crowds—" He exhales wistfully, as if memories are taking him elsewhere.

"You make it seem like you've watched the stars somewhere other than town before."

"Well, no—but there was a year I did watch the stars alone in an unexpected clearing. I was eight or so. My father and I were arguing that night, so I snuck off after the feast because I was cross with him. I climbed onto the roof of my house through my window and stayed put until the stars fell. The view was spectacular, even worth the trouble I got into from my father afterward."

I chuckle. That stunt appears to be out of character for the Liam I know, who is a stick-in-the-mud when it comes to reckless behavior or disregarding parental authority. "My dad would be cross with me also if I pulled a stunt like that, which is too bad. A view from a roof seems tempting."

Shadows and sunbeams bathe the rooftops in a honey-colored light, making them seem as inviting as ever. Climbing them is a reckless idea—one I'd never usually approve—but my siblings aren't around to follow my lead, and I have Liam. I'm tempted to ask if we can watch the sunset from the rooftops. There's something about the idea that's appealing. Climbing a roof is childish, but it could give me one last reckless thrill before my adult life arrives. It's certainly perilous, but I'm confident I could pull it off. The view would be rewarding.

"Maybe back then," Liam begins. "Our fathers are right to look down upon doing something so unsafe. One misstep could lead to a bad accident. It's not worth putting your life at risk."

He's right to be concerned. If my siblings, Jonavan or Aliah, suggested we all climb roofs, I would be the first to oppose it. They're still children.

Oren's fall crosses my mind. Not long before his disappearance, he fell from an apple tree and paid for it with his ability to walk. Perhaps if that incident hadn't transpired, it would be us two on this stroll. Regardless, he was a youth then. I'm not a juvenile anymore. I can care for myself.

"Technically, we'd be looking down on them since we'd have the high ground." I laugh, but Liam doesn't find me humorous.

"Brenda, I wasn't suggesting we watch the stars from the rooftops." His smooth voice morphs into something stern.

"What if I chose for us to watch the stars from a rooftop? It is my choice, isn't it?" I ask with a smile, hoping to lighten his confrontation.

Liam stammers, "It is your choice, Brenda, but I expect you to have the sense to pick a spot that doesn't come with endangering each other. Say you fell, or worse. I would feel responsible. Everyone would hold me responsible. I think we should look at the field you told me about."

"You wouldn't be responsible if it were my choice." My tone lurches from the friendly, light manner I've been using.

"Even if it were solely your choice, the public would surely scorn me for taking my lady friend on my roof and letting her fall! It would reflect badly on me, and I have a reputation to keep up for Seren. You know that!"

"I do know that, but I certainly don't want our relationship or decisions to be based on what people think of us. Is all I am to you your prestige?"

"No!" he blurts out immediately. "No! That is not what you mean to me. You are so much more. Brenda, you are my world, my stars in that night sky, my flowers in those fields. I only wish to keep you cared for and happy. So—" His face scrunches as he shakes his head. "If you wish to watch the stars on the rooftops, then I'll fulfill that wish for you to the best of my abilities."

"I was only going to suggest we watch the sunset from the rooftop."

"Well, then, we should hurry. There's not much time until the sun sets."

"Race you to your house?" I question playfully, to lighten the mood.

"After a meal like that?"

"I would win. I already won a horse race today, so I understand if you're backing out because you fear losing to me."

"Hey now, I have a few wins under my belt!" He grins.

"Then racing me shouldn't be a problem," I banter flirtatiously, leaning my face toward his.

"I guess it shouldn't." He leans closer, inches from me. His full lips form the most subtle smile.

I focus deeply on his robin-egg-blue eyes, locking him in before I take off running down the street. He'll have to follow me. I scoop Stella off my shoulder and into my hands so she doesn't fall.

"Brenda!" he shouts from behind.

I keep sprinting as fast as I can, and by a mere three seconds, I emerge victorious in the race. I celebrate by cheering and dancing while he's still trying to catch his breath. It's quite amusing to see how winded he is and how beads of sweat polish his forehead. His usually neat brunette hair is disheveled from the exertion of running.

I could have easily run farther.

We wind through his house and up the stairs to reach his bedroom. I've only been in his chamber a few times. So, I find myself observing it with a keen eye. It's meticulously organized and well furnished. His books and papers are neatly arranged on his desk, his bed is spotless, and the décor of family portraits and geographic maps adds a touch of personality to the space. If we get married, will our room be similar, or will this house be ours?

Will we move to a different one?

Liam unlocks his window and climbs up the sill.

"Hold on," I whisper to Stella, scratching my finger against her blue feathers. At first, I felt confident, but there's a shift when I put my upper body through the outside of the window. All it took was looking down. It's an elevated enough drop to recall Oren's fall again. He thought it would be fun to climb that tree. Likely, he never questioned his ability to do so. After the results, he regretted that decision more than anything.

The thought has my heart thumping.

"Liam?" My eyes dart to him. He sits on the roof, his hand outstretched toward mine. When I grasp it, he hauls me to safety. I grab Stella from my shoulder and drop onto my back. The buzzing sensation I felt surges through a deep gasp, which quickly transforms into guttural laughter.

"Quite a rush, isn't it? Kind of makes me feel like a child again."

"Yes!" I nod, tugging at my hair. That's exactly how I wished to feel, like a kid again. "It's amazing!"

Liam nudges my shoulder. "The sun is setting. Come see."

I sit myself upright, before returning Stella to my shoulder. The stunning, glowing round sinks into the horizon like roots into fertile soil. The colors of deep pink, orange, yellow, and purple swirl all around it. The sun's rays caress my skin, infusing me with warmth akin to a flower basking in spring's embrace, and I allow its beams to nourish and enrich my being. All the fear inside me melts from the warmth of the sun. My breath catches up to me as my heart rate steadies. This is the finest I've felt all day. "It's beautiful."

"I don't believe I've ever seen one as grand as this." Liam's fingers spread and weave into mine as he squeezes my hand. "I'm grateful for the privilege of sharing this moment with you. I apologize for my hesitation. You were right. This is spectacular. I wouldn't change a thing."

I clutch his hand back and smile. This grand sunset and him admitting I was right is all too satisfactory. "I'm glad you took me up here. The view is amazing, thank you."

"It's my pleasure."

I lean against Liam's shoulder while the sun descends past our view. Only illuminating rays keep the variation of pastel colors alive before they dull away into dusk. The heat of the rays dissipates from my skin, and in their place, a cool breeze sways my hair.

Now I understand how Liam and I operate. The exhilarating rush of scaling this roof mirrors our relationship. It's perilous at times. There are moments when a single misstep could ignite a dispute that I can't overcome, or instances where I'm satisfied by my own triumphs. However, the best times of all are when we can see eye to eye and enjoy victories together. Those rare beats are rich in excitement and adrenaline, like this one.

Regardless of what state we'll find ourselves in, no matter what life has in store, he will be by my side. It's going to be fine. It must be.

"Liam." It's time to get down.

"Brenda." His eyes connect with mine in a steady gaze, absorbing the tones of purple and red in the sky. It's as if the sky is embodied in a pair of stunning eyes, while his bronze skin glows in the sunlight.

Instead of feeling sensations in my skin from the sun, the flutters are deep in my stomach. My lips part as my nerves escape them through a quaking breath. His mild expression is unlike anything I've seen from him—it's equally curious and startling. His gaze lingers until he leans closer and closer, and his eyelids begin to flutter shut. I indulge my curiosity and find myself doing the same thing until our lips collide.

The contact is short-lived, as fear drives me back.

Something is off.

Several roofs away, a shadowy being lurks. The moment my

eyes meet theirs, the figure ducks out of my sight. Whatever the shadow was, it seized a shrill fear through me as if I were dangling off the roof again.

"What was that?" I ask, lunging to view it better, but there's no one.

"What was what?" Liam obliviously turns around to where I was looking.

"I could have sworn I saw someone on a roof a few buildings down."

"I don't see anything, Brenda. Are you all right?"

Am I? The sight of the figure pulsed fear and stress throughout me. The kiss was no remedy to any of it, which is beyond disappointing.

Behind us, bonfires light up the square, creating an ideal ambiance for another romantic rendezvous. Instead of hastily returning to the square, we leisurely stroll hand in hand down the same path we came.

I'm trying to focus on the romantic atmosphere instead of the suspicious person I saw. I'll hold Liam's hand, kiss him back, and indulge in his feelings, hoping to experience them myself. My doubts must be suppressed.

The festive atmosphere is filled with clapping, percussion, and stringed music. We join in the joyful dancing, and amidst the crowd, I spot my parents dancing together. Their love for each other is evident, though they couldn't be more different. Father is stubborn, extroverted, and charismatic, while Mum is shy, calm, and compassionate. Their personalities complement each other so well that I yearn for a love like theirs. I suppose not everyone gets that privilege. With Liam, I know there will be times when we'll clash. We're both stubborn and opinionated, which makes us prone to disagreements. However, we've chosen to dance together because we believe that our differences can be overcome.

It will take some time and effort, but that's what engagement is for—to prepare for marriage.

Mum and I make eye contact during a turn, and she smirks at me. She and Dad understand Liam's agenda and are pleasurably monitoring it.

Dad alternates between dancing with Mum and my little sister, Aliah. Mum, in turn, dances with Dad and my not-so-little brother, Jonavan. Jonavan's spindly body makes him awkward in dance.

Strangely, I'm not part of the dance rotation anymore. I don't get to waltz with Jonavan, spin with Aliah, or dance with Mum. Dad isn't twirling and dipping me like in the past.

Of course, it's my time to go. I'm an adult now.

Change is odd—it can be beneficial or detrimental. In this case, it's good, right? I'll get married and start a family while residing in the same town as my parents and siblings. I've yearned for this, and I'll never be too far from my childhood. I'll release it, knowing it won't run too far from me, and sometimes even come back to visit.

Right now, Aliah rushes over, asking to dance with me. I'm midway through telling her yes before my parents rush onto the scene.

"No, honey, Brenda is spending time with Liam," Mum objects.

"Anyways"—Dad scratches his thin blond hair—"we should set up our blankets to watch the stars about now, don't you think?" The mention of stars has Aliah happy not to be dancing with me.

"Brenda, come on, let's fetch our blanket!" the ten-year-old exclaims.

"Aliah! Did you not hear Mum? The two lovebirds want to be alone!" Jonavan laughs.

I roll my eyes at him before redirecting my attention to Aliah. "Sissy." I kneel, frowning. "I'm watching them with Liam this time."

"Will you both sit with us?" Aliah's round brunette eyes plead.

"Aliah, trust me, you don't want us there. You know how sometimes Mum and Dad kiss under the stars, and you look away? I might be trying that with Liam. You don't want to see that!" I smirk. She smiles and shakes her head with disgust. "I'll see you when I get home."

"We'll do bedtime snuggles?"

"Mm-hmm, I promise!" I weave my fingers through her brown curls before turning back to Liam.

"Are you ready to see the prettiest moonlit flower field you ever saw?"

"Please, lead the way." I take one of the blankets from Dad and begin to fulfill Liam's request.

"What did you tell your sister?" Liam asks as we stroll.

"Mm-mm! No one gets between sacred sister secrets, not even you."

"Sacred sister secrets?" My phrase curls his tongue.

Once we're far out of sight from the town square, a horn blast fills our ears. Followed by an unfamiliar, aggressive voice. *"Everyone, in the square!"*

Spooked, we both swerve toward the square. Distance prevents us from spotting anything out of the ordinary.

"That's not my father's voice, or anyone I know for that matter," Liam exclaims. He hesitates, fearfully staring toward the square, then at me. Outbursts erupt from that direction. The sense of dread I felt seeing the shadowy figure returns to me. This time, it's evident in Liam's expression as well. His brows knit together, and his square jawline clenches tightly.

A group of children sprint past us, unaccompanied by any adults.

"Hey! What's happening?" Liam asks them.

"We're under attack! Go hide!" a child blurts out, not stopping to give us any specific information.

Liam grabs my shoulders. "Brenda, you should see yourself home. If I see your family, I'll tell them you're safe and to go to you."

"No, I'll go with you!" I protest.

Liam, however, snaps back. "I don't know what's happening or if it's safe! Go home! Please! I'll return to you as soon as I'm able, but I must find my father. He could be in danger!"

"You want me to go to my house, alone? I told you I saw someone spying on the roof, Liam! I don't want to leave you. It's not safe!"

"Brenda, the activity is toward the square, not near your home. You'll be safer there than with me. As soon as I notify my father, I will return to you once I know it's secure. I'm not letting anything happen to you." He dismisses me by planting a kiss on my forehead. Afterward, he storms off with his fists clenched beside him.

I'm not staying here. He can't walk out on an unresolved argument and expect me to obey him. If there's danger, my family is there, and I'm not abandoning them like he did with me! If he wanted me home, he should've escorted me. I'm infuriated with him, but that's not my explicit concern. Who is this ignorant person belting in the square?

Liam blends with the group up ahead. I flow toward the square through a different street than Liam takes.

Outbursts of chaos blast from the crowd. Before I can determine the circumstances, a shady figure pins me to the ground. Stella hops off my shoulder to the dirt. I can't reach her, nor can she fly away.

The attacker's charcoal eyes are the only feature I can note. The rest of his features hide under black armor and a mask. It's the one who was on the rooftop! I knew I wasn't crazy! I kick him in the stomach before shoving him off and squirming to my feet. I cradle Stella before I sprint off.

"Liam!" The figures are chasing me. "Liam! Liam! Help!" He's nowhere around. Instead, a second figure pounces ahead. Dodging her is impossible, so inevitably I'm outnumbered and captured. They grip my arms with no mercy. Stella falls, and circumstances forces me to leave her.

I'm one of many abducted and taken toward the town square. Other masked intruders have dragged other women here, the stage from the play earlier. On the platform, they round us up, like sheep in a pen of wolves.

Out of the women, I recognize my cousin, Sophie, my friend Ulla, and Jahna, the baker's stepdaughter. All their hands and feet are bound by rope, while cloth tied around their mouths gags them. My fate becomes the same, which makes at least twenty of us bound up. One thing we have in common is that we're all eighteen. The reason we've been forced here is now painfully clear: these assailants are after Syann. They've taken every suspect captive, every eighteen-year-old female in Seren.

Between each of us are masked terrorists holding out swords. These weapons point to the space between two women's shoulders. If we try to escape, will the intruders slay us? The risk isn't worth it.

The curtains split, exposing the rioting crowd around the stage. At least twenty terrorists guard the front of the stage. A masked man stands front and center, with two shorter guards beside him. The center stage man's brawny build towers high. His mask hides his features, besides his red unruly curls, bound into a bun.

"I am a spokesman for Uxaar, the Shadow God!" He announces, with an outlandish accent that proves him a foreigner. "On a mission to retrieve Syann, the Goddess of Light! She's been discreetly living among you, but tonight, the stars will reveal her on this very stage, as the prophecy states! Syann is one of the women we display before you!"

The public rioting obstructs my attempt to locate anyone I know, until Liam and his father cut through the chaos. They both reach the armed intruders guarding the stage, who allow Byron up the steps.

"I don't know who you think you are, but you are unwelcome here!" Unafraid, Byron stomps toward the redhead, who is easily a foot taller than him. "Not only have you interrupted our cherished festival, but worse, you have also assaulted our dear women! You and your men will leave Seren at once, or there will be hell to pay!"

The redhead contemplates Byron's order, as he trembles and puffs for air. "Get off this stage while you still can, Byron. Uxaar is not a god of mercy," he warns our leader, sincerely.

"Spare me your absurdities! I'm not budging until you free our daughters and flee far away from here!" Byron demands through gritted teeth.

The intruder's attention is diverted from Byron. Someone else has captured it, yet his wavering eyes fail to meet anyone visible. It's as if he's watching a ghost that instills terror in him.

The redhead retreats from Byron, but the guard behind lunges at him. A blade pierces Byron's chest, releasing an oozy red liquid. I stare in horror, unable to look away.

Liam is screaming for his father, desperate to reach him, but several town folks drag him away. For a moment, his teary eyes meet mine, before he's lost in the chaos.

Someone else's eyes are on me, my father. He's as pale as a sheet, and frozen like a statue. The rest of my family must have fled home. Will I ever see them again? Will this be the last time I see my father?

The redhead and his men approach me and the hostages. Are we next in line to die? Hot tears stream down my cheeks as I puff through the cloth swathing my mouth.

"Quiet!" Byron's murderer roars at the crowd, who hushes at once. Pleased, he chuckles as he pivots toward the hostages behind him. "Ladies, I am a spokesman for Uxaar the Shadow God. You may not be able to see him, but I promise he is as present here as I am! He sees all and has been pristinely observing each of you to prepare for your capture. There's no escape! Your options now are allying with Uxaar by the Shadow Incantation or matching your fate with your former, weak leader, Byron Asbury. So, who will be the first competent one to accept Uxaar's offer?"

No response follows.

"No takers?" He clicks his tongue through an amused grin. "Well, then, Uxaar chooses you first, Brenda Fields. Uxaar has observed you, oh so closely. You're an intelligent, confident, and spirited woman. He has faith you have the intuition to heed my words." He removes the gag around my mouth, to allow me to speak.

"If Uxaar has watched my life closely as you say, he'd know I'd never follow you!" I spit at his feet. "Especially for killing my future father-in-law, you monster!"

The guard grins at my outburst. "Only to make an example, my dear. No one defies Uxaar without consequence. However, Uxaar understands humans withhold the compassion and soul that the Geron lacked. So, I will offer a deal to you, Brenda. If you say the Shadow Incantations, Uxaar will reverse the death of Byron and ensure no harm ensues upon Liam or your family."

"How should I know you have the ability to resurrect Byron?"

"Brenda, you have your heart closed off from the power of magic and have a foolish sense of denial! Do not doubt Uxaar or the power of the Underealm or Secreth, as you disregarded the warnings of Athena. This is no game. You either say the Incantations and Byron lives, or you refuse, and we kill you and all those you hold dear! Starting with her!" His blade points towards Sophie, and the guard behind her grabs her restraints and bears their sword up to her neck as she screams.

My cousin faces death's doorway. If I don't say the Incantations, we die. If I do say it, I might save Byron, but at what cost? My soul and the lives I'll endanger? I have to stall for time.

"What would I even say?"

A guard hands me a piece of writing carved into a deep purple crystal tablet. The tablet is as coarse and chilling as the murderer himself. Does this crystal possess magical properties? I'm certain these words audibly hiss in the air as I read them.

Set yourself free,
take over me,
Use me to make you higher,
In me have your way,
You get the say,
Do with me as you desire.

"After you recite these words, you will enter a brief meditative out-of-body state. There, you will select which Geron you'll bond with. So, what will be your choice? I've given you more than enough time to decide."

Sentencing myself is one thing, but my family, my loved ones? I can't. If Uxaar is real, Syann must be, too. I'll have to say these Incantations, hoping she'll save me and this town as soon as she arrives.

"I'll do it! Let her go!"

"Say it first!" the intruder demands. "Then she'll be free!"

I do as he asks, reciting the words. The more I say, the faster the Incantation expels. Slowing down is impossible.

As the spokesman described, my surroundings are no longer visible. A hazy light surrounds me instead. Within this light is an army of odd creatures.

The Geron.

Each one says their name simultaneously, yet somehow, I can comprehend each name. Uxaar's name is striking. His eyes and hair radiate an intense neon blue. His jawline and chin are the most elongated and robust I've ever seen. I must say one of their names, and it won't be his.

Something unexplainable in me tells me to say another's name. The urge is powerful and impossible to ignore. "Roe!"

Bright light overwhelms my surroundings, until it dims away

and I'm back on the stage. To my horror, the ghosts the redhead was so scared of now surround me. My eyes are now open to a supernatural realm I couldn't previously envision. The intruders were repeating words that the crowd couldn't hear, being Uxaar's spokesmen as they claimed they were.

Ahead of me is a Geron with scarlet-flame hair and neon-green eyes. Glowing freckles make his cheeks appear like the night sky. This creature, Roe, forces a sensation like no other onto me. He crashes into me, and it stings as if I've face-planted into a lake. Instead of Roe bouncing off, he absorbs into me like I'm a body of water. The violating sensation thrusts a loud whimper out of me.

On all fours, I dry heave profusely. The intruders are asking if the Incantations worked. The redhead says I'll be subject to the Geron's power once the stars fall.

A bright light shines far beyond the mountains, forming smaller, glimmering stars that pass through the atmosphere. These shooting stars plummet onto the stage one after another, forming a fading circle of light around my body.

My hands are left glowing like starlight.

4 *Brenda*

"Go and free Secreth, Syann," Roe says, forcing my vision to take a harsh hue of green. I'm incapable of seeing any other color, only various shades of green. This only lasts until Roe is through with speaking. As my vision returns to normal, Roe shoots off out of sight.

He's letting me go. Why? Does this explain why I was so compelled to call Roe's name when I said the Incantations? Does he want me to fulfill the prophecy? That goes entirely against everything Athena said about the Geron.

Other Geron shout, "She's the one! Syann, the Goddess of Light!" I want to ignore them, but my trembling, lit hands make that impossible.

Everything that happened since being forced on that stage should be impossible, but I'm living in this illogical nightmare. The prophecy I refused to believe is true. Syann really was living in Seren in disguise. She disguised herself so well that I was unaware that she was me. Now, she has claimed me against my will.

"No! This is madness!" I squeeze my eyes shut.

How is this possible? Did my parents know? No, how could they? I didn't even know that I was Syann! The prophecy states Syann's identity would be hidden until she came of age. What if they still somehow knew? Maybe my parents did an excellent deed that caused the Light to choose them to care for me. Perhaps there could be some intricate scheme I can't comprehend. This must mean my parents aren't my biological parents, while mine are long gone. Syann was a mortal baby born over a thousand years ago who died, and the Light chose her spirit to be its vessel. I'm the resurrected human baby, right?

It's too much to wrap my head around.

When I open my eyes, this illogical fantasy is still before me. Sophie is unconscious on the damaged platform, among the terrorists and other women. I rush to her side. Bruises and scratches taint her porcelain-like skin.

"Sophie!" I shake her, but she doesn't flinch. She's out cold.

I can't help but notice a striking green shimmer reflecting in her blonde hair. It reminds me of Roe.

I lift my arm toward my eyes. As I feared, the green glow reflects onto it and the ground. My eyes are glowing green. Roe marked me!

If I couldn't be more overwhelmed, the Geron won't stop hissing dreadful words. They say Uxaar is going to kill everyone I care about, and that Sophie is already as good as dead. Their overlapping insults and threats build a rage in me that erupts without warning.

"Stop!" I shout. "Please, for goodness' sake, not another word!" I glare around at them all. To my surprise, the creatures submit. They stop in midair and all silence themselves. Do I have the authority to control them? "Now go! Out of my sight!" As I ask, the creatures all flee, leaving the air clear. I only see what everyone else should see—no monsters.

My house isn't far. My family must welcome me back, even

with these magical scars. They can get help Sophie get the medical attention she needs, too. I won't be able to carry her on my own. So, I venture toward the edge of the stage to go home.

Bryon's corpse in a pool of blood stops me in my tracks.

My stomach wrenches into knots as my knees buckle at the sight. I've never seen this much blood in my life, and I hope to never see it in this quantity again. As a child, I could hardly stand eyeing a scratch without feeling faint. It requires all my willpower to drag my feet toward his body.

Uxaar didn't honor his end of the bargain by healing him, so I must try. I should be able to, but how? Maybe if I command with words as I did with the Geron? "Byron, wake up! Be healed!"

I wait, hoping for even a twitch of movement, but nothing happens. Maybe I need to touch him. I brush my fingers against his arm. The chilly temperature of his skin nearly robs my words from me. "By the power of Syann, I heal you, Byron!" I exclaim, feeling foolish as I do so.

Still nothing. Byron is dead. Liam's only family left is gone.

What is he going to think? How will I explain to Liam that I can't heal his father? Imagining the scenario sends me into a swirling panic that may bring me down like the many bodies in this wreckage.

A glint of familiarity ringing distantly begins to draw me from it. The voice is familiar, and not a Geron. "Syann!"

I despise that I react to *that* name with a turn of my head.

Jace climbs onto the stage, and Elouise isn't far behind. Of course, they're here. Jace needs me to heal him, too, I suppose. Too bad I can't. "You need to come with us. It's dangerous here. The terrorists won't be unconscious for long!"

I stammer, too overwhelmed to answer Jace.

"Can't you heal Byron?" Elouise asks tearfully.

"I-I don't know how," I admit shakily.

Jace senses my instability and gently pulls me away from Byron. "We're going to help you, but I need you to follow us."

"What about my family? Or the girls here? We can't just leave them!"

"We must. The Geron are after you, which will pose a threat to anyone near you. We can help you. My house is just outside of town—they won't easily find you there."

Though I've turned my head from Byron, his bloody corpse will forever be drawn into my memory. The last thing I want is for my family or Liam to meet the same fate because I put them in harm's way. Jace is right.

Jace and Elouise also have knowledge about Syann that I lack, and goodness knows I need any help I can get.

Jace leaps off the stage and offers a hand to help me down. He instructs me and his sister to remain silent until we reach his house. I do a sufficient job complying until we reach the street where I lost Stella.

I bolt off, telling the siblings to follow me as I do. I'm worried Stella will be gone to a horrible fate that I can't help her with. By some miracle, she's exactly where I dropped her. I pick her up, bringing her feathers to my face. "Stella! I thought I lost you!"

"A bird?" Elouise asks, which leaves me puzzled. Elouise adores Stella. She should recognize her.

"Stella. You know…" I hope my words will ring a bell in her head, but her features remain passive. "Elouise, you don't remember?"

"No, I'm sorry."

Come to think of it, neither of them has addressed me by my real name. "Wait, don't you remember me? I'm Brenda! I saw your play and gave you the flowers!"

Now instead of ringing bells, I've caused alarm, to Elouise especially. Jace discerns that and responds, "I know there is much to go over, but it will have to wait. We can't get caught."

How can neither of them remember me? If they can't, who's to say anyone can? Athena said the prophecy disappeared when the stars fell the first time, and no one remembered it. The reasoning for that was to keep my identity protected. That worked too well. I didn't even know who I was! Now that I do, did the stars strip away everyone's memories of my past identity? So, no one would try to hold me back here or endanger the people associated with me? That would mean my parents, Jonavan, Aliah, Liam, and all my friends and family would have no trace of me in their minds.

I'm jumping to conclusions too briskly, I hope.

Stella acts like she remembers me. She settles on my shoulder calmly as usual. I whistle notes from a folk song we enjoy. She whistles it back as always, which relieves me.

***

It's no mystery now that I never knew where Elouise lived. We are past the town's fence in a wood of oak trees. This end of town is opposite the area I go to pick flowers, so I've never been out here.

The deeper into the woods we get, the more the proud, towering trees evolve to humbled stumps until we reach a clearing. Surely enough, a cabin sits modestly on a far-off hill. I impatiently wish to rush to the shelter that hopefully has answers. I ignore the itch and walk to the porch at the same rate as the siblings.

The interior of this house is much more cramped than mine. A brief living space branches into a small dining area and kitchen, beside a hallway that must lead to the bedrooms. The décor is scarce, with only a few family paintings and assorted pots and pans mounted on the kitchen wall.

A woman at the kitchen table stands from her chair at the sight of us. Jace is a perfect likeness of her—well, a young, masculine one. They have the same nose and eyes. She must be their mother.

Our arrival seems to be a weight lifted off her shoulders. "Oh, you're both safe!" Her voice exhibits her profound relief. Jace and Elouise approach their mother's open arms while I linger behind the door.

"We brought Syann, Mum!" Elouise peeks back at me as she withdraws from her mum's embrace.

Elouise's mother makes eye contact with me. Awe drowns her countenance as she sinks into a bow. I've never felt more out of place.

"No need for formalities, please!" The words spurt from me as I offer my hand out to help her up. "Please call me Brenda. It was my given name that I would like to keep."

"Brenda." The woman rises to her feet. "You must have been through a great deal tonight."

That phrasing allows reality to settle in. My family is at home, either wondering where I am or completely without memory of me. Liam is certainly mourning his father, and potentially me, or the fact that he has no one to comfort him. One thing is for sure, my life has changed for the worse due to this unwelcome fate. *I want to go home.*

I nod. "I have so many questions. I'm not who you imagined I would be. I don't know who I am, and everyone forgot who I was."

"I'm sorry, Brenda, we don't remember a thing about you," Jace says.

"That doesn't mean we won't help you. We will do whatever it takes, but the time is now late. We should get you settled in and rested for what's to come," his mother suggests.

What is to come? Do they expect me to heal Jace? If that's even what he needs. Jace appears healthy to me. Is there someone after him and only I can stop them? I shouldn't worry about it now. I do need rest.

"Thank you, ma'am."

"Please, you can call me Valerie."

***

I wake up smothered by scratchy sheets. My fingertips search for Aliah, but there's only cold. I scan the room, and Jonavan's bed isn't across from mine as it usually is. It wasn't all a nightmare as

I hoped it would be. I'm still in Jace's bed (he's sleeping in the living room) and wearing his shirt as a nightgown since it fits me, unlike the girl's clothes.

I haven't slept well. Endless thoughts and questions wreak havoc in my mind. I yearn for the morning that will bring me answers. It feels as if I've been waiting an eternity for them when it's only been mere hours. Is that how life will feel like from now on? Or worse, could I die? Or could Syann brainwash me? Like how Uxaar does to his Shadow, who now has the power to go on a killing spree if I don't stop them.

"I don't want this," I whisper into my pillow as rage builds in me. *"I don't want this!"* I beat my glowing hands against the bed while bitter sobs erupt. I gaze at Stella through pools of tears. She's asleep on Jace's nightstand. That bird is all I have left of home. "I didn't even get to tell them all goodbye. What if I don't get to? They might have forgotten me, too!"

"Brenda." The voice sounds like wind.

Red-and-green light manifests before me, forming a Geron's body. The shade of green is identical to my eyes. It's Roe.

I sit up and gape at the creature approaching me. "You know my name." I wipe my eyes. "No one else does."

"For a moment, my mind was bound to yours. I know everything about you, Brenda. I saw it all, each and every memory of your life."

I shouldn't be conversing with Roe, but he also can't hurt me if I don't recite the Incantations again. I'm starving for any information I can get my hands on. "Try me," I challenge him through slowing tears.

"You knew Liam was going to propose, and you told no one. You even doubted accepting because you felt Liam wasn't your soulmate. You prefer the farm boy, Oren. You wished for him to return after his disappearance but feared you'd end up alone if you turned Liam down. You'd do anything to prevent being alone because it's your biggest fear—you'd even marry a man you don't love."

The truth crumbles my guard. Roe knows about what I never got to tell anyone. I don't love Liam. "So, you do know everything."

"I won't lie to you, Brenda. You have every reason to distrust me. What Athena said in her play was true—the fallen Geron aren't creatures worthy of trust. The only reason you thought to call my name…well, you wouldn't recall. I made a binding vow to you during the war that I would make my wrongs toward you right and help you in every way I can."

Contemplating the play is strange. Athena was telling my story, and I was clueless of it. "So, you did release me! A voice inside me told me to call your name. Syann must have remembered your vow."

"Yes, Syann's spirit resides within you. However, she won't always be clear to you while Darkness exists in you."

"Darkness exists in me?"

"Yes, you're a human who dwells in the Dusk realm. It's in your nature. So, until the Altar of Light purifies you, you won't be able to hear Syann's voice or control her power consistently. You must pursue the star. It will guide you to the altar."

So that's why I couldn't heal Byron. I would have never figured that out.

"Why are you helping me? You could've snared me and ensured victory for the Geron. If you help me, you'll return to the Underealm, right?"

"A fate I deserve. No thanks to Uxaar and those who joined them, many humans suffered gravely during the war, and now as a consequence of Uxaar's selfishness. Only you can mend what is broken by stopping Uxaar and restoring what's lost."

"I will follow the star, but as far as that goes, I have no idea what I'm supposed to do."

"Athena will welcome you and even know your identity as Brenda. She will show you your next steps."

"Why would Athena remember me? No one else can."

"I will let Athena tell her own story. I'll be watching you, my goddess, but now I'll leave you to rest for your journey. Find Athena, follow the star, don't trust the Geron or their followers, and don't speak the Shadow Incantations under any circumstances. I promise the other Geron won't be as generous as I am to let you go." Roe cautiously scans the room, then zips out of sight. I'm skeptical that Roe can still hear or see me, although I can't see or hear him. I try falling back asleep.

***

Coughs echo through the house. Is it Jonavan? No, that's not possible. I try returning to sleep, but the coarse outbursts become repetitive.

Who is that? Are they all right? My growing concern drives me to check on whoever it may be. Stella joins me.

One of the doors across the hall is open, which it wasn't before. Footsteps creak from the kitchen. A young man, certainly not Jace, hobbles toward the open door. There shouldn't be another man here. Who is he?

"Hey!" I startle him enough that he jolts. He scans me, starting with my eyes and stopping with my hands. They glow bright enough to illuminate the night around us. Shakily, he drops to his knees and bows. The act repulses me as much as when Ms. Valerie did so. "Please don't do that!"

The man coughs. "'M s-s-sorry."

Something about his soft voice and his face is a dream I dreamt long ago but never forgot. In fact, I clung to it as long as I could, even if memories and pieces of it faded over time.

He struggles to rise back to his feet, using a crutch to aid him. The crutch is the missing piece that unveils the man's identity in my memory.

Oren Silvius.

"Oren?" Confusion, excitement, and heartbreak overwhelmingly pulse through me. Has he been here all this time?

Does he remember me?

I vividly remember him as always. After all, he was my friend for five years—the kindest, most adventurous, and best friend I could ever ask for. Now, he's almost unrecognizable. Looking at him is like seeing a withered flower, starving for sunlight and water. His vibrancy is completely drained.

His thin frame suggests that he hasn't been eating enough, and dark circles under his eyes plead for sleep. Overgrown dark locks sag past his narrow shoulders, indicating a lack of self-care. His thin lips are heavily chapped. Oren is in rough shape, and it pains me to see him like this.

Despite growing deprived of sunshine, the features I once admired remain. Like a river in daylight, his gleaming brown eyes always reflected the world around him. His pale freckled skin contrasts beautifully with his dark locks. The features of his face are as soft as I remember his personality and soul to be. His nose is smoothly upturned. Although his face has lengthened, his triangular jawline is soft around the edges and lined with dark bristles.

His body trembles like leaves in the wind. He's scared of me. "And y-y-y'ur Syann. M-m-my sister ac-actually f-f-found you."

"Elouise? Elouise is your sister?" I ask more heatedly than I intended.

He nods. The resemblance between Elouise and Oren is obvious now, though there's little to none with Jace or Valerie. Still, I'm blown away. When Oren disappeared with no explanation, I was heartbroken. I cried myself to sleep the night that I found out he had moved from the farm village after his grandparents passed away. I even grasped onto the hope that we'd meet again one day, which made moving on from him nearly impossible.

What upsets me now is that I told Elouise about Oren some

time ago. She knew I had it badly for him until he disappeared without explanation and withheld him from me. That was the lie. She lied to me about not knowing Oren. Elouise may have intended on clearing it up yesterday when she told me her brother needed Syann, but why would she wait so long?

"You told me when we were kids that you had no siblings, yet you have a brother and sister? And Elouise never mentioned you to me when I told her about you years ago! I told her that I missed you and that I wished I knew what had become of you. She knew the whole time and never said a word!" My anger rises in my voice. I can tell I'm alarming him more. Oren doesn't remember any of that, but I wish more than anything he did.

"Wh-wh-what are you talking about? We've met b-b-before?"

"Yes, we have!" My pain-doused words shoot at him. *Breathe.* "There's much to explain, but we used to be *good* friends years ago before you vanished. My name is Brenda. The reason you can't remember is my powers stripped the memories of my identity. No one remembers Brenda, and I don't have memories of my life as Syann."

"You d-d-didn't know y-y-y' were Syann?"

"Oren, I didn't even believe in her. I deemed her a fairy tale."

Oren smiles subtly. "That makes t-t-two of us. Elly b-b-believes y-y-you could heal me. I n-never did. I've been ill f-f-for years w-w-with little relief."

"Since you fell from the tree?"

Oren nods. "I-I-I told E-Elly not to mention me t-t-t-t' her friends—It's c-c-c-complicated, b-b-but please don't bl-blame her for h-h-her secrecy. There m-m-must be more we can't rem-m-member."

I can't be mad at him—instead, my heart aches for him. At Elouise, however, I'm fuming. If she were in this room, she'd face my fury. "You have no idea how much I missed you. I grieved you! I knew you were ill and thought the worst had happened. You were my best friend! And I still want to help you, but I can't heal you yet. Not until I reach Secreth."

Oren nods, his expression surprisingly blank.

"I know because I already tried healing someone else, and it didn't work. But I won't give up hope yet." I try reassuring him with my words, and myself by rubbing Stella's chin. Her lively chirps grab Oren's attention. "Stella, shhh!"

"Stella?" Oren questions perplexingly.

Stella! Of course!

"You remember Stella, right? You gifted her to me!" My voice is desperate. Elouise forgot Stella, but she only interacted with her in my presence. Oren is a different case. He knew Stella before I did.

"Yeah, Stella. I th-th-thought she seemed f-f-familiar," he replies. "You're the one I-I-I gave h-h-her to?"

"Yes, you do remember me?" If he does, that would be everything. After losing so much, to regain an old close friend from long ago would be so healing. Hope twinkles in me as I step toward him.

He exhales deeply, slightly backing away from me. "Mm—n-n—w-well. No—er—but I have h-h-her feather in my j-j-j-journal."

"Yes, your journal! You might have written about me, too." I smile for the first time since my hands glowed. Oren potentially has proof of my existence as Brenda! Recorded memories! If Oren has evidence, indeed, my family should. "Is there any possibility you'd let me see?"

"Th-the feather?"

"Yes." I meant his writings, but I accept seeing the feather. If Oren doesn't remember me, he may distrust me with his writings.

He invites me to follow him to his room. It's a cool and minimalist space with a pleasant mint-and-oakwood scent. Apart from his desk, the room is sparsely decorated. However, there are enough books and writing utensils on the desk to keep anyone entertained. There's also an open journal with a pressed flower chain between its pages. "These flowers," I reach out to point to them. Oren pulls this journal closer while he searches through his other journals. "It's a flower crown from the festival my mother made. Did Elouise bring you this?"

Oren nods. She must have gone to visit Oren when she went home after the play yesterday. Did Elouise give Oren the flowers because he missed me? For now, I won't know. Oren couldn't answer that question if he tried.

He plucks the blue feather from his journal and passes it to me. No doubt it's Stella's. Oren continues to skim through the journal.

"Does the journal mention Brenda?"

Oren nods, wide-eyed. "Y-y-your name is all o-o-over it."

My heart races, and every fiber of my being yearns to seize the journal from his grasp and devour the words within. "Could I possibly see!?"

"Uh—I-I'm sorry. I—um—this i-i-is a-a-a lot to t-t-take in." He shuts the journal and sits it on his desk. "And my-my-my journal is pr-pr-private."

Whatever pressure he's experiencing is contagious. I yearn for the words in his journal more than anything. Instead, he's shutting me out! There's nothing I can do about it. I won't demand to barge in on his privacy.

"I understand." I force the words out of me. "But do you believe me now? That we were friends?"

Oren covers his mouth with his palm, nodding. "I-I-I—um— I think I-I-I should go b-b-back to sleep, Syann, um—sorry, Br- Br-Brenda—Brenda."

I nod, somewhere beyond disappointed. I always dreamed that when we reunited one day, we would spend hours catching up with each other. Instead, I only got five minutes before he shut me out. "Yes, it's Brenda. I should return to bed as well. Good night, Oren. I'll see you tomorrow."

"G'night."

5 Oren

I spent all night reading my journal after Brenda returned to bed. I knew Stella was familiar the moment I noticed her. So, I uncovered the story of finding the injured baby bird and how my grandma and I nursed her back to health. There I discovered writings upon writings about a girl named Brenda. That's what led me to pulling an all-nighter exploring my journal without the pressure of the goddess watching me.

First, I stumbled upon the story of how I gave her Stella, one of the countless tales in my journal. I approached it as if it were a brand-new book, untouched by time. These stories recounted our adventures. As I read them, I was astounded by the fact that I had experienced what felt like the most precious memories of my life. The act of forgetting her and these moments is a punishment.

Once I reached the point in our story where I moved, I thought the entries about Brenda would end, but several more followed. As I wrote, I reminisced about the past and wondered how she was faring without me.

The affectionate notes and portraits made me realize that I had seen Brenda as more than a friend. One entry, written yesterday afternoon, included the pressed flower crown Elouise had given me.

Dear Journal,

It's the Festival of the Stars once more. Things are the same as they are at each festival. So, I won't attend, no matter how much Elly wishes I would go. My one regret is that I can't bring myself to see Brenda, no matter how much I miss her. Five years have passed since I retreated into solitude, and neither my body or soul has healed from it. I know it well that I'll remain alone for the rest of my days as I face the rapid decline of my health. Even so, I can't help but affectionately miss Brenda, regardless of my knowledge that we're through. I look at this flower crown she made and am reminded of her wild beauty, her friendly, wide smile, and her sweet presence. Like a flower, her time in my life was beautiful but fleeting. I'm afraid my lifespan has the same fate unless Elly's hopes that my healing will occur tonight through a miracle is true. If so, could I see Brenda again? I want to hold onto hope, but I know better that waiting is safer. So, I'll press these flowers to preserve them, like how I'll always cherish my memories of Brenda in my mind for the rest of my days.

—Oren Silvius

Yesterday, I was deeply engrossed in thoughts about her and our past friendship. I sounded infatuated with Brenda, which is hard to fathom. Apart from Stella, there are no recollections of her in my mind.

If I once had feelings for her, could they resurface?

I can't deceive myself. Brenda is as beautiful as I described her to be in my writings. She radiates warmth like the sun, with golden hair and skin smooth and dark as honey. My journal states that her eyes were golden, too, but instead, they gleam emerald. The glow is unnatural—a mystical property, like her hands. It doesn't subtract the truth that they are uniquely breathtaking. Her lips are plump and soft, too. How would I know that? She kissed me on the cheek when I was twelve, and I enjoyed it enough to write about it.

Who knew I was capable of romantic feelings? I thought every emotional desire in me withered away, but now I'm itching to remember her.

This morning, I revisit my journal. The first thing I notice is the pressed flower chain that Brenda had recognized. It prompts me to head to my desk, where I find my other books. I had pressed my flower chains from past festivals in several of them.

I remember Elouise giving me each crown, and the happiness I experienced when she did. I felt joy, love, and value from my past, which made me want to hope for the better. Nothing else or no one else had ever given me that feeling, only Brenda. She's responsible for the sense of beloved nostalgia these flowers bring.

Even now, without recalling our friendship directly, I miss the idea of her. She was a friend who genuinely cared about me, who I could be my authentic self around and share joyful moments with her. Everything I read about her seemed too perfect to be true. I was content, a feeling I hadn't experienced since my days at the farm.

I can't recall my times with Brenda, but she can, after all those excruciatingly long years. Did I mean a lot to her as well? Do I still hold any significance for her now? She said she missed and grieved me.

These thoughts captivate me until a knock at my door interrupts them. I close my journal and place it on my desk. "Come in."

"Hey." Elouise approaches me. "Are you feeling any better?"

I glare at her as if her question is patronizing. Of course I'm not. "I'm confused—I met S-Sy-Syann last night. She—she had th-th-this bird. Do y-y-you remember the bird I-I-I found as a kid? Th-th-that me an-an-and Grandma t-t-took care of."

"She's the same bird?"

I nod. "Syann was m-m-my f-f-frien' Brenda, who I gave Stella t-t-to, but I can't r-r-remem-m-mber a thing a-a-about her!"

"She spoke to me about that this morning, harshly I'm afraid. She claims we were friends, too, and that she mentioned you to me. I didn't admit to her that I knew you. So, she's cross with me."

I huff. "I-I told h-h-her not to be up-up-upset with you."

"It's all right. She's going through a lot, Oren. I couldn't imagine everyone forgetting me. She must be terrified."

Though I'm unaware of exactly how it's like, I have a decent idea. I disappeared off the map. Surely no one in the farm village remembers me. My family is all I have, and now there's Brenda, too. If only I remembered.

"Are you all right?"

I shake my head. "I-I-I read every…everythin' ab-b-bout Brenda I c-c-could find—There was a lot. I m-m-miss-I missed her, even y-y-yest-terday b-b-before the festival, before we lost our-our-our memories of her, I—I wrote ab-b-bout her. But I-I-I can't feel any of-f-f any of it now. I'm h-hurt…that I-I had a f-f-f-friend and good mem-mem-memories, and I can't rem-rem-remember her. I wish I-I-I could."

"Well, it's clear having her memories restored is a great interest of Brenda's—So maybe she'll find a way to reverse it!"

Why should I hope for that? She couldn't even heal me last night. She doesn't know how to use her power.

"Don't get upset, it will be all right!" Her hand rubs my shoulder.

"I-I-I had somethin' g-g-good and it-it w-w-was t-taken from me. L-like everythin' else."

"Hey! Good is coming. She will find a way to heal you. Maybe you'll be able to remember her, too, and you can be friends again."

"Is—Will—M-may-maybe—"

"What?"

"All th-th-those words mean—mean something dif-dif-different. Some r-r-r certain, some 'r' not. M-m-m-my healing isn't certain. She s-s-said she couldn't heal m-m-me until she g-g-gets to Secreth."

"Oren, for once, don't you want to believe you'll get better?"

"Yes, Elly! I-I-I do. I do want t-to b-b-be better. I don't w-w-w-wi-wish this on me, b-but after all this—all-all-all this heartbr-br-break I'm-m not l-letting myself h-h-hope again!" My face is twitching. My throat tightens as emotions flood in. I hate fighting with Elouise more than anything.

"I know hope can hurt, but if we don't ever hope, we'll *always* hurt deep down. Hope is a motivator, Oren. Motivation is what you need. That's why I hope because I'm never giving up on you. And you shouldn't give up on yourself, either."

I inhale deeply, refusing to succumb to my emotions yet. "Every time I-I-I've ever hoped, it's al-always let m-m-m' down. I-i-i-if it w-w-works out, great! Th-that would—would be—" I wheeze into a smile. "Th-the greatest! Then m-m-maybe then I-I could be the brother y-y-you deserve a-a-an—need me to-to be." My smile breaks under the weight of the emotions I tried to conceal. "I w-w-would want n-n-nothing more t-t-than that Elly. I'm so tired of-of-of hurting you!"

"*You* are not hurting me." She embraces me tightly. I cling to her loosely in return, huffing for air. "I love you." She parts herself from me, meeting me in the eyes. "Let's go eat breakfast. Mum was telling me it's almost ready."

I scoff before I defeatedly nod. "Lemme g-g-get ready."

Before going into the kitchen, I swaddle a bandana around my neck, attempting to cover areas of my body I'm self-conscious of. I'm too thin.

My eyes meet the reflection in my mirror in disapproval.

Why are you trying to impress her?

I shake my head at the thought. I'm not trying to impress Brenda! I'm trying not to disgust her. That's not the same thing!

Squeezing raids my chest and spreads into my throat. It feels like air is expanding continuously, threatening to explode. A lump forms in my throat, making it impossible to swallow. My nerves are getting the better of me.

"You all right?" Elouise asks.

I nod untruthfully. Turning from the mirror, I head out of my room to the kitchen table. Elouise settles me in a chair before helping set the table.

The aroma of sausage is strong in the kitchen, and I can tell by the pot simmering that Mum prepared porridge. The smell revolts me.

My desire to eat is completely absent, even though my stomach feels hollow and leaves my body shaking. The lack of sleep doesn't help. Why would I want to fill the emptiness when I know it will only regurgitate?

"Hey." I turn to look behind me. Brenda stands there, with Stella on her shoulder. She's now wearing the outfit I lent her this morning—a white shirt and gray trousers. Although the outfit is unconventional for a woman, she looks much better in it than I ever could. Brenda's charm and beauty can effortlessly complement any clothes.

"Hi," I reply, not able to restrain myself from grinning at her.

"Where should I sit?" Brenda questions while twisting her hair. "There are only four chairs." She's right, there are only four chairs, and five of us.

Initially, her asking for my help bewildered me, but now it makes sense. I'm the only one not doing anything.

Involuntarily, I stand up. "T-take mine, I-I'll fetch another from m-my room." It will be challenging to retrieve my chair. I'll fall if I rush, but I won't be rude. I'd rather fall flat on my face than be rude to her.

"Don't be ridiculous," Brenda blurts out, unaware of how these words pierce me. "I don't want to trouble you. You said it was in your room?"

"N-n-no, let me!" I raise my voice instead of reaching for her. Everyone in the room goes silent as they turn toward me. Heat rushes to my face as my heart drums. Why did I burst out like that? The lump in my throat might choke me now.

"Is there a problem here?" Jace walks toward us before setting our plates on the table. I expect a firm expression on his face, but instead, he's approachable. It's a show for Brenda's sake that I see right through.

"No. I was going to grab the chair from Oren's room so there's enough for everyone," Brenda replies.

"I-I told her t-to s-s-s-sit in-in my chair," I add frantically, hoping Jace doesn't think I was telling her to grab her own chair. If I hadn't said what I did, Jace would chide me with the "that's not how to treat a lady" speech. I know not offering a lady your seat isn't how to treat a woman.

"Brenda, take my seat," Jace's voice booms. "I'll get the chair." He sets the final plate and heads out before we can give input.

Brenda takes Jace's chair, scooting it beside mine. She leans toward me, whispering, "It was fine. I could have fetched it."

I was only trying to be polite. *Guests should never have to serve themselves,* that's what Grandma always said. "Sorry," I mutter as I sit.

I'm disabled, yes, but does that deem me useless? I know it

does in most situations to my family, but I still fight the label deep down. I wish to contribute. Instead, I'm as ineffective as a wet rag.

"You don't have to apologize. You didn't do anything wrong."

Then why act upset? Well, she's not bitter at me. I'm overreacting. Other than apologizing again, what can I say? I remain silent.

Mum approaches the table and sets the large bowl of porridge in the center. She asks whoever is at the table if they want a helping. I automatically get a scoop plopped on my plate, along with an intense gaze from Mum. "I need you to eat." She pushes the dish before me and offers Brenda a scoop. I slouch disapprovingly, disgusted by the mush.

Everyone at the table is seated with a plate of lamb sausage and porridge in front of them. The tinkling of silverware, the sound of small talk, and the chewing of food fill my ears.

I haven't taken a bite yet. How could I with my raging emotions twisting my stomach into knots? I couldn't even get my stupid chair or have a civil conversation without shutting down. If I eat, I'll throw it up.

Why am I here? *Why?*

Everyone here has something to contribute but me. I'm the root cause of my family making this arrangement. Do you know how much easier it would be for everyone if I stayed in my room and was no one else's concern? It's painful. I yearn to help and be more than the victim. I could have gotten that chair for Brenda or helped with breakfast. That is if anyone would accept my help. None of them would. Brenda and Jace are prime examples. Even when I tried helping myself yesterday with the bucket, Mum stopped me. Am I that pathetic to everyone?

I want to shrink away, like the food on everyone else's plate. Instead, I will end up like mine: barely touched while going cold over time.

Things have never changed, and they never will. Why should

I believe that one day things will be different?

"So, Brenda." My mum sits into her chair. "What are your thoughts?"

"My first is to seek out Athena before I leave Seren to help me as a guide. I'm sure she knows more about these stories than anyone around here."

"Mm-hmm! Athena has this big journal, about the realms and Syann, that she's extensively studied," Elouise adds.

"Yes—" Brenda agrees. "But I don't know how this plays out for Oren or if Athena will know a way for me to help him. As far as my knowledge goes, I can't heal him until I reach the altar."

"Which is why I was going to propose a suggestion, Brenda. Would you be willing to take Oren with you on your journey? Along with Jace. We have a horse that Oren can ride as well."

Of course, I have a bite in my mouth when Mum says that. It was the only bite I've dared to take. The proposition ricochets shockwaves through me. Uncontrollably, I cough, sputtering out the one bite I swallowed. Everyone is used to my fits by now, except for Brenda. She's the only one who seems concerned for me.

Elouise is too occupied by leering at Mum as Brenda agrees to Mum's suggestion. "Mum, me too, right?" Elouise questions, baffled.

"No!" Jace snaps. "You saw the terrorists last night, Elouise. Not only that, but the Shadow is also now at hand. It will be unsafe!"

"I didn't ask you, Jace!" Elouise fires back at him. "Mum, I must go! I know more about these legends than Jace or Oren does. I can help!"

"Elouise, honey," Mum's voice wavers. "Jace and I discussed this while we were fixing breakfast. It's already a huge burden to bear to send your brothers out there. I don't want you to risk your life if you don't have to."

"Then why should Oren or Jace go? Brenda can return once

she reaches the altar. Right? Then she can heal Oren!" Elouise gazes at Brenda, who appears taken aback by how the conversation spirals into an argument.

"I will if that's possible."

"I'm not saying this to frighten you, Brenda, but I don't know what will become of you. The prophecy doesn't specify. I only know you are Oren's only hope left. I'm not passing up what might be his only chance at life."

Brenda is too stunned to reply to my mother.

"Oren, what are your thoughts?" Mum turns to me.

"You're right, th-th-this may be my on-only chance. If-f-f I d-d-don't go, and she doesn't c-c-come back—I don't have much longer t-t-to live. So, I'll g-g-go to Athena's, and see w-what she thinks, b-b-but you both need Jace. He sh-sh-should stay, too."

"I need to be there to take care of you," Jace insists, which surprises me.

I shake my head. "No, y-y-you take care of them."

Jace sighs heavily, scratching his facial hair. "I will take you to Athena's. Once we have more knowledge of this situation from her, we can reevaluate there. If you decide you don't want to continue, we can go home, or if you want to continue with or without me, we'll lead with that."

After breakfast, Mum instructs Jace to pack a bag for me.

Elouise assists Brenda in packing enough supplies to last her for a few days. Since I'm closest to her size, I volunteered some of my clothes for her.

Inside my bag, I have a water canteen, spare changes of clothes, some dried fruit, meat, and nuts in a small drawstring bag filled with mint leaves. I'm surprised Jace was so thoughtful. It would make more sense that he was trying to avoid secondhand embarrassment from my breath reeking of vomit. The only other items I can think of adding are my journal and a pen. I'm not sure if I'll use them, but it would be helpful to reread some facts about Brenda or sketch if I get bored.

Now, I sit on my bed, nervously fidgeting with the straps of my backpack. Brenda opens the door. She wears a pink scarf tied around her waist and a black hooded cloak with purple trimming. I recognize the cloak—it was Elouise's birthday present from Jace about two years ago. It has a wooden flower-shaped button he carved. Stella accompanies her.

"Hey. How are you doing?"

I shrug, oblivious of how to answer her.

"I overheard Jace saying he's ready. He's out feeding your horse."

"Oh—" Jace's behavior has been confusing. I'm unsure whether his help is motivated by genuine care for me or a show for Brenda. Though I'm sure he's the last subject I want to discuss. Still, I need to say something. "Um—h-how are you—an-and Stella?"

For some reason, she smiles briefly, as if she found my question amusing. It probably felt out of place or ill-timed, or maybe she appreciated that I asked. "This is all so strange. Last night was frankly traumatic. I'm still processing it." She glimpses at her gloved hands. "As for Stella, I asked your mum if she could stay here. So, she'll be fine. Thank you for asking."

"Oh uh—heh, y-yeah, you're welcome." I can't help but wonder where Elouise is. She and Brenda have mostly been together this morning, yet Elouise is not here now. I haven't seen her since I left the table. "Do y-y-you know wh-wh-where m-m-m-my sister is?"

"She told me how upset she was that she wasn't allowed to come with us. I wouldn't be surprised if she's trying to persuade Jace or your mum to let her go."

I shake my head, knowing Jace and Mum aren't going to budge, no matter how hard Elouise may beg.

"What's your opinion about Elouise staying behind?"

The truth? I'm terrified I'll never see her again, that when I tell her goodbye, it will be for the final time. I find myself dreading leaving for this reason. "It-it-it-it's f-for her o-o-own good," I mumble.

"It's certainly not the safest situation. The people who attacked Seren last night were dangerous. I wouldn't want my little sister out there either, if I were you or Jace." Brenda's countenance becomes stiff as if she drowns in thought. My journal educated me enough that Brenda had a little sister named Aliah. She was born briefly before our first encounter, and Brenda was over the moon. Brenda must miss her dearly.

Jace summons us. Brenda and I follow him out the front door with our bags. Elouise sits on the stone outside in the front yard— "Rocky" she calls it. She always sits on Rocky whenever she wants to be alone. I've even gone out there a few times to comfort her when she's sat there too long. As I predicted, she must have failed to convince Mum to let her come along.

"Elouise! It's time to say goodbye!" Jace calls for her attention. She sprints over to us by our horse, Mindy, where Mum waits.

"You all have everything you need before you leave?" Mum observes each of us, finding that we are ready with our bags. "Very well, then."

Elouise steps closer to me, acknowledging our time to part has come by tugging on my sleeve. "This isn't goodbye. You'll return once you're healed!"

I want to hide from her contagious tears, so I thrust my arms around her. "I love y-y-you, Elly. If I don't—"

"Shhh, no." She squeezes me tightly. "We will see each other again. I promise."

"Oren." I pull back from Elouise at Mum's voice. The sight of her, the sorrow she wears, digs up the emotion I tried suppressing from Elouise. She approaches me and plants her hands on my shoulders. "I'm proud of you. I'm so proud that you're stepping up and going through with this. It's going to pay off. When we see each other again, you'll be like the happy little boy I used to know."

"Mum." My tears linger in my eyes. My voice strains as I try to hold them back. "W-w-what if something happens?"

"Shhh." She lifts her index finger to my lips, which leads her hand to my cheek. "No what-ifs! You have Brenda and Jace with you to keep you safe."

I sniffle and wipe my face to try to conceal my falling tears. Mum's arms wrap around me, which feels foreign. We rarely embrace, so the feeling touches me. "I l-l-love you, Mum."

"And I love you." We share a tremor of fear in our voices, stemming from the intimidating question we ask both ourselves—

Will we see each other again?

"T-take care of Elly."

She releases me. "We're both going to be fine. Now, go along."

"G-g-goodbye…M-mum."

"Goodbye, son." She leaves me with a kiss on my cheek. The gesture shakes my core with emotion and fear. If I die, will Mum's heart completely break like Grandma's? Or has she accepted my fate and detached her heart from mine? I haven't detached mine from hers.

"All right, Oren, let's get you on Mindy," Jace says.

I've maintained the knowledge of how to mount a horse, but knowledge alone doesn't give one strength. Before Jace can take his turn exchanging goodbyes, he must help me mount on.

I can't help but keep glancing at Elouise, fearing something might happen to me and that I won't see her again. This fear intensifies when Jace arrives and pulls on Mindy's reins.

"Oren, it will be fine! I promise! I'll see you soon," Elouise calls as we trod away.

I hope her promise to me is fulfilled more than anything, but like my sister said, with hope can come hurt.

6 *Brenda*

My journey begins as my feet stamp into blades of green, parting ways from the Silvius's home. Who knows what transpires next? For once in my life, self-doubt saturates my mind.

Syann changed everything, that was made clear as I fled town. I'm now known there by no one, and I'll have to face that reality again when we arrive.

Even if someone could recognize me, I've disguised myself enough that no one should notice at first glance. The hood of my cloak conceals my glowing eyes and hair, which is pulled into a low, messy bun. Leather gloves cover the glow of my hands. Jace believed it would be best if no one recognized me after last night, and he's right. However, I despise that I've become a reflection of my current state—confined and forced to conceal my true self for the sake of others.

Every memory of me is inaccessible to anyone else. They reside solely within me, and the journal of a disassociated boy. Disassociated is an apt description of Oren at this moment. He hasn't uttered a single word since bidding farewell to his sister and mother. However, certain pictures convey messages beyond words. His antagonized eyes mirror the internal conflict within him, to the point it sickens him. Considering the emotional intensity of his goodbye to his family, it wouldn't be surprising if he believes that he may never see them again. He can't be confident in Jace and me to safeguard him in this journey, which hardly makes me confident.

I'm also scared that death will deter me from living out the future that was at my fingertips. How is it now so distant from me? My family and Liam have been torn away, stripping me of any clarity around my future. I crave reassurance. If Aliah were here, she would let me ramble as long as I desired and absorb every word I said. Likewise, my parents were always my rock when I didn't know where to turn. Jonavan also always knew how to cheer people up in his unique way. Right now, I have no one to comfort me.

I had hoped the silence would eventually break, and Jace would initiate a conversation, but he remains stone-faced. I can't help but recall all his condescending interactions with his sister in the past, and I can't help but wonder if he's capable of having a casual conversation.

If you want something done, you have to do it yourself. "Oren, how are you holding up?"

Oren hardly shifts his head my way. His eyes don't even skim me. Instead, my question triggers a daze, which he shrugs off. That's it? A shrug? He must be struggling harder than a shrug-worthy response.

"To me, you seem stressed, which it's fine if you are…" *Nothing.* "This is an intense situation. I'm stressed, too." I continue to prod him with my words, only for the awkward silence to stretch on.

"Brenda, I wouldn't expect much chatter from him," Jace remarks. "He hardly ever says anything."

Oren shrinks in posture at Jace's remark. I pity him, but at the same time, I don't know how to help Oren if he doesn't talk.

Our path leads us to a cluster of oak trees. I recall them from last night. Above the branches of the trees, a gray, cloudy sky hangs. The wind whistles a melancholic tune through the wooden arms of the trees.

Unlike before, Oren's eyes focus upward, gazing at the nature stretching above him. Only if you were searching for it could you see the slight creases curl upward in his mouth, forming a smile. It's the tiniest smile I've ever seen, but it's still a smile. He continues to gaze at each tree around him with curiosity and admiration, as if he were riding the horse alone in the grove.

A squirrel scampers on a branch ahead, captivating Oren's attention. His eyes never depart from it as he approaches the tree holding the animal. Oren appears cautious about encountering a living creature. His smile has been replaced by a slight gape in his mouth. When the squirrel scampers across the tree, Oren's eyes follow it. The rodent leaps to the branch across. Only under Oren's breath does a single chuckle escape his lips. It's barely audible, but I catch it. The observant, nature-loving boy I knew is still there.

I swing my head away, realizing that my lingering feelings for Oren have led me astray. Why do I hope that our friendship can somehow blossom into its former glory, when he has no recollection of me or won't even speak to me? The truth is, everyone forgetting me is isolating. I yearn for someone to care for me and alleviate this pain and loneliness. Could Oren be the one to fix this? Despite his forgetfulness, he possesses tangible evidence of our past friendship in his journal. That's more than anyone else can offer. He once genuinely cared about me enough to document our adventures.

"This weather isn't the best," I comment, hoping the generic statement inspires someone to say anything. The quiet allows me to overthink. With the situation at hand, I could do with a lot less of that.

"I bet it's going to rain sooner or later," Jace replies.

"Where do you think I'll be going—after Athena's? Obviously, to follow the star, but where exactly does it lead?"

"I can't be sure, but anything is possible."

"Yesterday, I denied all of this being possible. Syann's existence, magical realms, or creatures. Now, I wouldn't doubt anything being possible."

Elouise diligently searched for answers, relying on her hopes for these tales about Syann. She firmly believed that all her hard work and aspirations were, without a doubt, true. And indeed, she was right.

I was wrong, no matter how much I wished to deny it. Even now, with help, I don't want this. I yearn to go back home to my family and wake up from this nightmare, but the one thing that would haunt me if I took it back is Oren. If this all hadn't occurred, if Syann wasn't real, would Oren and I have ever crossed paths again? Why does my mind keep fixating on him?

Oren heaves deeply, leaning onto the horse's neck. "Buh-kt."

"Oren, it hasn't even been ten minutes," Jace grumbles.

I'm still struggling to understand what Oren meant. "Is he all right?"

"He's fine," Jace replies dismissively.

Oren's skin drains of color as his shaking breath intensifies. Something is wrong. "I don't think so! Mindy, woah! Stop!" I instruct the horse, placing my hand gently on her snout.

"Brenda! This is typical. Trust me. There's no point in stopping. We'll never move if we wait until he feels at ease!" Jace pulls on the reins agitatedly, signaling Mindy to walk again.

I pursue Jace heatedly. "It's a recurring issue for Oren, but his sickness is not normal by any means! Isn't that why I'm here to help him?"

"I know Oren is different!" Jace points a strong index finger at Oren, before grabbing a bucket hanging from Mindy's saddle.

"I choose not to baby him like Elouise does, so he can be stronger. I understand he isn't feeling well, but that's constant. So, if he wants to achieve the healing he needs, he must push through that. Otherwise, we're never going to make it. You know all those people you saw attack the festival yesterday? They're still out there. They're after you and any of your allies. We must put our best foot forward. Even if we don't have two good feet to stand on, we all must pull our weight."

What a jerk. I puff offensively, "The right thing to do if someone you care about doesn't have two good feet to stand on is to give them a shoulder to lean on. Supporting someone who can't support themselves isn't babying them! R—" The sound of Oren gagging interrupts what would have been a heated scolding. One thing leads to another, and he's profusely vomiting into the bucket. He violently coughs once he's finished.

"See, I knew what he needed," Jace declares cockily, somehow proud that his little brother vomited. "If it weren't for the bucket I gave him, he would have spewed everywhere. Now that that's out of his system, he should feel better for a bit." Jace's eyes shift to Oren. "Are you done?" Oren nods defeatedly, and Jace takes the bucket away from Oren. "I'll be back." Jace steps away toward a bush to empty the bucket.

Sadly, I glimpse at Oren—his cheeks have taken on a rosy shade. "Does Jace always treat you that harshly?"

Oren hesitantly nods. He sluggishly reaches for his backpack, taking it off his back and placing it in his lap.

"Now it makes sense that you never mentioned him to me."

Oren remains silent, his attention on retrieving an item he's seeking from his backpack. He extracts a water canteen and a small drawstring bag.

"You and Elouise are close, though, right?"

"Mm-hmm," he hums sentimentally, before swigging his water.

"You miss her, don't you?"

Oren nods again. His mouth is full of water, and he doesn't seem to be swallowing it. Instead, he hides his face and leans away from me as he spits it out. "S-sorry."

"You're fine." I don't blame him for trying to rinse his mouth out. He closes the cap of his canteen, then reaches into the bag, pulling out herbs—mint. "I miss my family, too." I scratch my shoulder, which feels bare without Stella. "At least we're in this together. It makes things a little less lonely." I grin at him.

Oren makes eye contact with me for the first time since we left. It's brief but noticeable. As his gaze falters, he nibbles on the leaf.

"That's mint?" I don't mean it as a question but as a conversation starter.

He nods again, continuing to chew. Oren has no intention of replying to me. It's all right. At least we had a little moment. I don't need an explanation of why he's eating it. Mint smells good. Vomit doesn't.

"All right!" Jace bursts out, breaking the silence between me and Oren. He walks back toward Mindy and hangs the empty bucket back on her saddle. "No more stops, and straight to Athena's."

***

Our arrival in town is as peculiar as I imagined. It resembles a ghost town. Typically, the day after the festival, the town is filled with people diligently tidying up the decorations. However, wreaths and banners hang limply on doors and lampposts, swaying in the strong wind.

Is everyone still hiding in their homes? Have the people left? Seeing the town I once knew as a welcoming haven abandoned because of me disturbs me deeply.

When we arrive at the square, we discover everyone's whereabouts. It's as crowded there as the festival stage was yesterday before Uxaar's goons showed up. Instead of the usual buzzing and colorful throng, this one is eerily silent and dressed in dreary black. Why are so many people here? Curiosity getting the better of me, I can't resist treading closer.

"Brenda. There's nothing to see here," Jace scolds me.

I ignore him and bolt toward the scene.

Someone speaks in the center of the crowd. His voice is too familiar—Liam's. He and a few men I recognize as some of Byron's councilmen stand by the well in the town square. It must be some sort of funeral for Byron.

The sight freezes me. I can't help but imagine Liam discovering Byron's body, which I had abandoned. He must have been devastated and felt more pain than I'm experiencing. If only I could have healed Byron or at least offered Liam an apology that I couldn't. The knowledge that I will never have the chance to speak to my friend again makes my heart sink.

My family stands at the forefront of the crowd. My mother holds a bouquet of flowers. Aliah clutches a basket of flowers tightly in her arms, tears streaming down her face as she rests her head on Jonavan's shoulder.

Liam's eulogy to his father sounds strangled yet strong. He doesn't dare shed a tear in front of the crowd. Liam is too prideful for that. Even so, his expression sags lifelessly, while his eyes hold no passion.

This is an expression of pure heartbreak that I've never witnessed in Liam before, yet I deeply empathize with his grief. Like me, he has no family. His mother passed away during childbirth when Liam was just four, along with his infant sister. I can only fathom the tears he shed last night—the most heart-wrenching tears that leave you breathless. He had no one to comfort him because I wasn't there for him. I feel like a mere stranger now.

Jace places a firm hand on my shoulder. "We need to leave at once!"

I shove his hand away angrily.

"Brenda! Don't! No one remembers you!"

I disregard Jace and venture deeper into the crowd. With Oren riding Mindy, he won't get through the gathered people. Jace won't even attempt to pursue me if he's to remain with Oren.

Against my logic, Jace chases me, grasping my arm.

"Unhand me!"

"No! This is a waste of time that we can't afford!"

I shove myself away from Jace. "They were all so abruptly stolen from me! I didn't even get to tell them goodbye. I will have that! Even if I can't speak to them face-to-face!"

Jace continues to protest, but I leave him, Oren, and Mindy behind to enter the crowd. I have an unobstructed view of Liam and my family.

Liam concludes his eulogy by unveiling an engraving of Byron's name on the well in the square. The entire gathering falls silent during the dedication, and they are all deeply moved by the weight of his words.

The crowd scatters when Liam leaves. I take my turn approaching the well. The carving of the message reads—

**In memory of
Byron Liam Asbury,
"a Father of Seren."**

My eyes well with tears as I read the latter line. I know Liam had to have chosen that. Like me, he feels fatherless now and burdened with an unexpected weight. His is to lead a broken town under a colossal threat. Mine is to face this said threat: Uxaar—he caused this. If it weren't for Uxaar, I would have never left my goddess form, right? I wouldn't be in this pain, and neither would Liam.

I'm supposed to be the goddess who saves us from Uxaar, but I'm only human. Silent tears escape as I kneel.

A clatter of hooves creeps behind me. Jace and Oren were able to make it through the scattering crowd. "Wh-what happened?" Oren asks.

I glance back at the brothers, wishing I didn't have to explain—but I won't ignore Oren, even if he ignores me sometimes. "This town's leader, Byron, um…was killed last night at the festival, by one of Uxaar's followers."

"We need to go, now!" Jace scorns me.

"Jace, s-she's up-upset," Oren stammers defensively.

I glance at Oren, vulnerably hearing him defend me. *He cares.*

"So am I! Since when did you care?"

Oren mutters frustratedly at Jace.

I'm ready to interrupt Jace and Oren's quarrel until a little girl catches my eye. Aliah scurries beside me, grabbing a fistful of blue flowers from her basket. She sprinkles the blue petals around the well.

Forget-me-nots.

How painfully ironic.

I grasp a cluster of the delicate blue flowers in my fist. At funerals, my family has always brought forget-me-nots as a token of respect, a symbol that the deceased are never forgotten. When her father died, Mum told me that when we bury the dead, they become one with the Earth. As the forget-me-nots grow from the ground, they serve as a reminder from the Earth to never forget those we've lost, as they continue to be a part of our world.

"You know what this means, Brenda?" my mum asked me back then.

"What, Mum?" I questioned.

"This means I will never forget you, and you will never forget me. We will forever be loved and never, ever forgotten."

The memory surges tears to my eyes without warning. Mum forgot me, she broke her promise to me. She said she would never forget me, yet my family sits beside me, not even acknowledging my existence. I bring the blue flowers to my chest as I cry.

"Oh, Aliah!" my mum calls. "Give her some room. It's not proper behavior to barge in on people." Her worn eyes dart at me. "I'm so sorry!" Her tone is apologetic and gloomy.

I gaze at Mom, noticing that her dark, coiled hair is in the same braid I wove for her yesterday. Even through her veiled hat, her warm, brown eyes and apologetic smile still send a comforting wave through me. If only that comfort were enough to melt the icy feeling that prickles my heart.

She really doesn't remember.

"It's all right." I sniffle, tugging my hood farther over my eyes. Mum never saw me last night—this is our first interaction since the stars fell, and I fear to say something wrong for once. "These flowers are beautiful."

"Oh, thank you, dear," Mum replies. "Are you all right?" Mum was always kind and ready to jump in at the first warning sign of negative feelings in others, even strangers. How did I become one to her?

"Everything is falling apart."

She sighs with a heavy nod. "This loss struck us all, along with this new threat among us, but all hope isn't lost. Byron and what he stood for will never be forgotten."

I twist the forget-me-not in my fingers. "Forget-me-nots grow from the ground, from the dead in the Earth, as a reminder to never forget the ones we've lost." This analogy could spark her memories, like how Stella sparked Oren's.

"That's why my family brings them to funerals. Who told you that about forget-me-nots?" Mum, surprised, asks me.

"My mum promised she would never forget me, but—" I'm interrupted by my own sob. "She's gone."

The air is silent between us for a moment. "What's your name, dear?" Mum asks me, so I tell her. I hope she'll remember when she hears it. My mum smiles bittersweetly. "I've always loved that name—it was my firstborn's name."

What? My heart skips a beat when she admits that. She acknowledged she *did* have a daughter named Brenda! "Was?"

"She's unfortunately no longer with us. She was only a babe. She passed on her birthday, only three days before the stars fell eighteen years ago."

My chest clenches tighter. This realization leaves me speechless.

I wasn't their Brenda.

My "parents" had Brenda, but when she died, I replaced her after the stars fell. When I lived with them, it was as if, in their memory, Brenda never died. I was nothing but an imposter instead of their real daughter, using her identity to hide my real one.

My family was always my sanctuary, a place where I felt truly at home. Even now, seeing Mum and Dad behind her, I find it difficult to doubt that feeling. Their love has always been a constant source of strength and identity for me. I believed that I was an integral part of them, and no one ever doubted that. In fact, I feel like a harmonious blend of both of them, physically and psychologically. I inherited Dad's stubbornness and Mom's compassion. My physical appearance is even a testament to this. I have a fusion of my mother's dark skin and my father's light skin, and Dad's exact arched nose, and my mother's nose freckles.

How was it all a lie? Is my appearance part of a disguise or a coincidence? Regardless, the experience was real to me, and I grieve the loss of it deeply.

"I'm sorry for your loss." That is all I can get myself to say.

"Thank you." She smiles. "During that time, it felt like everything was falling apart, too. Years before losing Brenda, I struggled with infertility. I was devastated and felt that all hope was gone, but now my husband and I have two beautiful children and a daughter who's joined the fields of flowers. She will never be forgotten and will always be a part of my family, part of these flowers you see." She gently places her hand on the flowers in mine, and tears cloud her eyes. "What I'm saying is, Brenda, don't give up. Hope is never gone. Neither are the love and memories people had for you."

I was determined to make my family remember me, but their

memories have erased me. The forget-me-not reference and my name didn't work. My family is convinced that Brenda is dead, and they should be.

I'm not her.

My dad stands right behind us, along with the Silvius brothers. For now, the logical move is to leave.

I can't help but cry. I yearn for the comfort my mum would always give me when I was broken. I wish to stay and be mothered and not leave.

Not caring what she might think, I embrace Mum tightly, knowing this could be my last time seeing her. "Thank you, thank you for everything."

This is it, the goodbye that I've longed for since last night.

She holds me back. Thank heaven, she holds me back. "Things will turn out, Brenda. Hold on."

I wish to hold on to her and never let go.

Her grip loosening from me is the unwanted signal that I must withdraw from her. Dad places a hand on Mum's shoulder, leading her to her feet. Step by step, they trod away. I listen to their footsteps until my racing heartbeat drowns them out and watch them leave until my tears blur them away.

I hoped I could prove to them I was their daughter, that I could jog their memories as I did with Oren. Even more, I hoped they hadn't forgotten me at all. The opposite transpired. I'm brokenhearted, sobbing against the well.

"I tried to warn you they wouldn't remember you!" Jace exclaims.

"I wanted a proper goodbye! That's all I wanted."

"Sometimes we don't get what we want, Syann."

"It's Brenda!" I snap fiercely through tears. I know I'm wrong, I'm Brenda's imposter, but how could I let go? I can't. I can't admit I'm wrong.

"No, it's not! You heard Petunia. Brenda was her child who passed. You're not her! It was all a disguise to protect you. You must accept that!"

"Jace—" Oren bursts in meekly.

"You don't get to tell me who I am or what I must do!" I snap at Jace, springing onto my feet. "I didn't ask for your opinion!"

"It's not an opinion, it's a fact!"

"Isn't th-that enough, Jace?" Oren's question freezes Jace and me. The defensive aggression in his eyes surprised us both.

"Yes, it is enough! Enough with the arguing, according to Jace, we've wasted enough time already!" I shout, before storming down the streets.

I intend on not saying another word before reaching Athena's, even if that means the silence will torment my mind. That's better than letting Jace belittle me.

As I always did with flowers in the past, I weave the clusters of forget-me-nots into my hair while I let my tears fall.

7 Oren

"This place reminds me of your old farm." Brenda isn't the only one who feels that way. Athena's stable evokes a nostalgic feeling reminiscent of my childhood home. This longing for my past—my grandparents, the farm, and my health—taunts me with the realization that it's unattainable. Even if I recover, my grandparents and those cherished childhood years are lost.

"I forgot you ever saw that place," Jace replies. "But indeed, it does." Jace steadfastly holds out his arms to help me down. I swing my good leg over the saddle and land softly and steadily with his assistance. Once I receive my crutch and Mindy is securely tied in a stable, we head toward the exit.

Brenda's voice, a distant echo, rings faintly in the hazy past reality that swirls in my mind. The horse before me, a familiar presence, stirs memories of carefree moments. The wind rushes through my hair as I gallop briskly through a field, a girl's laughter echoes in my memory. Who is she?

A hand waves in front of my face, jolting me out of my reverie. Brenda persistently asks if I'm all right, but I remain silent.

The horse is still there, right in front of me!

It can't be.

A grin disperses across my face. "Moo?" I gasp out the name.

The white-speckled horse has a smaller frame and a large spot by its right eye. It's Moo, my childhood horse!

"Seriously? The cow runt horse!" Jace snickers.

"Moo!" Brenda beams, following behind me. I set my hand on Moo's snout as the horse trots in place excitedly. He recognizes me.

"Hey, boy!" Moo nudges my shoulder, now neighing joyously. This makes me laugh like a child. "I-I-I missed you, too, bud!"

"You know this horse, too?" Jace asks Brenda. I know the answer to that. My journal mentioned we rode Moo together frequently.

"I learned to horse-ride on Moo. Oren taught me everything I know." Her tone slithers back into its previously spiteful tone. She's still angry at Jace. When she faces me, her expression at once lightens with a smirk. "So, the horse race I won yesterday is all thanks to Oren."

It's kind of her to give me credit for her victory, but I don't think I could have made that much of a difference. Our riding days were years ago.

Jace glares at us as if he's not buying it.

"It is nice to see Moo again." She reaches her hand to pet the horse.

I chuckle and say, "Y-y-yeah, it-it is. I-I-I wonder how he got here. D-d-d-id Elouise ever mention t-t-to you h-h-he was here, Jace?"

"No." Jace crosses his arms. "But Uncle Charley must have sold him after he inherited Grandpa's belongings. I'm not surprised if he did so, he's a runt!" Jace chuckles. He always teased Moo for being a runt. Although it frustrated me back then, hearing Jace say it now is pleasantly nostalgic. "Do you know why he's named Moo, Brenda?" he asks. "Because when he was born,

Oren—"

"Mistook him for a cow!" Brenda and Jace jointly finish the sentence. I'm partially relieved when they laugh together. Hopefully, the tension between them is fading. I say only *partially*, because they're laughing *at me,* which is embarrassing.

"I-I-I was si-six," I stammer defensively.

"He was always my favorite out of your family's horses because of how many fun adventures we had with him together," Brenda says to me.

I long to know what those childhood adventures were like. As my fingers trace through Moo's coat, they get lost as my thoughts do, colliding straight into Brenda's hand.

The touch is a spark, one I wasn't prepared for. Warmth hurries to my face, as my hand and gaze retreat to my side.

If the timing of Jace telling us to go hadn't overlapped with that moment, I would've apologized to her out of habit. Instead, I'm speechless.

After bidding farewell to Moo, Brenda regales me with tales of our cherished rides on him. These stories ignite a sense of anticipation to see Athena. Perhaps she holds the key to reclaiming my memories, or Syann possesses the ability to heal me sooner than expected.

Brenda knocks on the front door, which a stout woman with coiled hair opens. "Brenda! Oh, thank the heavens you're here!"

Huh? How does Athena remember Brenda? Brenda never mentioned it, but she also doesn't appear surprised that Athena remembers her. Instead, the stress in Brenda's body eases.

We're welcomed inside Athena's home without hesitation—urgently is more like it. Her home is similar to mine, cabin style, yet much more furnished. Many painted pictures, flowerpots, and books are on the shelves. However, Athena's room presents a different picture—a much messier one at that. It's a whirlwind of open books and scrolls scattered across her desk, some even lying on the floor and her bed. Despite the clutter, the room exudes a delightful scent, reminiscent of curling up with a good book in a meadow of wildflowers by the woods.

"I apologize for the clutter. Other than Elouise, I don't get much company here. Most of my time I spend studying."

"It's quite all right, Athena," Jace responds. "We appreciate your welcome."

"The pleasure is all mine." Athena's passionate eyes dart to me. "So, you're Oren?" I nod in response. "I could tell! You much resemble your sister. But she never mentioned how many freckles you've got!" She leans toward me, retrieving my left hand and observing it closely. "Why, you've got as many as the stars in the shower skies!"

I exhale harder than I'd prefer to exhibit, as my hand flees into my pocket. Would she find it proper if I tapped her nose and pointed out the freckles of her own? I hope not!

Athena is a prime example of why I conceal my body as much as possible. People judge far too easily. I should have worn gloves.

"Anyhow, it's a privilege to finally meet you. Elouise has told me a great deal about you. I've been hoping we'd meet for a long while. Sincerely, this is an excitement!"

A fabricated chuckle evades me as I stride back. I'm oblivious to how I should react to Athena's enthusiasm toward me. I cling to the fact that this attention on me will be short-lived. Brenda will be her primary focus, not me. Then I will finally figure out if I can be healed here or if my journey will continue. "It-it-it's n-nice to m-m-meet you, Athena," I force myself to say.

She smiles at me nevertheless before offering me to sit at her desk, an offer I won't deny. I thank her and take a seat.

"Athena," Jace begins, "Elouise has made you aware that Oren is ill and that we intended on seeking out Syann to help him. Is it possible for Brenda to heal Oren in her current form? Or will it have to wait until she reaches the altar?"

"When Elouise and I would discuss this matter, I was always unsure if Syann could heal Oren immediately. I didn't know how exactly Syann would come to be or how her powers would function. Neither writings nor prophecy specified. The only clue is the star. In the prophecies, it was a sign of protection. For the past eighteen years, it protected you, Brenda, through memory loss and blocking the Shadow's powers. Now, I believe it's directing you toward Secreth. It's even forcing you out of Seren by causing everyone to forget you. Within those mountains the star hovers over are a system of caverns leading to the Dawn realm. Within the Dawn realm is the entrance of Secreth. Only you pass through it. That must be the key."

"So, I can't use my powers to the fullest until I reach Secreth?"

"You don't know the Incantations of Light, do you?"

"No, only the Shadow's."

"Then I can't determine what powers you possess or how to use them."

My heart strums sadly. Brenda can't heal me yet. I should have known. Why would I be gullible enough to hope otherwise? The joy of seeing Moo again swayed my emotions. After years of guarding my heart, how did my guard crumble so rapidly?

Why does Brenda make me feel things I refused before?

Athena asks Brenda to remove her gloves. Brenda not only strips off her gloves but also her hood. Her face is meticulously depicted, showcasing her bun that tightly restrains her curls.

I recognize a point I named in my journal—her ears. I wrote that she had prominent ears, which I always liked. She never quite grew into them. The thought triggers a grin on my face.

Athena grasps Brenda's hands, observing from her fingertips to her palms. She even rolls up her sleeves to the point that the glowing stops, which is beneath her wrists. "I've never seen anything quite like this! They glow because, unlike any of us, your spirit is free of Darkness. However, your body and soul hold Darkness as we all do. This explains why only your hands glow instead of your body entirely. Now that her spirit has awakened in you, the stars are no longer blocking the Shadow's powers, because Syann herself now protects you. If I'm not mistaken, your flesh should be impenetrable."

"Impenetrable?"

Athena takes a pen and scratches Brenda's arm without any precaution.

"Ow!" An expression of awe swallows any frustration her face previously exhibited. "It hurt, but there's not even a scratch! Do you have a knife?" she asks Jace. Jace offers his dagger to Brenda, who grazes it across her arm without any effect. Undeterred, she tests Athena's theory by attempting to stab the tip into her forearm. Initially cautious, she soon realizes that the dagger is like trying to cut through a diamond. We conclude that she can feel pain from blows but is not physically harmed by them.

Brenda returns the dagger to Jace, who asks, "So, there's no other way for Oren to recover except for getting to Secreth?"

Athena hesitates to answer, uneasily admitting, "There's one. My journal speaks of a river flowing throughout the Dawn from Secreth. The pools the river empties in contain its healing powers, exactly what you need." She glances at me before grabbing an ancient book from her desk. Athena spreads open the journal and invites us all to take a look. On the page is an intricate illustration of a pool surrounded by crystals and trees. Within the pool is a drawing of a human observing their hand as if it had been miraculously healed. The illustration is breathtaking, and for some reason, it evokes a sense of familiarity in me, reminiscent of my own art. The artwork bears a signature: *Akira Dai.*

"There's a village of people from the Dawn. They've used these pools to extend their lifespans, even for hundreds of years. Many people dating back to the war on Secreth centuries ago are still alive because of it." Athena sighs, turning to me as she shuts the book. "I hated withholding this knowledge from Elouise, but I didn't want you both to make the same mistake my friends and I made by attempting to embark there."

"You've been to the Dawn?" Brenda asks.

"Indeed. Roughly two decades ago. That's the very reason I remember you, unlike anyone else. The Dawn is the grounds where the Geron are visible. Exposing yourself to them is one of two ways to gain the ability to see them in any atmosphere."

"Oh!" Brenda interjects, the logic of Athena remembering her clicking in her mind. "So, you can see the Geron?"

"Aye, except for now. Since you arrived, they've left me. For the first time since it began."

"After I broke off from the Shadow Incantations, they swarmed me. I got mad and told them to stay away from me. I haven't seen one since."

"They listen to you! I've only been able to listen to them. They've swarmed me like bees half of my life."

Brenda's face sags remorsefully. "I thought the five minutes they swarmed around me was hell. How did you get through it for two decades?"

"I barely could at first. It is a battle focusing on my surroundings, seeing them all around me while they tell me horrid things without end. None of you know what it's like to see a whole other world against you while no one else is even aware. No one could. I clung to the truth that Syann one day would come and end the fallen Geron, as foretold. And on that day, I'd have peace that would make all the nightmares worth it forever more. In the meantime, I distanced myself and studied."

A pang of guilt gnaws at me. I'm completely unaware of the Geron's nature, but they must be foul creatures. Now, it all makes sense why Athena is so focused and touchy with her surroundings. The Geron distract her.

I shouldn't have been so taken aback by her enthusiastic greeting.

"You didn't know before going to the Dawn that you'd be able to see the Geron?" Jace asks.

"We knew but underestimated the price because we were desperate. My friend Ebony, her mother was from the Dawn. Her name was Akira Dai; she was one of the many Shadows from the war in Secreth I mentioned earlier and the author of this journal. When the Geron invaded the Dawn after a thousand years, she left and decided to make a new life for herself in Seren. That she did. She settled and remarried and had Ebony and her older brother. They both grew up hearing stories about the Dawn from Akira, until she passed when Ebony was seventeen. Ebony inherited the journal, and we both became infatuated with its stories and the idea of embarking to the healing pools to restore Ebony's fiancé's, Philip's, sight. So, being the reckless teenagers we were, we all went through with it without telling anyone. We thought we had nothing to lose but each other, but that we did lose. Upon our arrival at the Dawn realm, we discovered the Geron had accumulated a band of followers since their return, and we were attacked by them. I got separated from my friends and was fortunate enough to be rescued by the village's soldiers, but my friends weren't so fortunate." Athena's eyes become tearful. "I still wish the roles were reversed. Ebony and Philip had such bright futures waiting for them. I never saw two people more in love. They both wished to be married and have a family, but now they're either dead or oppressed by the Geron's men. The Geron have sure never let me forget that it's my fault." Grief pours from Athena's eyes. "It wrecked me. I was so close to losing all hope, all until the stars fell for the first time half a year later. I knew then that Syann was here on Earth, and that she'd set things right."

The stars falling six months after Ebony and Philip's disappearance was no coincidence, right? There were over a thousand years of silence from the Geron until they escaped from the Underealm. Only one generation later, enough time for the Geron to recruit followers to attack Philip and Ebony, the incantation was said. It's too coincidental.

"I-I-I hate t-t-to say this, b-b-but, erm—um. I-I don't think th-th-them being ta-taken and the stars falling, um—s-s-so shortly after is, um—a-a-a coincidence," I mutter.

"I hate to agree with you, freckles, but I fear the same." Athena shakes her head.

Freckles? I hate that.

"Oren, you think Ebony or Philip is the Shadow?" Brenda asks. I nod.

"When the Dawn soldiers rescued me from the attack, their leader warned me that the Geron's men had been kidnapping their people to try forcing them to say the Shadow Incantations, which was why they attacked us. It would be better for them to be dead than have that fate."

"Why? Can I not save the Shadow?" Brenda asks.

"During the war, Syann was able to destroy the Shadow bonds and banish the Geron to the Underealm with the Light Incantations and the altar, but you don't have access to either. So, until you reach Secreth, the answer is unclear."

"Then Ebony and Philip had to have known the risks, right?"

"They did. Which is why I hold on to hope the Shadow isn't either of them, like how I've held on to hope that you were going to come save us."

Brenda sighs softly. "I will follow that star and try my best to help you all. I want to avenge Ebony and Philip and make sure you or anyone else are never harassed by the Geron again, Athena! And I wish to heal Oren, but I can't help but feel that this is all bigger than me."

Brenda is fighting for a cause that I'm too afraid to stand up for. She stands by what's realistic and doesn't make empty promises, unlike Elouise. Instead, Brenda only genuinely offers to try her best. She wants to help me, but she doesn't offer what she knows she might not be able to provide. I respect that so much.

"You experienced life as a mortal human, so you would hold the compassion in your heart to rescue the people you are destined to save. Now you know you are part of something much more. You must have faith in who you are and truly see Syann for who she is. The power in you created the Geron. That power can rule over them, as you have already proven. You are bigger than them!" Athena points a strong index finger to Brenda's chest. "You are bigger than Uxaar or his Shadow, and you will bring them to his defeat! You must believe in who you are, Syann, the Goddess of Light. Once you believe that, you'll have peace and faith that you'll be able to make things right. As I've said, I would have given up so long ago if I didn't believe in you. You're what kept me going," Athena says.

Brenda sighs, staring into Athena's sincere eyes. The air is painfully quiet until she asks, "Will you go with me? To the Dawn. I don't want to go alone. Your knowledge would help."

There's much pain and desperation in Brenda's voice, which triggers a realization in me: *I don't want her to go alone, either.*

"Brenda, it would be my greatest honor. I'll need to briefly pack some things for the journey if you don't mind," Athena replies.

"Not at all," Brenda replies. Athena nods before leaving the room with her journal and bag. Brenda turns to me as the door shuts. "So, what's the plan now? There are two options. We go to the pools, or you both go home, and I will try my best to return."

"Oren, it's your decision." Jace puts me on the spot.

I want to stay by Brenda's side, but I couldn't endure such a journey, right? Unless maybe I could? What if I made it to the healing water in the Dawn? Syann is real, meaning Secreth is real, and the pools. I can't be passive with that! Best of all, if I reach the Dawn, I'll be able to remember Brenda, too, as Athena does!

This indisputable idea pounds in my head. This trip has the potential to fulfill my yearning for healing, peace, and a fulfilling life—all of which I have been denied.

Familiarity is a comfort zone, but staying home, what do I gain? I'm lying in bed for days at a time, not knowing if I'll live to see tomorrow, and I can't eat without vomiting. I'll return to the same old life, hoping that Brenda will return to me before I die. If

I do go, I might get healed, or I might die. Either way, my suffering is finally over, and that's what I want.

"What if I—" I stammer shakily. "What if I went with you? If-If there's h-h-healing water. M-maybe it's my b-b-b-best bet. If I-I get healed t-t-t-there, I'll be able"—I cough—"be-be able to defend m-m-myself."

My answer shocks the two of them; their wide eyes tell that much. I don't blame them. This suggestion must be opposite the person they know. It even amazes me, but I'm tired of waiting. If I die, I'm hastening the inevitable, and giving myself the peace that my death wasn't at my own hands. Elouise would have never forgiven me for that.

"Are you serious? You want to take the risk?" Jace asks in disbelief.

Breath rattles out of me. "What if this is m-m-m-my only chance? We don't kn-kn-kn-know for sure if she will re-re-return. If she doesn't, I m-m-m-must make the journey an-an-anyway."

Brenda peers at Jace as if wanting his approval.

"All right, then. We'll go." Jace nods.

"No. You sh-sh-should go home, Jace. There's no point in-n-n-n risking your life for m-m-m-me. Mum and Elly need you."

"Only if Brenda agrees. If she needs me there to help you, I will go."

"Go home, Jace," she replies firmly. "He's right. Your family needs you. They've lost enough already."

"Oren, are you sure? It's going to be perilous. You might not return."

"I'm sure." I'm most definitely not sure. Something unexplainable in me is saying this is the right decision. I couldn't fight it if I tried. Instead, I will fight for my life on this trip. "Tell Mum 'n' Elly I-I-I-I love them. Thank 'em f-f-f-taking care of me. B' it's t-t-t-time I take care of-f-f-f myself."

8 *Brenda*

We spare little time before heading off. Judging from the heavy, gloomy clouds, this sprinkle will evolve into a ruthless storm. Getting seized by its rage is far from ideal. For Oren's sake, it must be bypassed. Only seconds of walking in the rain have his teeth chattering. I decided to give him Elouise's hood to help warm him.

Athena leads her white horse, Comet, out of his stall. I convinced Athena to let Oren and me ride Moo together to cheer him up. I'm unsure if this idea will work, but it's worth a try. I long to restore the happy farm boy I once knew, not only physically but emotionally. I want to see the old him, before things went downhill, and I know he's in there. I've sighted it twice now, back in the oak grove, and when he first saw Moo.

Oren now stares at Moo with wavering eyes. Perhaps it's not that he's worried about riding—maybe he's frightened about the journey, like I am.

Athena's presence provides reassurance that I lacked before.

I expected her to have much valuable knowledge, but I underestimated her. Her journal even has a full map of the Dawn realm, and my eyes itch to consume it. She promised to show it to me once we reach the caverns.

Beyond Seren is nothing but open fields, which are dull under the gray, cloudy sky. A blanket of fog swaddles the distant mountain I could have pristinely viewed last night. Only the beams of starlight peek through it.

There's a slightly nostalgic feeling to this, clinging to Oren as we ride off. Back then, wind danced through my hair as we rode. The sun kissed us with warmth, and my heart drummed with delight. Now I'm cold. My hair is as bound as my heart, which is broken.

"It was raining when you gave me Stella, like it is now. Every time Stella has seen rain since, she says, *rain!* Each time she did, I thought of you," I say into Oren's ear, my chin resting on his shoulder. "Every time."

I missed Oren dearly when it rained. Storms always left me pondering what had ever become of my friend after he had left the farm villages.

"I-I never enjoyed the r-r-rain, unless m-m-maybe I-I did with y-y-you."

Several memories of Oren and me in the rain pop into my head. Most of them ended in us running into a barn and keeping cover.

"You did enjoy the rain. What you did not enjoy was getting wet. When you were little, you nearly drowned when you went swimming. So, we usually found cover where we watched the rain and talked. You always told me you thought the rain was fascinating."

"I-it-it is."

I can't help but smile. "Once the rain stopped, you enjoyed playing in the mud with me, especially making mud pies. Yours were always better than mine. Also, our parents would be upset with how dirty we got."

Oren chuckles. "I-I nearly forgot a-a-about mud p-pies—I-I loved making—making those—Once I-I-I tracked muck i-in-in the h-h-house and J-Jace, my mum, ev-even my grandpa was cross a-a-at me."

"So was my dad when I soiled my dress and shoes, but it was worth it."

He chortles sweetly. "D-d-do you, um—remember a-a-anything else?"

Our conversation puts distance between me and my worries, which is exactly what I need. Oren's interest in our past doesn't stop. He continues to ask questions as I continue to answer. It's fascinating how he remembers the events I'm referring to but can't remember my presence. Regardless, he believes I was there and am the missing puzzle piece he lacked from the memory. It's sweet to return to little old memories from so far away. I treasured those times for so long. I know he once cherished them, too.

We come to a halt underneath a cluster of evergreen trees for a rest stop for Oren. The mountain under the star is getting much closer. All that's between us and the caverns is a clearing of grass and wildflowers.

We're over halfway to the Dawn. Instead of the sight of my future drawing me, I defeatedly sit in the damp flowers. They remind me of times picking flowers with the family I can never return to. My mother, well, Petunia, pointed out how when I'm nervous I'd twist my hair. She was right. The movement of my fingers calms and distracts me now, as it did back then. The crunching grass alerts me that Athena is approaching. She comes to a stop beside me.

"Athena, I'm not who you expected Syann to be like, am I?" I ask, uprooting a fistful of flowers out of the ground.

"Not at all." Athena stretches, before sitting against a tree. "You're much better."

Better? I heard her inaccurately, right?

"You have this feistiness in you, this stubbornness. Oh, and I know when it's used correctly against the Geron, and you believe in yourself, you will be unstoppable."

"For most of my life, I felt unstoppable, until now," I admit.

"Why not now?"

"Is it bad to say I miss my family and old life? And leaving that is scary? Handling the fate of Seren and this world entirely is larger than any responsibility I ever carried. Before today, I helped my family get by and lived my life. And I did it confidently because it was easy. *This* is not!" I made a decent-sized flower chain throughout that ramble.

"What you're fighting for now, Brenda, is for all the people you love and care for. They depend on you. You know that, don't you?"

"Yes, the biggest responsibility I've ever had, I know, Athena! I just don't know if I'm capable of fulfilling it."

"Say if you weren't guaranteed to defeat Uxaar, and your family still did remember you back home. Would you still embark on this journey if you knew of this danger and that you were the only one who could stop it?"

"Yes! I'd do anything for my family!"

"Then you can do this for them. You can save them."

It's not that simple, is it? Even so, she's right. I desire to believe in myself. Athena sets her hand on my shoulder, giving me a reassuring smile. I smile back as she stares at my flower chain.

"Enough gloom, huh?" The seriousness flees her voice through a grin. "This! This is how you made the crowns yesterday?"

"Yes." I nod, weaving the stems together.

"Can you show me how?"

"Of course." I instruct her to take some flowers and stems, and she eagerly follows my instructions. Athena rambles about how beautiful the plant life in Secreth is, according to her journal.

Oren lingers by Moo, contemplating whether he'll join us.

I give him a push by asking, "Oren, you remember how to make these?"

He nods. "'Y' taught me."

"Yes." I smile.

"You taught Oren? When?" Athena asks curiously.

"It's complicated," I answer. Oren hesitantly sits next to Athena. "But in short, Oren and I were friends for several years when we were kids—"

"But he doesn't remember you anymore!" Athena interjects. "I see!"

"Only through his journal, he knows that we were friends. Remembering Stella is what made him realize that."

"Journals are lifesavers, I'll always say. They preserve the past unlike any other. Memories of the past war in Secreth and the Dawn civilization, even through the eighteen years the stars affected Seren's memories. Now, a friendship that could've vanished. How incredible!"

I smile and turn to Oren, who's now weaving a chain of flowers, too. I catch him gazing at me with a shy grin. His eyes retreat toward his chain.

I stare at him like I did when our hands touched in the stables. I'm not afraid—if anything, I'm quite the opposite. "Oren's a talented artist, too. His sketches are marvelous!"

Oren stiffens, as if my compliments embarrassed him.

Other than praising Oren's journalism, I have no contribution to this discussion. The closest thing I had to one was Stella. On the occasions I needed to rant about a forbidden topic, she was all ears.

For Oren and Athena, though, it's clear how journaling benefits them after all they've been through. After this whole mess, maybe it would help me to journal all my thoughts and frustrations about this experience that no one else can relate to.

"Oh! Do you have any I could see?" Athena questions expectantly.

Oren blushes while bashfully rambling, "Eh, erm-m-m, uh, I-I-I dunno—M-m-maybe w-when-when it-it isn't raining. I-I don't wanna g-g-get it wet."

"Once we get to the caverns, then!" Athena elevates her finished crown over her hair with a laugh. "How does it look? It feels a bit small!"

A lightning strike robs our attention from her. We must go.

I gaze back at Athena, who's no longer concerned about the crown on her head. It's too tiny to cover her hair but much better than anything Jonavan could have crafted. "We should get going."

Athena aids Oren onto his feet. Through coughs, he mumbles a sentence to her that I can't make out. Athena beams while thanking him.

Oren abandoned his crown in the grass. It's simplistic, with daisies and clovers neatly woven in a pattern. I retrieve it, intending to return it to him.

Athena calls me over. She and Oren are both heading toward the horses.

"Yes, Athena?" I ask, catching up.

"Take Oren to Moo, please, I'm going to mount Comet." I do as she requests, resisting the urge to ask what Oren told her. I can ask Oren myself. Hopefully, he will tell me.

I link arms with him, which causes him to jolt at first. "What were you and Athena talking about?"

"Oh, um—sh-she—" He clears his throat after coughing. "I told her, um—th-that h-h-her—" He pauses, struggling to retrieve any words. "Her fl-flower crown was nice. Th-the lightning d-d-did interrupt her."

I wasn't expecting that, but I smile. "You mean the lightning stole her thunder." My joke hangs in the air with awkwardness. It was pretty bad.

He stares dead at me, before he picks up on what I meant. He forces out a chuckle, before hard coughs follow.

"Are you all right?"

He nods, weathered eyes peeking at me.

"Speaking of flowers, you left this." I display his crown to him as we stop beside Moo.

"Oh, y-y-yeah. It-it-it's not my best work."

"You're too humble. I think it's lovely." I offer it back to him.

He hesitantly accepts it. "Really?"

"Oren, I don't lie. If I say something, don't question it."

Oren apologizes, bowing his head down shamefully.

"You don't have to apologize. It's really all right." I grin.

He gazes at me as if he's tiptoeing on eggshells, then back at the flower crown. "Um…w-w-well, th-thank you. That's what I-I-I should've said. Um—if-if—I want—" He coughs again. "Take it. Um, if you fancy it, then I want you t-t-to have it." He tries handing it back to me.

Is this a sincere gift? Or is he trying to hand off a trifle he doesn't want? I wish to believe in the first, so I take it and place it on my head. Still, he won't be empty-handed.

"I do. Thank you." I remember his flower chains pressed in his journal, and how much he cared for the flowers. Maybe it's a gesture in return? "I'll treasure it, like you with your bookmarks—Speaking of, it's only fair that you have one to wear like Athena and me." I hand him mine. "Since we're all in this together."

"Are you s—" He stops himself. "Right, d-don't question it."

I chuckle. "Here." I gently place it on his head.

This reminds me of when we were younger. We would make crowns, necklaces, bracelets, all sorts of things that we'd exchange between ourselves.

I study Oren's attributes, and his growth since we were children. Notably, he's slightly taller than me now, unlike back then. I begin to notice the same vibrant energy radiating from the flowers on his head within him. His spirit is blossoming, and I eagerly anticipate the growth and color that will emerge with increased sunlight.

The limitation I perceive is reminiscent of his smile, which is genuine yet timid. I yearn to witness Oren Silvius in his full potential—his full bloom.

"It's nice on you. Now, let's get to those caverns before the rain gets worse. You're freezing." I tug the hood over his forehead.

"I'm—I'm fine." Oren shies from my gaze. He turns toward Moo, attempting to climb on as he did back in the stable. However, he's struggling to make any progress.

Athena, already saddled on Comet's back, watches intently. Her eyes seem to implore me to help him, which I am set on doing.

"Do you need help?"

Oren shakes his head, disappointed that I asked him.

His bad knee buckles when he launches up. If it weren't for me holding him, he would have fallen. He groans softly, bending and grasping his knee.

"Let me help you! Before you hurt yourself further."

"I-I-I'm fine," he lies. He's hacking terribly.

"A thank-you would suffice! You would have fallen if it weren't for me."

He only huffs and puffs while red rushes his face. I embarrassed him.

I exhale regretfully. "I apologize for snapping. Do you need a moment?"

He shakes his head stubbornly.

Athena asks if he's all right. I couldn't answer her; I was too busy pushing Oren up. With my aid, he successfully mounts Moo.

"See, there's no shame in asking for help. Everyone needs it sometimes." I take a cleansing breath before pulling myself up.

Everything turns white as a clash roars into my ears. Goose bumps rise on my arms as alarm bells ring throughout my body. Are my powers acting up again? Or Uxaar?

Moo throws me and Oren onto the ground before bolting away.

Oren crashes onto me, groaning at the impact. He frantically scrambles off me as soon as he realizes he has me pinned down. "Brenda, a-a-are you all right? I'm s-s-sorry!"

"I'm indestructible, remember?" I grin a little, taking his hand to get my upper body off the ground. We sit on the soaked grass. "But you're not! Are you all right?"

He gazes off into the distance, alarmed at the sight of Moo bolting away. "Moo!" he calls for the horse before his coughing fit takes over. He grips his head, groaning.

"What's wrong?"

He hacks, "Moo's gone, so 's-s-s-s-s Comet 'n' Athena. H-h-horses fear lightning. It m-m-m-m-makes 'em stampede."

"I know, Oren! I meant if you were harmed!"

"J-j-just dizzy." He bursts out coughing.

"Like the room is spinning, sort of dizzy?" Oren nods at me. "Do you think Athena can get back to us?"

"I dunno."

"Well, we should head for shelter before the worst of the storm arrives."

"We'll never make it t-t-to the caverns in time o-o-on foot. Not w-w-w-with me! My crutch is-is w-with Moo."

I stand up, offering my hand to him. "I will help you. Do not try talking me out of it."

I sense it's against his wishes for me to help him, but he takes my hand anyway. He denies leaning on me for support and walks on his own. Very slowly and crookedly. If it couldn't get any worse, it isn't long before the wind whips against us. Weighted, pouring rain follows. Such brutal weather has never caught me in my life. There's no escaping it. The caverns are still a long distance away, I think, at least. My visibility is limited. Only yards of grass stretch in front of me before it's lost in the mist.

Oren stumbles, unable to walk steadily in such heavy winds. I grab him before he collapses. Instead of pushing away, his shaking hands cling onto my shoulders. He's terrified. I know it. There's no way I can comfort him, either. He's soaking wet, unable to walk without me, and far from home. There's nothing I can do to change that.

The wind even turns walking into a struggle for me. The rain is pelting us so hard the droplets are like hundreds of needles continuously poking me. It's difficult to even look upward without the precipitation striking my eyes.

I bellow Athena's name, hoping she can hear me. Heavy rainfall, Oren's coughs, and thunder rumbling is all I can hear.

Oren comes to a hard stop.

"Oren? We must keep going!"

"Y-y-you didn't see that?" Oren doesn't have the time to warn me. A sack swallows my head, stealing my little visibility left. A grip on my shoulder tears Oren and me apart. Among the sound of the rain is a loud thud, immediately followed by Oren grunting painfully. "N-N-No, let her—hmm—let her go!"

A grip on my shoulder and another on my opposite wrist captures me. Trying to wriggle away is useless. Terrorists are here to attack us blindly. The sudden extreme weather against us had to have been Uxaar's doing.

"No! Stop!" My cries are muffled by the sack.

I'm slammed onto the ground so hard the wind hisses out of me. Before I can recover my breath, immense pressure on my chest follows. The weight pins me to the grass. I try grabbing the source to push it off and discover my attacker has their foot stomped onto my chest. My hands were my only hope of pushing them off, but the attacker binds them together.

The attacker cackles maniacally, sending a chill through me. "You're so weak," whoever has a hold on me says. I've never heard this voice. He's not the redheaded man from the festival. This voice is much grittier and more brutal than the other. No indication of sympathy is in his voice, which is something that radiated from the redhead. I'm in danger.

My breaths sound like a storm wind hissing through a drafty

wall, fighting to press through. Oren is screaming on my behalf to free me throughout all the thuds of violence. Unless my powers come through or Athena does, what chance does he stand?

The pressure grows greater as a presence draws near. His breath is close to me, like a predatory animal sniffing its prey. I'm vulnerable, with no defense, left to be eaten alive by this wolf.

"I could slit your throat, end everything right here and now, ensuring victory for the Geron." He lifts what is undoubtedly a blade to my neck. It feels thin yet durable. "Or you can say the Incantations to Uxaar, and I'll let you go free. All of this will stop, as you've asked."

"I already said the Incantations once and freed myself," I pant out. "What's the use of it? I'll only do it again."

What a heap of lies. Roe freed me willingly. I'm unsure if I can free myself. Finding out isn't worth the risk. My death doesn't outweigh the horrible outcome if I say the Incantations and am bound to them. The world would be doomed. Or what if I did recite them? What if I told them to Roe again? Roe seems to be a well-intentioned creature.

No. Athena and even Roe said not to repeat them. I must trust myself. This terrorist wants me to tell them to Uxaar, not Roe. Dedicating them to another, like Roe, might not get this terrorist off my back.

"If you won't surrender, then dead is how Uxaar wishes you to be."

Something dreadful must be causing Oren to scream, but I don't know what. *No! Don't touch her! Stop!*

A sharp and powerful clash impacts my chest, causing me to screech loudly as tears prick my eyes. The sword is sharp, landing a blow incomparable to any pain I've felt in my lifetime. This should be fatal, but my skin is like a shield, restraining the blade from bloodshed.

"I am the Light, a power that no sword or mortal power can overcome!" I growl. This statement comes from the powerful feeling inside me. Without that, I'd only be screaming. "I am immortal, and I will be Uxaar's demise!"

"We'll see about that!" The terrorist lifts his blade away from my neck.

"Don't you understand? The Geron will curse us all! He wants this world, your home destroyed! I only want to help!"

"The world beyond the Dawn was never my home! If you say the Incantations, Uxaar will have mercy on Seren. If you refuse, surely Uxaar will send the Shadow to diminish the place into ashes. Like Byron, everyone you ever loved will be deceased because of your insolence!"

"I will have no part with Uxaar! He cannot be trusted! I won't be the unraveling of my home, and neither should you!"

His presence radiates closer. A new sensation of pressure, but this time on my neck. What's different is that it's not a thin, sharp blade. Instead, gloved, large hands are there to choke out the little amount of air in me that's left. It's impossible to breathe.

"St-stop!" I try shouting, but it comes out as a breathless plea as silent as a whisper. "I-I—" He blocked my airways, and I can no longer speak or breathe. That should suffocate me. One can't live without air, yet I'm not giving out as the moments tread on. It's an odd, unpleasant feeling. I desire breath instead of demanding it. My lungs aren't burning in discomfort like I've been holding my breath for minutes—it's as if I were swimming underwater and didn't need to come up for air. My powers must be keeping me alive, renewing the oxygen in my body. There is no other explanation.

My attacker continues to threaten me to get me to recite the Incantations, but I can't speak. It's impossible to with how hard he presses on my neck. He ought to know by now, as well as I do, that I can't die. He grumbles a string of curses before drawing me up by my arm. He must be much taller than me. He has the strength to dangle me like a rag doll. He drags me along, his grip not faltering despite my efforts.

"You don't realize what you're doing! The Geron are using you! If you stop this, I can end this and help you and everyone in the Dawn. The Geron won't threaten you or your people anymore! Let me go free!"

"You can't save me! You can't even save yourself!" he hisses. "With Uxaar's shadow, we're all under his control! You're too blind to realize it."

He must be bluffing. Every attempt to kill me has failed—I'm not under anyone's thumb.

Before I can reply, everything stops at the croaking of a gag that didn't come from me. The grip on me releases at once. I begin to descend with no way to catch myself. There's no explanation for what happened, not yet.

A new set of hands slows my fall, and we stumble into the grass together. Who's holding me? Am I safe? In more danger? I'm breathing too hard. The sack is stripped from my face, revealing Oren. He's received a black eye, a slit on his cheek, and a busted lip.

The man who attacked me is slumped over in a pool of red. Oren killed him. Another limp body lies in the distant grass.

How?

I underestimated Oren. He *saved* me.

"B-B-Brenda! B-B-Brenda rrr—you al-al-all right?" Oren asks me before a cascade of coughs leaves his throat. He lifts my upper body from the ground. His grip on me is tight yet shaky.

"You're alive!" My broken voice echoes into his shoulder.

I sit steady in Oren's lap. He grabs my wrists and reaches for Jace's knife in my pocket. "He's—gone." Oren exhales laboriously. He tries to steady his hand to cut off my restraints, but he's vibrating too intensely. "H-H-He—won't—he won't-t-t-t hurt you! He w-w-w—" Before he can speak another word, Oren passes out.

9 Brenda

For hours I've pleaded for Athena to help, but she never comes. Oren lies limp in my bound-up hands, not coming to. None of my attempts to wake him or to break my wrists free work. On the positive side, when I listened to his chest for a heartbeat, I wasn't disappointed. Oren survived, but until he wakes up, I'm stuck here.

Oren could have been killed. It's a miracle that he wasn't. My powers proved useless in defending us. Perhaps Oren managed to defend himself sufficiently, or more likely, my abilities were simply ineffective in protecting him. What will I do if the latter is the case? I'm the only one left to defend him, aside from the miracle of Athena's return. Or worse, what if he never wakes up? Will I have to continue alone?

"Roe!" I cry out. "Show yourself!" He's my last resort, the only one I can think of to get clarity from.

The Geron doesn't spare a moment before appearing. "I'm here."

"What happened to Athena? Where is she?"

"The lightning was a strategic attack by Uxaar to drive you apart. Uxaar's followers abducted her, along with the horses. They're already in the cave system toward the Dawn. You need to go there as well. You've spent enough time waiting for him to wake already."

"What are you talking about?" I blurt out in disbelief. "I told Oren I'd protect him. His brother left me in his charge! I'm not leaving him to die!"

"If you don't, the Shadow will surely catch up to the two of you! Oren won't stand a chance against it. He's already as good as dead."

"Athena told me to believe that I will know what is right and to believe in Syann. Syann longed to save every human she could. I'm not leaving him!"

"Then I hope you're right, but don't think Uxaar won't take advantage of your feelings for him. He's used similar tactics in the past. Uxaar threatened Ebony to recite the Shadow Incantations to save Philip's life, despite Athena's assumption that she'd be wise enough to resist. I hope you don't disappoint Athena, too."

The information widens my eyes, and Oren coughs even more. He's regaining consciousness.

My eyes dart toward Roe, but he's already gone.

No matter, I got the knowledge I needed.

My attention returns to Oren. He gazes at me, disoriented. "Wh-wh-wh-what happened?"

"You passed out for a few hours after the attack, but you're fine. You're fine," I repeat, to reassure myself.

"Wh' 'b-b-bout Athena?'

"She was captured. I know you are tired and have many questions, but we must get out of this rain."

"Y-y-you sat out here th-th-that long?"

"Never mind that now. Can you help me out of these bounds?"

Oren helps me free my wrists, and in return, I get him onto

his feet. As we walk, I fill him in on everything—how Roe revealed that Uxaar's followers abducted Athena and her journal, and the unfortunate truth about Ebony reciting the Incantations. He listens quietly, offering little feedback. The responses Oren does give are slurred and muffled by the rain.

He's far past exhausted and traumatized. I can tell by how he deadpans at the downed terrorists' bodies that it wasn't easy for him to do what he did. He killed a man. He stares at the sword he used to do the deed in disgust as he picks it up. "I can use this as a-a-a cane." He pins it to the ground with his left hand.

***

As dusk descends upon us, we finally arrive in the caves. I assist Oren in sitting down, and upon realizing my own frailty, I take a seat beside him. My feet throb from the arduous hours of trekking through the storm. What's worse, a profound sense of guilt gnaws at my heart, stemming from the failures I've inflicted upon Athena and Oren.

The only obstacle between me and sleep is the empty void that is my stomach. Fortunately, the leather bag Elouise lent me protected my belongings from the rain. The first thing I take out of it are dry changes of clothing for both of us. Once we've both changed privately, I get us our supper.

Oren breaks the silence. "Thank y-y-you, Brenda."

I smile slightly. "I couldn't leave you. Consider it my gratitude for saving me, and an apology that you were harmed—Moo as well, I know you were excited to see him again." I hand him some dried meat and fruit, before taking my first bite.

Oren's face falls. "I knew it-it-it wouldn't last. T-T-That soon e-enough and he'd b-b-b-be gone again."

That's a painful way to perceive it. I never considered that perspective before, but I understand it now. Oren is acquainted with the repetitive nature of loss. I can empathize with that feeling now. It's excruciating, and I yearn for protection from it. Detachment is Oren's strategy to safeguard his heart. Can I achieve that level of detachment? Attachment is my driving force. I can't fathom becoming a recluse, living separate from the world like he does.

"You don't think that about me, do you?"

His mouth gapes in realization, as if he's inadvertently revealed a forbidden secret. He takes a bite of his fruit, perhaps as a temporary respite. "I dunno w-w-w-what's gonna happen."

"I wish I could tell you I did, but I'd be lying. All I can say is I will try my hardest to protect you and not fail you again."

The oozing wound on his cheek mocks me. It's a striking reminder I couldn't keep him safe.

"You're the one who saved me. I'm grateful, but I also feel guilty. It's strange. I don't feel like myself. I usually don't feel this much guilt or blame myself for things I didn't do, but I feel responsible for Athena and you."

Oren hesitates to answer. "She kn-kn-knew the risks of coming along. She w-w-wanted this. The same goes w' m-m-m-me."

"You're fine with dying?" The silence that follows scares me. "Oren?"

"I-I want m-m-my suffering to end. Whether it be healing, or-or not."

I swallow. "I'm not all right with it! I've lost everyone else. I can't lose you, too!" I can't discern if he's hesitating or blowing me off. "Your family doesn't want to lose you, either!"

"I'm a burden on-n-n-n them. I-I-I always have been. If I'm h-h-healed or I die, they don't have t-t-t-to worry anymore."

"Oren? They love you! Do they not? Whether they must care for you or not shouldn't change that. There is value in who you are now. Your family must see it! I see it."

His eyes sag dispassionately as a passive frown withholds a response.

"Do you not see it?"

He exhales while shaking his head defeatedly. "What if I d-d-don't see it? Wh-what if I agreed t-t-to this trip, b-b-because wh-wh-what happens to me d-d-d-doesn't matter. B-but wh-what happens to you does. I didn't want you t-t-to go alone."

"Can I ask why? Why I matter to you?"

"I-l-lost you once. I can't rem-m-m-member how it felt…All I h-h-h-have are words on pages, b-b-b-but they meant s-s-something. I didn't want to l-l-l-let them go and lose you a-a-a-again. I w-w-want to remember."

He was willing to risk his life to restore his memories of me? I knew I meant a lot to him before, but not currently. I assumed he wanted to take the gamble of getting healed, but it's actually because he doesn't value himself. I'm more afraid of his death than he is.

The more I observe him, the more torment and heartache I see. It bleeds through his eyes, where the wound in his soul is visible. What regret and hurt has haunted him all this time?

"This guilt and self-blame I'm experiencing—That feeling has burdened you for a long time, hasn't it?"

His eyes gloss over, which speaks more than any words could. He's carried guilt for a lifetime. It's gnawing at him.

How can I comfort him? Why am I questioning my ability to do so? This has never been an issue before. My confidence is shaken once again.

"I'm sorry, Oren. You've been through it. You're far from home and your family. We trudged through a storm for what felt like eternity, and our futures are uncertain. But don't question even for a moment that you aren't worth fighting for. You are!" I place my hand on his shoulder, realizing he's trembling. He closes his glossy eyes, sighing deeply with no response. He's hit his breaking point, and I won't push him past it. Not yet. "…We should rest, now that we've eaten."

***

I jolt awake to a faint rumble echoing through the caverns. Oren is already awake, and I'm not sure how long he has been. He was asleep when I dozed off myself, but now he holds a journal in his lap. As soon as he realizes I'm awake, he closes the journal. "You f-f-felt that, too?"

I nod through heavy breaths. "A tremor. We should move." I rise.

"D-d-do you think Uxaar h-h-has anything to do with it?" Oren asks through a cough. He returns his journal into his bag before trying to rise.

"It's possible," I reply, offering my hand to help him up.

I anticipate him releasing my hand once he stands up, but he maintains his fingers intertwined with mine, forming a bridge between us. Surprised and captivated by the moment, I freeze, before I gently squeeze his hand back. My heart pounds in my chest.

I can barely distinguish a faint smile beneath the expression of urgency on his face—it's both profound and comforting.

"Since Athena isn't-t-t-t here to say it, remember to b-b-b-believe in yourself, n-n-no matter what Ux-xar throws at us."

Now I'm the one who's nodding back as if I were mute. I never imagined he'd take my hand and soothe me. He hardly spoke or looked at me before.

Finally, I got through to him.

"Thank you. That means a lot," I tell him. "Athena felt like, well, I'd think the way you feel about me in this situation—the one who remembered the forgotten things, who kept that alive. If you didn't remember something, you could ask me. If I didn't remember something, I could ask Athena. Now I don't have that. We were so close to reaching here with her, before Uxaar drove us apart. He didn't want me to get to read that journal. He knew how important it was for me to see it. Also, who knows what the terrorists are doing to her. She's probably mortified!"

"I'm s-s-s-sorry, Brenda, I-I-I really am."

"It's not your fault, Oren, so don't be. I'm glad I didn't lose you, too." I squeeze his hand, causing Oren to grin sweetly.

Ahead, the trail splits. The right path is bathed in a soft glow. A misty veil, hovers above it, casting a glimmering light on the path. This sight fills me with peace. Syann's power hasn't forsaken us after all. The Light continues to serve as a beacon of hope.

As we venture through the lit path, it appears as if a blanket of stars stretches overhead. While it may not match the breathtaking beauty of the night sky, it exudes an enchanted ambiance.

Oren agrees. I can't help but feel a pang of sadness that he never experienced a star shower festival in town. We would have had so much fun together.

Farther into the cave, the tremors occur in unpredictable intervals. Each one causes my heart to race, urging me to take deep breaths. I've reminded Oren to do the same, as he's visibly tense. He can't walk without leaning heavily on me as the rumbles intensify. Each tremor that passes seems to drain his strength. Oren nearly collapses during each one and has to stop walking to maintain his balance. He wheezes, grunts, coughs, stumbles, and even yawns to the point that he's slowing us down.

What if we can't escape? If Uxaar sends this cave into collapse, I'll survive. As for Oren, he got lucky once. I can't risk his life again.

This method of supporting Oren works for a few minutes until the tremors reach their peak. Cracks and breaks in the rocks send plummeting pebbles and dust from the cave roof. Oren's legs are next to fall. He plunges forward, dropping his sword-cane. I managed to break his fall, but we are now on our knees. Given the intensity of the earthquakes, it will be difficult to rise back up—impossible for Oren.

I try making the impossible possible by getting Oren upward, but it's no use. The dust rising from the ground sends Oren into a fit of wheezes and coughs. He stops cooperating with my aid, kneeling on the ground on all fours. I try helping him still, but he shakes his head.

"Oren, we have to go!" I shout. I listen for a response. He only coughs before saying the word *go*. "I'm not leaving you!"

"G—" Coughs interrupt him. He's trying to tell me something but can only gasp. "Go, Brenda!"

"Oren, I will drag you out of this cave, I swear on my life!"

"I c-c-c-can't!" He coughs and grunts. "It-it's fine."

"No, it's not!"

I curl up beside him, hoping he'll cooperate. I can't allow these rocks to suffocate him. The Geron listened to me at the festival. When they surrounded me, I was exasperated and screamed at them to leave me alone. I haven't spoken to one since, except for Roe. Perhaps that's the key.

"Stop!" My voice is weak and shaky. I must be strong. I place my glowing hands on the cave floor, squeezing my eyes tightly. "Uxaar, stop the earthquakes!" I yell as loud as I can.

My hands radiate brighter, seemingly condensing the quakes. My desperate outburst achieved its intended purpose! Impulsively, I fling my arms around Oren, disregarding his need for air. The thought of losing him too was unbearable, and that fear overshadows everything else.

"H-h-how did you do that?" he asks in awe.

"It was my only hope to protect you." I bring him to his feet. "I had to hope the Geron would listen to me."

A rumble echoes through our conversation, and before we can react, the cave floor explodes. A figure of shadow emerges from the ground, leaving a trail of debris and dust in its wake. Although I'm sure the dust is the culprit behind my coughing, the heinous shadowy figure swoops in front of me, her scent, sulfur-like, burning my nostrils. The figure possesses a pair of piercing blue eyes, reminiscent of Uxaar's, and she's thoroughly corrupted.

My heart grieves at the sight of this beautiful blonde woman, Ebony. She has lost her soul.

If only I were holding on to Oren tighter. The monstrosity sweeps him from my hold. Oren lunges his sword toward Ebony but misses. In response, she grabs him by the neck with one hand, while holding a fistful of blue sparks in the other. I imagine by Oren's wincing that the sparks are deadly to the touch. She's using them to pin him in place.

"Say the Shadow Incantations to me, and I will return him safely to you. If not, he goes down into the depths," the Shadow growls. Her voice sounds like a haunted wind, toneless, relentless, like a storm ready to level cities.

I grasp Oren's sword, pointing it toward Ebony. "I will never say the Incantations! Bring him back to me because I said so!" I hiss heatedly.

The woman glares at me. "Such passion from a broken flesh bag who doesn't even know who in the universe she is. You dare expect me to listen to you when you don't even believe in who you are?"

"I am Syann! And you will listen to me! Let him and Ebony go, Uxaar!"

"You told everyone to keep calling you Brenda. That's who you wish you were in your heart, yet now you claim to be Syann? To get what *you* want?"

"I said, let Oren go! I'm the one you want!"

"Let him go?" The corrupted woman sneers into a grin. "All right, perhaps I'll listen to your instruction." She cackles. Letting him go is too gentle to describe what Ebony does to Oren. She slams him through the chasm she came from. I'm next, as the cave floor collapses from underneath me.

10 *Brenda*

The sensation of claws and feathers tickling me brings me out of my sleep. Familiarity prompts me not to question it. Regardless, the sight I behold makes no sense. Usually, it would, but after recent circumstances—

"Stella?"

How is Stella here? She should be back with Oren's mother.

I scan my surroundings—my old bedroom. The window beside my bed presents a familiar view of cobblestone streets lined with rows of wooden and stone houses. The remaining beams of sunset bathe them in a warm, golden glow.

Across from my bed lies another bed, where a familiar teenage boy sleeps. He has warm skin like mine and brown, wavy hair that spills over his straight, freckled nose. Jonavan! It's him! I've never misidentified his obnoxious snores.

How am I here? I called this place my home two days ago, but so much has transpired since then. Those events caused my exile from this bedroom.

Stella perches on my oddly normal hand. The texture and

sharpness of her claws feel so real it's hard to doubt them, but why are my hands not glowing? The confusion overwhelms me, causing my head to throb.

Cuddled beside me is my little sister, whose brown eyes peek at me. Excitement surges across her round face, propelling her to her feet. "Jon! Brenda's awake!" she exclaims, shaking her older brother before scurrying into the hallway. "Mum, Dad! Brenda's awake!"

My eyes prick with tears at the sound of her voice. She's using my name as if she remembers me. I'm not a stranger at the well anymore.

She scampers back into our bed and immediately into my arms. "Brenda!" Aliah smiles with deep relief.

I'm lost for words. I missed Aliah more than words can convey, but this can't be happening. I'm too shocked to embrace her.

When I thought I couldn't be more overwhelmed, the rest of my family calls out my name as they rush to my bedside. "Oh, Brenda, you're all right!" Petunia gently caresses my face and kisses my forehead.

"What happened?" I ask hoarsely, holding Stella in my trembling hands.

"There was an attack at the festival. Liam left you to see what was happening, and you fell and hit your head while you were trying to escape the intruders. Elouise found you unconscious."

"You've been out for two days," Jonavan adds.

"The terrorists, they were trying to find Syann," I reply.

"The goddess from the legends, yes. It turned out to be a bust. They never found her and eventually left."

There is no physical evidence I'm Syann now. My hands have reverted to normal, so why should they believe me? Nonetheless, after everything, I can't act as if it didn't happen, for Oren's and Athena's sakes.

"What? No!" I scoff. "This is going to sound insane, but I—

I am Syann! The attack, they took me and killed Byron! Then, when the stars fell, my hands started to glow, and so did my eyes! Everyone forgot who I was, including all of you! Elouise did find me as you said, but she took me to her house. The next morning, I journeyed with her brothers to find answers about my powers. The day after that, we ended up in these caverns, where we were attacked. Then I woke up here."

My "parents" exchange concerned glances before their eyes return to me. "You hit your head pretty hard, Brenda," the man I once called Father says, rubbing my shoulder. "You must have dreamed it."

"But Byron did die," Aliah whines pitifully.

A heavy sigh leaves her dad, Grover. "It must have happened before Brenda fell. That would explain why she remembers."

"There's no way I could've dreamed it!"

"Shh!" Petunia sets her hands on my shoulders. "I know yesterday was terrifying, and I'm so sorry about Byron. It was shocking to us all. I know it hurts, especially for you, but please know we will never, ever forget who you are. We are always here for you. I've always told you that, Brenda."

"Maybe some food would help," Grover suggests, with an inviting sparkle in his sky blue eyes. "You must be starved."

He's correct. I haven't eaten anything since last night in the cave, if that even happened. I'm on the fence that this is a crazy dream, but I sense their touches and voices. This is too vivid to be a dream, but my adventure with Oren and Athena was even more so. It was a nightmare, and I desperately wished to return home. That is, until I realized the weight of my responsibilities and the immense need Oren and Athena had for me. I can't abandon them.

"I have some leftover grits," Grover adds. "I'll bring a hearty bowl right to you." He leaves me with a kiss on my forehead. His beard tickles me as it always does when he kisses me.

As I wait for the grits to be ready, Petunia explains that the town held a memorial service yesterday in honor of Byron. She recounts how she stayed home to watch me while the rest of my family attended.

I'm glad I don't have to relive that again. The thought of seeing Liam races shivers down my spine. What could he be thinking? I fell off a roof and ruined his plans to propose to me. Dare he try proposing if he sees me? I hope not. I couldn't accept it in a situation like this, not in this world where I'm unsure if it's real, or one where Oren is still in the picture. Oren was the one I always loved. Before, I thought he was gone, but now I know he isn't.

Grover returns with food. I'm disturbed by the good taste and warmth in my stomach. The grits are buttery, hot, and textured.

This is exactly what I had always wanted, right? To be reunited with my family? It feels like a betrayal now. I'm leaving Athena, Oren, and everything I'm responsible for behind. In this bizarre reality, how are Oren and Athena faring? Is Oren still alive? Would he recognize me? How would Athena be doing with Syann's absence last night? Would she believe me if I told her that I'm Syann? Or would she be able to break me out of this trance? Is she even alive? If she is, I must find her.

After eating, I ask if I can get some fresh air. Grover informs me it's been raining for several hours, so I must stay inside.

"Rain!" Stella squawks.

That word could be powerful enough to stop everything in motion.

We went under the tree in the rain, where he gave me Stella. I loved him then and… I still do. I never stopped.

In the storm yesterday, Oren saved me, and look how I returned the favor—he's dying! This is my first opportunity to reflect on the events in the caverns, and I regret that I must.

The thunder clapping outside persists. Instead of seeing flashes of light, I see flashes of Oren. For a brief moment, he clings to my hand as tightly as possible, smiling at me in the cave.

But then, the tremors started. He believed he was too much of a burden and wanted me to leave him. No matter how much I yearned to protect him and change his mind, I couldn't succeed. The thought of it sends shivers down my spine, and tears to my eyes.

"Brenda, what's wrong?" Petunia questions.

"Uxaar was right. I don't know who I am anymore." I tug at my hair, realizing it hurts my head to do that. Gently, I twist my locks instead.

A hopeless expression of confusion scrunches Petunia's face. I've seen this countenance too often in the past twenty-four hours. She turns to Grover and whispers to him. He nods and excuses himself, Jonavan, and Aliah out of the room.

"Brenda, you've always been such a strong and happy girl. Why are you feeling this way?" Petunia sits on the edge of my bed.

"Because my whole life got turned upside down! Magic and demons are real! I'm the goddess they're after! I didn't want to be." I shake my head. "And I went to Byron's funeral! It was by the well in the square, which they dedicated to him. They carved the words 'The Father of Seren' on it. You were all there! You all forgot me! Liam did the same! Elouise's family only took me in because they needed Syann's help. It was like Brenda was wiped out of existence! So, when I'm finally beginning to accept that I'm Syann, I'm back home with no explanation, and everyone thinks I'm Brenda again? I don't know what's real! If this is a dream that the Geron are torturing me with, or if me being Syann is a dream. But I know I can't abandon it. Oren depends on me! Everyone does!"

"Oren? The boy from the farm?"

"He's Elouise's brother. He's ill and needs Syann to heal him. Athena was taking us to Syann's realm, but then"—I choke up—"I lost them! Athena and Oren are probably dead because of me!" My words perturb Petunia. Her expression stiffens. "What? What is it?"

Her eyes shine as her head sinks. "Athena's gone, dear."

No! I need her to be alive! She can't be gone here, too! "H-how?"

"After the attack, many people came to her home, seeking answers on why the attack happened, or if she was associated with it. It wasn't long before news came that she disappeared. No one knows where."

That's parallel to what happened to Athena in my reality. She was taken. If it weren't for Roe, I wouldn't have known that. No Roe, no explanation. I could sure use Roe's help now.

Petunia ends the silence. "You're overwhelmed, dear. A warm bath should clear your mind."

***

The rippling bathwater against my trembling body evokes memories of Oren. His constant shaking was a stark indicator of his trepidation. Did he always endure such intense emotions?

His suggestion for me to leave him behind in the caves could be depicted as a selfless act, or even a tragic suicide—a noble way to alleviate his pain. Was everything becoming too much for him to bear?

This is too much for me to bear.

Can I be hurt? I couldn't before. The sword couldn't penetrate me—could it now? I couldn't suffocate earlier when the terrorist's hand tried to strangle me. Nothing could kill me.

That's a way to discover my true identity. If I am Syann, I won't die. So, I submerge my head in the water with my eyes open, waiting for the urge to breathe. Instead, I detach myself from my thoughts, completely unaware of how long I've been underwater. The memory of losing Oren repeatedly plays in my mind.

What if I begin inhaling the water? Will I drown? My lungs start burning, but not as intensely as my head aches. Sobs leave me, causing me to gasp for air. I force myself out of the bathtub, coughing out the water I had inhaled.

I didn't suffocate, but I was on the brink of it. I couldn't bear to hold my breath any longer, but the chokehold I was in during the storm attack was equally excruciating, and I lived. My experiment failed.

My body still shakes even after I've dried off. The girl staring back at me in the mirror is terrified. Her golden eyes, which should be green like my nightgown, are now puffy and bloodshot. Her lips quiver in fear, and her posture collapses. All my confidence, faith, and hopes are shattered. She's not Brenda or Syann. The mirror shows a broken stranger.

The sight of the scissors resting in the drawer makes my heart race. Petunia trims our hair with these scissors. It's been years since I've drastically cut mine. These blades can test if my skin is still impenetrable. With trembling hands, I stare at the metal twin edges in my grasp as I slowly grind them into my skin. The sensation is unpleasant enough to cause me to wince, but not so bad that I stop myself.

The skin surrounding the blemish inflames painfully. I refuse to believe it, so much so that I'm willing to try again. My skin couldn't be cut before. There must be some logical explanation.

In the same drawer, I uncover Grover's knife, which he uses to trim his facial hair. It's much sharper than the scissors. I try not to yelp as I slash it across my left hand, but a sharp gasp escapes me. I'm certain that it drew blood. I peek at the welling red from this self-inflicted wound.

I cover my mouth with my hand to muffle the sound that escapes me, a mixture of a gasp and a gag. The sight of blood nauseates me, and it's now running from my hand and onto the floor.

"This isn't funny, Uxaar! You hear me? This isn't funny! Make it stop!"

There's no way my family is deaf to my episode. I sway in unsteady circles, sobbing loudly. Uxaar and Roe fail to appear, despite my pleas.

Grover and Petunia call my name as they pound on the door.

I ignore them while frantically searching for a towel to clean the blood off the floor. I wipe away the blood as they barge through the door.

The sight of my bloodied hand alone makes Petunia gasp, and Grover's pale skin turns a shade of red. I attempt to conceal my hand, but Petunia is already approaching. Her eyes quickly dart to the counter, where the bloody knife lies. I had forgotten to hide the knife. My attention was solely focused on cleaning the floor, but I had completely overlooked the most crucial aspect—the knife. This blood on the floor could have falsely swayed them that I was on my menstrual cycle, which might have partially justified my mood swings. I should have hidden the knife!

Outside the door, Jonavan asks about the commotion. Grover shouts at him and Aliah to go to bed. Who knows what my parents are about to do? I look like I've gone mad.

Petunia calls my name. I've never sensed such worry in her voice for me before. The soft, shaky whisper haunts me. Grover follows suit, firmly shutting the door behind him. I must escape, but there's no window. There's only the door they're blocking.

"Brenda! Why are you cutting yourself?" Grover questions discreetly.

"It's not like that!" I whine. My thoughts only come out as babbling. How can I convince them I was trying to prove I was invincible by self-harming? They might as well send me to an asylum now.

"Brenda, what's happening?" Petunia questions.

I'm suffocating, and the walls seem to be closing in on me. My parents—who aren't really my parents—are blocking the doorway, and my reflection hovers beside me. I'm tempted to resort to the same desperate act the terrorist attempted to do to me with the sword. If I end my life in this reality, will it finally end this dream and transport me back to the cave? Or is this a cruel twist of fate, and not a dream at all? What if being Syann was a distorted reality, a twisted reflection of my true desires?

"Grover, we should get Mr. Higgs!" Petunia exclaims in fright.

"We can't leave her in this state!" Grover argues back.

Mr. Higgs is one of Seren's finest physicians and apothecaries who resides a few streets away from us. If they took me to him, I could escape.

"No! Let me go to him, pl-please!" This could be my escape. "My head!" I lift my fingers to my head. "It aches."

The gaze they give each other shows my suggestion worked like a charm. Now, I must escape successfully.

Grover suggests he'll take me while Petunia stays home with the kids.

I'm fast and have great stamina. Grover is quick, too, but his stamina and physique have deteriorated with age. I could outrun him. All I need is a head start. Once I shake Grover, I can make a break for Oren's house.

The sun has set, leaving behind puddles of muddy streets. The weather remains the same as it was earlier today—cool and rainy. There's no time to devise an escape plan. Mr. Higgs's house is just two streets away. I must locate a window and make a hasty retreat.

If Grover catches up to me, I'll have to resort to physical combat. My agility and youthfulness are advantages, but his strength is a significant factor. I'm uncertain which trait would overcome the other in a race. Considering my current state of dizziness, if Grover manages to seize me, I won't be able to escape. There's no room for error.

As we approach the last street turn, I realize this is my best chance. As he turns left, I swiftly turn in the opposite direction and sprint away. I anticipate that the wet streets will cause him to lose his footing and provide me with a head start. However, he swiftly grasps my injured hand as he frantically cries out Brenda's name. He tightly clasps my forearm with his other hand and pulls me back into his grasp.

I kick and thrash, desperate to break free, but he only tightens his grip on me. He encircles my waist with one arm and my mouth with the other. I remain silent, realizing that my efforts have failed.

I agreeably enter Mr. Higgs's house when we arrive. Hopefully, he'll refuse to serve us at this late hour, but Mr. Higgs and my parents have a long history. He delivered the real Brenda, Jonavan, and Aliah, and he's good friends with my parents. So, there's a good chance he'll do us a favor. In this case, he does. He cordially welcomes us and invites me to sit in his office. The room has a distinct smell, like fresh herbs. Without sunlight, only dimly lit lamps and candles illuminate his space.

On the shelves, numerous bottles of herbs and ointments sit. He grabs a balm container and applies it generously to my wound. As the fresh blood from the injury mixes with the balm, it transforms into a congealed pink color. After the application, he begins to stitch the wound together.

His beefy hands are rough yet steady. Despite the steadiness, I feel pain. The sensation of the needle piercing the wound makes me squeamish. You'd think this wouldn't bother me after all I've been through, but blood is a fear of mine. I try to dissociate as much as possible through my thoughts.

"Brenda, please, if you will, explain exactly what you think happened last night. Your father told me his perspective. It's important that I hear yours."

Grover explained the situation to Dr. Higgs as he started stitching my hand, but he didn't delve into my viewpoint. He only mentioned that I've been experiencing delusions since my head injury and that I'm self-harming.

"Well, it wasn't delusions or imaginations, if that's what you think!"

"It? Elaborate for me," Higgs requests calmly, unbothered by my harsh remark. His voice, light and smooth, contrasts with his hands. His dark eyes are accompanied by a pair of glasses. His skin and brunette hair are warm, while his facial features are very square.

"Well, I was at the festival with Liam when the suspicious

activity began. He left me to see what was happening. I tried following him, but the terrorists attacked me. He said I escaped them, but that was untrue. They dragged me onto the stage with all the other women my age and told us all that one of us was Syann."

"The goddess you claim to be?"

"I am her. I didn't believe it was possible until my hands glowed. After that, my old friend Elouise and her brother approached me, insisting I go with them to hide from the terrorists. I soon realized they didn't remember me or our past interactions."

"Elouise—Have you had any recent interactions with her? Before the incident specifically."

"There was a play at the festival she participated in."

"The play about Syann, that Athena, God bless her soul, choreographed. I heard about it—say, was it your first indoctrination about Syann?"

"Yes. I disbelieved it. I found the story laughable really, especially when she said Syann would be a girl my age and could be me. Elouise, however, was confident Syann was real. Which is why it made sense I was at her house after the incident. She rescued me from the terrorists."

"Did she mention why she believed?"

"Yes, she mentioned her brother was ill. I assumed she meant Jace, but she actually has another brother, Oren. She hoped Syann could heal him."

"This was after the fall, or before, when you met Oren?"

"After."

"You had never heard of this boy before discovering you were Syann?"

"No. I knew him as a child. He was my best friend."

"Yet you didn't know he was Elouise's brother?"

"No."

"How long have you known Elouise?"

"Why is that important?"

"Because the mind is a strange place, Brenda. I hope to see if I can find connections that will prove that this whole side of yours is a psychological scenario you've created, or reality as you claim it is. So, if you could please answer all my questions."

"Fine. I've known her since I was fifteen, several years after Oren."

"So, how did you not know they were siblings?"

I sigh deeply. "They simply never mentioned each other. Oren said he wanted to be unmentioned after they moved. However, Elouise did mention to me before the fall that she had been dishonest with me. Although she was interrupted, I'm confident Elouise intended to tell me about Oren."

"You mentioned you knew Oren previously. How so?"

"When I knew Oren, he lived in the farm village. My father was and still is an importer of goods there. He would take me with him since I was about eight. You remember Oren." I turn back to Grover.

"How could I not? He was all you talked about after those trips."

I look back to Mr. Higgs as he replies, "So, he was a close friend."

"She was practically in love with him," Grover answers.

My throat contracts at his words. "We would see each other weekly when I visited the farms with my dad. That lasted until we were twelve. Oren grew ill due to an accident that left him crippled. When his grandparents passed later that year, he and his family moved to Seren. I was unaware of this and thought he had disappeared. I had no idea what had happened to him. When I met Elouise three years later, she never mentioned him, either."

"I see," Mr. Higgs says. "How did you take losing him?"

I sigh. "I—I never moved on. I tried forcing myself to, but I always missed him. My pet, Stella, was a gift from him, so she never let me forget. I would occasionally go on those trips with my dad to see if maybe—" I sigh. "I never saw him. Not until yesterday when I went to Elouise's house. It all made sense to me, because Oren was ill when I last saw him."

Mr. Higgs gazes at me, perplexed, rubbing his chin. "Moving on. Did you engage your family in any fashion after going to Elouise's house?"

"Yes. I went through the town square where crowds had gathered for Byron's memorial service. I saw my family there placing flowers at the well. I was desperate to get them to remember me but realized no one did. I was able to speak to my mother. She saw me grieving and asked if I was all right. I was honest and told her everyone abandoned me. That's when I discovered who I really was. She mentioned how her daughter Brenda had died days before the stars fell. I then knew that I was Syann, that the stars gave me to my parents to raise as their daughter Brenda, to keep me safe and disguised. So, I left, knowing that I wasn't Brenda."

Mr. Higgs seems baffled by my explanation. "Then where did you go?"

"To Athena, who guided me about Syann and where I needed to go. And she discovered I was invincible because of my power, which was the only reason I cut myself. After that, Oren, Athena, and I followed the star. Athena was lost, but Oren and I continued into the caverns. Inside was an avalanche. We fell, and I woke up here." I sigh, viewing my stitched hand that Mr. Higgs places a bandage on.

"Did Oren ever cross your mind during the festival? Before the incident specifically?"

So much.

It's a vulnerable conversation. One I don't prefer to venture into, but if this is a hallucination like I passionately believe, does it matter? He simply dropped everything I said to ask me that.

"Brenda? Did you think about him?"

"Yes. I did," I admit, frustrated.

"How come?"

I sigh. "I overheard my parents speaking to Liam at my house that morning. He planned to propose to me after the festival. I felt overwhelmed, so I went for a stroll. I-I no doubt thought marrying Liam would be the smartest decision, but I couldn't help but miss Oren. Despite that, I never held the same deep feelings toward Liam that I felt toward Oren. I was uncertain."

"So, he was relevant in your mind, likewise how Syann was because of the play. Elouise spoke to you after the play, claiming you could be Syann. The evidence is all there."

"I'm sorry?" I say in disbelief.

"You were so worried about Liam, and in grief about Oren, you're convinced you saw him again. Not only Oren, but the stress of an upcoming marriage also brings many emotions. Surely you had thoughts and fears about leaving your family."

I freeze. He can't pristinely point this all out. He can't! I don't care if he's a physician! Uxaar must be behind this!

"Which stands behind why everyone forgot and rejected you in this scenario you've created. You were afraid to part with your family by marrying Liam. And Elouise, you said she claimed the possibility you could be Syann. Now you think by being Syann, you can undo all the harm done to this town and rid it of these terrorists when that isn't possible. There's no star. Athena's gone, and you're not invincible." He gently grabs the underside of my injured hand. "Everything you've claimed is simply not possible. Sufficient evidence supports you creating this scenario to conceal your trauma, or that it's a delusion from hitting your head."

"What are you? A physician or a dream interpreter! I didn't dream it! This is a false reality made by Uxaar, and he speaks through you to try to convince me I'm not Syann to trap me here! To keep me from saving Secreth and this world from the Geron! I won't fall for it!" I shout, standing out of my chair. Grover sits me back down and scolds me. For how bold I sound, it doesn't mean I'm not convinced. I'm scared Mr. Higgs is correct, but I can't be wrong. "I can prove it. Oren is Elouise's brother. I didn't find that out until after the incident. If he is her brother, that supports my claims!"

***

I never imagined being confined to my house overnight. I had hoped to meet Elouise after Mr. Higgs, but Grover insisted it was too late. Now, I find myself trapped in my bedroom, with the diagnosis of a concussion and delirium. In three days, I'm to revisit Mr. Higgs to assess if my mental state improves. If not, this situation could escalate into something serious.

Is it true that I snapped and went insane due to the stress of the festival day? Mr. Higgs presented a well-reasoned argument supported by evidence, which is why I'm skeptical. Either he's an exceptional physician or Uxaar is craftily deceiving me. The only piece of evidence that invalidates my claim is the cut on my hand. It shouldn't have occurred, but it did. I lack the means to prove that the cut on my hand is an illusion, so to everyone else, I'm mad.

Suppose I can't find a way to get back to reality, I'll be trapped in this one. If I keep searching for means of escape, my reputation will be ruined, and I'll be taken to an asylum at this rate.

Giving up on Syann now would still ensure a bright future. Liam would marry me, and I could move on, but at the expense of my happiness. The knowledge that Oren is just a few miles away is something I cannot ignore. If it weren't for the inescapable nature of my room, with my parents constantly guarding me, I would be seeing him right now.

If only it were possible.

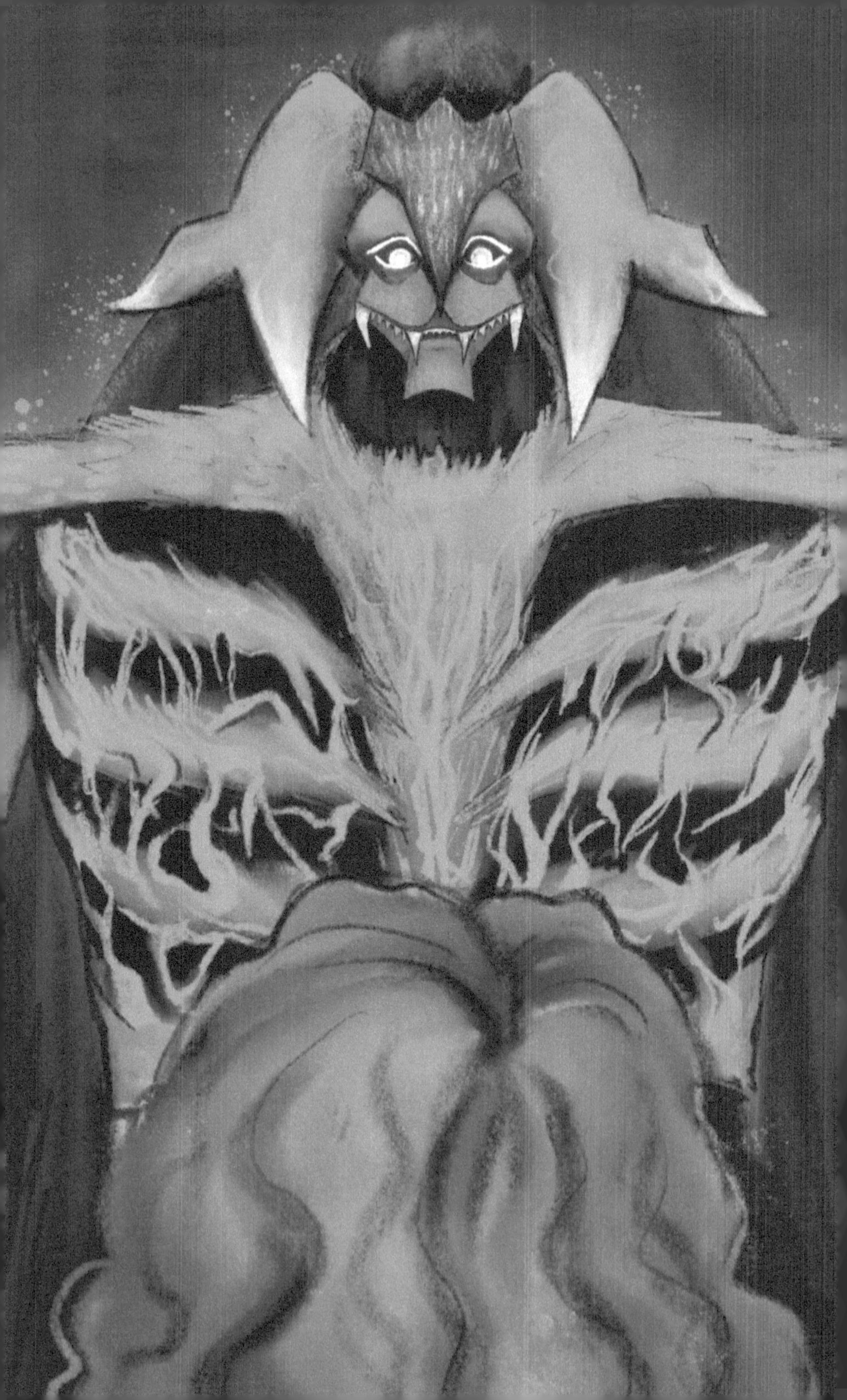

11 *Brenda*

At the breakfast table, I ate a meal I had nothing to do with making, which is strange at this house. I usually make breakfast or at least help. The omelet and mixed fruit are delicious, though. I'll give Grover that.

Circumstances have been awkward since leaving Mr. Higgs last night. Grover and I had a one-sided argument the entire journey home. He questioned my desire of not wanting to marry Liam. My defense unsurprisingly went unappreciated.

The kids didn't speak to me last night, and not much this morning, either. I suspect they're afraid to. That's also my motive for not talking to them—fear—fear of becoming attached to the illusion. I detest feeling guilty for the unease I'm causing them. My remorse suggests that I believe I'm hurting their feelings. If they're hallucinations, they lack emotions. Consequently, I shouldn't empathize with them.

Now I'm like Oren, becoming aloof to protect my feelings overall. That's what he said about Moo, right? Seeing him, it was a dream that he knew he'd eventually wake up from. That's precisely what this is. I'm afraid the more I attach myself, the longer I'll be stuck here, and the more I'll hurt.

Speaking of Oren, I'm desperate to reach him. I've only nagged Grover to escort me to him every time I've spoken to him. We've agreed that Grover will take me to Elouise's house after breakfast.

These circumstances have triggered my stress-eating habit. I devour my food so quickly that everyone in my family has at least half their plate left when I finish. Passively watching my family eat makes me uneasy, so I reach for a second helping. Even before I can savor that in peace, a knock at the door startles me.

I flinch as if I'm about to rise and answer the door. Reminiscing about the morning of the festival brings me to a halt. The same person who knocked that morning could very well be at the door now, Liam. I try not to jump to conclusions, but if this is an illusion, Uxaar will unleash everything to confront me. Even if this isn't an illusion, Liam would be worried about me.

Grover is never hesitant to let any expectant guest at the entrance inside, but now a glare of caution replaces the usual gleaming hospitality in his eyes as he opens the door.

The deep, soothing voice, laced with longing, confirms my suspicion of Liam's arrival. Grover tells him that this isn't a good time. However, Grover's persistent attempts to deter him indicate Liam's not taking no for an answer.

The back door entices me more than the scene at the front door. With Grover occupied and my chair positioned on the opposite side of Petunia and Jonavan—I could swiftly escape with a head start. I outran Liam when we raced on the festival night. Why not now? Well—Uxaar might not play fair if this is an illusion. Nonetheless, what more can I lose?

Commotion erupts as I rise from my chair and sprint toward the back door. Voices echo Brenda's name, and footsteps follow closely behind.

The wind tousles my hair, and my lungs expand deeply as I

stride forward. Undoubtedly, this escape commences more promisingly than my failed attempt last night, yet the outcome remains the same. Approximately halfway across town, I'm apprehended by a hand grasping my wrist. Jonavan has ensnared me.

Figures, being the youngest among the pursuers, yet he's always been surprisingly swift on his lanky legs. That doesn't make him stronger. I can still defeat him in an arm wrestle on a good day.

Glancing into his piercing blue eyes is a grave mistake. His elongated face now reveals terror instead of the confident, practical, and humorous gaze he usually wears. A wave of guilt surges through me, making me yearn for escape. I'm almost successful in pushing my brother away, but he manages to stall me long enough for Grover and Liam to catch up. Grover latches onto my other wrist, while Jonavan refuses to let go of his side.

"Brenda! I told you we would go after we finished breakfast! What you did was reckless!" Grover's tone is harsh but hushed to a whisper. He doesn't need to draw any more attention. Luckily, the streets are nearly empty. People are afraid of the terrorists. Well, that assumption lines up with reality.

"What's wrong with her?" Liam asks.

"Liam, if you have any discernment, this is a tense situation. I need her home and to keep this situation as low profile as possible. She's unwell and clearly upset, and I'm trying to contain that."

"First off, if anyone gives you problems concerning Brenda, they can take it up with me. Second, I see she's upset. You know her significance to me, so I have a right to know what is going on."

***

My appetite for a second helping vanishes once I return to the breakfast table. Now, Liam sits across from me, patiently waiting for my family to finish their meal before we engage in the inevitable conversation about me.

149

I don't wish to go through explaining everything again like I did with Mr. Higgs. That is if I even have a voice in this conversation. Chances are my parents will paint the picture for Liam, while I'm ignored. Part of me doesn't even want inclusion and wishes to leave like Jonavan and Aliah. It doesn't matter anyway. Why waste this time and sit here? I need to get to Oren.

"You said that after breakfast I could go to Elouise's house. I propose Liam takes me, and I will explain to him what happened. I trust him to keep me safe." My eyes lock onto Grover.

"Like he did from the terrorists?" Grover snaps. Silence fills the room at such a blow. Grover has always treated Liam like a son. I've never heard him say a hostile word to him.

Liam stammers at the insult. "I will never let it happen again. She won't leave my sight."

"Brenda is not currently stable; until that changes, I want her under constant parental supervision."

"I'm not a child!" I snap at him.

"You're my child, still living under my roof!"

"I'm not your child. If we go to Elouise's, I can prove it!"

"Whether that boy is there or not, that doesn't prove anything! Brenda"—Grover's voice softens—"I know you are confused, and you hit your head really hard and—"

"Oh, quit with 'I hit my head'! I know that!"

"You do not interrupt me when I'm speaking to you! You are out of place!" Grover roars.

I rise out of my chair. "I know it well!" Grover tells me to sit down, but I continue. "As of yesterday, you trusted Liam enough to hand me off to him for the rest of my life. So, you should trust him very well enough to take a stroll with me! Please!"

"Brenda!" Petunia scolds my uncouthness.

"You told her?" Liam glares at Grover and Petunia in betrayal.

"No! She improperly eavesdropped on our conversation!" Grover replies.

"We told her nothing," Petunia adds.

"It doesn't matter who knows what. That doesn't change the fact that he can take me."

Liam huffs and takes a stand behind me. "I can do what she asks. I promise you she won't leave my sight."

I nod along, a lie on my part. I have every intention of leaving him.

Grover sighs. "You won't let her leave your sight," he declares firmly to Liam. "And you won't try to escape!" he demands to me.

"I promise!"

"Liam, have her back here within the hour. She doesn't need to be out for too long. She needs rest."

"Absolutely. She can ride my horse as well. She won't have to walk."

Before we leave, I head upstairs, put on my shoes, and fetch Stella so she can join us. I wonder how Oren will react to seeing me again. Stella put the pieces together before, perhaps she will benefit me again. Even if she doesn't, her presence brings me comfort, whether this is real or a delusion.

Liam and Grover exchange a conversation about me that abruptly ends when I descend the stairs. This silence persists until we reach Liam's horse. Liam attempts to assist me, but I push his hands away from my waist and help myself. Despite his apparent offense, I remain indifferent.

"I'm ready. Their house is outside town, toward the west side."

"I'm aware of where the Silvius home is." Liam unties the reins from the fence. "We'll get there as soon as we can."

I nod, watching the distance from my house grow further as we leave. My fingers fiddle gently with Stella's feathers, calming my jitters. I can't tell my relationship with silence anymore. I always hated it, but now it's all I long for, to get to Oren's house without a word uttered from Liam. If only that desire weren't so unrealistic.

"You dare think that you're the goddess Syann? Brenda,

you've always been the most practical woman I've known. You've never believed in such things as magic."

"That is all Grover said? That I believe I'm Syann."

"No. He included that you think Elouise and Jace rescued you so that you could heal their little brother, who was your childhood friend. Then he mentioned you think this is all a delusion created by the—" He sighs forcefully. "The Geron to keep you from reaching Syann's destiny? And you learned that Brenda was a facade and was your parents' miscarried child? It's madness!"

"So that's all you know?"

"Other than the reason we're out on this endeavor is so you can prove your claims by the existence of Elouise's twin brother. Which would hardly prove anything."

"I didn't expect you to believe me."

"Did you want me to? Or better question, do you want to believe it?"

"At first, I didn't, until I knew how much everyone relied on me. The people I must save is a responsibility I can't ignore or run from."

Liam exhales deeply. "Brenda, we can't save everyone or the ones we lost, my father included. No matter how much we wish to deny they're gone, convincing yourself that this reality is false and that the losses are recoverable will only hurt you. It won't save anybody."

It's clear the message Uxaar is trying to convey here. I'm psychologically ill and using this Syann story as a coping mechanism. Mr. Higgs and now Liam have approached it that way. I must stand my ground and encourage nothing.

"Brenda…"

"That isn't my name anymore."

"Please, listen! I already lost my father to this incident. I can't lose you, too. I will stand by you and help you through this in whatever way I'm able."

"I need to see Oren. So I can protect you and everyone from

the dangers beyond this realm. Uxaar is coming."

"I don't need your protection. It's—"

"Yet I need yours? Because you think I'm unstable!"

He's hyperaware he's treading on thin ice with me, but that never stopped Liam in the past. "Dear, you're recovering."

I scoff at his sugarcoated tone. "That's much better!"

"I'm the leader of this town. I'm the one who's responsible for protecting this town! It's not your burden to bear."

"Why do you think you have to do it alone? If I were to marry you, your burdens would be my burdens! As well as mine, yours. We don't need to be so infatuated with protecting each other—instead, we should be working together!"

"Brenda, leading the government here will not be your responsibility to worry about. Neither is this whole idea that you are a goddess. You have head trauma, you should be resting and not worrying about any of this."

"Yes, I shouldn't be worrying about anything right now. We can continue this conversation if Oren doesn't exist, and you prove me wrong. Until then, I'd appreciate silence. I have much to process."

My request is granted, and the rest of the horseback ride is silent.

As we weave through the oak grove, my heartbeat is audible. Oren's house comes into view, which multiplies the thoughts in my mind. What if Uxaar pulls strings here? What if I don't get to see Oren? Jace or Elouise might not cooperate.

The horse halts, and my feet touch the ground. Liam and I approach the door, and I knock until it opens. I'm greeted by a pair of agitated green eyes—Jace. My stomach churns at the absence of Elouise and even her mother. If Uxaar were to manipulate the situation, it would likely be through Jace.

"Hello. Is Elouise here?" I ask. My index finger continues to ruffle Stella's chest feathers. She sits on my shoulder.

Jace's expression hardens. "I won't be bothering her."

"I'm sorry?" I ask.

"You've heard of Athena's disappearance? Elouise is grieving and wishes to be alone. Athena was her best friend."

"What about Oren? Can I speak to him?"

"Excuse me?" Jace's expression morphs into a challenged glare.

"Elouise told me about him. I know everything."

"I don't know what or who you're talking about!"

"Jace, I know your brother Oren! That he's ill and your family has kept him hidden, but Elouise told me!"

Jace seems peeved, which concerns me. "Brenda, now isn't a good time. I'm going to have to ask you to go."

"Can I see your mother? Please!"

Liam grabs me, trying to pull me from the door. "I'm sorry for the disturbance. We'll be on our way."

"Liam, let me go!" I try wriggling free. "Jace, please! I'm Syann! I'm here to help Oren! Like Elouise wants!"

Liam grabs me with full force and picks me up. I'm thrashing and trying to break free. Stella squawks while flapping her wing. She's going to fall off my shoulder if Liam doesn't stop.

I'm prepared to break into the house without permission to demonstrate my argument, but Liam intervenes, allowing Jace to slam the door. I loudly protest, but Liam forcefully silences me with his hand.

"Shhh! Shhhh! Brenda, compose yourself!"

"N-N-Nmh!" Stella falls, jumping onto the grass.

"I'm not letting go until you quit resisting!"

I can't beat him, so I comply and go limp in his arms before he sets me down. I take a harsh step back, heatedly bending and retrieving Stella.

"You heard Jace, there's no Oren, and Elouise can't see you! We must go home!"

"No! I must see Elouise!" I return Stella to my shoulder. "Jace is lying about Oren. He has always been incredibly secretive about the situation. I would only expect him to lie. Please!"

"We are not currently welcome in their home! There's nothing we can do. I'm sure you'll be able to see Elouise eventually. We must give it time."

"I don't have time! I don't! I must get out of this!"

"Brenda, you're taking this too—"

"Stop calling me Brenda!"

My outburst freezes Liam. His eyes widen as a frown sags on his face. "Honey, come home. We can fix all of it!"

"You can't fix anything! I'm not leaving here without getting what I came for!" I try turning away, but Liam grabs my wrist.

"Don't make me force you! The last thing I want is to be harsh to you, but I promised your father I'd return you home safely."

"Let me go!" I'm not going back to Seren. Who knows how long I'll be stuck there if I do? "Help!" I yell repetitively. I fervently hope that someone in the house pities my pleas. It's my last resort. Liam tries to silence me, but I refuse. He attempts to cover my mouth again, but I resist, struggling to get him off me in any way possible. I kick, thrash, stomp on his toes, and bite his hand, doing whatever I can while simultaneously trying to reach Oren's window and yell his sister's name.

It takes me a few minutes of wrestling before the door opens. Elouise, Ms. Silvius, and Jace rush out, catching my attention. Liam releases me when he sees them approaching.

"Syann?" Elouise bellows.

My name evokes an extraordinary sensation—a sharp shiver runs down my spine, accompanied by a sound akin to cannon fire. This sound drowns out the commotion among Jace, his mother, and Liam, who's attempting to explain the unfolding events. Amidst this chaos, a faint glimmer of light emerges from the direction of the mountains. In perfect synchronization with this flickering light, my heart races with an intense drumbeat. Could it be? Was it the star, shining for a fleeting moment?

No one else seems to be affected by the noise or light as I am.

They must be unable to perceive it.

Valerie approaches me; I think she asked me what I was doing here.

"I need to see Oren, your son. Elouise told me he needed Syann's help, which is why I'm here."

We're invited inside and led to the kitchen table, where everyone sits down except me. Oren is nowhere to be found. He must be in his room.

I've been through this before. The morning after the festival, I had spoken to his family about how to help Oren. There's no need to relive this ordeal.

I bolt down the hallway, scurrying into Oren's room. I don't care if anyone is chasing me or not.

When I open the door, initially it appears to be Oren's room. However, as I step through the doorway, the ground beneath my feet vibrates violently. For a brief moment, the room transforms into the cave.

The overwhelming sound of rumbling drowns out all other noises. I am uncertain whether the room is shaking or if it is my own body. My skin becomes rough and icy, while the only warmth I feel is the wound on my hand gradually diminishing, as if a flame is extinguishing. My hands radiate a brilliant, scorching glow, resembling stars burning intensely.

The next stride I take transports me back to Oren's room. The star shines brightly in the sky through his window.

My heart races as I stumble into my next step, and I feel the heat from my hands radiate throughout my body. With each step I take, my surroundings flicker back and forth, alternating between the room and the cave, and the hot and cold temperatures. One thing remains constant—Oren is ahead, whether he's covered in a blanket of cloth or surrounded by rocks.

I'm almost there. All I have to do is reach him.

"Brenda!" The voice booms like a storm from above. Like a strike of lightning, my surroundings flash into Oren's room to stay. Between Oren and me is Uxaar in his true form. He's colossal, towering at least seven feet tall, and radiating an otherworldly glow. His piercing eyes radiate hatred.

My heartbeat is in my throat, yet I must assert dominance here. I can't look scared. Too bad that I am. "I'm not Brenda! You failed!" I snap.

"It's not too late to return and embrace this way of life. Beyond that door, you can return to your family and escape this burden. I know you're terrified of it," Uxaar offers soothingly. "I'll give you a second chance. Not only that, but you can have whatever you wish. If you yearn for a happy life with Oren, where he is free from his ailments, I'll provide it. If you wish for Athena's safety, I shall grant it. All you must do is let go, leave this conflict behind, and forget Syann exists. You'll be happy, truly."

I turn back, seeing the door to Oren's room. It resounds with the knocks pounding on it. Voice after voice echoes from it—my family, Liam, my friends, begging me to come back.

"And live a lie?" I sharply pivot toward Uxaar.

"You've always lived a lie, yet you adored it. It meant everything to you. Why abandon it now?" Uxaar asks.

"Because, unlike before, I know the truth! That I am Syann, the Goddess of Light! And you, Uxaar, will free me from this illusion!"

Uxaar vanishes in a flash of darkness, which bleeds into the surroundings of the caverns. There I gaze upon Oren, embedded in a pile of boulders.

12 *Oren*

Lightning crackles as I shakily grasp a blood-bathed sword.
I've been here before, a moment I detested so much that it haunts
my mind more than I care to admit. This time, however, the
reenactment feels different. It's vivid and real, almost as if it's not
a dream.

The eyes of the person before me mirror my own—dark irises
concealed beneath hooded eyelids, and above them, a pair of
bushy brows. His frantic eyes reflect the terror of death, and I can
sense it deeply, as can he. The sensation is a sharp pain in my gut
that intensifies so strongly that I groan. Throughout the
discomfort, my eyes squeeze shut. When I finally reopen them, I
find myself in a different place—Brenda is standing before me.
I've changed places—no, I've changed bodies. I'm gripping onto
her tightly, just as the terrorist had, and black armor clothes me.

I yearn to utter her name and apologize for my obstinance in
the caverns, but no words come to my lips. Instead, a metallic
essence envelops my tongue. Instead of the words I desire to
speak, blood gushes forth. A sword has pierced my abdomen, and

now red seeps into my armor.

My head is like a cloud scattered by wind. Chimes blow and jingle in its current. Is it death taking me? I don't want to go. I thought I did, but not here, not like this. I don't know what *this* is! None of this makes sense, and time isn't gracious enough to give me understanding. Instantly, I collapse.

No matter how hard I struggle, breathing is impossible. My rhythmless heart delivers my body into a state of paralysis.

In front of me stands Brenda, safely in the arms of her rescuer—the real me. His soaked hair cascades down his face, dripping over his injured features. A crimson ooze emanates from his right cheek, and above it, his eye is swollen shut. His trembling lip is split open. What strikes me most is the way his slender arms enclose Brenda as if she were a precious treasure.

Relief washed over me when I realized I had saved her, even though the thought of murdering a man made me feel sick. I prioritized her safety over my own. I succeeded in saving her then, but is Brenda all right now? The last thing I remember is Ebony throwing me into a chasm. What has happened to Brenda? What has Ebony done to her?

For over an hour, I've been lying here, paralyzed and breathless. All I can do is think, which is my least favorite pastime. Brenda cries out for help until Roe arrives to talk to her. I can't see him, but she talks to Roe until I finally wake up.

When Brenda and I eventually leave, this body I possess is left alone. Chilling raindrops patter onto my body, but I don't shiver. I can't, even if I should be shivering. The aroma of dirt, grass, and blood is constant. I simply surrender my environment as I bleed out. This feels infinite, until it isn't. Another figure comes onto the scene. She's strikingly familiar. Her eyes are green as mint and her hair is as light as linen. A dark mask nearly disguises these features.

She scurries over, sliding down beside me. Her face contorts in agony. "Gunter!" she wails. "Gunter! No! No!" She frantically prods all over me, checking if I'm still alive. Suddenly, I realize who she is—the terrorist I had first fought and knocked unconscious. She's the one responsible for all the injuries on my face. Now that I know her identity, who is Gunter? The one I had killed must be him. I find myself lying in his place.

Now I understand. Whatever this is, it's trying to load on the guilt of what I've done—the murder I committed. I had to do it to save Brenda, but that doesn't mean I wanted blood on my hands.

The girl realizes I'm dead—or well—Gunter, I don't even know. She's wailing while hopelessly leaning on me. "Uxaar promised to keep us safe!"

"I'm sorry, brother, I'm so sorry." She cries again; it sounds different yet familiar. It's a cry I'd chase to comfort every time I heard it.

A lightning bolt illuminates the sky, casting a bright glow over me. As the light fades, I find myself face-to-face with Elouise.

Now I am devoid of any rain, moisture, or blood. I lie lifeless on my bed, while Elouise's cries pierce the silence.

Her voice is filled with anguish and despair. Tears stream down her round, swollen face. "Oren! I can't lose you!" she sobs, her voice trembling with emotion. "I can't!"

If I died, I never thought I'd witness Elouise's reaction. I could only imagine it in nightmares that prevented me from ending my life. Seeing it now is the most horrifying experience I've ever had. My sister weeps uncontrollably, finding no solace. My mother would be consumed by grief, unable to provide Elouise with the support she needs. Jace never cared for me the way Elouise did, so he would never be able to empathize with Elouise's pain enough to offer satisfying comfort.

I'm forced to watch while not speaking a word of consolation or giving a single touch of affirmation. Cruelly, I'm playing dead, making her believe I'm gone, but I'm not. I'm trying to move, but my mind has lost all control of this body.

Panic that I've never experienced crushes me. There's no rush of breath, increased heartbeat, or physical symptoms of it—only a deep sentiment of despair and perturbation coming as strong as gravity I can't fight.

What if I am dead? Who's to say one loses consciousness at death? I still have mine, yet I have no use or control of my body. What if this is the fate for all who've died? That's preposterous, yet there's no proof against it. No one knows what's after death, except the dead ones and the gods who rule over Light and Darkness. That uncertainty was a reason death terrified me, even when I craved it.

If this is a dream, it's the most intense one I've ever had in terms of sensory overload. Everything feels so real—each strand of Elouise's hair that brushes against me, her tears, the warmth of each stifling breath from her cries, and my scratchy blankets beneath me, too. She sits beside my bed, holding my hand, with her lip pouted out as far as possible.

"You deserved so much more than what life granted you." She shudders. "You were so kind, the gentlest person, and so creative. I'm going to miss the times you drew portraits of me and braided my hair. You were always better at braids than I was. What I'll miss the most is how you always listened to me, no matter what. Mum and Jace n-n-never understood me as well as you did—Though you are gone, I know you never wanted to leave me. You fought harder for me than anyone ever could. For that, I'm so grateful—You can finally rest now. You don't have to fight or feel any pain ever again."

Make it stop. These words reduce me to shreds. My stiff fingers make the longing to squeeze her hand back impossible. There's nothing I can do to show her I'm here with her, that I'm not done fighting for her, and I'm still in agony over her.

Footsteps and Jace's melancholy voice fill the air. "Elouise, it's time."

Elouise clings to me tighter, sobbing harder. "No. No! Please, no!" Elouise begs quietly to herself. My sister knows she's defeated, that she must let me go for good.

"Elouise, it's getting close to sunset. We must bury him," Mum says painfully. I can't see her. My sight is limited to the angle of my face, toward the ceiling. "We've said our goodbyes. It's time to say yours. I know it's horrendous, but it must be done."

Elouise envelops me in a tight embrace, kissing me on the forehead. "Goodbye, Oren!" she whispers, her lips barely parting from my head. With one final glance into my eyes, she brushes them shut with her hand, leaving me in complete darkness.

Elouise's wails echo through the room as sturdy arms lift me out of bed. There's no doubt they belong to Jace. Despite my small stature, I'm still taller than Elouise and my mother. Neither of them could lift me on their own.

I succumb to his grip, limp in his arms. I'm unable to fight, run, or willingly cooperate. My fate is sealed.

Jace lays me into the dirt, and the soil encloses me, stealing my ability to hear and suffocating the air I once sensed. I'm crammed tightly in the darkness, with only my tormenting thoughts as company. I can't dig myself out, scream for help, or express my emotions. I'm on the brink of exploding.

This is the bed I lie in. For how long, who knows? I hope my consciousness dies next. First was my ability to speak, move, see, and now hear. My consciousness is all that's left to lose before I'm nothing.

***

I'm liberated from the earth after what felt like an eternity confined within its depths, but the dirt isn't dirt anymore, it's heavy stones. As the bright light draws closer, air shrouds me, and I burst out, screaming. The emotions that had been bottled up for so long are now escaping like water rushing through a busted dam. Elouise's name is the only word that escapes my lips as the air fills my lungs.

A young woman sits in front of me, and I'm so bewildered

that I can't even recognize her. Where am I? A sharp pain in my abdomen jolts me as soon as I sit up. My head throbs, and my hearing is muffled. Am I reliving my death all over again? How much blood have I lost?

"Oren! It's me, it's Syann! I mean—Brenda! I'm right here! I'm here!" Her words are a blur. My heart rapidly pumps panic throughout me. The woman steadies my frame with a firm grip on my shoulders. Her hands are as bright as stars. "Oren!" She repeats my name until I look at her. "Breathe! Breathe, it's over! It's over!"

The realization hits me like a hailstone to the head—I'm back in the cave with Brenda. Whatever I went through is over, as she had promised. This closure gives me the space to process my emotions instead of letting them overwhelm me in a chaotic panic. The aftermath is filled with sorrow and confusion, so evident that my face flushes with tears.

Brenda can't see me cry! I shield my face with my hands as I curl up into a small ball. Crouching downward intensifies the pain in my stomach. I recoil upward as I cry out, tears streaming down my face. I'm in so much pain that I can't even hide it anymore. Was I stabbed? The pain feels exactly the same as it did in my dream, in the same spot.

"What's wrong?" Her hands reach for mine, moving them out of the way. Her gasp that follows is loud. "You're bleeding!" She begins to unbutton my shirt before I raise my hands to stop her. She grabs my hands, gently setting them aside. "Oren. I need to see your wound. Please."

My only response is a grunt of pain and a nod. I'm self-conscious about her seeing or touching my abdomen, but we've moved beyond the point where my embarrassment holds significance.

"No!" she whimpers, grimacing and shying her gaze away for a moment. "Oh no, no." Her voice breaks as if she's about to weep, yet she takes a cleansing breath and gulps it down.

She tries leaning in closer before squeezing her eyes shut. An extensive abrasion is below my left rib cage and above my belly button. It's not bleeding much anymore, instead scabbed over with green pus. A deeper wound oozes with red in the center of the abrasion.

She inhales sharply, forcing herself to observe my wound again. "This is bad. It's infected."

"Wh-what happened?" I whisper, longing for clarity more than anything.

"You don't remember Ebony attacking you?"

"Um—" I nod. "But after th-th-that?"

"She threw you in this avalanche, so I went after you. It took me some time to find you."

My lower left leg is underneath a large boulder. Attempting to wriggle free only ends in an outburst of pain.

Brenda realizes I'm stuck. "Don't move."

I try to stay still, but when she attempts to roll off the stone, I groan through clenched teeth. The intense pain in my leg evokes the distressing memory of my fall from the tree, which makes me feel helpless.

Brenda groans as she pushes the rock until it finally yields. She takes a moment to catch her breath before our eyes meet. "Oren, I'm so sorry this happened! I thought I could stop her!" she says firmly as she unties the scarf around her waist. Next, she pulls out her water canteen from her backpack. The water she pours onto my wound is cold.

"It isn't y-y-your fault."

Her wide eyes sparkle with tears, as a panic I'm acquainted with overwhelms her expression. Behind her wavering lips and shaky breaths are inconsolable thoughts swarming her mind. She doesn't deserve that. I wish I could take it away. "I know. I just have a lot on my mind."

"The blood pr'bly isn't helpin'—I know it s-s-s-scares you."

Brenda glares at me as if I said something wrong. "How did

you remember that I'm afraid of blood? Your journal?"

That's easy! When we were children, Moo threw her off, and she got a gash in her knee. Brenda cried, panicked, and even grew faint. It was obvious she had a fear of blood. She confirmed that to me once we got her wound bandaged up. How does she not remember? "When w-w-we were kids—"

Oh. Brenda! Me and Brenda, at the farm, our friendship—I remember!

The realization is significant, causing her name and all my breath to be knocked out of me. "Brenda?"

She's not the girl I used to know anymore. Brenda has matured and grown beautifully. Her green eyes stand out more now, especially here in the dark. They're like a set of glowing jewels. I get lost in them as the unlocked memories of her saturate my mind.

"Oren! Y—" She begins, but for once, I interrupt.

"I-I-I remember!"

"We must have passed the border between the Dusk and Dawn realm!"

Above me, the hole I fell through in the ceiling isn't visible. Instead, it's like a starry sky. As she had said, we must have passed through the border. My eyes dart back down as I grunt in pain from looking upward.

"Hold still. I'm going to wrap your wound up. It will be tight, but the pressure will help."

I inhale as she wraps Elouise's scarf around my core. "Thank y-y-you."

She nods. "This isn't ideal timing, but I missed you. I always did."

I exhale as she ties the scarf. "I—m-m-me too." I smile sadly. It's a small smile, which is all I can offer. My energy is depleted, I'm burning with fever, and pain pulses through me, yet she's a light worth smiling about despite it all. If only I had had the guts to reunite with her sooner. I was a fool.

She returns a smile as she buttons my shirt up. "We must get you to the healing pool as soon as possible. You're burning up." She sets her hand on my forehead. I wince when she raises her hand, not that the touch hurts. The light bothers my eyes and head.

I wish to adjust myself to stand up, but I already know I'm too weak to rise on my own. Unfortunately, I need her help, and for once, I should ask for it. "Can y-y-y' help me u-up, p-p-please?" I hold back every apology I long to say.

She smiles proudly and nods. Circling behind me, she removes my backpack and puts it on herself. She grasps beneath my arms to lift me.

I attempt to use both my legs, but my left one fails me. My right leg only keeps me from collapsing.

Brenda pauses. "Slowly, let's take this easy."

I nod. My next attempt at stepping onto my left leg ends in an intense outburst of pain. Immediately I shift my weight off it.

"Oren, your leg!"

"Brenda, I-I-I'm—I-I can't walk on it," I admit defeatedly. The last thing I want is for her to have to carry me. "Do you have m-m-my sword?"

"Yes." She reaches to the ground for it. "Here."

"Thanks." I bring the blade to my side.

"I'm still going to help you walk. Your leg must be broken. We don't need you falling and making it worse."

"I-I should be—" *Fine*, was what I was going to tell her, before I met her begrudged expression. "Pl-pl-please say if-if-if you get tired."

She trudges along with me at a slow pace. Walking on the rocky terrain with one leg would already be difficult. Even with Brenda's assistance, I'm struggling. The impact of each hop on my abled leg causes excruciating pain in my stomach. Additionally, I'm severely weakened due to the lack of food. I have no idea how long I've been confined to this pit.

Together, we venture down the path. As we move past the rubble, the path becomes easier to walk, but it's still not an easy task. Brenda walks at a steady pace, while I hold on to her and use my sword as a makeshift cane.

It becomes exhausting, so I'm grateful we stop to refresh ourselves before resuming our journey. Brenda sits me against the cave wall before positioning herself close across from me.

I'm filling the silence with loud chatters again, though I'm not even cold. I'm actually sweating, yet these chills up my spine come from nowhere.

She digs through our bags, collecting bandages, water, and food. "You need to eat."

I take the items from her, realizing she's only intending to feed me. "You—you need t-t-t-to eat, too."

"I will after I make sure you're taken care of. Infected wounds aren't anything to dawdle with. I'm going to remove your boot, too, so I can observe your leg as well. You aren't hurt anywhere else, are you?"

I shake my head, suppressing a scream as she struggles to remove my boot. I'm certain I'm biting my lip bloody to keep quiet as it comes off. A bright purple-green bruise has overtaken my shin, and my ankle is swollen, with a significant bump above it. My gut feeling is that my bone has snapped, which has distorted my leg. It's a coarse reminder of how my knee appeared after I fell out of the tree. I'd be lucky to have my leg return to its previous state. I could sort of walk on it. Now my leg is useless.

Brenda struggles to maintain a steady gaze on my injury, appearing queasy. Despite this, she wraps my wound with steady, gleaming hands. She also ensures that I eat while she bandages it up.

My stomach is tense, and I'm battling the urge to gag. Brenda is right, though. I must try to eat.

A sense of remorse squeezes my heart. Brenda's actions are so selfless. I don't deserve her kindness. What she deserves is to nourish herself, instead of dealing with me, yet I know apologizing to her would upset her.

If our roles were reversed, I'd happily do the same for her. So I'm trying to accept that this is all right; it's a foreign concept that I can't fully digest.

Brenda is essential to the world's rescue, while the world hardly knew I existed. The world needs her, so why should she waste her time on me?

"Are you all right?" She wraps bandages from my heel to my ankle.

No? Yes? I don't know. She's helping me. That's making circumstances better, yet that illusion shattered me. The fall handicapped me. I'm not fine. She's the only reason I'm close to fine. She's the Light among the shadows, the good memories I forgot I had, and the love I somehow became oblivious to. Can we pick up where we left off almost six years ago? We were children then. I'm different now and so is she. She's grown stronger, and I've broken down. Remembering her is a blessing and a curse. Things can't be the way they were. I want them to, though. I swallow the dried fruit I was chewing. My lips waver as I try to form an answer for her.

"It's all right to say no."

I nod. Before, I yearned to remember her so intensely, but now I'm apprehensive about it. What if I let her down? I fidget with my fingers, attempting to channel my fears nonverbally.

She silently focuses on the bandage. The hush drags on to the point it scares me as much as the speaking and listening did. I won't be comfortable. So, I should at least try to ease her.

"Thank you…f-f-f-for doing th-th-this. B-b-b-Brenda." I huff. My stutter is so embarrassing that I grimace at it.

She notices. "You needn't be embarrassed of your stutter."

"It's g-g-gotten worse since we l-l-last met."

"Do you remember what I would always tell you?" She grins. That's when I remember Brenda's reaction when I built the courage to talk to her after my accident. I remember being so scared that my grandpa had to explain the situation to her beforehand to ease my conscience. Turns out, I was frightened for nothing. Brenda so kindly said, *"Your stutter is nothing to be ashamed of. I think it's cute."*

Those sweet words mended the broken pieces I thought I was. Never would I forget that feeling. Remembering it makes me smile. I nod.

"Tell me, then."

"You s-s-said it-it-it was cute."

"And I still mean it." She smiles. "Don't be embarrassed."

Her compliment swells my heart and spreads a wide grin across my face.

"Another thing, I know I asked you and your family to call me Brenda, but after—well…I'm unsure what illusion Uxaar put you through, but I had an illusion, too. It made me realize many things, and I wish you to call me Syann now. Jace was right. Brenda was a disguise. She's not who I am. I can't pretend anymore."

Jace was right, but he was unnecessarily cruel to her back at the square. It made my blood boil.

"S-Sy—S-S-Syann." The name clumsily rolls from my tongue. If only I could enunciate it as beautifully as the name is.

"You can call me Sy, too, if that's easier," she says with a slight grin. "I know the name Syann is one you've probably not come across too often."

"No, it-it-it's pretty."

"Thank you."

When I reunited with her, I couldn't remember Brenda. I regarded her as the goddess Elouise told me tales about. Now that I remember Brenda, the girl I wrote stories about, she's abandoning the name. If anything she saw in that illusion was close to being as horrid as what I went through, I understand her wanting to forget so badly that she'd disassociate herself from her given name.

"A-are you all right? The illusion? M-m-mine was—" I blink uncontrollably, trying to process the experience. There's no word that can truly encapsulate the sheer terror and devastation I felt.

"I wasn't. I went mad. Uxaar nearly convinced me that I wasn't Syann, that everything was my imagination. I was back home with my family. They remembered me and loved me as they always did. It felt so real, but I couldn't let you and my responsibility go. I couldn't get that out of my head. My family didn't believe that I was Syann, so I had to escape, which took almost an entire day to do. When I finally did, I found you—that's when Uxaar showed up, and I broke free. I knew after that I had to dedicate myself completely to one identity and not teeter between two. So, I chose Syann. I chose to save you and this world and to leave my old life behind." She tears the end of the cloth, securing my bandage in place, like how she had to tear herself from her old life. It couldn't have been easy.

"I'm sorry, th-tha—y-y-you had to go through th-th-that."

Syann smiles thoughtfully. "Thank you."

"Are y-y-you going to eat?" I ask, now that my leg is bandaged.

"Not yet. I need to replace the scarf with bandages; it was only a quick fix—Are you all right with removing your shirt?"

I nod, knowing that I don't have much of a choice if I want my wound taken care of. Besides, I trust her to take care of me. I only hope she won't think less of me.

My unsteady fingers attempt to unbutton it. Syann steps in to finish the task. Her hands are much more graceful, though she has every reason to be as shaken up as I am. She's so strong.

"I don't want to pry, asking you what happened in your illusion, but did yours take you home, too? When you woke up, all you said was Elouise's name repeatedly."

Forcefully, I nod as I pull my arms out of my shirt's sleeves. "N-n-n-not at first…um…" I freeze in place, trying to control my rousing emotions. If I go any deeper into my illusion, the emotions will be in control of me. I'll be more vulnerable than I already am somehow. Which is hard to imagine, since I'm unable to walk, wounded, and shirtless at the moment.

She gapes at me, patiently waiting for me to finish my thought. The palpable tension between us is undeniable. It's the same tension I experienced when our hands brushed against each other in the stables, or when she's caught me goggling at her. However, unlike me, she isn't intimidated by this tension. I'm so nervous that my jaw locks up.

"I understand what it's like to miss family, to be scared you'll never see them again." She breaks the silence, with the canteen in hand. "It hurts, Oren. Even though I can't return to mine, I hope I can return you to yours."

I sniffle before bursting out into coughs that antagonize my stomach. The coughs are challenging to stop, and goodness, I want them to. I long to be well, but I'm not. The coughs remind me how poor in shape I am. The burning in my throat and abdomen brings oceans to my eyes.

The cold water splashing onto my wound only distracts me from my vulnerability for a moment, a short enough window for a tear to break free. I wipe it away instantly, as Syann dabs my wound dry.

"It's all right to cry." Her eyes dart up at me.

I shake my head as she grabs the bandages. She tightly circulates them around my core as her statement waits for an answer. Jace always said I was weak when I cried and couldn't bear anything without breaking down. As a result, it always felt wrong to burden others with my emotions. I already was enough of a burden. I don't want to burden her.

"When are you going to realize I won't judge you, Oren?"

When I stop judging myself. I can't tell her that.

"My illusion made me cry, too. You've seen me cry! Remember my meltdown at the town square? This journey is stressful. And it will be even more so if you bottle up your emotions. I'm here for you, Oren."

If I say anything, I'll burst open. The lump in my throat is like a secret I can no longer keep, but admitting it will make me weaker than I already am.

"Please be transparent with me. We used to tell each other everything long ago. That does not have to change," she desperately begs me. I've been unresponsive long enough that she's nearly finished sealing my wound.

I can't lose you, Oren. Elouise's voice replays in my head, cruelly as vivid as life. It sends a heavy storm that clouds my vision, but Brenda's sympathetic gaze shines through it like sunlight. That light, that green light, is what causes my tears to rain down. "I-I-I thought be-b-before." I inhale. "I-I-I was—fine, w-w-with dying." I shake my head, having difficulty saying the rest. I look at her, then my gaze wanders to the starry ceiling. The lights are vast and countless.

"You're scared?" she asks.

I nod, inhaling intensely as I continue my finger game. "I-I-I experienced it, dying—being dead, in my illusion, yet I-I-I was aware. I-I-I couldn't move—I couldn't breathe. I felt so empty." I sniffle, trying not to sob. "Elly—Elouise, she sat beside me—grieving. It w-w-was torturous! I-I-I-I can't l-l-leave her, n-n-not after th-that."

She tears off the bandage and sets it aside once she's securely fastened it. That's when her hands find mine, ending the game my fingers play with themselves. Fear skips a beat in my heart. My hands flinch initially, but I quickly relax them into hers. "It made you realize she's not better off without you."

I huff, frustrated, before gazing at her. "Sh-she should be, b-b-but sh-she loves me. I l-l-love her, t-t-too, enough t-t-t-to fight through chr-chr-chronic pain. I-i-it was always f-for her."

"She knows you're worth fighting for." She lifts her thumb to wipe away my tear with it. Like when she held my hands, I jolt, before surrendering to the foreign, comforting sensation. I'm not used to anyone touching me or hugging me, except Elouise.

Sometimes, it felt like a prison. I longed for affection at times, yearning for one more embrace from my grandparents. The deprivation of touch transformed it into a fear.

Earlier, I held her hand, hoping it would provide some solace. It was the first time in a while that I had initiated physical contact with someone other than hugging Elly. Syann made me feel significant in some way. I wanted her to experience the same feeling, but I lacked the right words.

Once she had fallen asleep after our exchange in the cave, I couldn't help but admire how peaceful and elegant she was. In my journal, I wrote about her and the things she said to me. Her presence even inspired me to sketch her in my journal.

"Elouise has fought for you. She found me for you. She studied with Athena for years in hopes of helping you. That's what people who love each other do. They fight for each other by making sacrifices."

I stare into her glimmering pair of emerald eyes. I fought for her in the rain. I'd do it again, as much as it terrified me. Is that because I love Syann?

She's proven that the feeling is mutual with all she's done for me. That could only mean—"You l-l-love me?" The question slips out of my mouth as quickly as the sacrifices she's made for me came to mind. She let me accompany her on her journey, rescued me from the rocks, assisted me in walking, and bandaged my leg and stomach. All of these acts were done for my benefit. Still, why would I ask her that? I lost control of my tongue.

"I never stopped loving you," she admits softly. "Even when I thought you were gone, thoughts of you wouldn't leave me be. It was torturous."

I sigh guiltily, remembering how much she occupied my thoughts the morning of the festival. The crown of flowers I had written about in my journal, the words I had penned about her there—"Then I t-t-tortured the both of-f-f us. I'm s-s-so sorry." My gaze drops to her hands holding mine.

"When you couldn't remember why you wrote about me, I wondered if it was because you missed me."

I nod. "Wh-when Elouise g-g-gave me one of those flower crowns, y-y-you were all I-I-I could-d-d thi-think about. S-s-sometimes I-I-I th-th-thought about um—um—coming to Seren to see you."

"Why didn't you?" The tone of the question borders on condescending.

I gaze at her. "I-I thought y-y-you'd be better off. Th-that you'd m-m-move on—it was hard wh-wh-when Elouise said you hadn't—b-b-but I d-d-didn't want t-t-to complicate things…for you. I-I-I was really s-s-sick."

"I could have helped. I would have been there for you, like before."

"I-I know, but then as y-years went by, I-I heard y-y-you were with someone el-else. So, I gave up t-t-the thought c-c-completely. I wanted y-you to be happy and to not b-b-be in your way."

Syann sighs regretfully. "I always had doubts about me and Liam. I missed you, but I thought I'd never see you again. So, I tried forcing myself to move on and make a life for myself, yet no matter how hard I tried, I never forgot you. It's like my heart knew you were out there and needed me, and I wasn't listening to it. Instead, I tried ignoring it. Liam was going to ask to marry me while the stars fell. I overheard it and, quite frankly, I freaked out. He didn't ever make me as happy as you did, but I also didn't want to spend my lifetime waiting for someone who may never come."

I nod. "I-I'm sorry th-th-that I caused you p-p-pain. I was only t-t-trying to protect you."

She nods, accepting my apology instead of denying it. That pains me for once, because it signals that I hurt her. "Thankfully, Liam never proposed, and now I know where I belong. I thought I knew before, but my old life was so much smaller than this."

"So, you're h-h-h-happy?"

"If anything, I'm scared, and I am hurting. Losing my old life in such a flash was shocking. I miss many things about it—my family and Seren, yet when Uxaar brought me back to it, I felt so out of place. I can't go back after all I know. I want to save you and this world and go to Secreth. That's what I'm supposed to do. When I do fulfill that, I will be happy. Even amidst the pain now, you being here with me brings me joy."

"Y-y-you make me h-h-happy, too. I only w-w-wished I had come to m-m-my senses sooner." I robbed myself of her.

"You don't have to shut me out anymore. I can be here for you now. You don't have to feel regret. We can't change the past, but we can change our futures. This is what I want, to be alongside you. What is it that you want?"

For the first time in my life, should I consider what I want? Her? Syann's presence in my life has ignited a profound desire within me—to be by her side. It's a sentiment she openly expresses on my behalf as well. This revelation stirs a combination of emotions within me—hope, worry, and zeal to take action. I recognize that my chances against this urge are slim.

Amidst my inner turmoil, the part of me that gazes directly into her eyes and impulsively asks her daunting questions without hesitation takes over and embarks on the unthinkable.

Gradually, I inch my lips closer to hers in a moment of exhilarating confidence, but amidst my joy, a lingering fear creeps in—what if this is too rushed? What if I overwhelm her? What if I inadvertently scare her away?

Instead, her lips find and press against mine. When her eyes flutter closed, I shut mine, too.

I've never kissed anyone before. The only other people I've ever witnessed kissing were my grandparents. Elouise always found it repulsive and deterred her gaze. In contrast, I always admired my grandparents' love and yearned for something as sweet and tender as that for myself someday. Without a doubt, this is what it tastes like—the love I've always longed for and never believed I could attain. She's bestowing it upon me, and I'm eager to explore it all until I've memorized every aspect of her. I'm overwhelmed by my desire, allowing its passion to engulf my senses like a fiery inferno.

Her kiss serves as the most effective remedy for my pain. Her sweetness elevates me far beyond the bitterness of my past wounds. I could relish this moment indefinitely if only time would allow it. However, an irritating sensation in my throat begins to drag me back into the harsh reality that I can't escape.

I gently pull back, clearing my throat as softly as possible to postpone my cough. "Syann, I-I-I know I-I-I don't want t-t-t-to lose you again." My lips are only inches from hers.

"You're a surprising individual, Oren Silvius," she whispers.

Nodding feels shallow at this point. Should I tell her I surprised myself, too, or kiss her again? I'm lost. I only know that I love her and can't lose her. I always want to remember her. "I-I don't k-kn-know what g-g-got into me!" I grin bashfully, turning my head to the side to finally cough.

"I do. You love me, too," she says confidently.

"I-I-I do! I r-r-really do."

She beams before her smile turns bittersweet. The grip of her right hand releases, and she lifts her hand to my cheek instead. Her thumb grazes right underneath my cut. "I don't want to lose you, either. I want to protect you," she declares passionately. "But I'm scared that I can't."

"I'm scared too…" I nearly died in my attempt to keep her safe last time. The only thing that comforts me is her. I rest my forehead against hers, allowing her presence to intoxicate my worries. "But at-at the same time, th-this is the-the most h-h-hopeful I've felt in years. I d-d-don't know how long th-th-that will last, but we're here now."

"And I will soak that in," she adds.

We stay like that for a moment, one sweet moment that flies by too fast. I'm injured. Syann is hungry. Those things must be taken care of.

13 ~~Brenda~~ *Syann*

I'm fortunate I have an appetite after all this medical work. If anything makes me queasy, it's the sight of blood. I experienced the most exposure to the fluid in my lifetime. Much effort was required to hold myself together, but I pushed on with all my might for Oren. After caring for his injuries, and getting him a new shirt and red vest, I joined Oren in eating.

I'm gorging on my food, like a ravenous dog compared to Oren. He's nibbling on nuts while I bandage him up but not consuming as much as I had hoped he would. I'll take the small victory that he hasn't thrown up, despite the few scares of him gagging.

For one thing, I'm starving. That full, warm feeling in my stomach from my illusion shriveled into a void when I arose. Second, this is—well, *should be* our last break before leaving the caverns. That makes me nervous. What will our arrival at the Dawn realm mean for both of us?

Fears of Oren meeting an undesirable fate, as well as me losing my humanity, creep up on me inevitably like a cat to a mouse.

I'm determined to keep the treasure I've found.

I can't lose Oren.

I finish my food and lean my head on his shoulder. With my eyes closed, I'm transported back to a familiar place—the field by his farm. We're sitting against a shady tree, enthralled by a lengthy conversation. I'd be naïve to deny this as merely a daydream, but I can't help but wish it were our reality. Instead, Oren is dying. If I want to turn this fantasy into a reality, I must save him by facing the risks that lie ahead.

The farther we venture through the cave, the more its structure transforms. Glowing crystals of every color imaginable embed the cave walls. Instead of the usual silence, a faint, monotonous hum reverberates throughout the cavern.

Another source of light, the Geron, appear one by one until they're like a swarm of bugs in the air. "G-G-Geron?" Oren mutters, wide-eyed.

I nod before the Geron speak like a cursed choir. I'm taken back to the time after the stars fell and crashed into the stage. I was running for my life as the Geron told me horrible things.

We'll destroy Seren. There won't be a soul safe from the Geron!
Elouise will soon be ours. Your family will die!
The Dawn will be the end of him!
You won't be able to save anyone.
You will both die!

Oren hyperventilates as the Gerons' words harshen, leading him to stumble. I nearly fall as I catch him. "Go! Stay away from us!" I command sharply. As desired, they all scatter. Oren observes our surroundings as he stands back up, ensuring they're gone. "Don't listen to them."

He's shaking uncontrollably, imprisoned by the words in his head. He doesn't respond to me.

"They can't touch Elouise or your family!"

Oren pauses to ponder my words before responding. "But Ebony c-c-can."

"That doesn't mean she will. She's after me, not them. It will do you no good dwelling on the worst of possibilities. Remember how you told me you had hope? Hold on to that." I lock eyes with him.

He sheepishly meets my eyes. "Elly—Elouise t-t-told me, hope—that th—" Bursting coughs cut Oren short.

"Do you need a moment?" He doesn't answer for himself, but it's clear he does. "Catch your breath." As we stop, he labors for breath, releasing me and grasping his wound. I feel pity for him. Even simple tasks like breathing and walking are a chore for him.

Once he regains his breath, he finally speaks. "Um, Elouise w-w-would tell w-w-with—say hope can—fear a-a-and hurt. B-b-but if we don't, we'll a-a-always hurt. I'm-m—only now realizin' she w-was right. It's sc-sc-scary."

"Of course it is, but doesn't it also feel good?"

"In a way," he replies sadly.

I chortle. That's ironically relatable.

"In-in-in—another w-w-way it f-f-f—" He gasps for air before leaning his head down into his hand with a groan.

"Oren?" I question fearfully. He struggles to finish his thought, but eventually I'm able to understand what he's trying to communicate—for him, hope is alarming, like a war raging in his head.

"You're right. It is scary. *This* is scary. Hoping can be against all odds, a desperate wish for the best to happen when it seems impossible. But I'm not going to sit here and accept that you might die. No, I'm going to do everything in my power to stop that." I put my arm underneath his shoulders to support him. "I wish you had time to rest, but we can't afford it. You're getting worse."

I hold him closer to me, taking extra care to guide his steps. Despite all his afflictions, the hope I give him brings a smile to his face. This feeling is special, and I wish I could relish it for longer. If only time were kinder, I would kiss and talk away his worries.

The light from the cave's end extinguishes the cave crystals' light. Past it, a skyline emerges, crowned by trees and plants. From a distance, they don't resemble the foliage we're accustomed to at home. Instead, they glow with unnatural colors—not green, but hues of blue, purple, and white.

Examining the horizon distracts me from the cave floor, which abruptly branches off into a water pool ahead of us. Oren can't swim, especially in his current state. If we're lucky, the water may be shallow enough for us to walk through it.

I tell Oren to lean against the cave wall so I can assess the water's depth.

The ripples from my step into the water appear unnatural. They intensify until the water toward the center swirls and ascends, shapeshifting into a peculiar figure made of water. Without hesitation, it waves at me.

"Hello." I wave back. Heat rises within me. My inner power surges an overwhelming desire to reach out and touch the water creature. My hand extends toward it, and it reciprocates the gesture, gently caressing its cool, flowing palm against mine.

Flashes of scenery appear in my head. This creature swims gracefully through the crystal-blue waters, and splashes the luminous plants rooted upon the riverbanks. The imagery evokes a sense of warmth and affection.

The creature spreads her hands, splitting the pool in two, leaving a dry trail for Oren. That's when I snap out of my trance. My hands slightly dim. I hadn't even realized they had brightened during the trance.

"What w-w-was that?" Oren asks in awe.

"An aquinne." Somehow, I know the species name. "She's been in hiding, waiting for me to return."

Before the trance, I had no clue what an aquinne was. Now, I recall the water creatures. Those flashes I saw weren't dreams or visions—they were fragments of memories from before my reincarnation. Secreth was more beautiful than I could have possibly imagined.

I approach Oren and help him up. "Let's go."

We reach the end of the cave through the dry passage, and the Dawn realm is before our eyes. The sky is a dark, vibrant gradient of blue, orange, and pink, like before the sunrise. Only there's no sun here. I even question if the plain above is a sky with an atmosphere or something else entirely.

Bordering the land are towering cave walls that stretch high like a mountain. As they ascend, the wall crystals blend seamlessly into the sky's color. From these walls, high above, branch out bridged fortresses. I'm uncertain about the extent of these bridges. Do they span the entire border, reaching the opposite end, or do they have a support halfway across?

Beneath the swaying trees, large crystal stones peek out from tall, feathery grass. Surrounding the pool's bank are sapphire-toned flowers that glow like stars. They're some of the most beautiful flowers I've ever seen. I'm tempted to pluck one, but a herd of massive creatures appears, grazing on the grasses and flowers, drinking from the pool.

"Harjins." I say the name that pops into my head.

These creatures are enormous, at least seven feet tall. Unlike horses, they have reptilian scales, a slender frame like a leopard, and paws instead of hooves. They have a long neck and tail resembling a lizard, and large horns protrude from their front shoulder blades, resembling wings. They're what I'd imagined a dinosaur or dragon to look like, yet their faces are intense and elegant, like foxes. Oren and I could swiftly reach the pools on one, but how am I going to get Oren onto its back?

As soon as Oren and I step onto the bank, like the aquinne, the harjins approach me. This time, the intense sensation or loss of control doesn't occur. Instead, I feel a profound peace, knowing exactly what to do here. My heart rate gradually steadies.

I pluck a flower from the grass to show Oren. Before I can present the flower to him, the petals dim.

"It-it-it only g-gl-glows if it's r-r-rooted." Oren frowns.

"Yeah," I answer disappointedly, holding out the flower. "Hello." The animal consumes the flower from my hand. Their eyes are an intense amber. "My friend is injured. We're in need of a ride to the healing pools. Please." The creature closes its eyes before kneeling. This will make it much easier for Oren to get on. "Thank you."

I help Oren walk toward the creature and climb onto its back. Once he has settled, I follow him up and position myself behind him. My chin gently nuzzles into Oren's shoulder, while I hold him securely by his waist.

"This-s-s lot bi-bi-bigger than a horse." Oren chuckles, sounding intimidated. That is obvious when the harjin stands up on its paws. I'm two feet higher than I would be on a horse.

"I know." I giggle, patting the harjin on the side. "Steady, fella. To the healing pools."

I've noticed that the star appears closer than ever before, but we're traveling in the opposite direction. The pools must be located on the opposite side of the Dawn realm, which is unfortunate, but it could also be advantageous. Athena mentioned the existence of a civilization near the pools in this realm. There's a chance we'll encounter them, and they might be willing to help us.

Oren and I are abruptly thrown off the harjin. I'm not sure what has caused it until a vine whips through the air as I'm plunging toward the ground. The impact aches, especially when Oren falls face-down on top of me. Two sounds make my heart skip a beat—Oren groaning in pain and the harjin running away. That was our ride! The ride Oren desperately needed!

"Hey." I smile tensely at Oren. "Are you all right?"

Oren pushes himself up using his arms and knees. His face is mere inches away from mine when he nods gently.

Before I can assist him, the vine snatches Oren from my grasp and suspends him in midair. Oren's screams echo as he frantically swings his sword, attempting to sever the vines. However, the vine swiftly wraps around the sword's handle, flinging it away from him.

I pop onto my feet, yelling, "Hey!—" Another vine from the dark tree grabs onto me. As it swings and tosses me, I manage to lock my eyes onto Oren. "Bring him no harm! *Gently*, put him down!" Thankfully, the vine does precisely what I ask, bringing Oren back to the ground carefully. However, the predicament isn't over. A sea of mangled black vines attacks me. The tree they grow from is hauntingly dressed in the coarse dark green crystal.

"Syann! G-g-g-get out of there!" Oren yells.

The vines encircle my mouth, trying to silence me.

I must remain composed if I'm going to defeat Uxaar. But how can I if I can't defeat a tree? I cling to the vines that muffle me, but that doesn't stop them from crawling into my mouth. Terror washes over me as they tunnel down my throat, causing me to gag. With all my might, I try to pull them out of my mouth, but they venture as far as my stomach.

I concentrate deeply on the thought, *Set me free!*

My hands flash in response, and in the blink of an eye, I'm thrown into the air as the rugged vine slithers out of my airways.

Another tree branch catches me. Initially, I fear that the battle isn't over yet, but I sense something different about this tree. Its crystal is radiant, unlike the first one. Moreover, its bark is pearly white and smooth.

The tree sets me on my feet, but I collapse right by Oren. My throat and stomach burn from the vine traversing my insides, and tears sting my eyes. If that had happened to a mortal, it would've killed them. Continuously, I'm retching on all fours, fighting against the urge to vomit, but everything I ate in the cave violently erupts out of me.

Oren's soothing hands rubbing circles on my back is my focus as I battle for my composure. He's behind me, comforting me, which is all I could ask for. I know he's alive. The tree failed to kill him. "Syann! Breathe!"

When the vomiting ceases, I bring myself to my knees.

Oren's hands perch on my shoulders. "Syann, are y-y-you all right?"

I wipe my mouth with my sleeve, turning toward him as tears blur my vision. "That was the most gruesome thing I've ever felt."

"I'm so sorry, I-I-I'm s-so sorry, Sy, but hey, y-y-you stopped it! You kept us s-s-safe." He wipes my tears away. "You're l-l-learning your powers."

I smile, realizing I did execute my commands exactly as I needed to. If I can keep that up, we stand a chance. "If I hadn't just thrown up, I would kiss you right now," I admit through an exhale.

Oren chuckles and plants a kiss on my forehead. "There's mint i-i-in m-my backpack if y-y-you want some. It always h-h-helps me feel b-b-better."

"That would be delightful."

The light branch pats my shoulder, similar to a child persistently poking with their finger. I rise, offering my hand to Oren, but he shakes his head.

"I suppose I owe you a thank-you for catching me," I tell the tree.

A branch extends itself to Oren, expecting him to reach for it, but he only leans away.

"He can't walk right now," I tell the tree. "But soon, once we get him to the healing pools and his foot is healed, he'll be able to." I gaze at Oren with a smile, but he isn't returning it. Instead, he's groaning under shallow breaths while reaching toward his stomach again. Concern wells within me.

The tree brings a limb toward Oren's foot, curious, observing the bandages. The stalk sways to Oren's level and fascinatingly grows in length before breaking off. Another limb catches this broken crystal branch and offers it to Oren.

"I think it's a walking stick!"

"Oh!" Oren hesitantly takes the stick from the tree, half smiling as he sets it in his lap. "Th-thank you." He nods to the tree with a cough.

"Would you like to try it out?" I ask.

Oren hesitantly nods again and grasps the tree branch to rise. Once he's on his feet, he places the rod beneath the crook of his left arm. "Th-th-that is nice."

I thank the tree, before asking, "Which way is it to the healing pools?" The tree points one of its limbs to my left. "You've been so helpful, thank you again." I take one of the limbs, emulating a handshake. The tree goes along with it. "Goodbye, friend."

We both tread in the direction of the pools. I discover the reason Oren seems off is that the fall from the harjin made him dizzy. He asks me to talk about anything to distract him. So, I ramble about the living trees, wondering if the ones in Secreth are alive, too. The one-sided conversation distracts me as well, to the point that Oren fainting catches me off guard.

"Oren!" I scream.

He descends face-flat. I roll him over face-upward, and he's unconscious. My heart clenches and doesn't ease until I put my ear against his chest. His heart beats slowly and steadily. Thank goodness. He isn't dead yet, but I don't know how long he has.

"Oren! We are almost there! Please! Wake up!" I shake him, but soon realize my effort is useless. Even if he does wake up, he won't be able to walk, nor can I carry him. "I'm going to get help! It's going to be fine!" I assure myself through panicked breaths. Roe was there for me last time. "Roe!" I call. Immediately, the familiar green-and-red glow presents itself. "Roe, Oren needs help! We're so close to the healing water Athena told us about, and I'm getting him there!"

Roe sighs disappointedly. "There are two adolescent boys some yards that way by the river. They're from the village here.

They should be willing to help you, but you'll have to go to them quickly before they're gone."

"What about Oren?"

"I'll guard him. If anything happens to him, I'll inform you immediately."

I don't like this, but do I have much of a choice? "You'll do exactly what you've offered and keep him safe."

Roe nods. "Run in that direction." Roe points to the right. "They're straight ahead and close by."

I nod before turning back to Oren. I drag him toward a crystal structure and lay him to sit against it. "I'll be right back." I gently cup his cheeks and kiss his forehead, grasping onto hope that he'll be here when I return.

The Light among the Shadows

14 *Syann*

Two boys around Jonavan's age hike through the forest. They are undoubtedly the ones Roe referred to. Both of them examine me cautiously. The taller boy steps back, while the other stands forward to confront me. He assumes a defensive position, drawing a dagger once I'm about a yard away from him.

"Woah!" The sight of the knife takes me aback. I don't know why, it can't hurt me. That realization emboldens me to step toward him, straight and tall.

The armed kid has shaggy dark hair, warm brown skin, a small, hooked nose, wide steel-blue eyes, a lean frame, and crooked teeth. I'm surprised by how stoically he maintains his expression for his age. He exudes fearlessness and readiness to fight. However, his tense expression softens when he sees my hands, replaced by a starstruck gaze. He lowers his knife. "Your hands!"

The taller boy, who's slightly older, I presume, grins. "You're Syann!" He steps toward me, but the knife-wielding boy holds out his arm to block him from getting closer.

"Yes, so listen! My friend is dying! If he doesn't get help soon,

I fear the worst! I need help getting him to the healing pools at once!"

"If you're Syann, why do your eyes have a Geron mark?" the shorter boy says. "You could be tricking us."

"I'll explain everything on the way. If you will help me, I need you to come now! Follow me!" I sprint off. Thankfully, the two boys follow.

"All right, you told us you'd explain on the way!"

"Before the stars fell, my town was attacked by Uxaar's men, who threatened me into reciting the Incantations. When the stars fell and revealed my identity, I was able to break off my bond with the Geron, which left the eye mark. What are your names?" I ask, hoping asking a question distracts them from questioning me.

"Gene," the dark-haired one answers.

"Kipper, or Kip is fine," the tall one adds. "As for Gene, it's short for Eugene." Kip, bald with braided sideburns and slightly lighter skin than Gene's, has a round, fleshy nose sprinkled with freckles. They both wear baggy cotton shirts tucked into moccasin pants and boots.

"Well, I don't give people the option to call me that, Kipper!" Gene snaps. "It's Gene and only Gene!"

"Nice to meet you both. My friend should be just ahead." He is! Oren is slumped against the rock like I left him. Roe isn't far from him, watching. As soon as the boys come into sight, Roe vanishes.

"A Geron!" Gene exclaims.

I ignore Gene and rush to Oren's side. He remains unconscious.

"Woah! What happened to him?" Kipper asks sadly.

"He's been ill, so I brought him with me so he could be healed at the pools, but the journey here has been rough."

"That Geron beside him had the same eye color as you!" Gene chides firmly, standing with crossed arms. Unlike Kip, Gene is utterly unfazed by Oren's condition.

"Are you helping me or not?" I snap back.

"Gene—" Kipper's brown eyes plead compassionately. "She's right, he's in bad shape. It's not like Master Floria lacks the mark."

"I didn't say I wouldn't help! Master Floria, however, wants us to have nothing to do with the Geron."

"Master Floria will be pleased to see her! Trust me!"

"Please. I can't carry him myself," I add.

"We'll help you take him to the village. Afterward, we'll find a way to get him to the pools. The pools are a bit farther away than the village on foot," Gene declares. "We have some remedies at the village that will stabilize him."

"Thank you."

The three of us carefully lift Oren, as if carrying a log. Kipper supports Oren's legs, Gene lifts his back, and I hold his head and shoulders. This way, we carry him to the village. We leave his new walking stick behind, as I'm told he won't need it.

The village appears in the distance. The fence around it is made of crystal stakes planted into the ground, woven together with rope. It sturdily reaches to eight feet tall.

Beyond the crystal fences are clustered huts made of gray crystal logs and white-moss-covered roofs. These houses are illuminated, like the flowers I saw earlier. This village appears to be surrounded by gray and blue trees, but they are none within the fence. Clusters of glowing flowers surround the houses. Not a single Geron is in sight, either.

As we approach the village, our presence draws the attention of everyone around. Four guards, each clad in intricate crystal armor with scaled shoulder pads, helmets, and a crystal spear in hand, stand vigilant at the entrance, guarding it from the outside.

Two guards head toward us. Their glares could burn through me. "Kipper, Eugene?" a guard addresses them. "What's the meaning of this? Who are these outsiders?" His voice is coarse but muffled by the helmet. The only facial features I can make out are his almond-shaped brown eyes.

Gene has that defensive gleam in his eyes he had when I first approached him. "Dick—" Gene clears his throat. The guard rolls his eyes at him. "I found them in the forest. She claims to be Syann, and this is her friend—"

"Oren." I cut in. "He's wounded and needs immediate care. Please. I don't mean any harm to you or your people."

The guard, Dick, I presume, gives the other guard a side-eye, muttering something I can't quite make out. I'm sure the names *Floria* and *Syann* are in the sentence. Dick turns back to us. "All of you are coming with us to speak to Master Floria regarding these outsiders. This fallen one, however, we'll take to our physicians, and he'll receive our best care."

The guard summons a stretcher. A human-sized mat sewn onto two poles is brought out. Oren is maneuvered onto it by the guards and carried into the village. The boys and I follow right behind them.

Gene whispers insults concerning the guard who spoke to us. He explains that his name is Dyke, but he calls him Dick to spite him for calling Gene by his full name. Kipper laughs, but I'm too worried for Oren to find Gene's joke amusing.

The medical hut, the second building to the right of the gate, has a door made of draping vines that you walk through. As I enter behind the guards with Oren, two women approach his side while the guards place him on the table. I assume the women are both physicians. One physician observes Oren and asks me about his injuries, while the other goes to a cupboard and retrieves a box. She brings the box over to the table.

The guards leave Oren with the physicians and approach me and the boys. "You three will be coming with us to see Master Floria."

Fear strikes me at the thought of being separated from Oren. I don't trust these people alone with him yet, but my protesting is shut down by Gene immediately.

Begrudgingly, I follow two guards out with Gene and Kipper, knowing it's my only option. If I want these people as allies, I must comply.

As we walk, my eyes trace the medical hut until I lose sight of it. I should be relieved. Gene and Kipper assured me they have advanced remedies and good physicians to stabilize Oren until he can go to the pools. That did ease my conscience a bit, but the guilt of leaving him with strangers gnaws at me.

I also yearn for the company of someone I trust. Everyone we pass stares at me like I'm an alien.

In the center of the town is a larger hut. According to Kipper, it's Floria's house. A pair of soldiers guard the doorway, which is also draped in vines.

Once we enter, Dyke instructs us to sit at the table as Floria arrives. She's tall, slightly taller than me, I dare say. I rarely meet women who are taller than me. She's shaved bald except for a silver ponytail behind her head and braided sideburns like Kipper's. Her clear skin is dark, and her frame is muscular, but her arched eyes stick out the most. They're the same blue as Uxaar's—sharp and piercing like them, too. She models the same armor as the guards but wears no helmet. A matching crystal spear is strapped to her back.

A lump forms in my throat in her presence. She must be over a thousand years old, being one of the people from the war Athena mentioned. She could beat me to a pulp with her eyes shut if I weren't invincible.

"She's a sight, huh?" Gene snickers.

"Eugene and Kipper Hernandez." Floria says. She has a thick accent. I'm unsure where it's from.

"Master Floria," Gene smacks, crossing his arms.

"You found this girl?"

"More like she found us."

Floria paces slowly toward me. The closer she gets, the faster my heart beats. My palms even sweat. Her expression deepens, like she's reminiscing deep in her mind. "Syann."

"Yes."

"It has been over a thousand years since I saw you, yet the memories of you are so clear. You look just like her, but dirtier," she remarks with disgust as she withdraws a step from me.

Embarrassment fills me, especially when Gene snickers. I've been so fixated on Oren's safety that I've been blinded from the fact I've been wearing the same clothes for days. I do not smell pleasant—instead, I smell like dirt, sweat, and blood.

"Dyke, escort her to my quarters to be cleaned. I have spare armor that should suit her fine," Floria commands.

***

I had no idea how much I craved cleanliness until now. The dirt and grime covering me appeared insignificant until I removed my soiled garments to take a bath. They had contaminated my skin and beneath my fingernails.

I try to savor the tranquility of this solitary moment in Floria's bathroom. This might be the only relaxing moment I'll have for a while. I grab a towel and gaze into the mirror. Strangely, I'm accustomed to the green eyes and radiant hands now. Seeing the signs that I'm Syann brings me a sense of peace, a peace that I hope will endure.

My hair is soaked, and there's no time to dry it. Briskly, I do a messy braid behind my head.

Next, I put on the armor Floria loaned me. The undershirt and pants are lined with green scales. The clothing is heavy, but flexible enough. I'm grateful Floria gave me a belt—otherwise, these pants wouldn't have fit.

The armor pads are intricate. I'm not sure where to start putting them on. Fortunately, Floria helps me out. She dresses me in the armor within five minutes while explaining its functions to me.

The ice-blue pads are crafted from a sturdy hybrid of crystal and metal. The shoulder pads and belt are made of green dragon scales, the same scales that line the undershirt and pants. Floria explains that these scales are flexible and sturdy, repelling harmful magical blows just as effectively as the crystal-metal. The shoulder plates and tasset drape with white glowing vines woven into thick yet short tassels.

It's an odd feeling to view myself in it in the mirror. I look like a warrior, a goddess of a warrior ready to face her destiny head-on.

I'm escorted to the kitchen table made of stone, draped with a lavender netted tablecloth. The four of us, Floria, Gene, Kipper, and I, are at the table. We each get a plate of roasted meat, along with scrambled eggs, and some—well, I'd say mixed greens, but they're blue.

Gene's and Kipper's mouths are watering over their plates as if it were the first thing they've been offered to eat all day. The feeling is mutual. Having a plate of hot food in front of me is a luxury I haven't had since breakfast at the Silvius's home. That feels so long ago. So much has happened since then, not like any of it feels as important as it used to be. Walking through Seren like an outcast, fighting in the rain, struggling through an illusion, and getting Oren out of the avalanche, it all feels mushed together now. The overall goal stands out—save the world and Oren.

Kipper is excited. "Oooh, you have no idea what any of this is, do you?"

"I can't say I do." I shake my head with an expectant smile.

"We have roasted mukner, a mammal we farm here within this village, and get this, scrambled dragon egg and a beet-grass salad."

"I would say that sounds delicious, but I haven't an idea what any of that tastes like." I chuckle.

"Nothing is stopping you from finding out," Gene says nonchalantly.

Gene is right, so I eagerly take a forkful of the roast and bite into it. The flavor is unlike any meat I've ever tasted. It's firmer in texture, not dry, and has an earthy taste with a subtle spicy kick. It's quite enjoyable. The dragon egg, on the other hand, is a bit runnier than I would have preferred and has a peculiar, subtle sweetness. The salad is bitter, but it pairs well with the egg. I mix them together, which earns me a strange look from the boys. Gene teases me about it, while Kipper decides to give it a try. They also gave me a cup of pink juice. It's quite strong in flavor, reminiscent of grapefruit, smooth like milk, and not very sweet. Floria claims that the juice is a highly sustainable energy source derived from the Light trees.

I can tell I've calmed down when I notice I'm eating slowly. The boys, however, mow through their food in mere minutes.

"So, you've been to Secreth?" I ask Floria. "I've heard of you and this civilization of people. You date back from the war on Secreth."

"It isn't a fond memory, but yes, I have. Unfortunately, through Uxaar's control," Floria answers.

"Is it like this place, or Earth? Or completely different?"

"It has the forestry of the Earth but the enchantment of this place. The environment lives and breathes there. It's glorious. The palace where you lived was grand and beautiful. It's much more impressive than any structure I've seen in my lifetime. I wish I could tell you what the colors were like in Secreth, but through Uxaar's eyes, I was colorblind. Everything was blue. I couldn't tell you if the grass was green, brown, purple, or white. With the mark on your eyes, I'm sure you understand."

"Oh yes! Everything was green! You would have no idea what color anything was seeing it for the first time in that perspective."

Floria shakes her head. "I'm excited to see Secreth with my own eyes if I make it." My heart tugs, wanting to promise her I'll make that happen, but I can't. "My people would be safe there. I've lost so many to this place over the years," Floria adds.

"Really? Couldn't anyone who died be taken to the pool?"

"There are some bad areas in this land. The trees here are

unlike the ones on Earth. They live off the power, whether light, dark, or a mixture. When the Geron invaded this realm after the millennia of silence, many of the trees were influenced by their Darkness. These dark trees have strangled innocents that couldn't be retrieved. Fishermen have been dragged to their deaths by leviathans, and hunters eaten alive by wild beasts or swooped by dragons. Many young children who've ventured past the village have disappeared over the years, likely abducted by the Gerons' followers and never seen again. It has amounted to hundreds of deaths in my lifetime. Senseless deaths that would all stop if we settled in Secreth."

"The followers kill the victims they take?" I ask, thinking of Athena. "They recently took my friend, Athena, who came along with me. I haven't seen her in days."

"Did she have any past ties to the Geron?"

"Yes, she said almost nineteen years ago, she ventured here with two of her friends, Philip and Ebony. Uxaar's followers attacked and captured them, but Athena was rescued."

Floria's expression lights up. "Athena! Yes, I remember now. It was my people who rescued her and brought her to me. She begged for our effort to retrieve her friends, but I had to break it to her that we had many of our own missing. Though I assured her that if we ever were fortunate enough to rescue them, we would return them to her."

"Ebony is the Shadow, Floria. She's the reason Oren is in such bad condition."

Floria's thin, white brows furrow. "How do you know this?"

"I was able to get the information from a Geron. They made it seem like Uxaar threatened Philip's life and she folded under pressure."

"That falls in line with the past tactics Uxaar has used—fear, abuse, and manipulation. When the Geron invaded after the peaceful millennia, everyone fell victim to the Gerons' verbal harassment. There was no escape; once you've entered the Dawn you can't go back to Earth without the ability of seeing the Geron, like those who are born into it. So many resorted to suicide. Several who died were brought to the pools, and when they awoke, they said the fate after death in the Underealm was even worse than before. So, droves of people opted to serve the Geron in exchange for the harassment to stop. It took over thirty years for them to find a victim who was willing to recite the Incantations, so it's safe to assume the victims before Ebony were killed. As for the victims now, they target the children more than anyone because they are easily manipulated. So many have been raised by the Gerons' troops and have been deceived."

"That doesn't surprise me. It seems Uxaar's followers do the deeds they do because they assume they don't have a choice if they want to live."

"The thing is, they do. The people here in the Dawn have found relief from the Gerons' tyranny. Over ten years after the Geron invaded this realm, the war between this village and the Gerons' followers was at its height. There was much bloodshed, and my people had the advantage because the healing pools were in our territory. So Uxaar and I made an oath that the Geron would leave this village undisturbed if we let his followers use the pools on the outskirts of our land. For the past fifty years, the very peace the Gerons' followers wanted, we have, while they are under the Gerons' thumb and have no real peace. They are slaves to foul creatures who hold no physical power over them."

"They are likely afraid that Uxaar's agreement is fragile, if Uxaar even allowed them to be aware of the agreement at all."

"The peace *is* fragile, regardless of whose side you stand. Uxaar's Shadow is on the rise. That's why we keep this place heavily fortified by guards to prevent attacks or kidnappings, but now that you're here and the Shadow is at hand, there will be attacks very soon. If not today!"

"If I'm to save you all from Ebony, I can't spend much more time here. So, I'm going to be straight with you. The only thing keeping me from continuing my journey is Oren. He needs to be taken to the healing pools, as I promised him and his family. After I do so, we're going to head straight to Secreth."

Floria pauses in thought. "Then I have an offer for you. The Geron are dangerous. I'm afraid you're unaware of their capabilities. My troops and I are from our time, being bound to them hundreds of years ago. We will come along with you as protection and escort your friend to the pools. Once he's well, we'll return him here. He will be much safer than he would be if he were by your side. Then we, and the troops, will head to Secreth and end the Geron. That way, you have protection and guidance on your way, and your friend has somewhere safe to keep refuge on the sidelines. How does that sound?"

How does that sound?

I couldn't ask for a better outcome.

15 *Oren*

I wake up drowsily but in less pain than expected. The room has this hazy glow that convinces me I'm dreaming. A woman prompts me to be still. I realize why—my slight movement sends searing pain to my stomach.

My vision is limited by lack of movement, but I'm pretty sure Syann is missing, like my clothes are. Only a gray blanket conceals my nakedness. The realization brings heat to my face and coarse chills everywhere else.

"W-w-what the—Why d-d-did you st-st-strip me? Who a-a-are you?"

The two women calm me down. They introduce themselves as the village physicians and claim that they had to thoroughly examine my body for injuries. While I was unconscious, they medicated my stomach wound.

As for Syann, their leader is questioning her, but she will return after.

I ask if I could have my clothes back, but they refuse. They will provide me with clean clothes at the end of my treatment.

The physician re-aligns the broken bone by gripping my ankle and pushing it back into place. That makes me groan louder than when Syann took my boot off. They place a cool towel on my forehead to soothe me, which fails to distract me from my pain. What distracts me is my humiliation, which only grows. Others enter the room while I'm still being operated on. I turn my head slightly toward whoever's walking in.

"How's he doing?" a woman asks. She, a tall and muscular bald woman in armor, approaches the physicians. Her eyes glow like Syann's, but Uxaar's color, the same blue from Ebony's eyes.

Syann's voice follows, calling out my name. My heart skips a beat, pumping dread throughout me. I'm not presentable. She can't see me like this! Except she will—she's coming from the same direction as the armored woman and stops right by me. Syann kneels, leaning in face-to-face with me. "You're alive!" She beams. "How are you feeling?"

There are two teen boys by the doorway behind her. The taller one waves at me when I make brief eye contact with him.

Everyone is looking at me, causing me to freeze.

"What's wrong?"

I stammer hesitantly, unsure how to answer, but I imagine I'm flushed.

"Oren, are you all right?" she whispers in my ear.

I shake my head. "Can th-they wait outside?"

She's unsettled by my response, but nods. "Of course." She swoops her head toward the others, asking them if I can have some privacy. Everyone other than the physicians steps outside the hut. Syann shifts back toward me, not making eye contact with me. "What happened?"

"I w-woke up and y-y-you were gone, an-and the doctors t-t-took my clothes off w-w-when I was uncons-sc-scious, an-and everyone c-c-came in unannounced."

Surprise builds on her face. At least the blanket is doing it's job. "Oh! I had no idea, Oren! I'm sorry, we can all wait outside until you're dressed, I didn't mean to—"

"No!" I blurt out. "Please no, d-d-don't leave again," I request pitifully. "I w-w-was so worried about you, p-p-please."

She frowns deeply. "I'm so sorry I had to leave you before. I didn't have a choice. I found help after you passed out, but their leader, Floria, demanded to speak with me. She's the woman who was checking on you, with blue eyes. I tried staying by your side, but they wouldn't have it."

The leader of this town saw me half naked. I visibly shrink.

Syann notices. "What is it?"

I hesitate to say, "I'm 'mbarrased she saw m-m-me."

"Don't be. You know, the first thing she told me was I was dirty and needed a bath!" Syann smiles.

I chortle—somehow that eases me.

"I felt embarrassed, too, but you have no reason to be embarrassed. I honestly wouldn't have noticed if you hadn't said anything. The blanket conceals you fine. Regardless, I'm glad you told me what was bothering you. You never have to fear being honest with me."

She's right—Syann's never given me a reason to be scared of being open with her. Still, there are multiple times she's had to prod to get information out of me, even just now. That must change from here on out.

"It-it makes me feel w-w-weak. Th-this situation, m-m-my body, my-my health, everything—" I'm afraid if I admit more, I will cry, which proves the point I'm trying to make—I'm too weak to even express my feelings without breaking. My frustration radiates from me like the sun's heat.

"Everything?" There she goes, prodding me again, because I'm holding back from her. Shame on me.

"Ev-ev-everyone has t-t-to take care of me, an-and for once I wish th-th-that could change. That I wouldn't burden m-m-my mum or frustrate Jace with m-m-my weakness. I-I mean, it's s-s-so obvious! Look at me. I'm w-w-weak, s-s-small, a-and too sick to care f-f-for myself," I rant waveringly. "Everyone e-e-else is so strong. Stronger th-th-than me."

The curious tension on her face melts into empathy as she shakes her head. "Oren, you are not weak. You are one of the strongest people I know. You've endured some of the toughest pain, which most are a stranger to. Even then, you still chose this journey of bettering yourself. You are powerful, and you are not ugly or weak. You are strong, and you are beautiful. You are who I dreamed of." She says all this firmly, like it's a lecture. Though the words are some of the sweetest ones I've heard. She sets her hand on my cheek. "Stop listening to those thoughts in your head, and listen to me, please."

I nod, able to smile as I thank her.

Syann explains there's a group who's agreed to take us to the pools as soon as I'm ready, which I will be once the physician finishes wrapping my ankle. They ask Syann to wait outside while they dress me. They give me a long-sleeve indigo shirt, black trousers and boots, and a crutch.

***

Outside, I'm introduced to the new members of our party. There are two boys, the shorter one is named Gene, who's fourteen—almost fifteen—he insisted on adding. The second boy, Kipper—who's sixteen—has taken a liking to me for no apparent reason. I'm unsure what Gene thinks about me. He has a tough exterior for his youthful age.

The blue-eyed woman is Floria. Kip tells me she is the leader of this village and is one thousand and fifty-nine years of age. He also tells me she was the girl Uxaar used to create the Shadow Incantations. She was freed when Syann banished the Darkness out of Secreth and closed its borders. Kip says Floria is one of the Eleven people who remain in this town who were the Shadows of the Great War.

"Floria said they're coming with us to the pools and Secreth's gate."

Floria turns around, replying to Syann, "They're the best men and women for the job, sharp in combat, with personal experience with the Geron and Shadows. They'll hold nothing back against Uxaar."

We'll have protection for the rest of our journey. The faint hope within me has been ignited even more fervently. Even my chest feels lighter now. What a relief! I've been worried ever since I woke up in this place. Syann and I have no experience with this realm, but thanks to this guidance, our path will be clear and direct.

We approach the town's edge, where a gate awaits us. Beyond it lies a group of individuals in matching armor and wielding crystal spears, all standing beside Floria. Roughly half of them are accompanied by harjins.

Even from a distance, it's evident that each of these individuals has strikingly bright eyes, with a variety of colors. Syann fits right into the group, matching their armor and glowing eyes.

"That's them, the Eleven," Syann says.

"Lucam, Amran, Perri, Urias, Fenneth, Rowan, Darius, Amber, Yoli, Canyon, and Floria." Gene lists them proudly.

"Lucam is the one with orange eyes," Kip begins. "Amran's are pink!"

"Boys, how about we allow Syann and Oren to have a proper introduction to the Eleven?" Floria opens the gate for the rest of us to go through.

I'm intimidated by the thought of meeting so many people simultaneously, especially such vigorous and mature individuals. Even after my conversation with Syann, my lingering insecurity about being the weakest among them persists. While I might be stronger than Gene after the pools heal my injuries, I doubt it. Healing won't erase my scrawny frame and lack of muscular strength.

My insecurity magnifies next to Floria. She stands an inch

taller than me, and her legs and arms are twice as wide as mine due to her muscular build.

Out of the Eleven, four of them are taller and broader than Floria. Two of them even tower over Jace's height, which is terrifying.

Amran is the tallest—I assume it's Amran because of his pink eyes—with warm, dark skin, a bridged nose, and lengthy dreadlocks bound in a high ponytail.

Each of their eyes is bright and difficult to gaze into. Eye contact is already challenging, and the bright light gives me headaches. Marked eyes are a troubled combination.

Thankfully, the introductions only get as deep as the brief exchange of names before Floria declares we head off. With her index finger and thumb in her mouth, she makes a shrill whistling call. I wasn't sure to whom, until a herd of harjins bolt toward us. Floria personally demonstrates to me how to have one sit by gently placing my index finger on its nose and tapping it three times.

Within the minute, I'm on the back of the harjin with Amran's help. Syann sits behind me, latching onto my shoulders.

I've noticed that the other riders hold on to the horns attached to the shoulder blades of the harjins. Why didn't I think of that before? Holding them is like having reins on a horse but inherently attached to the animal.

Floria mounts up and leads the way. Then Syann and I, along with the other Eleven riding in pairs, and Kip and Gene follow closely behind. Their presence assures me that I won't be seized by vines again.

We ride through a vast field of glowing flowers. A stream flows through the area, its waters shimmering. The field is fenced off on the sides, but the land stretches so far that the end of the gate remains out of sight. Dozens of wild harjins trod within the sapphire grass, their movements graceful and elegant. The scene is breathtaking.

Once we reach the gate's edge, the harjins effortlessly leap over the border as if it were a mere obstacle. The impact of their landing jumbles my stomach, but the exhilarating sensation of the ride far surpasses any discomfort. It's as if I've been transported back to my childhood, galloping through fields with my closest friend on Moo's back.

Once we're past the fence, we merge onto a trail in single file. Floria, leading the line, slows our pace down.

"We're close," Syann whispers into my ear. "Are you excited?"

"Um—It's-s-s comp-p-plicated."

"You're not excited?"

"Um—w-w-well—I'm gl-glad w-w-we have help, an-and won't be-b-be going through the r-r-rest of the journey a-a-alone. B-b-but I—" I sigh. "I worry s-s-something w-w-will go wrong."

"Like this is too good to be true?"

I look past my shoulder at her, nodding. That's exactly how I feel.

"Well, I've been meaning to mention something that I discussed with Floria. Once you're healed, we're returning you to the village. You'll stay there with Kipper and Gene while the Eleven and I go to Secreth."

Huh? I don't want to leave her. My sagging expression shows it.

"You'll be safer that way. Floria says she and the Geron have made a truce for the Geron not to enter the village, so there's a lower risk of you being harmed if you stay behind."

"What about you? H-how w-w-will I know you'll be all right?"

"I'm going to believe in myself." Her smile intentionally references what I said to her back in the caves. I can't deny what I said. "I'll be all right."

This idea of her heading off with strangers make me uneasy. "W-w-what if I also w-w-wore the armor? Th-th-the attack b-b-before they trapped you…I—" I scoff, surprised at myself for even considering bragging about saving her during the storm, but it's true! I hold my tongue even so.

Not that it matters; Syann is able to read the desperation in my eyes. "I know you saved me then, Oren, and I'm grateful, but you also nearly died doing so. Not to mention during that attack, I lacked a dozen warriors as a backup. Look, I don't want to leave you, either, but it's for your own good. I need you to stay safe. When I reach Secreth, I will do whatever it takes to return to you and return you to your family."

I know it's safer to stay back. I don't have the ability to protect her well as the Eleven will, but I don't wish to be oblivious to her well-being or whereabouts. Regardless, what argument do I have? All I can say is I disdain the thought of parting from her.

"Remember when Elouise didn't want you to leave her, but you told me it was for her good? This is no different. There's no benefit for your well-being to go. You're going to have to trust that I'll be fine, like how Elouise trusts that you will be. You're protecting yourself for her—and me."

I detest that she made that statement. It has concluded the debate. I had already said it myself—it was for Elouise's good that she stayed home. Syann's analogy only serves to make me miss my sister more. Elouise and Syann are the only individuals who genuinely make an effort to understand me, and now I will lose both of them.

Ahead, groups of illuminated pools of water are surrounded by numerous guards and civilians. Luminous crystal rocks, flowers, and trees with glowing crystal bark brim the waters. The purple foliage of the trees resembles a weeping willow. The atmosphere reflects magnificently in the pools, like a dream I never got the pleasure of dreaming.

Is this it, where my problems wash away?

"This is a joyful moment for you, Oren. You can allow yourself to be happy instead of worrying about the future. Relax."

That's against my nature. My life could be forever changing for the better, and the thought makes me sweat. What will that even be like? For so long, my guilt convinced me that I wanted nothing to do with the outside world. I never imagined that would change, but now that the pools are in sight, my mind is allowing me to think beyond my healing. It's exciting, scary, and new. How do I process that?

Floria hops off her harjin onto the pool's bank. She gestures to Syann and me as we come to a stop ourselves. "Your hardships are nearly over, son," Floria says. "You must submerge yourself in the water, and all your physical troubles will be left underneath the surface." With Floria's aid, I get off the harjin's back onto the ground. Syann and I follow her to the edge. Anticipation creeps up on me and leaves my system through a shaky exhale.

"You're feeling as if this is real now, huh? You're trembling," Syann asks, after handing my backpack to Floria.

My fear stiffens my jaw, so I only give Syann a nod. She caresses my shoulder. "Are you ready?"

I bob my head. Syann guides me into the water. Unlike the cool lakes I used to swim in at the farmland, this water is warm to the touch. As I venture deeper, the air becomes increasingly difficult to breathe, even though I'm not submerged yet.

My mind is drowning in a sea of thoughts, clouding my senses. Syann's question is the only thing that pulls me out of this mental abyss. We're standing waist-deep in the water when she suddenly stops. "Anything you wish to say before you go under? Or is this it?"

I soak her in, fully comprehending the sacrifices she's made for me. Syann brought me here, going above and beyond to ensure my healing. She even found shelter for me while she completes her mission. What's even more remarkable is that she's caused the sun to shine on me once again. I'm not better off dead, as I once believed. Thanks to her, I'm loved and have a new life ahead of me. I owe it all to her.

The thoughts nearly leave me speechless. I can't let that happen. "I—th-th-thank you, f-f-for everything, Syann." My statement is insignificant compared to all she's done for me. I want to say more, but she speaks first.

"Don't thank me yet. You still must go under. Count of three?"

I nod. Syann counts down from three. As she says *one*, I hold my breath. She continues holding me as I cut underneath the surface.

My trembling transforms into a rattling. Surely, I'm causing the surface of the water to ripple. It's been only a second since I started holding my breath, yet my lungs are already burning. How can I already need to come up for air so soon? Is this the sensation of healing, pain surging through my lungs and rapidly spreading throughout my veins? Being underwater as my lungs burn brings back memories of when I almost drowned in the lake as a child. The pain is unbearable, and I can't take it any longer. I burst through the surface and gulp in a massive breath, letting the relief fill my lungs.

Syann clings to me as she exclaims into my ear. I'm too dazed to comprehend what she said, but her voice was filled with overwhelming joy.

It's immensely easier to breathe, no shortness, no seizing, only fresh air.

"Oren?"

Standing on my own two feet doesn't bring an ounce of pain. I can't believe it. I press my stomach where the wound was, feeling the pain is gone. The shock rattles my body.

"Oren!" She cups my face with her hands; their light doesn't agitate me.

My surroundings are so much more precise and vibrant. The sharpness and detail of the foliage on the trees in the distance is impeccable.

"Your bruises and cuts on your face are gone!"

What?

An overbearing sense of disbelief and joy washes over me. My heart is skipping like a young child. Is this what it's like to be happy? The swelling in my heart, the wholeness in my spirit, the welling of tears in my eyes?

These tears become pools like this one—pools of internal healing. The bitter doubts of me ever being healed scatter like a flock of birds. They leave a fluttering sensation in my chest. *Joy.*

Syann hesitantly brings a hand toward my core. She's as curious to see how it's healed as I am.

"You can look," I tell her. She's gained my trust, and for once there's no shame in revealing myself to her.

She gives me a nod back before unbuttoning my shirt. I free my arms from the sleeves and set the soaked cloth across my shoulder. She picks apart the bandage, revealing the wound that is no more. She gasps at the sight of it, grazing her fingers up my abdomen. Her hands wander toward my chest, as she admires me with transfixed eyes. It's strangely wonderful.

"Sy—" The croak of my voice beckons her arms wrapping around me tightly. I lean my face onto her shoulder, where I cry. These tears of joy result from her willingness to help me. "Thank you," I whimper through a sob.

"I would do it a thousand more times for this outcome, Oren. I have always wanted this for you, just as much as you longed for this healing. You won't have to hide anymore. As soon as this is all over, I will never have to miss you again." Syann loosens her grip, her hands still wrapped around my back. We are close, our eyes locked.

"I-I always wanted th-th-this, too—but I n-n-never allowed my-my-myself to think that way bec-c-cause I didn't th-th-think it was possible."

"Well, now things will be different. A good different." She lifts my chin gently, caressing it with her thumb.

A wide smile spreads across my face. This positive change will be everything. I can be a good brother to Elouise and go to town with her. I can work hard to support my mother. Jace and I could even have a fresh start. As for Syann, our relationship can continue. I cherish that thought above anything else. "I-I-I don't know h-h-how I'll repay you."

"You don't need to." She tucks the stray hair in my face behind my ear. "You know why I did this for you, and I'll never regret it."

I know, too, that's what someone who loves somebody does—makes sacrifices for them. "I-I love you, too." I gaze at her hand, which she keeps still on my face. I catch myself grabbing it and holding it in place. I could dwell in this moment forever. She leans in to kiss me, somehow making this moment even better.

"In f-front of everyone?" I blush, wishing for the privacy the cave provided. On the bank, we have a full audience. If it weren't for them, I'd kiss her senselessly, knowing no foolish coughs would prevent me from experiencing the pleasure of the taste of her love.

"Yes," Syann answers proudly, crashing her lips onto mine without regard. I realize I don't mind. My heart flutters with joyous delight as I bask in the pleasure she brings me. It's clear that this is the most extraordinary feeling I've ever experienced. My hopes soar high for the future. Having her by my side is everything. Losing her would tear my soul apart.

This realization pains me as our lips part, and I yearn to never let her go or stop kissing her. However, her mission is not yet complete, while mine has been fulfilled. I've been healed, which is why I was sent here, but I've discovered something even better, something more profound. Now, her mission has become mine. If only she felt the same way.

"Sy," I say. "You'll c-c-come back? Th-this isn't it?" I whisper, lowering her hand toward my chest. I hold it tightly still.

"I never want to lose you again. I'll do everything in my power to return to you, but this healing you have, I must protect it. Bringing you with me isn't doing that." She squeezes my hand firmly. It makes me think how she's going to have to let them go. The tears I shed can't be very visible since I'm soaked, but Syann can tell. "Don't be grieved. This is good, really good."

I smile. "I f-feel good. I just—getting h-h-healed is-is great—but I-I-I got something even better. Y-y-you, it's you. I don't want to l-l-lose that." If I had to choose between keeping my health or her, I'd forever pick her.

"You aren't going to lose me, and we don't even have to say goodbye yet. I'm going to ensure you get back to the village safely."

That's right, we still have to return through the trail. The realization demands a deep breath to recover from the lingering fear that creeps in again. What if Uxaar intends to raid us then? What if he deliberately waited for my healing to crush this newfound hope I have? I don't want to spiral into dire scenarios, yet that's precisely what I'm doing.

"Let's get back to the bank." Syann grabs my shirt off my shoulder and hands it to me. I put it back on as I go back.

I'm still sniffling, baffled by the fact I'm walking! My once-injured ankle aligned and good as new, my heart swells happily. Years of being crippled are underwater now.

All eyes cross me as we step onto the soil. Kip cheers, and even a few of the Eleven are lifted by my tears of joy. However, this attention is exacerbating my emotional imbalance. I cover my mouth with my hand, huffing tearfully. Kip even offers me a hug, but I politely decline.

On the way back to the village, Syann and I chat to occupy our minds. We discuss our futures, the unknown yet exciting nature of it. For example—how excited I am to show Elouise I'm healed, and my anticipation of the potentially better relationship I could have with Mum and Jace. The stress I caused will be gone. Also, now that I'm healed, numerous new opportunities have opened up for me. I'm determined to help my family and be there for Syann, but I'm uncertain about the specifics of achieving this. Given the fogginess of Syann's future, it's challenging for me to envision my own future with her. Syann herself is unaware of her life's possibilities or even if she'll have one once she reaches the altar. I share her apprehension about waiting for fate to unfold. Light forbid I lose her.

We return to the fenced land of harjins by the town, where all the Eleven dismount. "Syann, the rest of our journey will be on foot," Floria says.

I leap off the harjin, excited that I don't require assistance to get down. The grin on my face is as uncontrollable as a spooked horse. My arms swing out to Syann pridefully. At last, I can be the one who helps her down.

She slides down the harjin, right into my open arms. I try to twirl her in the air, but my performance is clumsy. She slips through my arms and playfully embraces me. I squeeze her as my laughter subsides. If only we could always be together like this. What if one day, nothing could ever separate us? We could become one, forever and always. Perhaps I'm thinking too soon, but how could this feeling within me be mistaken?

"Oren, Kipper, and Eugene, your journey ends here. Say your goodbyes." Floria returns my backpack. I had almost forgotten it.

My journey with Syann can't end. If we are to be separated, she must return. My hands linger on her waist, while my eyes are immersed in hers, unwilling to look away. I refuse to rush this moment, even if Floria is urging me to. "Thank you." I repeat those words, tightly embracing her.

"You're welcome, love. We'll be back together soon. I won't stop until we are together again, just like this," she says, as sweet as pie.

"I'll b-b-b-be here waiting."

Syann lets me go, and she's tearful, too. "In the meantime, they'll take good care of you here. I wouldn't leave you somewhere you wouldn't be safe, please know that!"

"Just tell me th-th-th-that you'll be s-saf-safe. That's all I care about."

"The Geron can't break me. I'm immortal, you know," she

teases, playfully.

I wish I could laugh with her now, but I only picture the horror that was Ebony. Ebony will pursue Syann, and I'm terrified. "That doesn't m-m-mean they can't capture you, Sy! Or-or-r-r torture you!"

"That's not going to happen." I wish that reassured me, but words are empty in times like these. I need more than words, to know she's well. She kisses away my single stray tear. "I love you, and I will not rest until I'm reunited with you."

"I—" I clear my throat and lean close to her, cupping her jaw and kissing her gently on the lips. I hope it's not the last time I can do that, or I'd be robbed of a lifetime of giving her my utmost affection. "I love you, too."

"Goodbye, Oren." She holds my hands until the distance between us becomes too great.

"G'bye, Syann."

16 *Oren*

As she ventures to lengths I can no longer visualize, my body freezes. I could idly stand here, waiting for her return. I'm already holding my breath for our reunion. My lungs burn as if I'm underwater again, except I'm not underwater, and my lungs are restored. Regardless, it feels like I've forgotten how to breathe. I'm convinced I'll only be relieved when Syann comes back.

"Oren." Gene's voice jolts through my spine. "Enough of longingly staring into the horizon. Let's get inside the village where you'll be safe."

I forgot Gene and Kip stood behind me. As I linger in place, I wipe my eyes to hide the fact that I've been crying.

"I know you're gonna miss her, but we'll give you a good time. I promise!" Kip sets his hand firmly on my shoulder. I shrink down. Kip doesn't take the hint that I don't want him to touch me and guides me through the gate.

Where do I start? I've never had any significantly younger male friends or siblings. I only know that they are supposed to look up to you, but I'm no role model for any man. Girls were always easier to get along with—Elouise, Syann, and my grandma, for example. I don't remember having many male friends. Jace would have surely turned them all against me, making them belittle me as he always did. Death ensured that my dad was a stranger to me, leaving the closest person I have to one being my tyrant brother. Of course, my grandpa was a great father figure, but death robbed him of me when I needed him most. How could I have anything to give Gene and Kip? How would they want to be my friends once they got to know me? To everyone, I was a damsel in distress, in a sickly man's body. How long will it take me to recover from that shame?

"Aren't you happy to be healed?" Gene questions condescendingly.

Of course, I am, but Syann is the reason that occurred. She's all I can think about. If something happens to her, it was all for naught.

The villagers gape at me, the outsider I've been reduced to. My arms cling to my body, attempting to provide some self-comfort.

"What's the matter?" Kip asks. I duck my head.

"I think he misses his girlfriend," Gene answers.

Girlfriend? I suppose we kissed in front of them, and we've professed our mutual love. Still, can I call her that yet? I'd like to.

Title or not, I do miss her, and Elouise, my mum. I might even appreciate Jace's presence right now, at least it would be something familiar. "I m-m-miss her, and-and home," I mumble to get them off my back.

"You miss home?" Kip questions. I nod, tightening my grip on myself. My fingers are rattling against my arms.

"Is it your family, or does this place not settle with you like Earth does?"

I shrug to Gene. This realm is a phenomenon, I'm only uncomfortable that I know no one. So, it is my family and Syann's absence that's spoiling my mood. If they were here, I'd be relieved.

It makes me wonder, what if Jace never left? It's for the best that didn't happen. He could have died in the cave, if not in the storm, or he could've been kidnapped like Athena. Also, Syann and I wouldn't have gotten the privacy to get as close as we've become. It's better that he's safe at home.

"Maybe you're hungry!" Kip exclaims optimistically. "We can go to my hut and prepare you something to eat. I'm a good cook, thanks to my mum!"

"He actually is," Gene chimes in.

I hadn't realized yet I should be able to eat without vomiting it anymore. My body is healed from the inside out. I'm starved, but the idea of eating casually is foreign; nonetheless, I nod at the suggestion.

On the way to Kip's house, the boys bombard me with questions that I primarily respond to with a nod or a shake of my head. I don't mean to be rude, but I haven't warmed up to them yet.

Kip asks if I can cook. As a kid, I used to help my grandma mix ingredients and peel apples when she made apple pie. That about sums up my cooking experience. Could I become a good cook with practice?

He also asks about my favorite food, unfortunately. My aversion toward eating is outstanding. It takes me a moment to deliver an answer, but I go with apples. The thought of peeling them brought them to mind. I also have numerous fond memories associated with the fruit—my family going apple picking, baking pies with my grandparents, and snacking on apples with Elouise and Jace when we were young. Of course, I fell from an apple tree, but I can't hold apples responsible for that. I refuse to let the one unpleasant memory overshadow all the positive ones.

What's interesting is Kip and Gene respond with, "What's an apple?"

Right, they've never been to Earth. We're in the inter-dimensional realm between Earth and Secreth.

"Um—It's a f-f-fruit," I answer, but Kip and Gene want more specifics. It takes them a while to get it all out of me, but I tell them it's about the size of a man's fist, that they can be red, green, or yellow, and they taste tart, sweet, and crisp. Their questions don't subside—Where and how do they grow? Do you cook or juice them? Or eat them straight off the trees?

I answer all the questions about apples until we've reached their front door. The house is similar in structure to the medical hut, built from crystal logs and comparable to the size of my house. However, this is homier, furnished, and decorated with trinkets and flowers.

"Welcome to my place!" Kip exclaims as we enter.

Cozy and inviting, the hut is decorated with several candles and family paintings on the shelves. A booth-style table in the corner of the kitchen adds to its charm. Handmade blankets drape over the chairs, while a similar tablecloth covers the booth.

I'm undecided about where to go once I step inside. I reach the front of the doorway but hesitate to venture farther. Even if they welcome me in, the thought of roaming freely makes me feel uneasy.

"Are Uncle Lonnie and Essy still out?" Gene addresses the empty room.

"Yeah, they're with Jodie. They said they would return for supper. So, we've got the place to ourselves."

I don't know what they're discussing, but I realize Kip and Gene are cousins. Lonnie and Essy must be Kip's parents. Do they even know I'm staying here? What if they aren't fine with it? I dawdle by the door.

Kip pivots back toward me, puzzled that I haven't followed them in. "Oren, please make yourself at home. Take a seat." He gestures to a booth.

"Um...I-I'm still w-wet," I mutter, clinging to myself a little tighter.

"Oh, right. If you need to bathe or change clothes, you can go freshen up in the bathroom. Do you have any clothes in your backpack?"

I'm down to my last pair of clean clothes, which are gray pants and a regrettably short-sleeved white shirt. It's still fortunate I have one more pair. I wouldn't have been able to borrow any clothes that would suit me. Kip is significantly larger than me, and I'm sure his parents are, too. Besides, I wouldn't borrow their clothes without their consent anyway.

I nod to Kip. A moment alone in their bathroom will benefit me. Hopefully, I'll be able to compose myself. Kip leads me to a room around the corner of the hallway. He welcomes me to take my time and tells me he'll prepare lunch for me while I clean up.

Being alone allows me not to be so tense. My arms drop by my side, and I can finally draw a clear breath.

The only person I encounter is my reflection in the mirror. For a change, I'm drawn to staring at it. The dark circles under my eyes have lightened. My lips aren't dry or cracked. My skin appears clear, free from acne, scars, or cuts, except for my freckles. The only improvement my physique desperately needs is weight gain and a haircut, but those are concerns for another time.

After getting clean, I dress myself and style my hair into a topknot. Finally, I decide to chew the last of my mint leaves. When Syann borrowed some, I was left with only a few. It's not the worst problem to have. I shouldn't need more.

When I exit the bathroom, the air has a subtle aroma that spurs my hunger even more. It's an unfamiliar smell, yet an appetizing one.

Kip is in the kitchen, scooping a strange paste from a bowl into a cone-shaped shell. I'm still determining what the dish is. He notices me and smiles. "Perfect timing! I just got your food ready. Sit at the booth over there. I'll serve it to you."

Gene is already sitting at the booth with a cup of juice in his hand. I sit on the opposite side, placing my hands in my lap.

Kip serves me a plate with the shell, a piece of pink bread, utensils, and two cups—one with juice and one with water. I assume one of the cups is mine, and one is Kip's, but I'm wrong. "I didn't know if you wanted to try the juice or if you wanted water, so I brought you both!" Kip says, setting the cups by my plate. He takes a seat by Gene. Neither of them has food. Why? Are they only going to watch me eat? I don't want to ask. "You don't know what this is, do you?" Kip points to my plate. I shake my head. "It's a dish called shellings. A shell is a type of edible fungi that grows here. Inside it is a savory filling that you can eat straight after harvesting. But it's common to take out the filling and stew it with mixed vegetables, which I did here."

So, a stuffed mushroom? I'm not going to mention it, though. That's asking for them to question me about mushrooms. They probably don't know what one is, likewise with apples.

"Even the outer shell is edible," Gene adds.

I nod, exhaling nervously. "Aren't eith-eith-either of you hungry?"

"No. We ate with Syann and Floria while you were with the physicians."

"So go ahead! Enjoy!" Kip adds.

Why am I so nervous about eating in front of them, or eating in general? I haven't enjoyed eating anything in years. Those emotional walls are still standing, and I want them to be torn down so I can have freedom. I can't do that by being passive like I was before.

"Is something wrong?" Kip asks.

My thoughts have held me captive for too long. Impulsively, I shake my head as I scoop a hefty spoonful of the filling into my mouth. The flavor is sharp, like goat cheese. It's seasoned with subtle herbs. There are some chunks of vegetables in it that probably shouldn't have been swallowed whole, but I did.

I cover my mouth with a clenched fist as coughs boom from

me. The last thing I wanted was attention, but I've certainly attained it.

Gene exclaims that I'm choking, and repeatedly hits my back while Kip lifts my cup of water toward me. I can't drink the water until the hacks stop. Thankfully, it doesn't take long until my airways are clear.

"Are you all right?" Gene asks, somewhat amused.

I nod, sipping the water. "I-I-I um—just s-s-swallowed too fast." I try laughing it off, but I sound unconvincing.

"If you don't like the shelling, it's all right," Kip says.

I shake my head. "N-n-no really! It's g-g-good." It did taste decent, but I'm scared to try it again. On top of that, my throat hurts from choking.

"Then what's the matter?" Gene asks.

I'm reluctant to answer. Who says I must? If I solve the problem by eating the food, it's over. Slowly, I take a bite as my sight drops to my lap. When I swallow, I shake my head. "Nothing."

"It's even better if you dip the bread into the filling!" Kip suggests.

I'm hesitant to give bread another try. I enjoy its taste, but bread always made me feel unwell in the past. My throat would itch and swell, and my stomach would ache after consuming bread. Years ago, I concluded that I had some sort of intolerance to it. Would that intolerance still be present?

No, it's fine. I'm healed.

"Wh-why is it pink?" I ask.

"What other color would bread be?" Gene asks.

"Um—brown."

"Brown?" Kip questions.

"That's boring." Gene adds.

I pick up the bread and pull it apart. It's much spongier than bread at home. It has the consistency of cake. Does it taste like cake? My curiosity barely drives me to try it.

"Do all people from Earth eat so slowly?" Gene asks.

"Gene!" Kip scolds, smacking his arm.

"Mm…actually no, your girlfriend scarfed her food down, not as fast as us, but still," Gene corrects himself. He's right, Syann is a quick eater, especially in comparison to me. "She did ask quite a few questions before trying it, though."

"Did she eat this?" I ask.

"No, we ate at Floria's," Gene answers.

"We had eggs, roast, and vegetables," Kip adds.

I sip on the water slowly, debating whether I should eat any more.

"Do you actually not like it?" Kip frowns.

Guiltily, I sigh. I suppose I should come clean. "It's not that. Eating is just—when I-I was sick…eating always made me-me worse. I-I-I threw up h-half the time. I'm not used to it."

"Oh." Gene scratches his head. "That makes sense. You're skin and bones."

"You need to try," Kip suggests. "You have to eat to live."

I sigh defeatedly, nodding. I've had much more intense discussions with Mum concerning my unhealthy eating habits. I did try to overcome my eating abnormalities, only to get the same results—irritation and vomiting. I know that shouldn't happen now.

I fork a piece of the bread and dip it in the filling. Hesitantly, I bite some of it off and chew it. It resembles the taste of cake. It has this sweetness that bread at home doesn't have. The spongy texture I felt earlier is evident in my mouth, too. I agree with Kip that this plate is much better with dipping the bread into the filling. It makes the filling less overwhelming in flavor. After I swallow, I let Kip know I agree with him about the bread.

It helps when the boys' conversation distracts them from my meal. So, I force myself to eat a little under half of the bread with some filling. Afterward, Kip leads Gene and me to his room, where they tell me I'll be sleeping tonight. For now, I sit cross-legged against the wall on the floor. I don't want to be rude by occupying their bed or chair. Kip takes the bed. Gene takes the chair.

"So, Oren, do you want to rest a bit? Or we could give you a tour of the town, anything you'd like," Kip suggests.

A tour might be the distraction I need. I'd love to stroll around and appreciate this place's beauty now that I can, but I also remember the drowsy, groggy feeling that melts me after eating. Both suggestions are good—take a short break, then go on a tour. "Um—I'd be al-al-all right with the tour, but maybe—um, I'll s-s-sit for-for a bit first?"

"Fine with me. I could personally use a break, too." Gene sinks in his chair with a relaxed grin. "It's not every day I get summoned by a goddess."

"While we're here, this can be a good chance for us to get to know each other." Kip suggests. I'm not surprised.

"Well, for us to get to know you, Oren," Gene says to me. "Me and Kip are already tight."

I pull my journal out of my backpack. The old pages bear lamentations of my life before. Would the author of these entries believe me if I told him that we got healed? No, he wouldn't. Knowing the impossible has happened stretches flashing glee across my face. "You're cousins, right?" I ask, pushing my involvement in the conversation.

So many blank pages remain, waiting to be filled with fresh memories and accomplishments. On the first blank page, I sketch a rectangular-shaped face with a triangular jawline, seated elegantly above her long neck. It would be an injustice not to name the rest of her features as elegant, since they all exquisitely represent her strength, beauty, and resilience. From her rebellious curls, freckled arched nose, and sparkling wide eyes, underset by a pair of full, focused brows. If only my handiwork could give justice to her beauty, but I can dream to try.

"Yep! But we're more like brothers," Kip clarifies.

"Since my dad passed last year, his family has taken me in," Gene explains. "My mum left my dad when I was young. So, I stay here with Kip."

The vulnerable statement surprises me as much as it resonates with me. "I'm sorry." I frown, as the loss of my father traces my mind.

Gene doesn't acknowledge my apology. "You have parents?"

"Um—" I gaze at the page, interrupting my pencil stroke. "M-my-my father died, too, but I never kn-knew him. I have a mum."

"Are you both close?" Gene asks with a longing in his eyes, perhaps from the unquenchable yearning of not having a mother there for him.

I couldn't imagine Mum abandoning me. Though I can't say we're close, either. Tension festered between me and Mum once I got ill. Maybe when I go home and things are better, we will be close.

"Is that a-a sensitive question? Gene didn't mean to intrude!" Kip scowls at his cousin.

"N-no, it's fine. My m-m-mum is nice—l-l-life has been hard for m-m-my family. She can only t-t-t-take so much."

"Because you were ill? And your dad?" Gene asks.

I inhale and hesitantly nod.

"How did that happen? You getting sick for so long?" Kip asks.

Strangely, no one has asked me that before. My sickness has always defined me. Everyone around me knew. "I-I hit my head in an ac-c-c-accident when I was twelve. I-I-I dislocated my knee and my foot, too, my head or-or leg never healed right. So, I-I-I got worse over the years. Then, my grandparents…"

"Your grandparents?" Kip follows.

"They-they passed." Forcefully I admit, "They were like parents to me."

"They meant a lot to you." Gene says it like he can tell.

I nod. "I-I was never the-the same af-af-after…"

"You felt discouraged?" Gene prods. "Depressed?" I nod. "That's how I felt when my dad died. I didn't want to get out of bed or eat. He was the closest friend I ever had. I wanted to be him, but he went hunting one day and got attacked by a beast and that was it…He was gone."

What a ghastly way to die… Gene is young, too, meaning his father being in his thirties or forties was plausible. My grandparents at least led whole, happy lives. Gene's dad's life was prematurely seized. That can't be easy for Gene to shoulder.

"How old were you when you lost your grandparents?"

"Twelve."

"You're seventeen?"

I nod. I'll be eighteen in three months, but I won't point that out like Gene did with his age.

I'm ashamed of how long I hid away. Five years, and I couldn't pick myself up. After a year, Gene is out and about, assisting a goddess of all things. In our short time shared, I can't know Gene's burden, but he seems to have fared better than me. "How did y-you deal with the loss?"

"After grieving for some time, I chose not to let it shape me and to keep moving like my dad would want me to. Whether that was distracting myself with tasks or hobbies or surrounding myself with friends. I chose to move on, and that doesn't mean it doesn't hurt anymore. Some days are harder to get through than others."

I tried shifting from my grief, but my sickness beat me to a pulp. When it felt like I had nothing left to give, I craved death, something I wouldn't give myself the satisfaction of. Forcefully, I persisted to stay alive, but did I really live my life to the fullest?

My sketch of Syann reminds me that she dwelled in Seren the entire time after I had moved. I could have had her, but I did exactly the opposite of what Gene did. I isolated myself from my loved ones and wallowed in grief. Fear barricaded me from my childhood friend and venturing to Seren with Elouise. How could

I have been so stupid?

"Are you all right?" Kip asks. He rises to his feet and walks closer to me.

I curl up smaller on the ground while biting my lip. Why did I get so vulnerable with them? It's as if I don't know what I even want! Part of me longs to cling to familiarity and wall myself off, but the other half is so weary of it. I'm betraying myself. "...I wish I had-had done that. I—I tried, un-until it-it um—got too hard."

"It's not too late." Kip sits on the ground, too, a comfortable distance ahead of me. "And now you're healed! Your sickness won't meddle with your life anymore."

"Yeah. Don't beat yourself up. Life beats us up enough. Why feed your suffering?" Gene questions, walking behind Kip.

Their words are an easing comfort that I'll hold on to. I should let go of my past pain and shame. I need to forgive myself.

It's as Syann said: *"You don't have to feel regret, either. We can't change the past, but we can change our futures."*

"Another terrific thing, when Syann returns for you, she's going to take you to Secreth. Secreth is a paradise realm where you can live forever. With forever, you can make up for the years you've lost," Kip says.

"Also, you must be doing something right—the goddess herself fancies you." Gene smirks. His reminder of Syann's love for me makes me grin. My smile lingers as I view my completed sketch. It's not perfect. Her ears are a little exaggerated. Her eyes aren't roundly shaped how they should be, but I can tell it's her— the one I love the most.

"Things will turn up!" Kip nods.

I thank them before returning my glance to my journal.

"Do you draw?" Kip is attentive to the fact that I've got my journal in my lap. His question makes me jolt and stammer.

"He can," Gene assumes confidently. "I knew he had a hidden talent. Quiet people always do. Like how Min can sing—pfft, Oren can probably sing, too."

I don't confirm or deny. Only Elouise and Syann know that answer.

"Can I see?" Kip asks.

"Um...I usually don't sh-share—"

"Please!"

"If you show us, I'll show you Kip's handmade scarves. I'm sure he'd even let you have one," Gene bargains.

Well, I do enjoy scarves or any clothing that covers my neck.

They're not going to let me be anyway, so I turn the sketchbook around. I planned on telling them not to flip through it, but their outburst doesn't allow me to speak.

"What in the Underealm!" shouts Gene.

Kip's jaw drops. "Y-y-you did that? Without her in the room!"

I'm overwhelmed. "Uh—um—"

"Wow!" Gene laughs. "That's incredible! It's the goddess herself."

"Um—Thank you," I shyly say, pressing the journal against my chest.

"Do you have more?" Kip asks.

I shake my head. "Um, no—I m-m-mostly write in it." That's a lie—well, not the journal's contents being mostly writing, that's true. There are more drawings in it, though.

"All right, a deal is a deal. Kipper, bring out the crochet!" Gene announces.

Crochet, I haven't heard that word in a while. Crochet was an art Grandma was skilled in. She'd weave clothes, blankets, and toys for me, Elouise, and Jace. I'm excited to see Kip's creations. Sure enough, he brings out a handful of scarves and hats. The display makes me realize he made the tablecloth and blankets I saw in the living space, too.

Kip lays out three scarves, a purple hat, and a gray cowl on his bed. I get to touch and try them all on before I get to pick the one I want to keep. The gray cowl suits my style, so I take it. Kip tells me he can teach me to crochet after the tour if I'd like. I'm actually excited for his lesson.

Out the doorway, the boys ask what my favorite quality of the Dawn's nature is. I tell them how much I've enjoyed the flowers here.

Both of their faces light up. "On the edge of town, there's a beautiful flower garden! We can start there!" Kip exclaims.

This time, I'm the one asking questions on our walk. I find out the reason their plant life glows. Everything here connects to their source of energy, called the core, which is made of crystal material entirely manifested by Light and Darkness. The trees here are part of the core that springs beyond the surface. The flowers are different. They aren't part of the core, but the roots being in touch with it causes the flowers to glow until they are plucked.

In turn, I explain to them the science behind plant life on Earth. Our plant life originates from seeds, which grow in soil with proper exposure to sunlight and water. The boys tell me they don't have a sun and that the core is the life source. While heat comes from these geysers that shoot out what they call beats. They're like purple fireflies that never dim their light.

A fence resembling the one by the harjins' field comes into view. Beyond it, clusters of flowers and feathery ivy climb structured arches. The fence separating us from the garden turns out to be a gateway. Kip opens the entrance, gesturing for me to go through first. I pause once I've crossed the gate and take in the enchanting view.

"This is-is beautiful." I wander closer to the arch of flowers.

"Different from home?" Gene asks.

I nod. This garden is extensive. Not only flowers but also roots and some type of produce sit in rows in the ground. We aren't the only people here. Civilians with baskets pick produce and herbs among the garden. "Is this a-a-a community garden?"

"Yep." Gene nods. "Where we grow our food and flowers. This garden is a mile's worth."

"Woah." I intend on seeing all of it. "Does anyone t-tend it?"

"Yeah, it's guarded like the rest of town, to prevent any of the Gerons' followers or wild animals coming to vandalize it. They'll pick any weeds or repair damaged structures, but no one has to water it," Gene answers.

"Yeah! The geyser trees water them," Kip adds. "You know what that is?"

I shake my head, though the title gives me an idea. A tree that spurts water?

"Follow us!" Gene jogs off, which thrills me. This gives me a reason to run—something I haven't done in years! The sensation is so exhilarating that it makes me laugh like a child. As we approach a towering crystal trunk, its top buds resemble a flower, and a gentle mist emanates from its crown.

"Here it is," Gene exclaims as he catches his breath.

"You don't have anything like this at home?" Kip asks.

"We have tons of these around. They're the source of water for all plant life," Gene adds.

My head shakes. "We have rain. It-it precipitates from the-the-the sky."

They both squint at me. "Precipitates?"

"Oh—it-it means it falls from the sky." I point up.

Gene weaves his brows. "I see. Does anything else fall from the sky?"

"Umm—other f-f-forms of precipitation, um, snow or hail. Snow is white, fluffy, and cold, and hail is-is chunks of ice, which is frozen water. Th-th-that doesn't happen often, though." I hush after answering the questions, to take in the view of this geyser. It's phenomenal. The two boys read the moment and stay silent as I view it.

Gene tells me several more geysers are around the garden. So, we explore further. I'm immersed in the flowers, plants, and even fairies fluttering around me like butterflies. Who knew fairies even existed? I suppose it's not far-fetched after all I've experienced.

Another pleasant thing is the fragrance. It stuns me when that pleasant scent transforms into a burning heap that clenches my nose. The familiar odor races chills down my spine.

"Ew! What's that smell!" Gene coughs, pinching his nose.

Ebony, she's the one who reeked of this sulfur smell. I gaze around, and a circular smoke cloud reels behind us. Two glowing spheres blaze through it. There's no one to protect us. Syann isn't here.

"Run!" I yank Gene and Kip's wrists as I dash away.

"Why?" Kip blurts out. I spin my head back. Through the darkness is Ebony, unhinged and foaming at the mouth.

Gene swings his head back and stammers a curse out of his mouth once he's seen her.

Kip also looks. "No! They aren't allowed here! Floria and Uxaar agreed!"

We all come to a hard stop as the darkness swirls ahead of us. Out of it comes Ebony. "I am a spokesman for Uxaar the Geron. Floria isn't here," she growls. "Nonetheless, the agreement only concerned the Geron, not their followers or Shadows."

"Help!" Gene and Kip shout. Gene jerks me backward before we bolt off as fast as possible. Our pleas for help catch the attention of some guards. Two of them run toward us with crystal spears in hand.

I pray they're enough against Ebony, but she is quicker and tackles me to the ground. She's almost too strong to wrestle free from. Fighting her brawny arms is a feeling all too familiar, like I'm battling the terrorist in the rain again. I conquered her; can I defeat Ebony, too? For Syann, I must try.

I'm silent through my attempts. The last thing I want to do here is get Gene or Kip hurt. It would be better if they escaped, but they realize I'm captured and steer my way. Whatever they try will be useless—my body ebbs into ash along with Ebony's, until all turns dark.

***

She plunged me into an inky abyss, and now I'm submerged

beneath its depths. I'm uncertain if this is water, but this sensation evokes a haunting childhood memory of the farm's lake engulfing me. If Jace hadn't intervened that day, I might have found myself here long ago—the Underealm.

Uxaar killed me. This is the fate death offers that I was always so frightened by. Horrendous shrieking, wailing, and pleas for help drench the atmosphere. Noise couldn't spread this legibly underwater. It's frigid, haunted air that swallows me.

What about Gene and Kip? Or the people of the village? Was Uxaar only after me? Or was I the beginning of the plot to annihilate the village after Syann left? I have no answers to these questions, only fears of the unknown. The entire new life I thought was ahead of me now is up in smoke.

"Athena!" I call desperately. The plea itself shocks me. Calling her name is my realization Athena might be here, too.

I try kicking and paddling as if I'm swimming. This way, I gain some ground—or air.

"Athena!" I weakly cough.

"Oren!" a voice echoes, but it doesn't sound like Athena. No, it's too soft and delicate. Behind me stands a woman. She's petite, with dark hair, clear olive skin, and hooded brown eyes resembling—*Elouise*. Panic clenches my heart. My sister can't be here! When the Geron first swarmed Syann and me in the caverns, one declared their intentions to capture my family. Did they succeed? The Shadow may have seized my family before they got to me!

"Elouise!" I bellow hysterically, paddling to her. "Elly— *oh*." She isn't my sister, but the resemblance is off-putting. She appears to be the same age. The primary distinction lies in her small stature compared to Elouise. Her eyes are also narrower, and her jawline is squarer than Elouise's.

Her anguished eyes plead as if I'm water in a desert, as my name again departs her lips. "You weren't supposed to ever be here!" She shelters sobs with clenched hands. One hand reaches out toward my cheek but passes through me like she's a ghost. She's nothing but a spirit. The woman breaks down through repeated apologies to me.

I'm perplexed by her and how she knows me. I've never met her in my life. I can't help but wonder how long she's been trapped in this realm—days, months, or even years? I feel sorry for her, yet she returns the pity. Has she done something to me? Is there a greater purpose behind why Ebony brought me here? "Who are y-y-you?"

She answered, but I failed to comprehend it as my consciousness faded into black.

***

Screams draw me from my slumber, if I was even asleep. The last thing I remembered was the Underealm, which scrambled my sense of time. It was like the illusion Uxaar put me under—it could have been seconds, minutes, or hours.

I'm no longer in the Underealm. The cries in the Underealm were collective, like a choir. This is one woman, loading the eerie air with her repetitive cries.

Air replenishes my lungs through a hefty gasp. I'm hyperventilating as I try to move, but the restraints I'm in show no sympathy.

I'm in a dome-shaped cave room. It reminds me of the caverns Syann and I traveled through together. Colorful crystals illuminate the cave walls. The crystals faintly hum in the background, barely heard behind the howling of this woman and the various blinding Geron around me.

A woman stands yards ahead of me. Her fate is the same as mine—she's also tied against a pillar. She's the one I searched for. *Athena is alive.*

The Light among the Shadows

17 *Syann*

Floria leads our group. The Eleven form a perimeter around me—three of them in a line in front, five in the middle, and four in the back. I fall in the middle of the center row, between Canyon, Urias, Amber, and Lucam.

I keep glancing back at the village, even until I'm nearly out of sight of it. Oren stands like a statue. He hasn't moved an inch while watching me depart. I know I'm hurting Oren by leaving him, which pains me in turn. Despite that, I'm grateful for his safety. I made the right choice.

Oren is far safer than I am now. I'm continuing to trudge into unknown terrain, like I have been for the past three days. With time, it hasn't gotten easier—if anything, it's gotten scarier. I'm about to face the worst of my journey now that I'm approaching the end. The Eleven's help eases my fears somewhat, yet guilt presses me about not being on the front lines. Unlike the Eleven, I'm invincible, while their armor can only protect them so much.

They came to help me willingly, knowing the risks involved. If any of them were to die, they accepted the possibility.

Nevertheless, I hope it doesn't come to that. Whenever Uxaar attacks us, I'll have an opportunity to protect them—I can only wonder when that opportunity will arise. Uxaar won't allow us to enter Secreth without conflict, and the entrance is near.

The others have the same idea. All have sharp, attentive eyes like a hawk, nested beneath furrowed brows. A weapon is ready in each pair of hands, including my own—a spear of shimmering crystal.

I divert my gaze forward when Oren is out of sight. Hopefully, he goes into town and stays put.

"He'll be safe. You shouldn't worry," Amber reassures me.

There's lots to fret about. The only preventative keeping Uxaar from attacking the village is a fragile agreement with Floria. I try to adhere to the fact that Uxaar is after me, not Oren or the village. Still, that doesn't mean Uxaar couldn't attack them to use that against me.

"I know it's for the best," I admit.

"It's hard to set aside significant attachments to an individual for the sake of the greater good, but that's what must be done," Floria says.

"Do you, or did you ever, have a significant other, Floria?" I ask, to make conversation to occupy my mind. Hopefully, this goes better than my painful attempt with Jace and Oren when we left their house.

Floria hums. "No, not once in my life have I. My desire has always been to nurture and protect my people. Investing in one person on an intimate level for my emotional gain felt selfish."

"Do you think my love for Oren is selfish, then?"

"It would depend on how you manage it. If you chose him over the greater good or even risked it for his benefit, with your power and responsibility, I'd say yes, that's selfish. You proved otherwise by making the right decision by leaving him behind. If you continue to let your love and responsibilities co-exist without conflict, then there's no harm in it. It can actually be beneficial."

I hope they won't judge the times I did risk the greater good for Oren's sake. My devotion to him has lengthened our journey, from waiting for him to wake in the storm, nursing his wounds, then carrying him through a cave. Without question, I'd do it all again for him.

He's done nothing but defend and care for me with all his ability. How could I do nothing less than that for him?

I understand that I have divine responsibilities, yet my humanity persists. Brenda's presence lingers, encompassing me with emotions and feelings. She is part of me. I chose Syann, but I want to choose Oren, too. Can't I have both? Or will the demands of ruling a realm and nurturing an intimate relationship be overwhelming? Or is my mindset simply too advanced? Oren and I only spent a few days together before professing our love, but years of unspoken affection and longing preceded it. We always loved each other.

"Syann was always fond of humans. That drove her to bring in as many humans as possible to Secreth. She didn't have a significant other, though. I suppose, in this case, that would be quite awkward," Rowan chortles.

"Well, before the war, I never experienced a life on Earth— where it's full of hurt and Darkness. Love is what motivates us to pull through it. I'm a human like all of you. I don't think it's strange that I desire affection, too."

"Nor do I," Urias adds. "Affection is good. And it seems you know how to balance it with your responsibilities, as Floria stated."

I smile. "So, what about all of you?" I ask curiously.

Urias smiles, holding out Canyon's hand, which is in his. "As I said, love is good and needed. Canyon and I have been together for seven hundred years. She's the light of my life."

"I'm married as well, to Yoli," Amran adds.

"Only I, Lucam, Fenneth, and Perri choose to be on our own," Floria says.

"I don't have that desire," Perri comments. "Never have."

"I was married once. I lost her three hundred years ago and could never bring myself to love another. I devote my time to protecting the civilization as Floria does," Lucam remarks. "It's a purposeful distraction to combat my loss."

"My story is similar," Fenneth says. "Yet much longer ago. I lost my family in the war of Secreth, my husband, and my two boys."

"You're from Secreth?" I ask.

"Yes, as well as Darius and Rowan."

"Do you mind me asking what it was like? Funny thing, but I don't remember any of it. I've seen glimpses, but very few."

Fenneth smiles. "Not at all. It was breathtaking," she begins. "My whole life growing up, my family lived in this wonderful home by this vast lake. It was consistently still as glass. The aquinnes would greet me every morning and play with the other children and me when we went swimming. You could swim out as deep as you wanted without feeling a hint of danger. In fact, all of Secreth felt like that. This serenity hovered over the land, and it never left. I felt it from childhood until I was married with my own children. I never knew fear or sadness. Not until the day Uxaar marched in with his army of Shadows, picking off the humans one by one. Isho, a Geron, deceived me into believing if I said the Incantations to him, my family would be spared. Instead, I slaughtered them with my own hands." She shudders tearfully. "The Secreth I knew fell to ashes—After all this time, I clung to the prophecy, knowing you would for the victims of the war, because I knew you, you were kind, good, and the most compassionate. Seeing you now, it's everything." Her voice breaks. "I know I'll get to see my family again, together in Secreth like we once were. I'll finally be home."

I wish I was confident that I'll feel that way when Secreth is in my reach. "I dread that I won't feel at home there, or that when I'm restored, all the memories I've had for the past eighteen years will disappear like everyone's memories of me back home. Oren only remembered me because he crossed the border into this realm."

"It will turn out how it's meant to, for good," Canyon affirms.

"Yes. The suffering will be over soon enough. Just one more battle on the horizon," Amber says.

I'm concerned that won't be the case for me. Even after witnessing several flashes from the past, the goddess feels like a parasite that will consume me. I fear I won't be the person I've always been.

A deep sigh escapes me, as I cleanse my mind of the thought. I must be prepared to fight Uxaar and not allow my mind to become clouded. Losing concentration could have a severe cost.

"Leave the prophecy out of mind for a moment. Tell your story, how you feel you should tell it," Canyon suggests.

I fancy this idea, for two benefits. One, we have nothing but ample time to kill until we're attacked or arrive at our destination. A lengthy conversation will help ease my mind. The second is obvious—the Eleven don't understand how I forgot my life as Syann. I will explain everything to the Eleven, all that I said to Floria, but in heavier detail. I will explain my past, who I thought I was, how I discovered I was Syann, and how it affected my past life. The effects it had on my family, how it ruined Liam's proposal yet reunited me with the one I truly loved. There's enough time to explain my journey and those who embarked on it—Oren, his family, and Athena. Time allots for me to explain everything until we're on the same page. What's nice is none of them judge me by my feelings or decisions. Instead, they seem captivated by my story and are understanding. The conversation doesn't die off, either, even when I've completed telling all the events that led me here now. With eleven people to ask me questions, the conversation stays stoked like a fire.

***

We come across a river bend flowing downstream. Floria informs us that the water will lead us directly to the falls if we follow it for a few miles. We're so close, the future is just ahead of me—or above me?

I shriek as my feet ascend farther from the ground by the second. This must be what it feels like to be prey, swooped up by predatory fowl. I'm unsure who the predator is, but it fastens me by my shoulders.

Urias manages to grab my leg, but his grip fails. The rest of the Eleven try catching up to me, but I'm too high up.

A blue-eyed Shadow with wings of smoke on her back holds me. They're as dark as the meaning of her name, Ebony.

I must think of a way down, fast!

The limbs of a Light tree extend toward me, snatching me. Ebony's grip is equally firm. I find myself in an unexpected tug-of-war. I'm uncertain of the winner, but I have an advantage—my spear! The fallen Geron lack healing abilities, so if I strike Ebony, she'll release me. My plan goes better than expected—As I jab the sharp blade toward her shoulder, she lunges before swooping off, abandoning me on the treetop.

The fear I experienced on the roof with Liam lurks in me. "I'm indestructible!" I whisper to myself repeatedly. "If I fall, I'll be fine!" I place my spear through the sheath on my back to ready myself to climb down.

Far out in the distance, crashing water streams down the edges of the dark crystal mount. That's it—my destiny right there. The star is directly above it. Surrounding the falls, like tiny ants from here, are at least twenty of the Gerons' troops. Initially, I don't understand why they guard this location until I spot a passage behind the cascading water. The entrance to Secreth must lie beyond it, and Uxaar is determined to prevent me from reaching it. These troops outnumber the Eleven. Do we have a chance against them?

Instead of climbing down myself, the tree limbs pass me down until I'm on the ground. The one that sets me on my feet nudges me toward the river. An intense wind blows me toward the stream. "All right, I'm going!"

The wind propels me forward, along with a trail of airborne leaves that guide me. War cries pierce the air, and my eyes meet Ebony, shrouded in smoke. A pair of blue lights pierce through her mangled blonde hair.

The Eleven are spread thin in the battle, with at least twice as many terrorists among them. I can't help but wonder if all Eleven are still alive. The bloody bodies I find on the ground confirm my suspicions—Perri and three of the terrorists were slain. Two of the terrorists in the river attempt to drown Amran. Yoli is nowhere to be seen.

"Uxaar!" I cry, interrupting it all. My being buzzes with energy. My spirit is calling out to nature, creating connections between me and it.

The trees seize Ebony by every limb, along with several of the terrorists. The water splashes and spits out Amran and Yoli—who must have drowned—while sucking the terrorists into the depths. The other terrorists who were unaffected halt with their hands raised. Nature is protecting me.

Ebony vanishes, only to reappear right in front of me. "Tell your remaining followers to surrender, or I'll force them to," I hiss at Ebony.

"I'd like to see you try," Ebony challenges.

Crystal protrudes from the ground, encasing each terrorist. The ones the tree abducted are hurled out of sight. The display even causes many of the Eleven to gasp in fear. Syann's spirit within me must be triggering all these reactions of nature. I have no idea what will happen next.

"Don't act so proud! Whatever you create! I can destroy it!" Ebony bellows, sending a whiff of black smoke toward the crystals, which slowly melts it.

"Enough is enough!" I grasp her arms forcefully, and in response, my hands shine brilliantly. Ebony shrieks in terror at my touch and vanishes into thin air. She frantically dives to the ground yards ahead of me, her eyes flitting between a likeness of Uxaar and her own green eyes. The shadowy smoke on her skin dissipates as she struggles in the grass. My touch has disrupted her connection with Uxaar!

Her cry is distorted, fading between Uxaar's and Ebony's voices. "You will never restrain me long enough! You can't get rid of me!" The shadows in her skin resurface. Behind her, the dark cloud has finished melting the crystal I've created. The victims inside collapse to the ground. A few of them gasp for air, but the majority are incapable of breathing.

The trees snatch her once more. Ebony's screams pierce the air as she frantically attempts to vanish, but her attempts are futile. She phases in and out of existence. Without hesitation, I rush over and grasp her head, causing Ebony to let out a deafening cry before she collapses.

Floria props Ebony up by her shoulders to examine her. Ebony pants as her eyes gloss over. The terrorists who've regained consciousness flee for their lives, knowing their champion is defeated. *I did it.*

"Uxaar is still in her! Her eyes aren't marked!" Floria exclaims. Before I can react, Floria sends her spear through Ebony's abdomen.

"No!" I bellow. I told Athena I would do everything I could to save Ebony. I was set on it, yet I failed Athena again. Devastated, I follow Ebony to the ground. "Floria!"

"It's the only way to stop her!"

I redirect my attention to Ebony, ignoring everyone else. She lies on her back, gasping. "Hold my hand, Ebony. As long as you hold on to me, Uxaar shouldn't control you."

She takes my hand with a discombobulated gaze. "Ebony?"

My eyes widen. Did Uxaar brainwash her so extremely that she can't recall her own name? "Is that not your—"

"Master Floria!" a distant voice booms through the foliage,

interrupting everything in motion. A dozen guards aboard harjins harshly stop once they've approached us. One leaps off their harjin, bolting toward Floria.

"General Sanyel? What's the matter?" Floria asks, stunned.

"There's been a breach in the garden! Testimonies claim the Shadow came and abducted Oren!"

"What?" I interject.

"Was anyone else taken or harmed?" Floria asks.

"No. The Shadow targeted Oren and vanished with him, but the people are scared now that our amendment with the Geron is broken! With actions such as these, they could return and attack!"

"No! We've taken care of the Shadow. There will be no more breaches!" I say sharply before turning to Ebony. "Where did you take him?"

"The-the Underealm."

"Oren's dead?" My heart stops, and dizziness overtakes me. It takes everything in me to prod Ebony with more questions. "Why? Why would Uxaar target him? Why would Uxaar go out of his way to kill him!" Tears rush to my eyes.

"There's another Shadow. I wasn't the first." She gasps for air.

"There's another?" Floria asks condescendingly.

Her head limply lies back. We're losing her, but I need more answers. "What's your name?" I ask her, squeezing her hand extra tight.

She stares off before shifting aloof eyes at me. She's gasping repeatedly, trying to answer me through wavering lips. "Olive." Her hand goes limp, and her eyes turn Uxaar's blue as she breathes her last.

My heart sinks before its beat courses violently in my body. Ebony is still out there. I haven't even encountered her yet! Olive was the girl in the caves.

I turn to Sanyel. "Take Olive and the other dead to the village. Once she is healed, have her fully interrogated in a secure area! Have everyone else prepared for battle. There will be more upcoming breaches!"

Sanyel veers his gaze to Floria as if he requires her approval. Floria affirms my command. Sanyel takes Olive's body to the harjin. The ones who fell in battle, Yoli and Perri, are also taken to go to the pools.

If Olive said the Incantations at some point, who's to say there aren't other Shadows I don't know about? Olive, the only one here who could have given me answers, is dead. When she's resurrected, I won't be present for her interrogation. There's only one other who would have the answers, and I must probe him immediately.

"Roe! Show yourself!"

249

The Light among the Shadows

18 *Oren*

"Athena, are you all right?" I ask.

I hoped Athena would've been happier to see me, but she's petrified. Who knows what's happened to her and what dreadful things she's heard since her arrival here? Physically, she appears unharmed. No visible injuries indicate otherwise, but I know better than anyone that some of the worst pain comes from the mind. With her history, Athena would know that, too. The potential psychological torture the Geron could have put her through in the time we lost her is daunting.

She shakes her head. "We've been played for fools!"

"Wh-what do you mean?"

The screams that woke me resume without warning, startling me, and Athena even more so. The cries clear all the thoughts in my head. Any curiosity about what Athena said is gone.

She grimaces, bowing her head as she stifles a sob. "We've fallen straight into Uxaar's plan from the start. It all began with me! What I did!"

Athena must know the truth about Ebony. That's what must have hurt her this badly. Finding out your best friend sold herself to the devil isn't light news. It would break me if I discovered Elouise had done such a thing. "You found out a-about Ebony? That she said the Incantations."

"You don't even know the worst of it!" Athena cries.

The screams in the background boom. The woman begs for help, before pleading someone's name specifically: Philip.

"Ebony!" he pleads weakly, yet desperately. Chains rattle through grunts of struggle. "Someone h-h-help her, please! Please!"

The voices only make Athena cry harder. Another new voice rings in the air, bringing me to silence. Unlike the others, it's soft and vulnerable but cries out as loudly as it's able. I haven't heard a cry like this since my days at the farm—a baby.

Why does the sound move me as much as it does? My heart clenches and sears like a fresh wound. Does this baby have anything to do with Ebony or Philip? Am I being toyed with instead? No—this baby is significant.

An intense sentiment bathes me, making me teary and sick to my stomach. As senseless as this sounds, this place is familiar. It reminds me of the caverns, but the familiarity is something else. Something happened here that impacted Syann in some way— and me. Is this what Syann meant when she told me her powers made her feel things? Is there some energy in here putting Athena and me in disarray? Or is stress making me mad?

What did Ebony do to me?

"Athena?" I can only call her name. I'm unsure what words should follow. Should I ask her what she knows or attempt to comfort her?

Thuds of heavy footsteps drown out my thoughts.

A towering man in dark armor enters the room. He stops in the space between Athena and me. Deranged red curls tumble to his chin. The freckles on his pale skin compete with the number of my own. His round yet worn-down eyes are intensely fixated on me. Does he know me, too? Or is he going to kill me?

All he says is my name before he swallows sharply. If I knew any better, he's queasy. The way my name leaves him is so strained and rocky, and it echoes through me. This follower of the Geron is terrified. He isn't as harsh as the ones I've encountered, yet is familiar as one I've seen in nightmares.

There's no need to ask him who he is or tell him who I am. He already knows all he needs to about me with the Gerons' help, yet the protracted silence gives me the intuition that I'm supposed to speak.

"Philip!" Athena shouts.

The man draws a commanding arm to his side to silence Athena. "No. I have to do this, Athena."

"Ph-Philip?" I stammer. "Y-y-your friend Philip?"

The expression Athena wears is not one of denial.

The redhead inhales painfully. "We have much to discuss."

No! I shake my head frantically. I don't want to be here. I can't be here. Syann will hunt me down if she discovers Ebony kidnapped me. That can't happen. I also want nothing to do with this conversation because I fear it. I don't have a role in this story! Syann is the goddess, Athena is the scholar and explorer who first ventured to the Dawn, and Ebony is the Shadow. I'm the sick boy who needed help. Philip has nothing that I need!

Philip draws closer to me, his gaze softening in a sorrowful way. He's deep in thought and unsure how to break out, so I do. "Why are you helping Uxaar?"

"To help the ones I love, who are as much under Uxaar's thumb as I am."

"Only Syann can save Ebony. So wh-why work against h-her?"

"You don't understand, so I'm here to make you understand."

"Understand what?"

Philip's chest rises and falls unsteadily. "Nothing is how it appeared to you. *Nothing.* There's a significant reason you were brought here from the beginning. You feel it, don't you?"

I stare at him, not wanting to admit I agree. Refraining from denying the claim is enough for Philip since he continues.

"There's a bigger reason than you being healed from a mysterious sickness. If anything, that was a cover-up, a trap designed by Uxaar."

"A cover-up of-f-f what? I was sick! How is that a-a-a cover-up?"

Philip claiming that my sickness is something more or less is triggering. My illness was traumatic enough.

Philip glares down to the ground, clenching his fists tightly. "There are"—he inhales sharply—"*two* laws of how the Incantations can be utilized. They can be said to oneself or recited on the behalf of your unaccountable blood. Meaning a blood-related child that is not yet of age to say it on their own behalf." He sighs painfully with closed eyes. When he opens them, he states something audacious. "Ebony said the Incantations over her son to Uxaar to save our lives… *You* are Ebony's and my son."

The woman who resembled Elouise in the darkness speaks the words I couldn't remember. "I'm your mother." She was Ebony.

A heavy gasp rushes out of me, leading to a series of shallow breaths that outpace me. I don't know how in the world I'm supposed to respond to that. I'm panicking, on a level comparable to the aftermath of my illusion. *That can't be true.*

I want to white-knuckle the truth I thought was mine, that I was the unfortunate, sick boy in a dysfunctional, lovable family who was healed by a magical goddess who fell in love with him. However, how can I argue? How can I let go? "No—I'm the— the son of Tobias and Valerie Silvius," I whimper tearfully, knowing my defense is untrue. The truth can stay far away from me. I don't want it.

"Tobias was Ebony's older brother. You're only their nephew."

Mum always told Elouise and me we took after our father,

Tobias, that he had dark hair and hooded eyes as we did. Those features were apparent with Ebony. I thought she was Elouise because she gets those traits from the Silvius side. And Philip, our resemblance is there—the freckles, the narrow jawline, and the heavy brows. I'm a clear mix of Philip and Ebony. My stomach churns at the thought, as my heart rejects it. "No! No, I was sick. You're ly-ly-lying. You're lying! I-I-I can't be the Shadow!"

"Oren!" Athena cries. "He isn't lying to you!"

"You know I'm not lying. You knew those voices were significant, as was this place. You were born in this very chamber. Those baby's cries, it was you. It was you, son—I'm—I am deeply sorry."

I shake my head. This changes everything. The news stoops me to a new low, lower than the past horrors I've experienced. I was a pawn in Uxaar's game. All those years, he played with me through bodily torture. I was his entertainment while he waited for Syann to come and his powers to be ready. "No! No! I-I-I can't be the Shadow. I saw her, I saw her! It-it—isn't me!"

"You weren't the only one," Philip says. "She was a diversion so that Syann wouldn't suspect you. She was the girl you outmatched in the storm. Uxaar strategically used you to kill her brother to manipulate her into reciting the Incantations. You know it to be true."

I do know now. The fight between her before felt like a horrid rush I could barely recall because I passed out. Only actually stabbing Gunter replayed in my head. Now it's clear—that battle was won with the power Uxaar lent me. That's why he blinded Syann with the bag so she wouldn't catch my glowing eyes. Uxaar wanted her not to suspect me, and he succeeded. He used his power through me to create those horrible illusions, too. It all makes sense now.

"I-I-I can't fight Syann!" I shake my head. "She trusts me!"

"That's precisely what Uxaar planned to do. Uxaar used you to gain Syann's affection and trust to make her vulnerable."

Was any of it real? If Uxaar had controlled me, could he have influenced my feelings for Syann? The kiss back in the cave—it shocked me when I did it. When I held her hand, it felt as if I had lost all my self-restraint. Is that why? Or was I flustered and in love like I thought? Was Uxaar behind it all, pushing me past my boundaries to think and act on things? What if it's even deeper than that? My depression following my grandparents' death, my hardships with eating and lack of motivation to leave the house—was it Uxaar inflicting me?

Not only has he made my life a living nightmare, but he also influenced my decisions and my emotions. I'm only a puppet, a doppelgänger.

I sob loudly before they morph into agonizing screams. The aches and the queasiness return all at once but greater than I felt before. The ropes around me snap as flame consumes me. Uxaar doesn't need to have me confined in rope. The control of my body is a much more effective restraint.

My clouded vision is now only in tones of blue, the color associated with despair. I can't move or speak, no matter how hard I try. It's like I'm in that horrid illusion again, where I'm dead and can't move, but this is worse. The grave now is my own body.

I would barter this destiny for death in a real grave. As Athena said, being the Shadow is a fate worse than death. If Syann can't save me, Darkness will torment me for the rest of my days.

Swarms of Geron enter the room, circling us like a funnel of wind. Chanting and laughter that I can't interpret booms. Several of the monsters brush against me, actually *touching* me.

Athena jolts against her pillar, muttering prayers under her breath.

Will Syann even be able to defeat me? Thinking of us as enemies shatters my heart into shards that will cut and hurt her, too. I hope she'll know, whatever Uxaar will force me to do to her, that I didn't mean a fraction of a second of it. It will be the deepest regret in my life.

Rage saturates me, one that's foreign in an intense nature. I charge toward Athena, readying to make a violent blow. "It's all your fault!" Unfamiliar concepts of vengeance, hatred, and agony target Athena. "My parents would have never ended up here if it weren't for you! We could have lived a good life if your foolishness hadn't destroyed it!" I yell.

Terror and sorrow drench Athena's eyes. I'd never wish to stimulate that. Yes, it's a fact Athena encouraged Ebony to undergo the trip where she'd meet our demise, but Ebony made the decision. Athena didn't force her to go or to say the Incantations. She didn't mean for this to happen. Never would I want to blame Athena for Ebony's choices. Even so, Uxaar forges a rage in me I can't overcome, no matter how I long to resist it.

Philip stops me, grabbing my wrists to block me from touching her. He's much taller and heavier built than me, providing good resistance, yet Uxaar's strength in me is an advantage. The smoke I'm emitting is burning Philip, too. "Uxaar!" Philip growls through his pain, knowing he's no longer speaking to his son. "Don't hurt Athena, please! She could still be of use to us!"

My hands swing Philip's arms around his back, twisting his shoulders. He cries out in pain. "Question your loyalty to me, and you will be next to face my wrath, Philip," Uxaar hisses through my lips. "I know what's best for my plan."

"I'm sorry, master. What would you have me do to make it up to you?"

"Send a squad of guards to deliver Athena to the Destination. I'm aware there is further use for her there. Then resume your guard here."

Philip gulps, lifting his head. "It will be done."

"Then go see to it." Saying those words is the last thing I remember before a burning dark flame devours me.

***

Uxaar leads me to the armory, where I put on armor as dark as shadows, crafted from durable crystals. I can only presume it's magic-resistant, like Syann's armor. I discover that I'm not alone in wearing it. I command an army of hundreds wearing the same. Only a dark cloak of smoke trailing down my back sets me apart.

We're heading to the village for a full-scale raid.

Athena's cries echo in my mind. Now they're taking her to the Destination, who knows what atrocities will be done to her there. I'm left with that knowledge and my repressed grief that I can't save her. I can't express any of it except through the tears flowing from my eyes. Even Uxaar can't stop me from shedding them.

Imagine if Elouise knew I nearly murdered Athena, or that I violently yelled at her. Athena is a mother to her, so in a sense, she was like one to me. We were not close, but she loved and helped my sister—well, cousin—so much. For that, I'm indebted to Athena. Instead of repaying that, I'm bringing her worst apprehensions to life. I'm the son who ruined her best friends' lives. What if Athena blames me for Ebony's death? And what has become of Philip? My existence was wrecked much more than I ever could have imagined.

"Soldiers!" Uxaar addresses through me. "We are after something greater than death—souls! Give every civilian a chance to say the Incantations to spare them from our slaughter. Anyone who refuses shall perish. I want no rebels to survive! Either dead or bound to incantation! Is that clear?" The troops cheer in response. "The goddess Syann will meet us in battle before you know it! I've allowed the soldiers sent to warn her passage so she will come and meet her true match. We will not fall to her again!" I roar. "Wait here for my signal. When you see the pillar of Darkness in the sky clear, you charge without mercy!"

My cloak painfully splits into wings, and I ascend high enough in the air to catch a glimpse of the village below. The fenced-in borders, clumps of huts, the harjin field, and the gardens I had shared with Gene and Kip all come into view. Seeing these familiar sights triggers a flood of memories. Only hours ago, I had first laid eyes on these places. Back then, I had no idea that my life was filled with untold lies. Instead, these fresh memories are connected to moments of optimism and joy. I was convinced that my life was about to pivot toward the better. But now, I realize that what I gained—love, healing, and friendship—are all about to perish.

Gene and Kip will fall by my hand if Syann can't save them. We could have been great friends if things had unraveled differently. The last happy memory I had was with those boys. Is it too much to ask that I can at least hold on to those memories? When they're dead, I will only remember how much I hate myself for destroying them.

Smoke surges from my body as sweat would. The pain it causes would typically make me roar, but Uxaar stoically presents me. The beads of black-and-blue fire pierce my skin like needles. These particles of smoke form into a cloud that swirls the more voluminous it becomes.

A funnel forms around me, drawing closer to the ground. I remain airborne, at the center of the storm I'm creating. From here, Uxaar will control me, and this tornado will sweep through the village. The wreckage it leaves behind will mirror my transformation—a broken disaster wrought by Uxaar. The funnel spins faster and faster, moving at a rapid speed. The jolting and tossing of riding a horse are nothing compared to this.

Even under Uxaar's control, I'm hyperventilating uncontrollably. With the funnel's speed, I'm unable to get enough air into my lungs.

I can only imagine how much damage this tornado has dealt to the village. Debris whirls around me, and short-lived screams echo throughout the funnel. Supernaturally, I'm surviving. The smoke deteriorates anyone in it, reducing them into ash.

As time passes, I descend toward the ground. The closer I get, the weaker the tornado becomes, and the duller the ache in my body grows. I had anticipated relief when the tornado stopped, but upon touching the ground, the sights before me weigh more than the pain Uxaar had burdened me with. Damaged homes and limp bodies stretch out as far as my eyes can see, through the blue filter of a monster.

I need Syann here. Despite my fear of her confronting the truth about me, she must stop this before the remnants of the town are eradicated.

Some of the houses still stand tall, thanks to the durability of their crystal walls. Distant screams and the approaching soldiers of the village prove there were somehow survivors. Their numbers are comparable to those in Uxaar's army, who arrive shortly after.

The terrorists who get past the village's soldiers storm into houses to do the obvious, to make the victims fall, either through saying the Incantations or death.

Several of the village's soldiers barge straight for me, and Uxaar boldly retaliates with my bare hands and magic. My armor protects me from their sharp spears, allowing me to inflict damage on them. Their armor, however, shields them from the deadly smoke I discharge, but for how long?

Uxaar's soldiers come to my aid, valiantly fighting for my freedom. However, the village's soldiers are formidable adversaries, having superior combat training and strength. I hope that's enough for them to emerge victorious against Uxaar, ensuring my capture and eventual demise. If only such a scenario were feasible. Uxaar possesses the ability to make me vanish and reappear as he pleases.

The absence of blue was the last thing I anticipated. I find myself in a familiar room, its walls painted in a dull gray and purple. This was the last room I was in by choice—Kip's!

I betray every desire to hide from the boys when I abruptly sling off my helmet. Uxaar suppressed my emotions for so long that I can't remain silent. My screams gradually transform into uncontrollable sobs.

"Oren?" Gene exclaims as he barges through the door. "You're alive!"

"G-g-get away from me!" I lunge back.

"Oren! What—"

"He's in shock. Who knows what they did to him!" Gene blocks Kip with his arm. "Oren, what happened? Why are you wearing that?"

"No!" I scramble into the corner, as far away as possible, before I meet the wall. "Please!" I must warn them, but I can't. As if they haven't plagued me before, uncontrollable coughs seize my ability to utter a single word. Pain grips my skin, but knowing Uxaar will force me to slay them hurts far worse.

"Oren!" When Gene touches my shoulder, he withdraws his hand as if he has touched hot coals. He yells agonizingly.

Kip is puzzled by Gene's outburst and frantically asks him what's wrong. There I stand before them, blue-eyed and all.

Gene blurts out a curse as he grips the situation. His hand is withered beyond use from my touch. Alongside Kip, they head to the door to flee, but I cut them off with a trail of smoke. They direct their helpless eyes toward mine, knowing they are cornered as much as Uxaar corners me.

"Oren, what have you done?" Gene asks in terror.

"Say the Incantations, or I'll finish you off!" Uxaar growls through me.

"I won't be a traitor like you and say the Incantations!" Gene roars. "I'd rather die!"

They think I chose this. It's a dagger in my chest. Never in a million lifetimes would I choose this.

"What about your friend here? Or is 'friend' not even a strong enough word? A brother is more like it. Kipper, he's your everything. Would you really allow him to perish because you wouldn't sacrifice yourself for him?"

"No!" Kip shakes his head. "Gene, no! Don't do it!"

"Syann will save us! Even if you must kill us first!" Gene

growls through gritted teeth.

"Kipper?" Uxaar asks through me. He shakes his head. Uxaar punishes Kip by having me shove him into the corner of the room. There, the smoke blocking the doorway devours Kip. Screams flood the air before the smoke clears away. Kip is nowhere to be found. I killed him, the boy who was nothing but kind to me. This is how I repay him.

Gene breaks down, bursting into screams of wrath and despair.

"Eugene, I can alleviate all your suffering with the Incantations—"

"I should have let you die in that cursed forest! I knew I should have never helped you!" Gene breaks into inconsolable tears. "Go ahead. Kill me. I'll never say the Incantations!"

"No. That would be far too merciful." I exit the room, leaving Gene alone to mourn one of the many deaths I'm bound to cause. The worst part is how I mourn them, too. No one knows that. No one cares, nor should anyone care. Everyone wants me dead now, including myself. What a place to be.

The Light among the Shadows

19 *Syann*

The glow of crimson and emerald shimmers over me and the remaining Eleven. They're alarmed by the creature's presence, yet I couldn't care less. "Did you know about Olive?" I demand.

"Yes. She said the Incantations shortly after your and Oren's arrival at the caverns. She was with the terrorist who attacked you and Oren in the storm. The one Oren killed was her brother. Uxaar used that, and her fatal wound, in their favor to persuade Olive to recite the Incantations, to save her brother and herself."

"Is Ebony the only one left, or are there more?"

"Neither. There is one Shadow left, and it's not Ebony."

"What do you mean it's not Ebony?" I shout. "You told me she said the Incantations back in the storm! You lied?"

"I never lied to you. She did say the Incantations, but I wasn't able to clarify that truth. It was too dangerous in the circumstances you were in. Oren woke up, and I couldn't risk him seeing me!"

"Him seeing you? What are you talking about?"

"Ebony had to have said the incantation on behalf of her offspring. It's the only way that is possible," Floria's face falls.

"Ebony didn't have any—" I cut myself off. Athena mentioned nothing about Ebony having a child or expecting one; maybe she wasn't aware that Ebony was expecting. Athena said Ebony and Philip wanted a family and were in love. It's possible, very possible, which is terrifying. The thought of the Shadow being a child with no choice is horrid.

"That was the reason Uxaar had Philip and Ebony taken, while Athena was left behind. Unknown to anyone at the time of her capture, Ebony was with child. Uxaar could sense it. He saw an opportunity to use the pregnancy manipulatively. Ebony could speak the Incantations either for herself or, better, for her child. So Uxaar threatened her to say the Incantations over her infant son by torturing Philip. Giving Uxaar the upper hand of having a Shadow that was unaware of their identity. A clean slate. You have all met the son of Ebony Silvius."

"What?" I blurt out. The name Silvius is an explosion within me. Everything becomes discombobulated by the impact, making grasping the realization impossible. I can't draw a breath. Instead, each beat of my heart booms in me.

Oren isn't dead like Olive said, but this update doesn't relieve me. Athena said being the Shadow was a fate worse than death. Uxaar can claim his mind and body and abuse Oren however he sees fit. It's now no mystery why Oren suffered so much in the past—the God of Darkness claimed him.

The Goddess of Light must claim Oren back.

"Oren is the Shadow?" Amran questions sternly.

"He was a trap!" I gasp for air. Doubting the claim is out of the question. "His sickness, his family claiming he needed healing, they had to be in on the whole thing! Whether it was willingly or by force, they sent Oren to me so Uxaar could make me an easier target!"

It worked well. Oren was the bait, and I fell for it hard. The lies persuaded me, and not only that, I fell in love with him. I fell in love with the one who was meant to destroy me, the enemy I was destined to defeat.

"You must understand I couldn't shed light on the situation until Oren was gone! Uxaar would have attacked through him without delay if I had. The best I could do was convince you to leave Oren behind, and I tried, but you wouldn't listen, Syann! You did exactly what Uxaar wanted, by sympathizing with the Shadow!"

"So, neither of us had any idea? We both came here blind!" I tug my braid as tears sting my eyes. Athena must have been clueless about Oren's identity, too, yet she had to have known Ebony and Oren's family were related. They all have the last name, Silvius—meaning Oren is somehow related to his family who raised him. That would explain why he ended up with them, but not how Athena failed to mention Ebony and Oren's relation.

"I would assume Oren knew nothing." Roe's words relieve me. "The Geron had strict orders to stay out of sight of Oren so he wouldn't see them. Even if he did see any, Uxaar could rewrite his memories. For example, how he couldn't remember you initially when he should have all along. Oren was removed from the Dawn when he was only an infant so that he wouldn't know his origins. Uxaar demanded secrecy."

That makes sense. The Geron weren't spotted until Oren reclaimed his memories of me. Uxaar covered everything, and I fell straight into his plan.

No matter how strong I'm trying to be, I can't keep from shedding my roused tears. I have a million questions about Oren and the situation his family was in, but there's no time. "We continue down the river to the falls," I force myself to say. "It's not far. I saw it from above when Olive snatched me. The only issue is that it's guarded by a larger group than the one we faced. Even if we overtake them, Oren will come. The only way I can stop Oren is to get a hold of him, which won't be easy."

"Your spirit has the power to influence nature. We can use that to our advantage. As for Oren, in the end, he's only human," Floria says.

"You seek to kill him? Like you killed Olive!" My voice peaks in agitation.

"I seek to do what it takes. Oren will be twice as powerful as Olive. When a Geron has possession over multiple beings, his power divides that manyfold. If I get a chance to kill him, I will. Besides, if his body is recoverable, the pools can restore him."

"And if he's not recoverable?"

"Remember what I told you, Syann!" Floria lunges toward my face. "Your affection for him cannot stand in the way of the greater good! You must be prepared to sacrifice if the world's fate demands it!"

When we discussed this earlier, it was easier to listen to because I believed Oren was safe. However, now that he's in grave danger, the thought of abandoning him makes me feel sick to my stomach.

Before I can respond, a grand tornado rises and whirls chaotically in the air, miles away. It's precisely where we came from, the village. No doubt Oren is the one causing it. In the funnel are surging sparks of blue. The winds become strong enough to whip the air around us. I can only imagine what destruction is ensuing in the village.

I'm the only one who can stop it, yet I'm supposed to follow the star. This is a diversion I can't indulge in. "We must keep going. Getting to the falls is the only way to draw him out of there. He'll come to stop me!"

Floria agrees.

I call for harjins, and moments after, a herd arrives. I don't hesitate to mount up, telling the others to do the same. We take off toward the waterfalls. Roe hovers beside me as I ride off at high speed.

It feels wrong that Oren isn't here with me. He was with me

almost every time I rode a horse (except the races). Now, I'm heading in the opposite direction of where he is. I hope Uxaar brings him to confront me, so I can save him from Uxaar's possession. If I can, he could dwell in Secreth with me and leave behind any horrors this life has brought him.

How terrible. I sympathize with Oren more than ever. We were in it together from the start of this journey. Now, our situations are more parallel than I could have presumed. Both of us are humans blindsided by taking on the power and burden of a god, yet his situation is far worse. The Light blessed me with its power, while the forces of Darkness vilified him. No one maliciously lied to me. Light's forces wiped away every trace of anyone's memory of Syann. Oren's family lied to him—not little fibs, either. These lies will have a profound impact on his life.

***

We continue to follow the river. The noise of the flowing current intensifies to the sound of crashing water, meaning we're close to the falls. This sound is even easier to hear when the wind's howling softens. The tornado is fading.

Beyond a cluster of bushes, the falls are at last in sight. Guards stand around the mouth of it. Boulders are scattered throughout the water, creating a path toward the falls. Before we can step any closer, Roe hovers before me, gesturing with his claw-like hands for us to stop. I do, matching Roe's gestures to the ones behind me.

"Go any farther, and the guards will notice," Roe warns.

"We should arrange a strategy," Darius says.

"Use nature to my advantage. Once I've thrown them off, we'll rush in."

"See, water surrounds them. It's as simple as sending a surge powerful enough to wash them away, if necessary. How far do you think their loyalty to the Geron goes?" I ask.

"In my experience, they were all either manipulated or scared to be killed," Fenneth answers.

"Most of them were kidnapped children," Rowan remarks.

"Olive seemed to be the exact case." I scratch my chin.

"So, what are you thinking?" Floria questions.

"I go alone and negotiate. I'll offer them protection to switch sides. If they hesitate, that's when nature will back me up. I'll show them that they shouldn't only fear Uxaar."

"Don't go alone. I will stand by your side."

"As will I," Darius bids.

"Fine, but the rest of you stay here and on guard. Your signal to reinforce us will be this tree limb hitting the ground three times. If the tree limb only hits the ground twice, it means the negotiations worked and we're clear to continue—Roe, I want you to be an extra pair of eyes on Oren. Warn us when he draws near."

"That I can do," Roe agrees.

I ascend to my feet, Floria and Darius after me. My posture is straight, and my head is high as I advance past the foliage. I stop on the rocks fringing the mouth of the falls. Each armed guard circling the entrance has their eyes peeled and focused on me.

"I'm here to negotiate!"

"What are your terms?" the one in the front asks.

"To let me through and stand by my side. You will be under my and my soldiers' protection and receive a full pardon for any acts of loyalty to Uxaar. The Geron will fall, and you will be free."

"If we don't?"

"I will show you that Uxaar isn't the only one you should fear!"

"Is that right?" a voice muses, but it doesn't come from anyone around us. It isn't the voice of the soldier who asked for terms previously. It's toneless—a Geron.

Out of the falls walks a slim frame clothed in charcoal armor. Narrow blue eyes blaze through his helmet. I know underneath the disguise is Oren. In his hands is a hostage held at knifepoint: Athena. Uxaar took her as a bargaining chip. "You said you were to negotiate?" Uxaar growls through Oren. "Take one more step, and I will cut her open!"

The sight of Oren weighs me down and constricts my throat. I don't want Athena to die, or Uxaar to make Oren murder her. I must touch him, before Floria can get near him. What's tricky is that the only exposed parts of Oren are his eyes and hands. Olive lacked a helmet.

"What can I do in order for you to free her?"

"You can take Athena's place. Then the Eleven and Athena are free to go and will be unharmed. That is, if they don't attack and give me a reason to harm them, meaning they are not permitted to come rescue you," Uxaar says. "I will swear under these conditions by an oath."

Before I respond, I review the words carefully. If I hand myself over, Oren will take me to Uxaar's fortress. I'd have to find another way to return to the falls. If I disagree, Athena dies unless I overpower Oren and his guards. That's highly unlikely. "On what force do you make this oath?"

"Pfft! Flesh bags have such pathetic memories! You've forgotten the laws of a binding oath. Why, it was only the result of the balance between Light and Dark that forged its existence!"

I glance back at Roe, who nods at me.

"Uxaar speaks the truth. We agreed by oath that my village was to be undisturbed by the Geron. In exchange for his followers being permitted to use the pools. An oath that Uxaar disregarded!" Floria hisses.

"You know very well, Floria, that I disregarded nothing! Not a Geron has ascended over your land. The oath excluded my fleshy followers, and you know it! You agreed to prolong your land's stability, knowing that the peace wouldn't endure!"

"Don't give this demon the time of day, Syann. He holds no honor."

"I don't have all day, goddess," Uxaar speaks over Floria.

"Fine," I interject. "I counter your conditions! They remain the same. Only the protection applies to everyone from the village. If you go back on your word and attack them with no provocation, you will set Oren free."

"They attack me unprovoked, then I'm allowed to fight back. I attack them unprovoked, then I grant Oren freedom from our bond."

"Yes."

"Syann!" Floria raises her voice. "This is foolish! You'd be casting us away from battle uselessly! We would be unable to rescue you."

I approach Floria, whispering, "It isn't me who needs rescuing. My powers will come through for me. This may be an opportunity for me to discover how to free Oren and remove our obstacle entirely. What I need from you is for you to take all your people to my homeland, Seren, and protect it. Uxaar plans to overthrow it next, yet with this oath, he can't attack you without losing Oren as his Shadow, regardless of your location. So you need to get there as soon as possible. When you do, you must warn my people of the dangers of the Incantations!"

Floria nods. "How can I get there in time?"

"I'll keep Oren occupied as long as possible. Roe can act as a messenger between us in case anything goes wrong and guide you through the caverns outside the Dawn. Worst-case scenario, if I desperately need help, we can disregard the oath entirely and resume this war we're already in. Trust me."

"Breaking the oath is not something to take lightly. It is a bad omen! It could get us killed!" Floria sighs, unexpectedly relaxing. "Fortunate for you, dying for this cause isn't beneath me. If you believe this is the right play, then I won't stop you."

"Thank you." I nod and turn back to Oren. "I agree to the terms."

"Then swear it on the balance of Light and Dark. Break the oath, and the powers will decide your fate. Most humans who've broken oaths perish in unforeseen circumstances, but we are not human, are we? We're gods. We are Light and Darkness. What we say of this oath, goes."

Perhaps, if the oath is broken, I can protect my friends from the consequences enough. Hopefully, breaking the oath won't be necessary at all. My objective is to make Uxaar break the oath.

"I, Uxaar, swear an oath on the balance of Light and Darkness. If Syann bonds to this oath, I will exchange Athena unharmed for the price of Syann in my custody. I also swear not to harm the people of the village of the Dawn as long as they remain neutral toward my army. Oren will be released from my bond if I fail to honor that condition. If the village fails to remain neutral, I am allowed to oppose them in battle."

"I, Syann, bond myself to this oath," I say, expecting something to happen, but silence follows.

Oren removes Athena's muzzle and chains before pushing her to me. Athena glances into my eyes before embracing me. "I am more than willing to die for this cause. You know that." Athena disappointedly parts from me.

"I have a plan. The people here need you. Go with them." I smile, letting her go. If only I didn't have to part ways with her so soon. I missed her dearly, and I have so much to ask her about.

Floria takes Athena by her shoulder, pulling her away from me. One of the terrorists does the same with me, furthering my distance from my allies. Before I can speak to Oren, I'm muzzled and stripped of my weapons. Next, they chain my hands behind my back. My two primary attacks toward Oren, my touch and voice, have been impeded. I'm unsure what happens beyond this point, but I must trust my plan.

"Remain at your guard here!" Uxaar demands through Oren.

The stench of sulfur whiffs around me through a fierce wind. Oren's cape splits into two wings that protrude from his shoulder blades. He turns and grabs the chains around me before we ascend.

Uxaar knows better to fly near any tree limbs. Oren shoots up at an altitude above the tree line before venturing in a new direction. Trees, harjins, and any ground-bound creatures are now out of reach.

Fortunately, one of the most powerful creatures is from above—dragons. Their emerald scales protect them from any form of magic. Combined with their immense size and fiery breath, they are undoubtedly the most formidable creatures bestowed upon the Dawn. These scales are the source of the armor worn by the village guards. Uxaar would find it challenging for Oren to defeat a dragon. If I manage to mount one, I can either return to the falls or the village. However, Oren cannot enter without violating Uxaar's oath with me. If I escape to the Eleven, I will become an elusive target.

It isn't but two minutes before two dragons soar into view. Oren veers into a different angle opposite theirs.

Oren tilts his head toward me, glowing eyes glaring through the helmet. "This is you, isn't it? Make them go at once!" Uxaar roars.

I ignore Uxaar. I cannot speak or control my spirit calling to the dragons. My only response is lowering my brows at Uxaar.

"I mean it!" Uxaar bellows as the dragons close in.

Oren abruptly veers in the direction we came from, attempting to outmaneuver the dragons. However, the creatures are faster than Uxaar anticipated, leaving him with no choice but to engage in a fight for escape. Fighting while holding me would be a taxing mission, and if he were to let me go, I would have the opportunity to escape. Even if Oren were to drop me, I could still manage to get away.

Cowardly, Uxaar keeps Oren flying away as long as he can, until a dragon reaches out and snatches me. The two engage in a fierce tug-of-war until the dragon emerges victorious. The second dragon swiftly snares Oren, swooping him away from me.

Uxaar uses his most obnoxious stunt, making Oren disappear. In moments, Oren reappears, not where I would've expected. He stands on my dragon's scaled snout, advancing closer to the creature's facial features. The beast tries shaking Oren off, but he remains balanced as he draws his spear. I'm helpless to prevent Oren's next move against the dragon. The spear finds itself in the one vital place the dragon has no armor—its eye. The dragon's grip falters as it roars in agony, and I find myself in Oren's grasp again. The second dragon hunts us from behind.

"Don't think I won't treat the other one worse. Make them go!" Uxaar orders. Oren returns the spear to the sheath on his backside. What's halting him from blinding another dragon?

The half-blinded beast flees. The other continues to track us, and is catching up. The dragon uses its large tail to whip Oren, but he cleanly dodges it. The dragon is angered, and roars ferociously at Oren. Oren howls back at it like a deranged animal, flying closer to its face. The dragon opens its mouth wide, sparks erupting deep inside its throat. As the fire pours out from the creature, Oren hovers, unmoving, forcing us both to experience the heat of a million suns. The fireproof scales of his armor protect him from any burns, as the dragon's skin protects itself from the dark flame Oren retaliates with.

I never could've predicted Oren would have found another area where there is no protection of scales for the dragon, yet he surprises me. He takes us both inside the beast's mouth.

What Oren plans to do here becomes painfully apparent— obliterating the dragon from the inside. Oren grasps the dragon's uvula while perspiring shadowy vapor to kill the dragon from within. The dragon roars ferociously in pain. The beast tries to spit us out, but Oren grips the dangly flesh. Little time passes before the shaking and boggling of its head goes limp.

The change of motion is as intense as the severing of my connection with the dragon. My heart twisted fiercely the moment the creature died, and now we're descending rapidly. The rattling frightens me, and Oren doesn't stick around for it. He vanishes once again. Alone, I'm falling from hundreds of feet in the air, in a dead dragon's mouth!

***

I have a fragmented recollection of my time escaping the dragon. There were the gentle flashes of light, the cold air that bombarded my damp skin, Oren's silhouette, and the sensation of being swept into his arms. Time seemed to crawl until exhaustion finally dragged me into a deep sleep.

I wake inside a circular-shaped dungeon with pillars all around it. The walls are made of rugged crystals. On the surface of the floor are bloodstains. Who knows what monstrosities happened here?

The Gerons' presence barrages this glowing room. They circle like a haunted funnel of wind. I lock eyes with one—Roe! The relief of seeing him is brief. How could he get me out of the chains that bound me to this pillar? Roe hovers around a particular guard near the room's entryway. I've seen him before—the redheaded man from the festival! He's attentive to Roe, fear rampant in his eyes. If I can turn the tides of loyalty in him and the other guards, the odds could tilt in my favor.

Uxaar doesn't notice the exchange. Roe blends in with the other Geron, so I'm not forcing them to leave yet.

Oren's illuminating eyes fixate on me. When the guards clear away from me, no one is in the way of my and Oren's stare down.

The voice that comes out of him isn't the gentle and stuttering tone I adore. Instead, it's the wind that howls from Uxaar. "Syann, there's been far too much runaround between us for my taste. I will be gracious to you and offer you one last chance to say the Incantations to me, or Seren is next to receive my fury!"

I shake my head, looking past Oren to Roe. I must buy Floria time to get to Seren. Roe will have to help me.

"So, you'll let me go off and destroy everything you love? While you sit and rot in my dungeon? Huh. Have it your way, then." Oren turns his back on me, only to face Roe. "Is this your plan? To collaborate with this downright traitor to take me down for you? Roe is weak!"

Before Oren can look back at Roe, Roe lunges at him with a sharp pair of claws, aiming for his chest. The force of the attack sends Oren rushing toward a pillar. If Oren collides with the pillar before Uxaar intervenes, the impact could be enough to pierce his armor and hurt him.

My role in this plan is to command the Geron to leave the fortress with my powers. I'm right on time. Uxaar furiously realizes that all his allies of his kind have left the room. I can sense his outrage from the roar that escapes Oren before he vanishes. Oren reappears right in front of me, shouting in my face, "Whatever you're doing, stop it! The Geron are under my command! They fight for me!"

I hoped Uxaar would react this way. The creature is too vengeful and hateful for his own good. He rewinds Oren's hand, rebounding for a sharp slap across my face. Instead of hurting me, the effect is the opposite—Oren's eyes flash as he collapses onto the ground. His body thrashes as distorted cries leave him.

Uxaar was so irate that he underestimated the dangers of touching me. Now, Oren is disoriented by the disruption of their bond. I've bought myself some time. I thrash, trying to break free from the chains and reach Oren. If I manage to get to him quickly enough, I can free him, but I won't be able to escape these chains without assistance.

The redhead rushes to the scene, unexpectedly stopping by Oren. Why does he care to check on Oren with such concern? Is he not coming to help me? Was he here for Uxaar's aid instead? I thrash harder to get his attention. He notices me and rises to come to my rescue! Only to be confronted by Uxaar rising in his true form behind him.

"Philip, if you betray me—and it will be the end of you!" Uxaar hisses.

Philip! Oren's father! He's the redhead?

"You want me to prove my loyalty to you, master? Once and for all?"

"How so?" Uxaar questions.

"You've taken everything from me! My love, our son, my home, all I have to offer is surrendering my soul. I'm tired of fighting!" Philip begrudgingly begins to recite the Shadow Incantations, his voice wavering.

My heart races. I'm flailing harder than ever, trying to persuade Philip not to do this—but the name he says changes everything.

"Roe."

Green illuminates Philip's eyes. My tension leaves through a relieved sigh. We've gained an ally, a powerful one who isn't bound by the oath. Uxaar knows, too, that he has a new enemy. He snarls loudly before Oren vanishes. I was moments away from saving him. Now he's gone again!

Roe unleashes a torrent of destructive smoke from Philip that severs the chains binding me.

Regarding Oren's liberation, wherever he may be, Uxaar must lack control over him. Uxaar's presence before us raises my suspicions of this.

Uxaar's anger boils over, lashing at Philip. Uxaar grabs Philip by the neck, intending to choke the life out of him before Roe makes Philip vanish—leaving Roe in his true form. "I won't have any more on my side betray me. Not Philip, not you!" Uxaar points at Roe with a sharp claw. "What will you gain by betraying the Geron? Tell me!"

"You are the one who betrayed the Geron! By dividing us and placing this curse of Darkness upon us!" Roe argues.

"If you break that curse, it will be the end of all of us. There is no chance of redemption for you, Roe. When a Geron changes sides, it can't be undone!"

"It will be the end of the Geron who betrayed the Light, as it should be! The loyal Geron have lost their purpose because of our deeds. Secreth needs restoration and freedom, and I can give it and know that I've fixed what I've done to our home, what I helped you do! Even if it costs me everything."

"Roe, you don't see it! You don't have to wander this world without purpose to bestow anymore. Neither of us has to continue that path! Do you realize what power you possess? You hold a soul that your power can be wielded through! After years of wandering in this realm and being nothing, you could be a hero, Roe. Use your bond with Philip against her instead of for her! Together, we Geron can reign in this world! Not be sent back to the Underealm after a thousand years of exile!"

"You're right about one thing. I could be a hero. Demolishing a whole other world alongside you will not be how I become one! Not one I'd be proud of being. I have no desire to inflict pain on these humans! While you have torn families apart with your ludicrous actions and animosity. You've devastated the lives of two once-thriving families! And you've driven Oren mad out of his mind! If I help you, so much worse will be done!"

"The humans destroyed our home!" Uxaar roars out. "For their own selfish gain! Why should I have sympathy for doing the same to theirs? Why do you? They stole everything from us!"

"The Light welcomed the humans into our realm! Your jealousy and hatred toward them are what demolished our home. It's what motivates you to eradicate this world. And I won't indulge you any longer. My loyalty stands to the power that created my very being! And that is with Syann! Not you!"

"And that, my old friend, will be your downfall, along with the humans, beginning with Seren!" With that declaration, Uxaar disappears.

20 *Oren*

I've returned to the Underealm, drifting like a released kite.
That's how I've become—cast out and abandoned—or maybe I
slipped away? Does it matter? It hurts either way. My first instinct
is to toss off my helmet and let it float away in oblivion. Frigid air
torrents toward my face, forcing a harsh shiver down my spine.
The void of Darkness and the wandering spirits among it immerse
me.

For what reason did Uxaar bring me here this time?

If only the last thing I remember would evade my mind. Did
I really strike Syann? My heart clenches at the thought. All the
things I've done since Uxaar took over were things I'd never dare
to do. When I hit her, deep grief ached in my bones. Though the
presence of her warmth and Light that she always gave me surged
in me, making the Darkness within me flee for a moment. That
must be why Uxaar sent me here.

So many souls from the Dawn are here, including Kip. He
wanders, frightened and alone, somewhere. Hopefully, we don't

cross paths. I couldn't bear to face him.

"Oren!" I turn back, recognizing the soft voice. Initially, it was delicate and then antagonizing. Now, this voice has more significance than it did before. The first time she was a stranger, the second she was a friend of Athena's, and now I understand she's my mother.

When I turn to my left, she's floating there. Ebony hesitates to shift toward me. Conflicting emotions burden me. Part of me sees an innocent woman who did what she had to save those she loved. If she hadn't said the Incantations over me, we'd both be dead, along with Philip, with no signs of Syann coming to rescue us. The other part sees a foolish, poor excuse for a mother who sold her son to a monster. Wouldn't the more selfless thing to do be to recite them on her behalf? Uxaar tortured Philip and me our whole lives as a consequence of her actions.

"You know now, don't you?" she questions tearfully.

Will inhaling deeply keep me from crying? I've shed too many tears today, but it's not enough. "Why?" I ask, through a lump in my throat. My question doesn't need to be specific—my tone conveys my anger.

"When you were born, you weren't meant to survive. After a failed attempt to escape the Dawn realm with your father, you came early and were as frail as a wilted flower. Uxaar was going to surrender us to death unless I gave him what he wanted. He demanded that I say the Incantations over you. I knew Uxaar would continue to torture others with no way of stopping it. The only way to bring Syann to be was for Darkness to rise. I held on to hope that she would come and save us all, and in the end, we could be together again." Ebony sobs. "I know it isn't that simple. You have every reason to hate me for what I've done. I wish I could have your forgiveness, but I know it's too much to ask for."

"I wish I w-w-was dead. I wish you'd let me die," I mumble gruesomely.

"I hope one day that changes. That life treats you with

something so special that it outweighs the troubles you've gone through."

I believed I could be with Syann once I was healed and forget the years I spent battling illness. Together, we could embark on numerous adventures to compensate for the lost time. It would all be worth it.

That feels inaccessible now. The two people I cherished I can never return to. Elouise isn't my sister—I know that now. As for Syann, she deserves better than what I have to offer her. Everyone does. I'm the most guilty and violent human to roam this Earth.

"Was there any good in your life?" Ebony questions tearfully. "He promised there would be."

Uxaar did? Why? "There was, b-but it was all lies."

Another chill jostles through me; Ebony, too. It was nothing ordinary. Something in this realm has shifted. A new presence has entered it.

"Ebony!" a voice echoes from afar. I'm taken back to the moment I heard the same voice echoing in Uxaar's fortress. It's Philip.

"Philip!" she belts out before turning to me. "Oren, where was your father before you came here?"

"The room I-I-I was born in. He's n-not dead. He said the Incantations to another Geron. One that pledged loyalty t-t-t-to Syann." As I speak, Philip comes into view. He soaks in Ebony more desperately than when Ebony first saw me. This is the first time he's seen her since she died. I try to imagine the weight of that. According to Athena, Ebony and Philip shared the deepest kind of love. They even had a child together. They had to have been head over heels for each other, only to be swept away at my expense.

"Ebony!" Philip bursts out. He swims to her, attempting to bring Ebony into his arms. She holds herself back, already knowing the truth that they can't touch each other. She's a ghost here. The painful realization hitting Philip is apparent. "Ebony?"

"Philip," she sobs. "Neither of you should have ever been brought here." She breaks down.

"We're not dead," he comforts her, eyeing me. "We were both sent here for protection, for how long I don't know. As long as I'm linked to a Geron, I can traverse in and out of this realm." Philip's voice breaks. "I wish I—I wish I could get you out of here with me! I'm so sorry, Ebony, I failed to protect you! There hasn't been a day that has gone by where I didn't think of you." He turns to me. "Both of you." He tearfully turns back to his love. "Ebony, Syann was so close to freeing our son. She's going to do it. She'll free us!"

Ebony's smile sags sorrowfully. "Oren told me you said the Incantations to a Geron! Why?"

"One that changed sides with Syann made a bold stand against Uxaar, which inspired me to do the same. I would have died if I hadn't said the Incantations to it."

"You mean I-I-I-I would have killed you," I utter gravely.

"No!" Ebony shakes her head. "You are not to blame. If you need someone to blame, I'm the one! I'm the one who caused all of this! You had no choice! You were only a babe!"

"Did you? Uxaar d-d-didn't give you a fair choice, did he? It was either say the Incantations to me, or the people y-y-y love die! Of course, you'd choose the latter. Anyone would! My only options in-in life were to suffer or t-t-to die. It will never be different because that is my fate!"

"No!" Philip objects. "Syann is going to save you! Just because we failed you before, Oren, doesn't mean we will continue to. She is going to fix everything. Don't think that you're exempt from that. You said she trusts you. She must care for you."

I'm fading away—it's simultaneously soft and sharp. My consciousness is leaving me gradually and dully, yet my body jolts violently. I experienced the same sensation when I touched Syann's face. My vision alternates between ordinary and blue hues. My parents call out my name as I slip away.

***

Aches take me from my slumber. How clanky and stiff I feel in this armor! My bed was never particularly comfortable, but—

Wait, what? My bed?

At first, the sensation is ordinary. My open eyes unveil the familiar room, dimly lit by the window. Days ago, I was here. Usually, I never question being in my room or bed. If I'm not at my desk, I'm always in my bed.

The sharp pounding in my heart is the first sign of panic. Why would Uxaar bring me here? He intended to take me to Seren, but why must my family suffer? Why must I confront the lies they fed me my whole life? Will Uxaar force exploding wrath from me like he did to Athena?

I can't let that happen.

My vision still flickers from blue to normal. Uxaar can't fully grasp me yet. I should utilize the time I have to warn my family! Dodging them is futile. If I run away, Uxaar will bring me right back.

Rising reminds me how much I want this armor off. It's protecting me from Syann. Therefore, it's my enemy. I try ripping it off piece by piece while fighting against the opposing thoughts from Uxaar.

Leave it on, boy! I'm not done with you yet!

I shudder. "Yes, you are!" I hurl the shoulder plate of the armor on the ground as hard as I can. I yelled way louder than I should have. Someone must have heard my screams and the loud crash on the floor. Right? "No!" I whisper to myself once I've realized.

I'm unavoidable, undeniable!

"Get out of m-m-my head!" He's taking over. My eyes remain blue longer in the flickers than they do my own. "Elly," I mutter and then whisper to myself frantically, "I won't h-h-h-hurt her. I won't hurt h-h-h-her."

You already have.

"No!"

My door swings open, and Elouise stands in the doorway. A myriad of conflicting emotions swirl across her face—concern, bewilderment, and finally, excitement. Each emotion leaves a residue of itself on her.

"Oren?" She paces into the room and closes the door behind her. Uxaar's presence in me melts away, as do the blue flashes of my vision. Uxaar doesn't want to reveal himself to her yet.

"Elly!"

Elouise runs and tosses her arms around me. "I wasn't sure I'd ever see you again! And you're standing!" She laughs. "Look at you! Did you reach the healing pools? Jace told me all about it!"

Elouise's hugs were always restoring. Part of me badly longs to hug her back, but I don't indulge the selfish thought for a moment. "Elouise, you need t-t-to find Jace and y-y-y m-mum! Get them out of here! It isn't safe!" I back away from her.

"What do you mean?" she asks. Of course, Elouise wants a full explanation before doing what she's told. I shouldn't be surprised.

"I—I don't have t-time to explain now! I need y—t-t-to— *Augh!*" My head aches excruciatingly. Screeching rings in my ears as my head throbs. I grasp my head while doubling over. I'm unable to form any words, no matter how hard I try. It comes out as groans.

"Oren? Oren! What's—" She stops and holds me around my waist, "Sit, sit down! I've got you!" She leads me to my bed, not leaving my side. "Did you not get healed?"

Undeniable! The word from Uxaar keeps playing in my head.

"Mum! Mum!" Elouise shouts in dismay.

I'm terrified. I'm terrified. This is what occurred before Kip's death. I suddenly appeared on the scene and lost control, subsequently killing Uxaar's intended target after luring them in.

Jace storms in first, reacting as Gene did by blurting out a swear the moment he lays eyes on the scene. From his reaction alone, I realize that Jace knows the truth about me. He sees his dear sister at the killer's side.

Jace swiftly intervenes, pulling Elouise away from me as their mum enters the doorway. He instructs her to leave, but Valerie promptly overrides his request. "Jace, take Elouise and leave this place!"

"Mum! No! You must go! You can't stay!" Jace screams back.

Amidst the chaos, my eyes flicker blue again. Uxaar brings me to my feet.

Elouise squeals at the sight. "What's happening?"

"I said go!" Valerie shouts. "There's no time!"

Betrayal and fear etch deep lines on Jace's face. Despite his resistance, he obeys his mother and exits the room with Elouise, who is struggling against him. Valerie closes the door, leaving me alone with her.

I'm terrified that she'll die, heartbroken that she and Jace were aware of the situation and chose to conceal it, enraged that they kept my identity a secret from Elouise, and spiteful that they allowed me to endure such a miserable existence. I'm consumed by fury that Uxaar shattered my family into fragmented, dysfunctional pieces. "You a-a-and Jace knew! You knew who I-I-I was!"

Valerie stammers, "I was forced to hide it from you! Uxaar swore to kill Jace and Elouise if I didn't! I already lost their father to Uxaar's followers. I couldn't lose anyone else! Jace only knew because he was old enough to remember the day his father died. Elouise was an infant when it all happened. I thought it was better that she never knew and got to have a normal life."

"A normal life?" I roar. "Sh-sh-she didn't have a normal life! Ever since I fell from that tree, she spent her life blaming herself for it and trying t-t-to fix me! You knew I-I-I-I couldn't be fixed! Yet you never told Elouise or me that! She wasted years of h-h-her *precious* life worrying f-f-for me! And f-f-for *what?* She's never gonna t-t-trust anyone again! I love her, a-a-and y-y-you hurt her!"

"You think I *don't* love her? She's *my* daughter, Oren! My *only* daughter! I know her better than anyone! She's not a secret-keeper. If she had told the truth to anyone, and I mean anyone, Uxaar would have had her and the people she told annihilated! Just like her father was!" Her roaring words are mighty enough to destroy the dam controlling her tears.

This is how she finally admits how Tobias died, after years of me asking about him, a forced confession of how it was my fault. I ruined their lives. It's no wonder Jace loathed me, and Valerie always estranged herself from me. Tobias died because of me.

I ruined everything. Ebony's and Philip's lives. Athena's, Valerie's, Jace's, and Elouise's were botched. The list of names may be infinite. Who knows how many other people I've hurt in my life?

Anger and turmoil manifest in the form of screams. Uxaar stirs feelings of hatred toward those who wronged me, to the point I can't stand it. This anger demands to escape.

My desk, under assault by my arms banging down on it, is the target of my blue eyes. The furniture rattles loudly, startling Valerie. Unable to contain my rage, I unleash a frenzy, swiping all the clutter on my desk—stacked books, drawings, bottles of ink, and writing utensils—to the ground, clearing the table in a single, uncontrollable fit.

"Oren—I'm sorry. I really am. Life wasn't fair to you."

My eyes revert to normal as I gaze back at her. Does she regret how I was treated? Deep down, does she love or pity me? "Son—"

My eyes flash back to blue fury with that one word. "Dare you have the *audacity* to call me son!" Uxaar roars at her through me. He is controlling my every action now. I'd run away and never return to this house if it were up to me. "You were never a mother to me! You never will be!" Uxaar drives me to say. Darkness surges through my body, engulfing the room in a matter of moments. Valerie scrambles to the door, promptly escaping before the smoke sweeps over. Darkness overtakes my vision, lulling me to sleep.

***

When you sleep, you're bound to have dreams. Many people have peculiar or even amusing ones. Elouise particularly enjoyed sharing her imaginative dreams with me. She usually did so when she brought my breakfast in the mornings if I was awake. Her dreams often involved adventures, humorous conversations, or odd occurrences in town.

My dreams were often nightmares. I usually kept them to myself, unlike Elouise. However, she could usually sense when I had a nightmare. They always left me extremely skittish and aloof, sometimes even teary-eyed.

Another dead giveaway was me screaming awake in the middle of the night. When that happened, either Elouise or her mother would rush to my side to check if I was all right. In those cases, I needed them to stay by my side until I could get a hold of myself, which usually took a while.

The reason I can decipher which dreams Uxaar creates is that they felt so real. Normal dreams are often hazy and elusive, but I rarely experience dreams like that. When I do, they usually resemble flashbacks from the past—Brenda and I embarking on new adventures, Elouise, Jace, and I exploring the outdoors like we were kids again, or sometimes I even have nightmares about drowning or falling from trees.

Currently, I can only presume that I'm experiencing a night terror, the ones Uxaar creates. However, I don't feel Uxaar's presence within me, and my vision remains normal.

My whereabouts is a cave. A tunneling cave that moans echoes of my parents' screams. I recognize them from before.

I'm reluctant to continue walking, but the tunnel is irresistibly drawing me in with each step. Upon entering, I'm met with a horrifying sight. In the dungeon room, with a circular arrangement of pillars, I find Philip chained to one. He's much younger, around my age. His hair is shorter, and his beard is disheveled. His youthful face is devoid of wrinkles or lines, instead bearing the marks of abuse. Blood streams from his nose, dripping down his chin and seeping into his torn shirt. His forehead and cheeks are bruised and blemished with bloody wounds. He's limp and exhausted, his strength waning. "Ebony!" he groans out, his voice filled with desperation. "Someone, please help!"

Ebony stands across from him, even closer to me. Her backside faces me, and her hands are cuffed behind the pillar. Her black, wavy hair cascades down her back. I inch closer, circling around to her front to face her. For a moment, I gaze at her before quickly turning away, as if I were about to touch hot coals. The pain from the sight lingers in me like a burn would. Her arms are tightly chained behind her, encircling her torso, underneath her breasts, and above her rounded stomach. Her legs protrude from her dress, spreading out as wide as she can manage despite her shackled ankles. She is giving birth and is in agony.

Birth is supposed to be a joyous miracle. I remember the instances with the livestock at the farm being so. The sight, however, makes me sick to my stomach. This was supposed to be a moment for my parents to cherish, but instead, Uxaar made sure the experience was traumatic.

I yearn to escape, but Uxaar materializes beside me. With one clawed hand, he grasps my face, while the other clutches my shoulder. This isn't a figment of my imagination—Uxaar is revealing my past to me.

"Watch." A tone of amusement douses his words. Uxaar's claws sink into my skin, drawing blood. How is this funny to him? It's demented!

"No!" I squeeze my eyes shut, yet Uxaar comes over me, forcing my eyes open. The sight is now in a hue of blue.

Ebony moans loudly, but not a single guard is in the room to help her. Couldn't Uxaar at least have the decency to have someone aid her? My mother shakes harder than I've seen anyone tremble in my lifetime. Her skin is like snow due to blood loss. Ebony lets out one last cry before her child enters the world. Uxaar shoves me closer, directing my eyes toward the frail babe I once was, lying on the ground wailing.

"Oren!" She tries to struggle free, as Philip once did. Like his, her attempts are too weak to be effective.

"Mum," I whisper, feeling a heavy sense of sympathy. I can't decipher if the emotions are sourced from me or Uxaar. How could I?

I attempt to touch her, yearning to liberate her from her chains and take us far away from this place. However, my hand passes through her like she's a ghost. I lean in closer, my eyes filled with tears, as I observe the infant through them. Undoubtedly, he's the tiniest baby I've ever laid eyes on. His skin appears to be a shade of purple and lacks the freckles I currently possess. Feathery dark fuzz sprouts from his head. His delicate, pouty lips quiver around feeble cries, and his eyes remain closed.

"Philip!" Ebony calls. Philip's only reply is bobbing his chin briefly. He tries to form words, but only a weak groan is heard.

The only one who answers her call is Uxaar. He appears right before her. "He's dying, along with you and your son. You three will all be dead by nightfall without any intervention. You hold the key to saving them. It all depends on which option you choose."

"Option?"

"In order for me to save Philip, I demand worthy compensation. Say the Incantations to me on your son's behalf, and I will save Philip, and your son will live. Refuse, and all three of you die. It's that simple."

"Let me speak them over myself. My son will not be bound to a creature as cruel as you!"

"I want him. The deal only applies with the son."

"Why?"

"You're weak, a vessel as small as you could be easily overcome by human warriors. As for the son, I can build him up to be exactly how I want him to be during the eighteen years. Because he won't even know who he is. Not until Syann is ready. The power of anonymity is a great one. I will not save Philip or your son if you say the Incantations for yourself." Ebony weeps, offering no response. "I'll give your son a childhood he can hold on to, full of good and happy memories. He won't know of me until after the last stars fall. Or he can spend the centuries in the Underealm because you surrendered his chance of life."

"You're lying to me! You won't give Oren the life he deserves!"

"Oren—if you recite the Incantations over him. You will be bringing Syann's coming. She could save your son from my grasp, or you can pass this up, and you three die out. Then I'll wait for the next unfortunate soul to wander into these lands that I can torment. Syann will not come until someone speaks the Incantations. Destiny brought you here, Ebony, don't ignore its call!" At the end of Uxaar's proposition, two guards enter the same way I did. They both carry swords, holding the baby and Philip at their points. "What will it be, Silvius? You will answer now!" Uxaar shouts so loud it echoes through the room.

Ebony startles, stifling a sob. "I'll do as you ask."

"Good." Uxaar directs his gaze to the guard next to the infant. "Uncuff her and hand her the child."

The guards obey Uxaar's command and hand Ebony her child. She weeps uncontrollably, holding the wailing infant close to her chest and kissing his head. "Please forgive me," she whispers, her lips pressed against the baby's head. "I'm so sorry for bringing you here. I'll never stop praying that Syann saves you." Ebony cradles the child against her chest before bringing him closer to examine his face. She gently caresses his cheek, then turns her attention to Uxaar. "What do I have to say?"

Uxaar replied with the words of the Incantations:

Set yourself free,
Take over he,
Use him to make you higher,
In he, have your way,
You get the say,
Do with him as you desire.

He continued. "Then you will enter a trance, where you select the Geron. There, you will call my name. Call another's name, and our deal will be disregarded."

Ebony follows Uxaar's instructions to the letter. However, the grief she carries is too overwhelming, and she succumbs to it, becoming lifeless before our eyes.

Uxaar swiftly takes the infant from Ebony's grasp and carries him away. I rush toward her still body. From this moment, eighteen years ago, until now, Ebony has been trapped in the Underealm, haunted by her actions.

I roar out, my gaze fixed on Uxaar with a furious intensity. He sneers back at me, and everything else around us comes to a halt. The guards, Philip, and no one else moves. I can't help but despise Uxaar for holding the baby, an innocent and sweet child who did nothing wrong. That baby's mere existence was a sin, and if he hadn't been born, none of this would have happened. I want Uxaar dead—I want myself dead.

"You wanted to hate your parents for what they did to you, but you can't. Instead, you're blaming yourself, aren't you?" Uxaar asks. "That your very existence ruined their lives."

"I h-h-hate you!" I shout through hot tears.

"I know," Uxaar taunts me with his coaxing tone. "This hatred shall consume you. Much of your past is still a stranger to you. I will introduce you as I regain my hold on you."

"No! I don't w-w-want to know!" Regardless, our surroundings resume their motion, and Uxaar doesn't acknowledge me anymore.

"Take Philip to the healing pools at once! I have plans for him. Keep him cuffed and return him here after he's healed! As for the woman, dispose of her corpse. She's no longer of use to me." The guards nod, unfastening Philip's unconscious body from the pillar.

The surroundings swirl into darkness once more, transforming into an entirely different environment. We find ourselves in Seren. The sun must have set approximately an hour ago, as evidenced by the sky's indigo hue.

Before us stands a modest one-story stone house, similar to many others in Seren. Although I've never been inside or seen this house, I must assume it holds significance. Its location on the outskirts of town is evident from the gates behind it, which guard the oak tree grove.

"You don't know this place," Uxaar states. "This is where the ones who raised you lived, before they moved to the farmlands. You're the reason they moved there. You'll understand soon enough." We observe two Geron guards, one of whom is holding the baby, who seems to have grown slightly.

"Three months have passed. This is the day after the birth of Elouise—July eleventh. I left you in the care of my guards for three months, waiting for the daughter of your aunt and uncle to be born. I planned to have them raise you as their own so you would be far from your past. So far, that you wouldn't even know of it."

The guards approach the door, pounding on it. A man I've only seen in old family paintings opens it. Tobias, the man I thought was my father. I spent countless hours gazing at those paintings, wondering about his life and what my life would have been like if he had been present. All that contemplation is meaningless now.

My uncle is alarmed by the guards, and especially the baby. He opens his mouth wide to speak, but the guard speaks first.

"We're sent on behalf of our master, Uxaar, the God of Darkness, to relay a message to you."

"I'm sorry?" Tobias scratches his beard. He turns his head back inside, whispering, "Jace! Stay inside with your mother and sister." Tobias closes the door behind him and redirects his attention to the guards.

"Your sister, Ebony, who went missing, passed away in childbirth three months ago."

"Childbirth?" Anger glints in his slim brown eyes. The guard displays the baby to Tobias. My uncle's expression is a concoction of grief, anger, and heartbreak, all blended into one—this expression I've seen in too many faces today.

"You will take the child and raise him on her behalf. Uxaar demands it."

"What did Uxaar do to Ebony? It's no coincidence this child was born the same month the stars of Syann fell. Athena said your men kidnapped her for a reason! It was the child, wasn't it? It's been nine months since she vanished!" Athena must have triggered the recollection of Syann's prophecy. A growl escapes his lips as he winds his arm up, preparing to unleash a beating on the guards. However, the guard not holding the baby draws a weapon, abruptly halting Tobias's escalating violence. "She said the Incantations over the babe, didn't she? Didn't she?" Tobias asks aggressively through clenched teeth.

"You must keep this knowledge confidential. You will raise the child, Oren, as your own on behalf of your sister. He will be known as the twin of your newborn daughter, Elouise. You will not tell him who he is. You will give him a normal life, or the consequences will be grave. I swear that to you! So, take him." The guards run off as soon as Tobias has the baby in his grasp, leaving him to panic at his doorstep.

Tobias runs to a wooden shed in the backyard. There, he grabs an ax. I can already tell what he's planning to do with it.

He darts past the fence and ventures deep into the oak grove, intending to commit a heinous act. Tobias lays the baby on a stump, intending to end my life permanently, but I am already aware of the fate that awaits me. It was not me who was destined to die, but the other. Tobias met his demise the week Elouise was born, and now I know how. Before Tobias can raise the ax, a knife strikes him squarely in the chest.

The guard responsible approaches to retrieve the baby, glaring at Tobias's dying body. "You don't listen to instructions well, do you? It was simple. Raise the boy with your daughter. By refusing to raise this child, you lose the privilege to raise your own!"

They abandon my uncle to die, returning to the same front door and knocking on it once more. This time, they endure an even longer wait before the door finally opens for them.

Jace unlocks it. He must be five years old and vulnerable as a lamb. For once, I pity him. "Where's my dad?" He asks timidly.

The guards don't entertain Jace and storm into the house, dragging the boy by the arm behind them. Throughout their walk to the master bedroom, the boy screams for them to release him.

There, Valerie sits in her bed, holding Elouise close. She appears significantly younger and livelier than I'm accustomed to seeing. When she realizes they're holding her son hostage, she springs up tensely, her voice rising in a shrill scream, demanding that they let Jace go.

"Listen very carefully," the guard demands. "Fail to do what we tell you, as your husband did, and your son dies next!"

Valerie muffles her outburst, covering her mouth.

The guard holding the baby steps forward, presenting the infant to Valerie. "This is your nephew, Oren, son of Ebony, and the prophesied Shadow of Uxaar the Geron. His mother passed away, and Uxaar demands you raise him as the twin of your newborn daughter. He is not to know of his identity, of Uxaar, or his true lineage. Instead, he is to be one of your own. Defy any of those terms, and your children's lives are at stake. Tobias died defying my terms. Don't think I'll hesitate to kill another."

"Let my son go!" Valerie screams in terror.

"Take the babe first!"

Valerie places Elouise on the bed and struggles to rise. She must be weak, having recently given birth to Elouise. She hobbles over to the guard as quickly as she's able and takes the baby in her arms. The other guard lets go of Jace, who runs to his mother in tears. He buries his face into her as Valerie strokes his hair. "I've done what you've asked. Go!"

"No one outside this house knows who he is. Defy me, and this family will be reduced to ash. From this day forward, Oren Silvius is your son, as Elouise is your daughter."

"Get out!" Valerie breaks into a sob. Her cries are the last thing to fade into darkness. I'm uncertain whether the darkness signifies the end of the nightmare or if I'm about to be transported to another part of my past. Instead, the darkness persists, and Uxaar remains within it. I collapse to my knees.

"They all cry, you especially," Uxaar says patronizingly. "It's a sign of weakness. It shows how weak and pathetic humanity is. The only strength you have is mine. Without me, you're nothing—nothing but a weak, broken boy who doesn't know who he is. I'm what makes you whole."

"You're a d-d-demented monster!"

"No. I'm a god! You are subject to my power. Soon enough, the universe will be, too. Syann will see the darkness humans are capable of and will regret the day she tried saving it on the backs of the Geron."

"She w-w-will destroy you!" I roar. "And make y-y-you pay!"

"If so, you along with me. We are one." Uxaar chuckles wildly.

I despise that I concur with one thing he said. If Uxaar were expelled from me right now, what would be left is an absolute storm of confusion. My heart would be smashed into a lot of pieces that no one would attempt to mend—not even myself. As for Syann, she will witness the true monstrosity I am and eliminate me along with Uxaar.

21 *Syann*

"Roe, what did you do to Philip?" I ask.

Philip reappeared before us but remains frozen on his knees. The only movement he exhibited was the spilling of tears from his eyes. As I fix my gaze upon him, I learn that the expression on his face isn't solely one of sorrow. It's bittersweet, like holding a fistful of forget-me-nots while reminiscing about someone you had lost. Before I could react, Philip made fleeting eye contact with me before succumbing to an emotional breakdown.

"I took him into the Underealm, where Ebony is kept."

"Ebony is dead?" I ask. I had hoped Ebony had survived, like Oren and Philip. As I bend down to Philip's level, I can't help but think of his son. Philip tries to hold back his tears with his palms, just like his son did. Inside the barricade, I see a tortured and heartbroken boy. I can't undo the past, but I hope to restore his family. However, if Ebony is in the Underealm, is it even possible to save her? "Philip, I need your knowledge to leave this place. You're my biggest hope to save Oren."

Philip drags his palm to his chin, revealing swollen red eyes that stare at me, aloof. "Oren was there, too, with us. Until he vanished, Uxaar was regaining his hold on him." Philip shudders, biting his full lip. "I failed my son."

"You did all you could, Philip. What matters now is focusing on how to stop Uxaar from making things worse." Roe redirects his focus to me.

"Where is Oren now?" I ask.

"I'm unsure. I would have to scout," Roe replies.

"Go. Philip and I will head to the falls. Your connection to Philip will keep us in touch."

"The guards throughout the fortress won't allow you to just walk out. Not without seeing you held hostage by a Shadow. I'll need to be in Philip until you have a clear exit."

Philip sighs heavily. "Roe's right. If they see you in custody of a Shadow, they won't dare intervene."

I don't like what I'm about to suggest. "Can't you do what Uxaar did and make Philip fly? We could escape undetected. You could blow a hole in the roof, right?" I ask Roe.

"I suppose. Still, to do that, I must be in Philip, meaning I cannot scout."

"Just get me in the sky. We must act now!"

Roe doesn't question me and disappears. Philip's eyes contort into a green, inverted shape, mirroring Roe's. Our escape plan is now underway. Philip clasps his hands together, conjuring a dark green smoke between them. This energy surges upward, transforming the cave stone into ashes. The room is enveloped in a cloud of embers and debris. As the smoke dissipates, a substantial tunnel emerges from the ceiling.

I'm unexcited when Philip sprouts wings, given how terrible my last flight was. I can only hope there will be no issues this time.

My back faces Philip so he can hold on to me. Roe doesn't hesitate to shoot into the air through the opening. As I had anticipated, a dragon soars right before us.

"Put me and Philip on, and you scout for Oren, Roe. We'll be safe if Oren isn't here. You and Philip's minds are forged. If we get in danger, you'll know."

"All right," Roe agrees, guiding Philip and me on the dragon's back. When we sit down, Roe exits Philip and gazes at me in his form. "I will find Oren and report to you his whereabouts." Roe goes, leaving us settled on the dragon.

"You really trust Roe?" Philip asks once we've taken off.

"Roe isn't like the others, I've learned. The power in me knows I can trust them. I can't explain it yet—If you hadn't said the Incantations to Roe, Uxaar would have killed you."

"I know. That's why I did it. I hope he lets me free so there's even a chance I can see Ebony again."

"Roe will free you," I assure him, focusing on the beauty below: purple and blue foliage and the glow of trees and embers. This is my first time feeling safe on a flight here. It is beautiful. "If not, then I will. I could free you right now if it pleases you."

"No, not if my connection to Roe helps you."

I nod. "Is this your first time riding a dragon?"

"Yes. It's quite a view—nothing beats the feeling of riding a horse, though. Before all of this, when I was your age, I'd ride out in the fields around Seren every day with Ebony and Athena."

"Your son would agree. He loves horses. We rode them all the time when we were children."

"You've known my son that long?"

"Yes. Since we were both eight, I considered him my best friend. I still care about him very much," I admit.

"Is it more than that, too?" Philip smiles. "I know that look."

I sigh. "I'd be fibbing if I said no—I love him. He loves me, too. I hope his guilt doesn't change that."

"I know a thing or two about having guilt about the one you love—It wouldn't stop me from being with Ebony. Nothing would."

"I hope Oren feels the same when he is set free, but I'm scared that Uxaar has completely depreciated him. He was finally lighting up again, and then Uxaar possessed him." Philip doesn't know what to say. I try to swerve on the positive side. "I hope you both get to meet properly one day. He's wonderful."

"I wish I could've taken his place. I wish that I could have saved Ebony," Philip mumbles sorrowfully.

"You weren't in that position, though, right? Roe told me Ebony said the Incantations to save your life."

He nods. "They beat me severely…When Ebony and I were first taken, they gave Ebony her own quarters and cared for her. I didn't understand why until we realized she was pregnant and that Uxaar wanted our child. He agreed to let me stay with her only if I joined his army. I consented because I hoped to use my training against them to escape. We tried escaping six months later. Ebony was getting too far along to wait anymore. So, we attempted to flee to the village, but our pursuers caught up to us. I fought them off, and even killed several of them, but Ebony got hurt and fell into labor prematurely. After my beating, when I came to, I was held by Uxaar's men at the healing pools, and discovered Ebony died after saying the Incantations over Oren to save my life. In that moment Uxaar gave me two options: to keep serving them, or die. I thought maybe I could find a way to free Oren or save Ebony if I stayed, but I was never successful."

"You're succeeding now."

"Eighteen long years later."

"You shouldn't blame yourself."

"But I do. I should have never let Ebony embark on such a dangerous trip for my sake. If I could be blind again and have her back, I would do it in a heartbeat. She was my—"

"Syann!" Roe appears beside us.

"Roe?" He's at my right in his form, Philip being unaffected.

"Oren is in his house. Uxaar has him under an illusion. The Darkness of it has completely overtaken and destroyed the house."

"Did anyone die?"

"Stella didn't escape, but his family managed to flee. I don't know how long Uxaar will hold him in the illusion."

I stammer, overwhelmed by the news of Stella's passing. The image of her being abandoned in a burning house, helpless to escape, tears at my heart. She wasn't just a bird—she was my friend. She had always been by my side, preserving the memories of me and Oren. However, I can't afford to grieve her loss just yet.

"We should be at the falls soon. Stay in sight of Oren. Let me know if he poses a threat and take Philip if you need."

"All right, be careful." Roe disappears again.

I grieve Stella inwardly. Philip asks about her. I tell him the story of how Oren found her and nursed her back to health before gifting her to me. Philip listens attentively as I recount how Stella played a key part in guiding Oren to his journal entries about me. Philip thoroughly enjoys the story, much as I relish sharing it.

As we approach the falls, I sense that the guards shouldn't pose a significant threat this time. Roe's possession of Philip should deter them. However, my powers have other intentions. A powerful surge of water from the falls scatters the guards, creating a clear path for me to approach. An aquinne emerges from the water and waves at me.

"Thank you!" I laugh, returning the wave.

"Woah! What is that?" Philip asks.

"An aquinne. They are water spirits from Secreth."

A feeling I experienced when I first spoke with Floria has lingered in me. My journey appears to be presented before me without any obstacles. However, this time, it feels more ominous. Last time, I was naïve enough to believe that everything was fine, and I was completely unaware of Oren's fate. Are there any more secrets waiting to be revealed?

Water soaks us as we stride behind the stream of water. A hidden passage is behind it—a tunnel, dark and elongated as far as my sight can reach. The light from my hands and eyes is all we have until we reach deeper into the tunnel. Like the caverns, crystal flecks line the cave walls, providing twinkles comparable to a starry sky.

Philip resumes our conversation. "It sounds like you made Oren happy."

I smile. "He was happy for some time. Oren and I would always play together, only us. It was like that for the four years I knew him, and by the end of it—I was in love with him. He loved the outdoors. Riding horses was his favorite. Swimming was— well, he refused to. Still, he would run and play like any other kid. Oh, and he could draw so accurately and sing, too. His voice was lovely on the rare times he would share it. It's been years since I've heard it, but I still hear his melody in my head. He was far too talented to hide himself the way he did."

"I used to sing to Ebony, too. She loved my voice. She always told me I'd sing the best lullabies if we had children. Though I never g-g-got to sing to Oren—" Philip tenses up, growing silent.

We've made so much ground that the entrance is out of sight. The tunnel got even brighter the farther we walked. Still, the end isn't in view.

"What was Ebony like? I've only heard a little about her from Athena."

"Oren takes much after her. When I saw him, I instantly thought how much he looked like her."

"Really? I think you look a lot like him."

Philip chuckles. "Maybe it's the freckles. Anyway, my family was from this country called Ireland, but my parents died when I was eleven, leaving me. I ended up in Seren after several years of being on my own. Athena's mother, bless her soul, took me in. She provided me with work and shelter at her stables, and Athena and I became like brother and sister. I met Ebony soon after that, and it was love at first sight. Though I couldn't see too well. She was tiny." Philip chuckles. "I towered over her." He gestures his hand to the height of my collarbone and under his chest, which makes me laugh. I suppose evidence of Oren taking after Ebony is his smaller build. Philip is much larger.

"Her family was overly protective of her, but that didn't stop her from doing what she desired. Her father disapproved of me, an orphaned, blind immigrant living in a stable. He didn't think I could care for her, yet she overlooked all of that and loved me for me. I grew to admire her for her independent and adventurous spirit as time passed. I felt like she should face or achieve whatever she put her mind to. She thought that, too. She thought we could go to the Dawn to heal my sight and…" Philip trails off with a weighted sigh. I sense his regret in the air. "I miss her more than anything—Do you think it's possible to rescue her?"

The weight he carries presses onto me. "I don't know, as far as I know, I can't go into the Underealm. The only way I could is by reciting the Incantations or die, and I can't do either of those things."

Philip's eyes roam past me. "Through there, you'll get your answer."

In our sights, a radiant gate stands before us. Crafted from brilliant crystal, it sparkles like a diamond, reflecting rainbows with every gleam. Within the stone panels of the wall behind it, a large white portal beckons us. On each side of the gates, three crystal columns stand tall.

"The gates." The gates of Secreth, I recognize them somehow. "Beyond them is the altar. Only I can go past them."

"Yes. Until the curse breaks, the gates won't open for anyone else. Anyone who tries instantly dies. The gate is too holy for anyone other than the Light to touch it," Philip says. "I've heard so many stories." The numerous skeletons near the portal account for that claim.

A shaking sensation sinks into my bones. I walk closer, seeing a majestic crystal bridge between us. Beneath it is a large chasm that stretches down beyond my sight.

It's silent until we reach the other side of the bridge. The gate is only feet away from me. The humming noise it's making leaves me trembling. "Roe." I stare into Philip's eyes. "Where's Oren?"

Philip's eyes flash green. "Still in the illusion, you're in the clear," Roe answers through Philip.

In the clear or not, I'm nervous about leaving everyone.

"You and Philip keep everyone safe until I'm back!"

"We will try."

A deep breath isn't enough to prepare me, is it? To venture into the realm where I belong? To completely sever myself from the world I grew up in, leaving everyone on Uxaar without my protection?

My heart races, and my hand stretches toward the gate. I anticipate a magical touch that will stun me, but surprisingly, it feels natural, as if I'm simply opening the front door of my home. The peaceful emotion swells in me, pricking tears of joy in my eyes.

Beyond the gateway lies a grand throne room, surpassing any room I've ever encountered. It spans the size of a field, making me feel like a mere flower amidst its vastness. To my left and right, towering crystal walls stand tall, adorned with doors trimmed with golden foliage. These doors proudly reach only two feet below the ceiling, creating an awe-inspiring presence. This ceiling transforms into a celestial canvas painted with rainbows, studded with diamonds that twinkle like stars. The marbled floor mirrors the dazzling colors of the ceiling, reflecting like a crystal mirror. In the heart of the room, the altar stands on a star-shaped tile, radiating a mesmerizing glow. Its gold surface reflects like a tranquil lake at sunset, captivating the eye. Beyond the altar, down a path of colored tile, lies my throne. Although bare, it exudes an aura of magnificence. Its shimmering surface mirrors that of the altar, adorned with diamonds and golden flowers that embellish the staircase leading up to it.

Two Geron guard each side of the throne, the two doors, and

the portal. So, besides the eight of them, I'm isolated.

These Geron are unlike the ones I've encountered before. Their countenance is serene and angelic. Meticulous golden armor adorns their frame, contrasting sharply with the calloused skeleton of Uxaar and Roe. Instead of a murky darkness emanating from their waist and head, a bright white illuminates them. Their light eyes radiate a profound peace that instills a sense of security within me.

A peaceful hush settles in my spirit. It's reminiscent of those serene mornings when I would watch the sunrise from my old window while everyone else was still asleep—but for once I long for those around me to wake up and experience it, too. How did I manage to go eighteen years without this tranquility? It's astonishing that I once believed I was happy before this moment. The mere thought of leaving this place devastates my heart. What's worse is knowing that multitudes are deprived of such bliss. Turning a blind eye to that would create remorse I couldn't possibly bear. For that very reason, I must save them all—Ebony and the countless others can't be doomed to the wretched Underealm.

I'm at a loss for where to begin, but time is wearing thin. Uxaar could awaken in Oren at any moment, and Roe can't warn me from here. The altar is the only clue I have about finding the answer.

The sparkles of crystals within the gold are mesmerizing. Lilies of white gold adorn the rims of it, creating an immortal garden beneath it. If only I knew what to do with such a magnificent structure.

"Two choices." The words muse loudly within me.

"What choices?" I respond. "Who are you?"

"I am the spirit that resides within you, Syann."

"Are you addressing me? Or are you *Syann*?"

"Both."

"Can you show yourself?" I ask.

"I'm afraid not. I'm forged inside you."

"All right, then. If you're Syann, what does that make me?"

"We lifeforms are composed of three parts—the body, the soul, and the spirit. The body and spirit are forms, the body being a mortal form, and the spirit immortal. The soul is what allows these forms to live in unity. What made Syann was the death of an innocent infant girl. Her soul was pure, so her spirit was fit to be the form of the Light while her flesh was dead. That's who you are. You are her flesh that I made rise once again, so through the Darkness, my spirit could enter the Dusk realm. Through you was the only way for me to traverse to Earth undetected."

"Why did you wait until the Shadow appeared to come to Earth?"

"Because without it, we can't save the people from the Darkness. The Darkness is ravenous, demanding a price be paid. The only acceptable price is the one that is of pure Light. Pure Light will destroy the Darkness."

"How will this be done?"

"I must journey into the Underealm. There, I will purify the spirits within it and serve as a bridge to Secreth for us all. After I bind the Dark Geron into the Underealm forevermore."

"I can't go into the Underealm! Only the dead and Shadows can go there!"

"You can't, but I can. The only way for my spirit to go into the Underealm is by you saying the Shadow Incantations. You would create a bridge for me and a connection to trap the Geron with me."

"Which would kill me. A spirit departing a body is the death of it."

"Don't think of it as death, but the beginning of something far greater. Our soul unites us both. You will be one with me and live in me."

I don't understand what that means or have the time to receive answers. That makes my breaths heavy. Secreth's calming atmosphere is a thin twine holding my composure together.

"Why didn't you do this before when I said the Incantations to Roe?"

"Roe didn't kill you. Instead, he set you free. Roe was unaware of the design of my plan yet made himself loyal to me by oath during the war. Since he didn't kill me, our spirit couldn't depart into the Underealm. Even if we could have, we needed to break Oren's bond to destroy the threat first. To save him and the world from Uxaar, his bond along with anyone else's must be broken. It's up to you if you want to save him, even if it means losing everything."

"If our souls are one—you know I want to save him more than anything!" I reply. "I only have to touch him!"

"It would only be a temporary solution. The Incantations must be destroyed, or the threat will rise again. Which can only be done if you recite the Incantations to Uxaar. From there, I will do what needs to be done."

"You'll make sure Oren makes it out alive?"

"Don't underestimate how much I care for him. I love Oren more than you could imagine. The same goes for every human in the Dusk realm. I would do whatever it takes to save them from Uxaar's grasp. Your mind is clouded with Darkness because of your human nature, it fills you with doubts that you must cast aside."

"Is that why I'm here? To get rid of my Darkness?" I ask. "Now that I'm no longer hidden, there's no use for it."

"Precisely. You must lay on the altar and eliminate the Dark nature within you. Then you will be completely in touch with our power. The power I've been using within you all along that you couldn't understand. You will understand and be able to control it. Your eyes will be open to what you must do to stop Uxaar and the Incantations. That is, if you are willing to trust me, yourself?"

I'm afraid, yet I've come this far. I must trust that I'll be fine, that Oren and every soul trapped in the Darkness will be free.

She's the one who spoke to me when I was lost, guiding me with signs and using nature to protect me. She also gave me a purpose to fulfill. I'm fortunate that I even got to live those eighteen years. After all, I was supposed to die as an infant. That was all the time I should've been allotted. The Light is the reason I'm alive. Therefore, I owe everything I have, my life, to it.

A tear slips from my eye, the contradiction of me agreeing to this. I want to know what it all means. Regardless, I must surrender myself. "Yes."

An altar is a place where sacrifices are made. In the stories, the individuals who sought purification would offer up their Darkness and their connection to Earth in exchange for eternal life in Secreth. In return, they would experience a life of unparalleled bliss and freedom. However, what did they truly sacrifice? Who would willingly choose to live in Darkness? They didn't miss anything. So, why do I believe I will? I am afraid of change, of letting go, and of surrendering myself to someone else. Despite my attempts to dismiss the identity of Brenda, I still yearn for her desires and grieve the loss of them. I had always desired a long life, envisioning a future with marriage, children, and love. I longed for countless more adventures, yet I fear that my time is drawing to a close. When I lie upon the altar, it feels like my deathbed or even a coffin. Despite my emotions, I am not dying yet. I still have one final objective, one final sacrifice to make in the Dusk realm.

My spirit invokes the Incantations of Light to purge me of the Darkness. I'm consumed by a radiant light, experiencing an internal fire that doesn't cause pain but rather a sense of relief and tranquility. The overwhelming thoughts that had consumed me dissipate, replaced by the echo of the altar breaking beneath me. I no longer require the altar for purification. The knowledge and power of the Light is at last accessible in my mind. I'm the embodiment of the altar, and I must undertake the journey to vanquish the Shadow Incantations forever more.

22 *Oren*

The sky is sunny and partly cloudy. The gloomy weather that followed my departure from Seren would be more fitting—reflecting the storm brewing within me. It would mirror the rage that would lash out at anyone in Uxaar's path. The radiant sky appears too optimistic, almost as if it holds a glimmer of hope. Perhaps it means Syann would arrive and prevent any harm I could ensue, or she would save me and still accept me despite my actions. However, this false hope is a dangerous illusion that I can't afford. I had allowed myself to hope before, and it had brought me unfathomable happiness from Syann. But somehow, Uxaar had twisted that joy into guilt and heartbreak—the deepest pain I ever beheld. I lost her, and the health I had believed I had gained. Everything Syann gave me is gone, proving that my distorted mindset was right. If I had never allowed myself to hope before or indulged my desires with Syann, would I be suffering this severely now? It would have been worth avoiding the more profound pain that false hope entails, not to mention the anguish I must be causing Syann. That's the crux of the matter. That's why

I concealed myself from her for all those years in the first place, to protect her. My arrogance in believing I could find happiness with her was now shattering her heart and mine.

Dark smoke billows from the rubble I stand amidst. This was my home, everything I knew before Syann came along. Now, my family is also homeless, unless they've managed to hide more than I could possibly fathom. Did they have a plan? A place to stay? Are they safe?

Even if I grieve or miss them, I will never properly bid them farewell. The thought of never seeing Elouise again under the circumstances we left off is jarring. She was all I had before Syann came into my life. Elly was my best and only friend for so long, and this is how I repay her.

I can't help but wonder what has become of my family. Where is Syann? If Roe was truly trustworthy, Philip must have freed her. I need her to stop me now! If she doesn't appear, I'm afraid of what's to come.

Smoke behind me crackles and hisses, a noise I've grown to despise and even fear. Instinctively, I want to close my eyes and detach myself from the blue hue that engulfs me, but I can't even do that. I have no control over my fate. The noise ceases, but I remain still.

"Uxaar. Let the boy go before things get worse." It's the voice of Roe. My father has become like me, with eyes that aren't his and speaking the tongue of another. Roe has taken over them. The green-eyed Geron knows I'm far gone. He was right to address me by Uxaar's name.

A hateful sneer spreads across my face, and words form that aren't mine. "You intend to fight me if I don't?"

"I'd prefer diplomacy before violence."

"Diplomacy!" I cackle. "We're far past that! We're at war, Roe! We've been in it for centuries! And I'm still struggling to see why you have chosen the wrong side at the height of it! You have the power to take control of the humans with Philip! To claim this world and never be powerless again! Instead, you want to sentence the Geron to death!"

"As traitors of the Light should! My mind is made, Uxaar!"

"Unfortunately, so is mine, and it would seem our desires don't align!"

"I'm not letting you destroy this realm!"

"Well, then, try and stop me!"

Philip growls and lunges at me. Uxaar refuses to let me bear it. Instead, I disappear and reappear in the town square. To my right stands the well from Byron's funeral ceremony. Regrettably, all around it are townsfolk who will soon become victims. They scatter and cry out in a chaotic commotion.

A surge of Darkness emanates from me, as powerful as I felt it when I attacked the civilization of the Dawn. Seren will meet the same fate. Who can stop me? I fear Roe can't, and even more so, I fear for Philip's life. I have no desire for more casualties or blood on my hands!

The energy blasts toward the well, obliterating it and transforming its remnants into a geyser. Boiling water erupts meters high from the site, drenching numerous people who are unable to flee swiftly enough, resulting in their being splashed by the scalding water. Their anguished screams reveal the excruciating pain they are experiencing as their flesh burns.

"Seren falls today!" Uxaar roars through me.

"You have to go through me first!" Roe's voice booms from behind. When I turn, I meet a fist to my face. The pain in my nose is enough to make me wince and recoil back.

"You think Philip enjoyed that? Punching his only son in the face! What happened to you wanting not to inflict pain on the humans?" A smile stretches across my face. A familiar red drips from my right nostril to my lips.

"I'm doing what is necessary to stop you from it!" Roe shouts through Philip, drawing out a sword from his sheath. "Philip knew what he signed up for when he said the Incantations. The boy, however, got none!"

"You're right. Ebony made it for him!" I speak for Uxaar.

"You gave her no choice!" Philip charges at me with a sword in hand. I retaliate with my sword, carved of Dawn Core crystal. His sword is forged of ordinary steel. It makes sense that Uxaar didn't give his followers swords that weren't immune to Darkness. Doing otherwise would allow them a chance to overthrow the Shadow like Philip is trying to do now.

I thrust my foot into Philip's gut. He doubles back and recovers with a countering blow—kicking my feet from under me. Mid-fall, Uxaar materializes me midair and drops me on Philip's shoulders. I presume Uxaar intended for Philip to fall upon impact, but only his knees buckle under the weight of me. I latch on to Philip's head with one arm and keep my sword pointed at his neck with the other. Before I could deliver the killing blow, Philip grasps my hand, grappling against my grip on the sword. My father is undoubtedly stronger than me, which is why Uxaar makes me vanish along with the sword.

I reappear facing the geyser. Between the eruption and me, Philip charges toward me. Uxaar is up to the challenge of combat. We clash our swords yards away from the well, neither side yielding.

Uxaar loses patience with the simple slashing of swords. Mid-swing, I use my other hand to grab Philip's hand gripping his sword.

Keeping his hand out of action is a struggle. He combats against my grip. I attempt to strike Philip with the sword in my left hand. However, Philip anticipates my offensive moves and grabs my hand before the blade can pierce through. Instead, the sword remains at the surface of his skin, drawing blood and causing him to groan. Nevertheless, it fails to weaken him. We are locked in a struggle that, if Uxaar doesn't intervene, I will eventually lose. We are holding each other's arms back, and it may not be long before Philip draws my blood. Overwhelmed by pain,

I burst out as my wings return to my back, releasing all the tension within me. I am propelled into the air and hurl Philip toward the boiling uprising of water. Before he can come into contact with what could have been his watery grave, Philip vanishes.

My wings vanish, and I plummet to the ground with an unusually stoic demeanor, my fist slamming into the earth with a deafening impact. The force of Darkness surging into the ground induces an earthquake, causing numerous buildings to bow beneath the force of the tremors. The distant screams that echo through the air haunt me.

"Uxaar, stop this!" Roe's voice begs, but where is it coming from?

Uxaar knows where Roe is. I turn left, and Roe is there in his form.

Philip is the one missing now.

"Did Philip need a time-out?" Uxaar patronizes through me, but Roe's retaliation is immediate. Rigid pain radiates through my right shoulder, the same shoulder I had ripped the armor pad off. Philip impales me from behind while the tip of the blade is exposed on my front side.

Uxaar swiftly repositions me to prevent the blade from causing further damage. Blood gushes from the gaping wound on my shoulder, seeping from both sides, I imagine. My vision momentarily dims, and I wonder if I'll faint.

Now, I face Philip, who is drenched and looks at me with panicked blue eyes. I can't tell if his wound has healed, but Roe must have teleported him to the pools. He didn't waste any time striking me on the shoulder when he returned.

"You're as destructive as I am, Roe. Give in to it," Uxaar says.

Philip shakes his head. His eyes flash green as Roe retakes him. "I won't!"

A gleam in his eye catches my gaze. It's not the usual glow a Geron gives someone's eyes—tears well within them. Philip is as tormented as I am. "I have to stop you, whatever it takes!"

"Stop me?" Uxaar laughs out of me. "It's too late! The work has already begun. Do you seriously think I came alone? I have many undercover followers in this town. You know this, Philip! You were part of the attack here! You were my spokesman on that stage! They've already gone to gather the helpless in this town. The victims will assume a good shepherd is helping them. Instead, they're cornered to be fed by the wolves. Others are reciting the Incantations as we speak. To spread out into new lands to begin the mass destruction! You will die along with everyone else in this miserable world!—Unless you take this opportunity of mercy I'm giving you. You take Philip and go, warn Syann, or do whatever pleases you, but you can't beat me, Roe! Why kill the man trying?"

"Who's the one that's bleeding out right now?" Roe asks.

"Oh, spare me! His blow was hardly fatal! Philip missed to spare Oren. You both hope to save him, which is foolish. He should have aimed for the chest while he could have!"

Flames rise on the opposite end of town. Buildings topple in the fire. Unfortunately, I believe what Uxaar says. I can't be the only Shadow.

Philip retracts his weapon as he rushes toward me to fistfight. Immediately, I draw my sword to pierce his abdomen. Philip dodges the attempt before grabbing my right arm. He squeezes at my wound before using his knee to jab my stomach. I get no time to defend myself before his other fist barges into my nose. I drop my sword after the blow, which clangs on the ground. While Uxaar tries to recover me, Philip uses his grip on my wound to sling me to the ground.

Roe's voice booms out from Philip. "Enough!" He retrieves his weapon and commandingly points it toward me. Philip stomps on my wound, so hard that spots overtake my vision.

"You said to aim for the chest!? Because that won't be a problem." Philip raises his sword shakily above my pinned body. Philip's wavering countenance exposes Roe's thought process. Neither wants to kill me, but is it worth letting Uxaar continue?

No! Roe knows that! Roe would kill me even against Syann and Philip's wishes. It's the right thing to do.

The blue leaves my sight, which was the last thing I expected. Uxaar couldn't have left me as an act of surrender—Uxaar has intentionality for everything. This is too easy.

My breaths become surprisingly steady. Through my blinking eyes, I take in the colors. The natural soft blue of the sky shines beyond the billows of flame. I despise blue. I didn't before, but now it's a painful reminder that stirs fear in me as vast as the sky itself.

The redness of my father's hair stands out as vividly as his mesmerizing green eyes. They relentlessly remind me of Syann and the captivating glow of her eyes. If my wishes come true, his eyes might be the last thing I see.

"Go ahead, i-i-i-it's all right." My voice breaks. "Finish it."

A tear strays from my father's cheek as he winds up the sword. A shadowy figure appears behind him, with a sword in hand.

My heart stops. "No!"

It should've been me! How close it was to being that way! I yearned for the relief of a sword piercing my chest, fatally severing my life from me. Philip should've struck me, sending my spirit to decay in the Underealm as it should—yet, Philip's blood is gushing from his back and stomach, contradicting the fact that he held the upper hand moments ago. Perhaps he never did. This entire situation is a game orchestrated by Uxaar. I'm merely a pawn, serving his whims on a platter.

Roe departs Philip's body in a burst of vibrant green emanating from his eyes. The Geron swiftly darts away as Philip tumbles onto me. I roll Philip off to my side, exposing the Shadow that stabbed him from behind to be a girl, no more than twelve years old. She's why Uxaar made me drop the sword. What a cunning snake. Her eyes are fluorescent yellow. Her skin is dark, along with her braided hair. Her blood and dirt stain her clothes. Her left hand is crushed, likely from the earthquake. Her emotions and innocence were exploited by a Geron. What stands out the most are the tears streaming down her face.

My father groans, stealing my attention from the Shadow girl. I sit up, grab Philip, and let his head rest on my lap. He lies in a pool of his own blood, his mouth trickling with the same red and labored gasps.

I can't decide which color is worse, bright blue or deep red. Maybe the deep navy blue that is as mysterious as the night sky or an ocean beneath it. The color of blood behind Uxaar's eyes.

Right now, Uxaar is forcing this moment upon me, and I'm at a loss for how to respond appropriately. I committed a heinous crime—murdering my father in cold blood! The realization of what I've done overwhelms me with a desire to flee, consumed by shame for having caused such a devastating event. However, my internal conflict lies in the guilt that yearns for reconciliation. I could stay with Philip, apologize for my actions, and seek help for him before it's too late—but I know that I'm no help. I'm a curse. My father will die.

Amidst my hesitation, he calls my name as he grasps my wrist. "Oren!" When my eyes meet his, the numbness I felt ceases. Emotion floods my soul, as tears overflow from me. "Son, listen." He grunts. "Syann will save us both. She's in Secreth now. When she returns, Roe is going to explain everything! He'll warn her!"

"You should have killed me while y-y-y could've!" I sob.

He shakes his head as he coughs. He struggles to lift his hand to my face. I help him, holding my hand against it. It feels strange, but I owe this to him. "Syann said you loved horses and could sing like me—and that you could draw. She is-s-said you were wonderful—I'm so gl-glad we g-g-get to speak face-to-face without being under their influence, even if it's just this once. I regret we didn't have more—more of that. I wish I could've b-b-been your dad and g-gotten to see you—grow up…I failed y-y-you, and your mother. I'm so sorry," he admits tearfully. "I'm so sorry, Oren. Forgive me."

"I'm sorry!" I whimper. "Don't go! Pl-l-lease, I can't t-t-take anymore. I-I-I've killed so many p-p-people!"

Philip shakes his head. "She's coming, son, Syann, gonna—she's gonna—" He convulses, his breathing resembles choking. "—save us. She-she loves you…and s-so do—I," he says, as his wound exiles the remaining life out him through one shaking exhale. He's gone.

"Dad?" I whisper to myself. I never imagined I'd address Philip that way. Earlier today, I assumed he was a stranger, a lost friend of Athena's. However, he turned out to be the father I had always longed for, the one who had always fought for me. Although he may not have succeeded, I know he tried. Look where that led him! This is the reward for helping me!

Darkness surges from my hands, belittling his frame into ashes. "No! N-n-n-no!" I stammer, clutching myself as I weep. "I'm s-s-s-sorry. I'm so sorry!" I slide to the gravel on all fours. He was speaking to me moments ago. Philip thrived before he was stabbed. Life is that fragile. I should know that more than anyone, but the truth still taunts me. "Why? Why d-d-d-did he have to die? Wh-why did Kip, T-T-Tobias, my mum, a-a-and my dad h-h-h-have to die!" I sob ferociously. "Let m-m-me die, Uxaar! Pl-pl-please! I don't w-w-want to k-k-kill anymore!"

Your time will come, but I'm not done with you yet.

23 *Syann*

I step into the Dawn realm, where I face a harsh truth—the peaceful atmosphere of Secreth made the news of my death easier to swallow. Without it, the wind is knocked out of me, and fleeting sobs mercilessly drag me to my knees.

How can I convey the profound impact the altar had on me? I feel incomplete, teetering on the edge of wholeness. I yearn to reach the final step to fill the one void that still lingers within me. The compulsion to do so is an irresistible urge. Each passing moment, someone is drowning in darkness, waiting for salvation only I can provide.

It's a weight I must carry, and it's too heavy.

I recall every detail now—the tranquility of Secreth, Uxaar's descent into Darkness, and how his war shattered the peace. Roe solemnly swore to me by oath that he would rectify his mistakes. Subsequently, I exiled the Geron into the Underealm. My long-awaited questions have finally been answered. I am one with the goddess, gaining her memories and powers.

Instead of only my hands glowing, my entire body is

illuminated. More crucially, I understand the path I must take to save those ensnared in the Shadows. I must take on the Darkness within me to protect everyone from its viciousness. If I fail and only sever the Incant bonds from its Shadows, the incantation will still exist and pose a threat. I must annihilate it.

The only obstacle now is getting back to Seren.

Roe and Philip are gone, too. This could only mean one thing—Oren woke up. "Roe! Roe!" I yell through tears. He doesn't reply.

I'm alone, against my wildest wishes. I desperately miss Oren, Stella, and my family. When I need comfort the most, everyone is gone. A sharp cold seeps into my chest. Whatever Roe's up against alongside Philip is more urgent than answering me. Uxaar must have a grasp on Oren again and is wreaking havoc on Seren. A frustrated groan grovels out of me as I force myself into a running stance.

"You're not alone," the Light says within me. The tension in me snaps, and my position of readiness to run melts. "I've always been with you. The Darkness can't blind you from that any longer."

"If the Darkness is gone, why do I feel so broken?" I sob.

"Emotion isn't Darkness. We're capable of sadness when involved in a dark atmosphere. The burden of knowing that the Darkness torments the ones we care for is large. We will feel it until the Darkness is defeated. To do that, you must hurry to Seren. You can catch Floria's group if you make haste."

***

Flight is the fastest way to travel, as I've discovered through many remarkable feats today alone. The star I once followed no longer graces the sky because I've found the Light. Now it dwells within me. Before, the Light and even the creatures within this realm guided me. The trees aided me in capturing Olive, and the dragons came to my rescue. That was all the Light within me assisting me. I couldn't comprehend it then, but now I do.

A few minutes of flight have already revealed the devastation wrought upon the village. Trees and the remnants of homes lie scattered across the landscape. Contrary to expectations, the village is not abandoned—instead, numerous soldiers survey the area. The healing pools are also teeming with people. Floria must have assigned a group of guards to revive the dead and provide medical attention to the wounded survivors of Uxaar's attack.

Floria and the remaining villagers come into view. They're approaching the border of the Dawn itself, the very cave mouth Oren and I had entered earlier today. Oh, how much has changed since then.

The dragon won't be able to pass through the border, so my only option is to travel on foot with Floria's army. However, this plan is contingent on Roe's arrival. If I say the Incantations to Roe, I could reach Seren in an instant. Nevertheless, I can't risk doing this without Roe's knowledge, as it could endanger Philip significantly.

Before I depart, I take in the sights one final time while I'm here. This will be my last expedition into the Dawn realm. I'm certain I'll never forget it. The dragon descends toward the ground to land ahead of the army.

Arrows from the army soar toward us. These arrowheads are crystal and can penetrate deep enough into the dragon's scales to cause pain. The dragon growls and flinches, nearly casting me off. They don't know that I'm on it!

"Don't shoot!" I wave my hands frantically, trying to get their attention. The racket is replaced by my name being called in a variety of tones, ranging from confusion to joy and everything in between. We land ahead of the front lines, where Floria and a few members of the Eleven are standing. "Don't shoot the dragons! They're good creatures!"

Floria holds her hand up toward the crowd, gesturing for them to stop moving. "Syann! You reached the altar." She gapes at my altered appearance. "Why are you here?"

"Oren is already in Seren. If you go, it will be considered an attack, and our oath with Uxaar will be broken. If any of your people came thinking they had sanctuary in Seren, it isn't so."

"You're suggesting that we turn back?"

"I was only warning you. If anyone is willing to continue, Seren will need help with recovering from the destruction there."

Floria hums perplexedly. "Well, then, we will all continue. Everyone who has come along is aware of the risks. The ones who chose to stay behind are providing relief to the victims of the attack. As for us, there is nothing left for us here. The village was destroyed. The best we can do is help another people rise from the ashes, no matter the cost."

"Then I have one more favor to ask. If my plan works, and Oren survives, he doesn't have much left to turn to. The only family he's ever known has betrayed his trust. He may feel he has only you and Athena. You know more than anyone about what he's gone through, Floria. Please be there for him. If no one helps him, I'm afraid he'll harm himself."

Floria nods. "You have my word. Anything else?"

"Is Olive safe? She wasn't recaptured, was she?"

"She's in General Sanyel's custody. We agreed we wanted her far from the action in Seren. Yoli and Amran stayed behind too to help with the relief. When the time is right, we'll send a group to retrieve the survivors left."

"Good, is Athena here?"

"She's in the center lines with Eugene."

"And Kipper, too?"

"I wish I had better news to give you." Floria's face falls.

My heart twists in my chest. Kipper is dead. I gasp sorrowfully. "No!" The thought of a sixteen-year-old child being killed is chilling. Oren forced to do the act is even more disturbing. "The attack?" My lips waver.

Floria nods. "Eugene isn't doing well. Kipper's parents also perished. The concerns you have for Oren, we have for Eugene.

He lost all the family he had left. Athena volunteered to watch him, along with a few guards."

"I'd like to speak with them."

Lucam offers to escort me. As I walk to the central lines, I contemplate how everyone in this crowd relies on me. I'm being stared at, whispered about, and cheered for. My radiant presence is undeniable in this sea of people. They see me as the beacon of hope, the one who will save them.

Seeing Athena safe and free is so surreal that my heart flutters with joy. I had been so worried for her. My feet stride toward her, and I embrace her without a moment's hesitation. It feels like I'm hugging my mother when I do. Everything she had told me was true—I needed to believe in Syann. At the time, I had failed to protect her, but this time, I mustn't fail again.

Her smile is radiant when she lets go to view me. "I knew you'd be all right, Syann!" she cheers tearfully. "Look how beautiful you are."

I smile, though my appearance is the least of my concerns now. "I didn't know that you would be all right! I was so worried when we were separated!"

"All is well with me." Her hands retreat to her chest. "Others here have lost much. Their home, their people, but you will make it right. They have faith in you, just as I do, and Oren is going to be all right. I believe that. Uxaar is not going to win."

I nod, shifting my gaze to Gene on Athena's right. He stares forward, not acknowledging my presence. Surely, Oren is a sore subject for him. Though the details of Kip's death are obscure to me. "Hey, Gene." I step beside him. His silent stare only hardens. A severe burn chars his hand. Why did he not go to the healing pool?

"What happened to your hand?" I ask, but Gene ignores me.

"He won't tell anyone. He refused to go to the pools or let anyone treat it," Lucam whispers to me.

"Let me see it." I offer my hand out.

Gene gazes at my hand before reluctantly extending his. I gently grasp it, focusing on alleviating his pain. As his burn heals, vivid voices and memories of Gene resurface in my mind.

Oren bursts into Gene's house, panicking. Gene tries calming him down, but his hand burns when he brushes Oren. Uxaar takes over Oren at once. Gene calls Oren a traitor, as Oren threatens to kill Kipper. Gene believed I would save them, but Oren annihilated Kipper in a heap of smoke. Gene breaks down in tears, wishing he had left Oren to die instead of helping him. Oren does exactly that to Gene, abandoning him.
"Syann will save us, even if you have to kill us first!"

All the pain he endured, I couldn't prevent. For the greater good, I couldn't stop Oren from killing Kip. Gene's statement of faith back then, which he didn't seem to believe afterward, crushes him. Now, he appears confused that I'm tearful and even more so that I've healed him. Amidst this confusion, there's a sense of peace that wasn't present before.

"H-h-how did you…? You couldn't heal before!"

"I had to go to Secreth to reclaim my powers. That's why I couldn't stop the attack on your home. I'm so sorry. I wish I could have stopped it, but that was what Uxaar wanted. The twister was a diversion to keep me from Secreth! Now that I have my powers, I will stop Uxaar, and afterward, I will save Kip and everyone you lost. That is a promise. Until then, will you believe and stay strong for me?"

Gene's eyes fill with tears. "I'm not strong." He sniffles. "I've always tr-tried to be the tough one, but I'm not! Uxaar took everything from me!"

"Come here." My outstretched arms invite him.

Gene practically jumps into my arms, sobbing in them. "I believe you can s-save them, but it hurts so bad!"

The others around us stare. They likely have never seen this side of Gene. My arms curl him closer to me to shield him from their attention. "I know, it hurts me, too. My heart aches more than you could know."

"I said horrible things to Oren, too! I thought he betrayed us! I had no idea his mum sold him out until Floria told me! Uxaar's been torturing him!"

I wasn't expecting Gene to bring Oren up, much less feel sorry for him. That relieves me. "I'm going to save Oren, too. Uxaar isn't going to win. And one day, this will all be in the past, and we can all move forward from it. Don't give up, Gene, even if it hurts right now."

Gene releases me, and his softened gaze rises toward my eyes. He doesn't smile, but a glimmer of hope illuminates his pupils. I believe he trusts me. "Do you think he'll forgive me?"

"He's going to be more concerned about whether you'll forgive him. I know Oren well enough that he feels guilty over all of this. He could use a friend while I'm gone."

Gene's expression contorts. "What do you mean when you're gone?"

Roe frantically materializes before us. Everyone busts into commotion at the sight of him. I coax the people, persuading them that Roe is on our side. Philip's absence and Roe's distress churn my stomach. If Philip isn't here, that could only mean one thing—"Where's Philip?"

"He was slaughtered in battle! We fought Uxaar with all our might and had Oren pinned, but another Shadow caught us off guard and stabbed Philip from behind. I couldn't transport him to the pools in his condition—therefore he perished! Now Seren is in flames, overrun with Shadows! They are dispersing to other towns and countries! By the time you arrive, there will be nothing left! Not just in Seren, but the realm."

I glance at Athena. The news brings her to tears. Her best friend and her home are gone. The news enrages me. "I must do what I did in the very beginning. I have to say the Incantations to you! There's no time to lose."

"No!" Gene bursts out. He isn't the only one. People murmur opposition all around me. Roe is included.

"Trust me! This is what I must do. You may not understand, but know that I do. The Light created the Geron! Don't think I can't overcome them!"

Athena's concern shifts into a smile. "You can do anything you put your mind to, Syann. Go."

I nod at her. "Athena, thank you." I set my hand on her shoulder, realizing this is goodbye. She doesn't even know it yet. The thought drives me to hug her again. "Next time you see me, everything will be made right. For the time between, while I'm gone, I trust you to encourage those left in Darkness before the Light returns."

She nods into my shoulder, sniffling. "Absolutely."

I turn to Gene. "Gene, you will see me again. I promise. Don't forget what I told you." He nods at my words.

I remember how terrified I was when I said these words the first time. I was desperate to save Sophie and my family. I was counting on Syann to come and rescue me from the Darkness. Who knew the instinct to recite the Shadow Incantations to Roe was from the Light? This time, as I speak them, I'm as scared as before. Numerous lives are on the line. Including my own and the one I love the most.

I'm brought into the stasis where I must choose a Geron. Each one gazes at me with an intense gaze, as if I'm the ultimate prize they're desperate to claim. Unbeknownst to them, this is their downfall. Uxaar is present, and he glares at me the most intensely of all. *You're a fool.*

"Roe!" I call, cutting myself off from the stasis of choosing. When I reawaken, my vision is still colored. Roe hasn't overtaken me yet. I don't think he will unless I ask him to.

"Tell Floria I had to go and to remain on course. By the time you arrive, I should be gone. The people of Seren will need help until I return," I say to Lucam. I don't wait for a response.

***

A blink was all it took for my surroundings to change. The town square is where I find myself. I traveled through the Underealm instantly, thanks to Roe.

Days ago, this place was radiant. Flowers and banners garnished every street corner. Lively people stood as far as I could see. The aroma of sweet florals and baked goods blessed the air.

Seren couldn't be more oppressive now. Every building has surrendered to raging flames. The smell of it is so strong that it forces up coughs. Sounds of screams and gushing water boom over the crackling of flames. The worst of all, the only perceptible people are dead or Shadows.

This was my home. I would have never imagined seeing it this way. Sorrow robs my strength from my knees, and tears tumble down with me. Why? Why did all of this have to happen? To think, this town isn't the only one suffering. Darkness is spreading like a plague throughout this realm.

"You don't ever quit, do you, Roe!" A voice rumbles from behind. "Philip is dead, so you get the goddess herself to say the Incantations to you!" Uxaar's voice storms Oren's lips. This would be the first time I've seen his face like this. His sharp blue eyes are full of spite, hatred, and tears. I would give anything to see his soft brown eyes again, but like me and the Eleven, he's permanently marked. His nose and shoulder bleed, and his freckled cheeks are streaked with tearstains. Oren won't be the only one marked by tears. Seeing him and the devastation evokes tears in me.

"Uxaar, I came to surrender upon an oath," I declare.

Uxaar chuckles out of Oren. "Please, enlighten me on said terms, oh Goddess of Light!"

I bring myself to my feet. "Every single person bound to any Geron is freed. I take their place. You can have my body, exactly what you want."

"That's it? You're going to sacrifice yourself to end it all?"

Uxaar chuckles. "You're far too noble! You have the power to fight without death touching you, yet you're a fool enough to squander it for humanity! You and Roe alike! I shouldn't be surprised, yet even this is a new low for you!"

"Do you accept or deny?" I question harshly.

Uxaar laughs. "I accept!"

A lump forms in my throat as memories of my fond childhood with Oren waltz through my head. I long to talk to that Oren one more time. If only life were so generous. When we trade off, I will die. The last time I will ever speak to Oren is like this— Uxaar controlling him like a puppet.

He will be without me for some time, this version of me forever. I'm afraid he will have difficulty moving on from that. I need to tell him to care for himself, keep going for me, and remember that I love him. If only I had time. I have to trust Floria will arrive in time to help Oren in my place.

"I swear, by the powers of Light and Dark, that I, Syann, will proclaim the Shadow Incantations to every Geron. That is if Uxaar binds to this oath, and every Geron under their charge frees their captive souls in my place."

"I, Uxaar, bound myself to this oath."

The bound oath is completed, and our next actions will be determined by the powers within us. Nausea rises within me. The words that exit me can't be halted or withdrawn.

Take over me,
And set Shadows free,
Use me to make you higher.
In me have your way,
You get the say,
Do with me as you desire.

The stasis realm is vastly different this time. Not only are there Geron but also the spirits they control. There are hundreds of people of all ages and backgrounds, all gazing at me with hunger in their bright eyes, yearning to be saved. Except for Oren, whose eyes are filled with guilt and tears. As the Geron pierce me like arrows into their target, the souls scatter to freedom. When I wake up, everything burns like hellfire. My glowing flesh turns black, and flecks of rainbow color engulf my vision.

Before me lies Oren, sprawled on the ground, the impact of his severed bond evident. His bright blue eyes dart toward me, their sight clouded with shame and terror that I yearn to alleviate. "Syann! No!" He tries rising to his feet, using all the force he has, but that doesn't compensate for his blood loss. "Wh-why? Why? Why w-w-would you do this? Sy! Syann! *Answer me!*" He sobs as he crumbles alongside his world. "P-p-p-please!"

I crave more than anything to soothe him, but the words are all stuck in my mind. My trembling lips can only manage screams of agony.

Dark recollections of the Shadows haunt my mind, the atrocities they inflicted on their homes and people. Uxaar subjected Oren to countless afflictions. If Floria doesn't find him in time, he'll die. Either he'll bleed out or destroy himself first. He's dangerously close to that fate now. If Oren rises and touches me, the smoke emanating from me will obliterate him. I'm exerting every ounce of my strength to withhold the Geron's power to protect him. The only course of action left for me now is to surrender.

Finish me, Roe, so my spirit can pass on.

It was an honor to fight by your side, Syann. Goodbye, my goddess.

This is our demise. Roe has chosen his side long ago, and there's no way to undo his fate. Humans, on the other hand, possess the ability to embrace both Darkness and Light. For the Geron, it's a choice. Once that decision is made, the corruption becomes irreversible.

Roe must dwell in the Underealm forever.

Oren rushes toward me, crying my name out as I fade away.

I pray Floria and her people get here soon enough to rescue Oren, and that in another life we'll meet again—the life my soul and spirit will live confidently as Syann, the Goddess of Light.

The Light among the Shadows

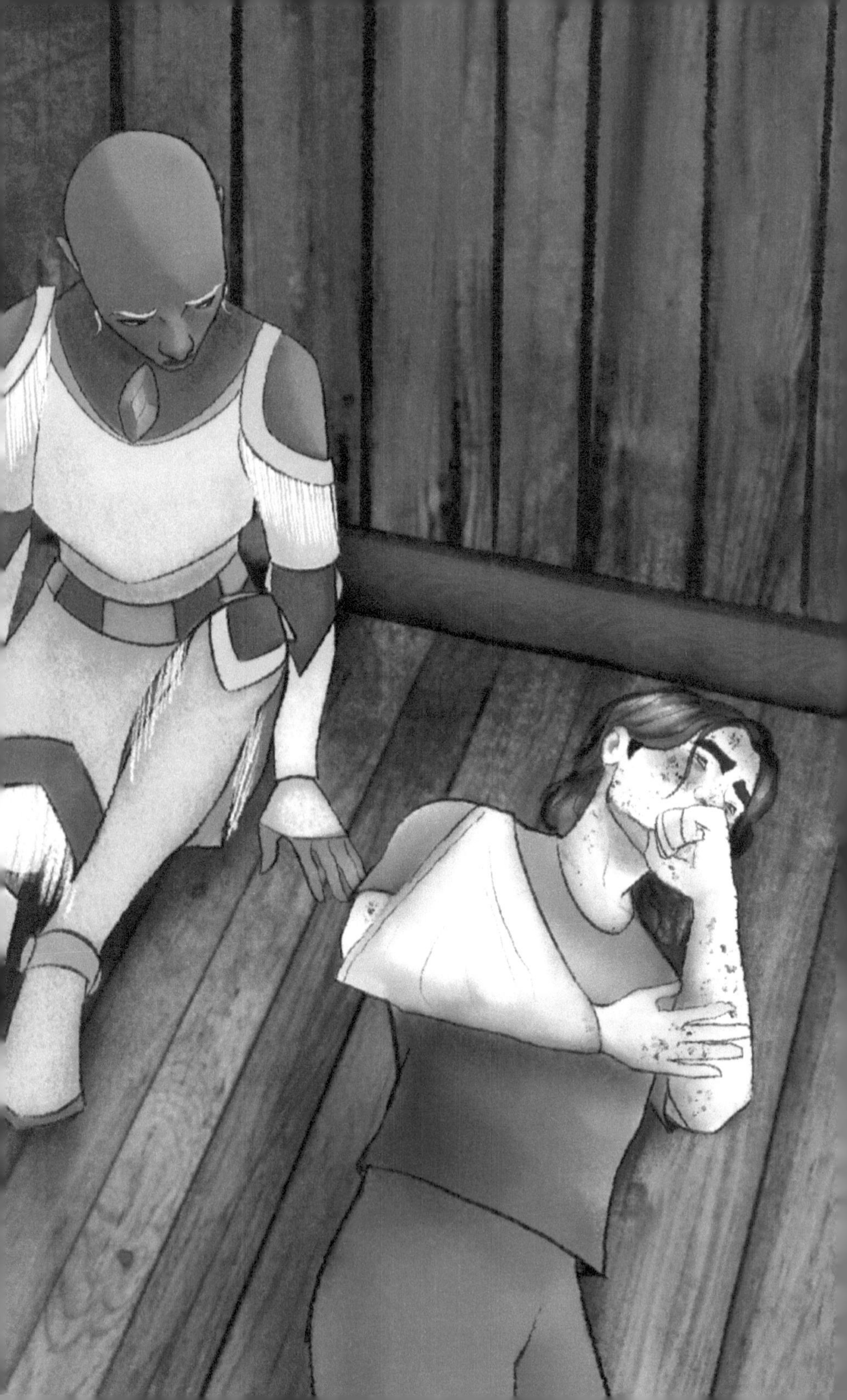

24 Oren

Syann deserved every blessing the realms had to offer her, yet she surrendered everything. She paid the price to repair my wrongdoings, to rescue the souls tethered to the Geron. Shrills of hundreds of Geron fled her as her flesh was scorched into ashes. All that's left of Syann now is her empty armor and ash blowing in the wind. There was nothing I could do to thwart her death. If there was, I would have done anything. There would be no question, even if I had to suffer endlessly to save her.

I state that as if I'm not suffering endlessly already.

My heart is too sick for me to lift myself off the ground. It's my hideaway from the atrocity this town turned out to be. My shame is too immense to confront anybody. This will be my place until my wound has no more bloody tears to cry. This is a sentence worthy of a murderer.

How did life become this way? In my wildest dreams, life would never be this horrid. All those years, rotting in my room, only scratched the surface of the anguish that has passed today. Back then, I was a purposeless burden, yet at least I wasn't physically hurting anybody. Only I was dying inside.

Now, my soul feels lifeless and devoid. Uxaar has vanished from my being, leaving me with fragmented thoughts and memories that I can't comprehend. Am I still the same person I once was? Or is my mind merely a reflection of what Uxaar left behind? Have I ever truly thought for myself? Did I genuinely love Syann? Do I harbor feelings of pity or hatred toward my parents? Or was Uxaar manipulating these emotions for his own amusement and entertainment?

Well, I currently love Syann deeply and miss her more than anything. She's the reason my weeping persists. As a child, I adored her before Uxaar discovered that Brenda was Syann. That signifies something. My feelings for her are an integral part of me, regardless of their origin. I cherished her above all else and everyone else.

Loud wailing and a desperate calling of names fills the air. It's possible that a mother is searching for the child I killed. There are countless possibilities for the voice and its origin, but the outcome remains the same—someone is deeply grieving on my account.

Smoke pollutes the air I breathe, transforming my cries into strangled coughs. Helplessly, I choke between them, each one intensifying my pain. I'm slipping away. Potentially, I'm perishing sooner than I thought.

***

Where am I? Hard ground supports my limp body. Perhaps I haven't moved? No, the floor is smooth, chilly, and wooden. I'm no longer in my armor, either. Soft clothing loosely swaddles my legs, abdomen, and arms. Bandages squeeze around my ribs while a sling cradles my right arm.

I find myself in a cabin, far from isolation, where at least twenty wounded people cram this space. All are victims of the destruction of Seren. Many of them have glowing eyes, a sign that the Geron had once corrupted them, while a few eyes retain their natural dimness. What unites them all is the overwhelming terror that radiates from each pair of eyes.

I shouldn't be here. If anything, I should be in custody, not hospitalized. There's been a mistake. Whoever brought me here must not know who I am, that I started all this.

Floria, she's here! The gasp that leaves me doesn't go unnoticed by her. She approaches me, crouching to my level. "Oren, how are you feeling?"

I wish to forget the events that make me feel how I do, or I wish all that occurred these past twenty-four hours was only an intense nightmare. Sure, it would still stick with me if it was only a dream, but this reality is one everybody must live with. I shake my head, turning toward the wall.

Floria doesn't accept that answer. She sits beside me. "I can imagine, not well. You're not the only one who's had Uxaar hijack their head. It's traumatic. Not to mention your wound—if we hadn't found you sooner, you would have bled out."

Her eyes terrify me. I can't bear to peek at them. They only remind me of Uxaar's eyes. That monster ruined my life by ending Syann. "Syann—died," I whisper. Tears raid my eyes.

"You think she's really gone?" Floria questions. For a split second, her words convince me Syann's death was all a nightmare. However, my skipping heart drops as she continues speaking. "The Light will never be gone. We haven't seen the last of her. We don't know why Syann sacrificed herself, but I'm sure she had a purpose that we simply can't comprehend."

I watched her die. Darkness devoured her and left her ashes as crumbs. As much as I wish to believe that I haven't seen the last of her, I won't be fool enough to hope again.

Floria sighs at my prolonged silence. "There are people in the square who want to see you."

I'm led outside to discover I'm still in Seren. The house I was in is one of the two left standing on this street. The smoke has cleared, and the fire, once raging, is deceased. It's dim out here as it was in the cabin. Judging by the pink tone of the sky, sunset is soon.

Floria escorts me to the town square, which is surprisingly crowded. Liam stands by the dried-up well, conversing with numerous villagers. Now that the Geron were exposed here and their curse ended, is Liam distressed about Syann, too? After all, he should remember her now.

He can't possibly miss her as much as I do.

This spot only reminds me how I lost her, and I yearn to evade the memories that hunt my mind down. Philip is as vivid as real life, half grinning in a pool of blood as his last breath flees him. He became ash like Syann did. Her screams boom louder and louder, deafening all the noise around me.

I'm bewildered when Elouise's voice scatters my thoughts. Behind her are her mum and Jace. I can't say their approach brings me pleasure. As for Elouise, I missed her terribly. That doesn't mean I wanted us to cross paths again. I never thought we would, but I somehow survived Uxaar.

How can I pick up where we left off? I can't forgive myself for how I've affected her life so negatively. The last thing I want is to make things worse.

I wish it were as easy for me as it was for her. She rushes to me, hugging me without a hesitant thought. Her constricting my injured arm makes me wince, but my emotions are far more pained by her hold.

I can't bring myself to hug her back. I don't deserve it.

She sobs into my chest, seeking my comfort. Why? I'm the one who made her cry and caused all her problems. Maybe that's why I should attempt to fix them. I owe her that, yet it would have been better if I had never been there. Would that be for the best now, too?

"I thought you were gone!"

"…Me too." I mutter hesitantly. It's the most neutral thing I could say. I can't tell her that I'm happy I survived or that I'm here for her. She would be heartbroken.

"I'm so sorry for what happened to you!" She peeks at me with pitiful eyes that pierce me. "I didn't know, I swear! They lied to me, too!"

I shake my head. "I'm s-s-sorry. I'm so sorry, Elly."

"No! Oren, mind none of the facts. You're still my brother, always. You're more family to me than anyone could be. You didn't lie to me all those years! You were always there for me! Nothing has to change between us, right?"

I retreat from her embrace, unsure how to answer her. How could nothing change? Everything is different now! "Forgive y'r m-m-mum and Jace. They did it t-t-t-to protect you from me. They were right to disregard me f-f-f-for your sake. They are your family."

"Is that your way of saying no?" Elouise fusses as if I've betrayed her. I'm protecting her!

The thought of severing ties with her forms tears in my eyes. She was the closest thing I ever had to family. "You're b-b-better off without me."

"You're lying to yourself! Family sticks together! We stick together!"

"Elly, I'm sorry. I-I-I-I love you, but I can't go back home after that—but you m-m-must." I can't bear to face the rejection in her eyes any longer. How is she naïve enough to think things can snap back to the way they once were? It's impossible! Without another word, I turn to run away.

Slam!

I was oblivious that Athena was standing behind me. She flinches back and grabs my arms to prevent me from trampling her. She says something, but all I can comprehend are the eyes of the boy standing beside her, the eyes that witnessed me killing his best friend. The sight of Gene instantly drains the air from my lungs, and I instinctively dart in the opposite direction, just as I had before. This time, Jace swiftly reaches out and grasps my good arm, restraining me with an iron grip.

"Please l-l-let me go!" I gasp for air.

Jace doesn't answer me. Instead, he speaks to the bystanders that are now watching us. "He's in shock." That's what Gene said before Kip died. Dark fumes overtook him. Gene said he wished I was dead. I wish I was.

I might suffocate. "Jace, please!" Jace doesn't release me.

All eyes are on me when I glance up. It's overwhelming. Instincts lead me to shield my face with my hands. The panic steals the strength from my knees. If I can't run, I'll hide. The ground is my safest place. It held me and caught each tear I cried before. I wish I could dig deeper into it. It would be even better if it could swallow me for good.

I expect Jace to slip degrading comments, but he follows me to the ground. Oddly, his large, rough hand rubs my arm to comfort me. I want him to stop and everyone to abandon me, but it's as if I'm a magnet luring them in. There's so much presence radiating around me. They give words that were intended to encourage me, but my soul rejects them.

Jace tells me to stand in a surprisingly kind tone. Maybe he even pities me, for once. I'm not cooperative. I only stand when my noncompliance leads to causing a scene. The last thing I want is for everyone in the town square to watch Jace drag me against my will.

Floria decides to take us all for a walk, which includes me, Jace, Elouise, Valerie, Athena, and Gene. Several of them try to engage me in conversation, but after my disinterest, Jace shuts them down.

Walking requires me to watch where I'm going, making the sights of the wreckage unavoidable. There are Dawn soldiers and civilians scattered around town. I overhear they're searching for the wounded to save.

Athena's stables, once a symbol of pride, now lie in ruins, a heap of burned rubble like everything else in town. The pain in Athena's and Elouise's eyes is palpable, and the number of memories they hold here is immeasurable. She's shared countless stories of her years here, from researching the lore of Secreth with Athena to cooking and tending to the horses together. Of course, there are also memories left unsaid, too.

Even the one memory of this place I have is worth mourning. My reunion with Moo was surreal. At that moment, I felt like a child again, ready to take my horse for a ride in the farmlands. All of that is gone, like the childhood I held dear. As for the other horses, they're either dead or on the run. I'm envious of the creatures for that. I deserved that fate, not them.

We sit against the fence around town. Beyond it is the expanse of green, reflecting the sunset's glow. It will be dark soon. So why are we out here? I'm not concerned enough to ask. I'm more tempted to run again now that Jace has released me. My arm throbs from the blood rushing through it.

"Oren. We're all here for you." Athena breaks the silence. "You don't have to keep the horrors to yourself. We are a safe place. You can tell us anything. Believe me, bottling it all up will do no good."

The words were intended as a sweet gesture, but they frustrate me. I've never felt truly safe here. I thought I did, but two of the few people I trusted deceived me. To survive, they had to. You could say they're trustworthy for keeping that secret for eighteen years, or that they did whatever it took to keep us alive, regardless of the impact on me. My conflicting bitterness is evident. The only safe places I've ever known—my grandparents and Syann—have all passed away. Elouise is an exception, but I'm more harm than good to her. She shouldn't trust me.

"He doesn't feel safe," Gene says. "How could you?" *How could you kill Kip?* This is how I process his question. I immediately apologize. *I'm sorry*, the first two words I've said since my conversation with Elouise. I surprise everyone with my words. I processed his question wrong. He was asking how I could feel safe. "Sorry for what?" Gene asks.

"Everything." My eyes retreat downward. "Y-y-you were r-r-right. You should've lef' me t-t-to die."

"No, I didn't mean that!" He blurts out the words in panic, before a forced sigh slows him down. "At the time, I thought you chose to say the Incantations and betrayed us. It wasn't until the Eleven returned with Athena that I found out what really happened. With everything you explained to Kip and me at our house, it made so much sense how you couldn't overcome your grief. Of course, you couldn't! You were possessed by Darkness your whole life. So, I'm glad, even if it was for just a bit, that I could help pick you up. I still want to help you and be your friend. It's what Kip would've wanted."

I don't know how to respond to that. I was convinced Gene hated me and was terrified of him. Is he really forgiving me?

"Oren," Valerie speaks up. "You didn't hurt anyone. Uxaar threw us in a bind that neither of us wanted a part of. Regardless, I didn't treat you as one of my own like I agreed to. My fear distanced me, and I lied so my family would survive. I'm so sorry to you and Elouise. Neither of you deserved any part of it. There's no taking back what happened, and I'm not asking for your forgiveness. I only ask that you forgive yourself. If you need someone to blame for your pain, you can blame me!"

"He showed me how I was—was brought t-t-to you." I refuse to say Uxaar's name. "How he killed—how he-he killed—" I fail to form Tobias's name. "You and Jace had every r-r-r-r-reason to despise me!" Tears brim my eyes. I can't keep them from falling. "I-I-I-I can't hate you f-f-for lying to me. You did it-t-t-t to protect Elly—Th-th-that's all that mattered."

Syann's voice in the back of my head argues that I do matter. Because of her, I once did.

"It was a twisted situation," Jace speaks up. "One I handled harshly. I took out my rage on you when you were only a victim of Uxaar, too. You weren't the monster, Oren. I'm sorry for making you feel otherwise." He turns toward Elouise, who sits by

Athena. "Elouise, I want to apologize to you as well. I hope you know that I love and value you immensely. I only wanted to keep you safe. I see now that my overbearing behavior strained our relationship, and I falsely blamed Oren for it. I was jealous that you got along with him better than you did with your biological brother. I felt that the bond we were supposed to have was sabotaged, and I wasn't allowed to tell you how I felt until now—There was so much I was forced to hide from you, and I'm sorry for all of it. I hope one day you both can forgive me."

I glance at Elouise, who passively nods her tearstained face. I yearn for her to accept the apology with open arms. She deserves to feel happy and accepted within her own family. As for me, the apology is hard to swallow. I don't doubt its sincerity, but could Jace and I ever be friends? He's always made me feel belittled. How will I overcome that? Ultimately, he deceived me with a lie that I believed for my entire life. He had to, but it hurt. He could have been kinder to me.

"It was a twisted situation as Jace put it," Athena follows up, holding Elouise's arm. "It's good we all get to talk it out after being unable to for so long. I know there's a lot of emotional walls built here, and it's going to take time. However, it's good we started here and now."

The conversation soon shifted to Floria providing us with updates on our community's next steps. In the morning, a group will set out to the farmlands for shelter, where Seren's rebuild will commence. Liam intends to remain behind until the final group of people departs and the evacuation is complete. As for tonight, we sleep under the stars.

I'm left to process everything. From our conversation earlier to going back to the farmlands—the land of my past. Everything that made it great is gone—my grandparents, Syann, and Moo. All that's left is the residue of memories I can never relive again.

My thoughts make me restless, and Jace and Gene sleep close by my side—I'm used to sleeping alone and can't help but feel like

I'm being guarded, especially since Floria has been awake this entire time. There's also this wound in my shoulder that's impossible to lie on. I'm left with the single option of lying on my left side. The fact that I can't roll around manifests my restlessness through a spreading panic in my chest.

When I eventually drift off to sleep, the horrid events of today reappear in my dreams. I see Kip fading away, Gene screaming at me that he hates me, my mother's anguish, my father's blood, and Syann's final cries. Not only does this nightmare jolt me awake, but the screams that emanate from me rouse everyone around me. They surround me, incessantly asking if I'm all right or what I dreamt. These questions I refuse to answer with anything but nodding or shaking my head. It turns out to be a ten-minute ordeal before everyone finally returns to sleep, except for me. It's as if I'm sixteen again, when my nightmares were consistently so horrible that I feared sleep. Now, at eighteen, there's no peace anywhere. Not when I'm awake, asleep, in silence, or even in conversation. This realization drives my mind to a dark place. There's one place I haven't dared to try and find peace. The solution I've been yearning for since I realized my identity—death.

Everyone is asleep now, so I can escape if I'm cautious. I wait at least an hour before venturing off. My eyes yearn for one of the two killers in Athena's stables—a rope or a blade. I spot a rope first—one that once guided a horse and its rider. Now, it will be a lifeline between me and death. It's charred from the fire, but it will suffice. From here, I will venture far into the vast, silhouetted expanse of the distant forest. In those woods, I will end my life. I will truly experience death firsthand rather than serving it to others. The Underealm will mete out the punishment I deserve.

"Oren!" A sharp whisper resounds throughout the wreckage. *No. I was followed.*

Behind me, Floria glares at me with those blue eyes. Uxaar's eyes stare me down. Does looking into my eyes scare her, too, or is she used to it? A thousand years of her reflection could have done that. Maybe it still haunts her all the same. Maybe her heart is beating as fast as mine.

"Oren! What are you doing?"

"I c-c-c-couldn't sleep." I can't admit the truth. She'll tell everyone.

"What were you going to do with the cord?" She gestures toward the rope in my hands. I don't answer. "Hmm?"

I was going to hang myself in the woods.

I don't have to tell her. The answer is fleeting in my eyes. Regardless, Floria expects a confession.

I want to run, but it would have to be a dream for me to outrace Floria. I lean against the charred doorway to hide. It shifts under my weight, failing to conceal me. In a fit of rage, I thrust the damaged supports to the ground and hurl the rope across the scene.

Shame tramples me for losing my temper in front of her. Shudders leave me, ones so loud they could strangle me in place of the rope. All the strength in my legs goes, and I collapse. Ugly, coarse sobs run through my throat. "Floria, pl-please let me die." My plea is soft. I don't know if she heard it.

Floria approaches, unfazed by my actions. "I know more than any other what you're going through. We solely share something agonizing, Oren. Uxaar mutilated us and twisted us into monsters, leaving us feeling broken and unworthy of anything good. Learning to overpower Uxaar's mindset is the hardest task of coping because it can't be done alone. It requires constant reassurance and resilience from people who care for you, which is difficult to accept when you feel like you're a burden to everyone around you. It leaves you feeling trapped in a battle that you want no part in, so you think the only way out is dying."

"You t-t-tried, too?" I mumble, tilting my eyes upward.

"I did more than try. The boy who Uxaar experimented with alongside me, Pollus"—she bites her lip, as if the name hurts to say—"dragged my corpse to the pools because he knew I was worth more than what Uxaar made me. Because Pollus chose to save me that day, he saved you, too."

Floria's voice is sorrowful. I can only imagine Pollus died. Wouldn't he have been a member of the Eleven if not? Supposedly, he was killed like Gene's dad, or maybe one day he succumbed to the anguish the Geron left him with.

"What if—if I don't want to be saved?"

"That's why it's so important now more than ever that you surround yourself with people who want to save you. The voices in your head are going to wound you and make you believe that you are only what Uxaar made you, but that version of you is dead. Don't allow it to live on inside you. You must let that version of yourself go and see yourself as someone new. There's no relief in suicide. It will send you straight to the Underealm where pain is unimaginable. I felt far greater pain than I ever did after my death. In the Underealm, I faced Uxaar again, where he mocked and terrorized me until Pollus brought me back. If you choose to take your life, Uxaar will undoubtedly do the same to you. Is that what you really want?"

It's hard to believe there is pain I can't imagine. Even if Uxaar tormented me for eternity, I couldn't cause anyone on this side any more misery. Still, Floria is right. I don't want to see Uxaar again. The sight of Floria's eyes sends clamps into my chest. I can only imagine what seeing Uxaar's would do to me. There's no peace or escape.

Distant footsteps crunch through the hay. I'm afraid of who it is joining us, so I hide my face.

"Your family is here. Don't shut them out," Floria tells me.

"Oren!" It's Elouise. My heart sinks. Elouise was never meant to discover this. She was supposed to believe I had vanished and forgotten about me, but I'm an idiot for even considering that! She would tirelessly search until she found my remains.

I wasn't thinking about Elouise at all when I ran away. My

heartache clouded my judgment, preventing me from focusing on my goal of protecting her. It convinced me that protecting her meant abandoning her. If I vanished, it would devastate her.

"Floria, what happened?" Jace asks. "Elouise woke me up crying that Oren was gone."

"That's right."

"Oren, what's wrong?" Elouise sits in front of me. Jace follows behind her but remains standing. They both witness the absolute spectacle I've turned out to be. I don't want to admit I was going to leave them behind.

I bury my face into my knees, squeezing my eyes shut. "You'll h-h-h-hate me," I sob. "Y-you already sh-sh-should!"

"There's nothing you could say or do to make me hate you, Oren. Please tell me what's going on. Please don't keep shutting me out."

Your family is here, don't shut them out.

Floria isn't going to speak for me. I must.

I sniffle. "I-I was, um—was gonna—end m-m-my life," I admit through defeated sobs.

"You made an attempt on your life?" Jace's voice booms out. I refuse to look up or answer him. However, my silence answers well. "What have I done?" Jace whispers to himself. "This is why you've been trying to run? Suicide, Oren?" Jace asks condescendingly, but I can tell it's out of a place of fear instead of anger. "Why? Why would you do that? To you or us?"

"…Us? J-Jace y—hated me! Wh-wh-what difference does it m-m-make to you? I was a burden! I still am to everyone a-a-and myself! I wanted everyone to b-b-be free! It would be b-b-better if I was dead!"

"Oren!" Elly's voice elevates through a dismayed cry. "You-you would be sending yourself into the-the-the Underealm! Right back to Uxaar! How is that better?" I won't look at her, but the crack in her voice tells me I'm making her cry. I'm so horrible, so self-absorbed.

"Syann's down there! A-a-alone!" My lips quiver intensely. "Suffering for my sins! I-I can't live with that! I-I-I can't! I'm s-s-so sorry!"

Jace grasps my good shoulder. "Oren, look at me! Breathe."

I barely comply. My breath is hard to keep up with.

"I'm truly sorry, from the depths of me, I am, about Syann and for how I made you feel. I know forgiveness is much to ask for after how I treated you. I'll be honest, I resented you, heavily. I felt restrained, that I couldn't live the life I wanted because Uxaar had a target on my family. I couldn't bring myself to marry or travel as I desired because I couldn't leave Mum alone in that situation. She needed me to take care of her and be the man of the house. I never once considered your feelings, only my own and what I had to sacrifice. Now I see how harmful that was to you and Elouise. She doesn't want you gone! She needs you! You are part of our family. I know, it's broken and wrecked, but that doesn't mean we give up on repairing it. I'm not going to give up on it. Each time you run away, we will keep on after you because we aren't better off without you! I was wrong! I was dead wrong, Oren. I was horrible to you and Elouise!" Jace's countenance is humbled by sympathy that drags his facial features into depths that are foreign to me.

"You don't have to run away at all! Like Athena said, we're here for you. Like you were always there for me!" Elouise adds. I finally muster the courage to shift my gaze to her, and as I suspected, wet trails of sorrow pave her face. After all this time of staying alive for her, I almost caved in.

"I tr-tr-tried to leave you. I told myself I n-n-never would, but I was weak—I-I-I am weak!" I whimper out. The weight of all the guilt became too much, and it only gets heavier. Now I must account for the pain I'm causing my cousins now. All while Syann's death relapses in my mind repeatedly. I wish she were here now. She'd know what to say.

"If you feel too weak to carry everything you're carrying,

Oren, instead of giving up, why not seek help? I've always been willing to help you!"

"Guilt," I answer Elouise.

"About Syann?"

I nod, breaking out in a sob.

"I'm so sorry." Elouise readjusts herself to sit beside me. I'm unsurprised she could tell what was disturbing me. "Athena told me how close you both became. Syann showed you the deepest kind of love by saving you."

"May I add," Floria says, "the last thing Syann told me before she left was to look after you. She didn't want you to face the aftermath alone, because she knew you couldn't do it that way. She wants you protected and cared for. Your connection to Uxaar never changed her perception of you."

"Or for any of us, for that matter!" Elouise smiles softly. "Uxaar is to blame for everything. You are innocent. Uxaar may not have let you think that, but he's gone now. It's time you start thinking for yourself." She clasps my hand tightly, so tight that she shakes it.

"I—um—it's all s-s-so jumbled, my head," I admit, peeking at her.

"We'll help you. You're not alone. Do not think for a moment that you are! You hear me?" Her widened brown eyes lock with mine before she squeezes me. "Don't you ever scare me like that again, Oren! Promise me you won't!"

Can I promise her that? No. "I-I can't yet."

The hope that lit Elouise's face darkens. "Please."

"Elouise," Floria scolds. " It's going to take time for Oren to heal. You will never be able to fathom the anguish Uxaar put him through. His heart and self-esteem are shattered. Be patient with him." Floria turns her attention to me, offering her hand out. "Let us return to camp before the others realize we're missing."

25 *Oren*

Since the evacuation happened, I've spent much of my time here in this clearing past my grandparents' old barn. It's far away from the farm village, which didn't completely escape Uxaar's destruction.

I sit beneath the solitary cherry tree in the middle of the clearing. The cherries, always sour and inedible, were a disappointment for Elouise and me. Despite our persistent hopes that their taste would improve year after year, they remained the same.

My grandparents used to take us to this spot for picnics every weekend. The tree provided ample shade and was conveniently located near our house. Those days were filled with joy and laughter as my family and I spent quality time with our grandparents. I cherish those memories deeply.

The painful memory of this tree is that Grandpa and Grandma were buried here. Since arriving in the farmlands two days ago, I've come to this grave spot every evening before supper. Not alone, although I wish I could go solo. If I could, I would vent my innermost feelings as if my grandparents were listening. My feelings are so dark and miserable that I don't confide them to anyone else.

Instead, I'm with Athena today. The last time I spoke to her exclusively was when I nearly killed her and told her that she ruined my life. Since then, I've felt tense around her. She also knows about my suicide attempt. Jace told his mum about it as well. From then on, I've been supervised constantly.

"What does this place here mean to you?" Athena pops a cherry into her mouth. As I anticipated, her face puckers as she spits it out. Still sour.

"Elly's grandparents w-w-were buried here." I sniff. "They never knew about Uxaar. Th-th-they were the closest things I had t-t-t-to parents growin' up. N-n-now I know I wasn't even th-th-th-their grandson."

"Their love wasn't a lie. Hold on to those times, cling to them dearly. We've learned that the times with our loved ones only last so long. The times I had with your parents mean the same to me. They were the best times I had."

"They're gone, t-t-too." Losing them is a jumble of complicated feelings with which I can't cope. "Athena, I-I didn't mean it when I said y-y-you ruined my life. It-t-t wasn't your fault m-my parents died. I'm sorry."

"It wasn't you, child. Uxaar said those things through you to hurt me. I didn't take them to heart. I learned to tune the Geron out long ago. So don't blame yourself. Ebony and Philip were responsible for their choices."

"I-it-t-t-t still wasn't fair."

"Would you want to discuss it? Surely, discovering the truth about them has been difficult for you. It's been hard for me, and I'm not even their son."

"Y' kn-kn-kn-ew 'em better than I did."

"Which is why this must be painful. No child should be separated from their parents at such a young age—they were wonderful people. I would have loved to have seen what it would have been like if we had never gone to the Dawn. It would have been so exciting. They would have been overjoyed to have you. I would have gotten the privilege to help them raise you." She laughs at the thought. "But this life will be good, too. Syann came, and the Shadow Incantations were destroyed. She didn't go to the Underealm for nothing, perhaps to save those in it, your parents. She wanted to believe she could, back at my house. And she promised to me and Gene that we'd see her again."

I don't believe Athena. I can't bring myself to hope for anything again without explicit proof. The only way I could believe it is if I saw her myself. Athena didn't watch Syann die like I did, so she can't understand.

Athena realizes I'm not ready to talk about my feelings about my parents yet. So she asks me to follow her. We go to the house she's lodging in during Seren's rebuild. "I have a gift for you," she says, displaying a beautiful leather-bound journal. "I know you lost yours, and in such dire times as this, you're in desperate need of a new one."

I accept it with a bittersweet grin. "Th-thank you."

"It will help you heal. I promise. The feelings you have trouble forming into words, jot them down. Don't hold back no matter how dark it may be. This book will keep those feelings safe until you're ready to share them.

Dear Journal,

You'll wish Athena had given you to someone else, a happy boy with a promising future ahead of him. My past journals were always my confidants, my sanctuary for expressing my sorrows and unanswered questions. But unfortunately, you won't be an exception. While many of my questions have answers now, I prefer to remain oblivious, even though my life before was so terrible. Desiring it back should reflect the depths of my current suffering. Uxaar manipulated everything from the beginning. He tormented my body for years and forced my family into acting out a lie for me. Aunt Valerie even admitted that many of the doctors I saw growing up were actors sent by Uxaar.

I'm left with countless exposed lies, losses, and almost no strength to endure. If it weren't for Floria, and my family's constant supervision, I would have taken my own life two nights ago. Now, I'm trapped in a cycle of despair, convinced that continuing only brings more pain. That's all I've accomplished in life, hurting my family. My parents are gone because of me. The pain is unbearable, considering I never knew them. However, with the few interactions we had, I could sense their love for me. They wanted me, but Uxaar tore us apart, just like he destroyed everything in my life. I don't feel like I belong in my adoptive family, even though they insist otherwise. All I can see is the unforgivable mess I've made. I don't understand how my family can forgive me for it. Syann's death is the most unforgivable sin of mine. When I had her as a companion my journal entries were filled with happiness. The stories we shared were treasures worth cherishing forever. But now, like when she left the first time, there's nothing joyful to write about. I didn't deserve her goodness or love, yet she gave it to me unconditionally. I try to comprehend how it works by convincing myself that if I were in her shoes and she were in mine, I would do the same for her without hesitation. However, when the roles are reversed back to how they played out, I don't understand because I'm not worthy. Syann was. She was worth everything. So why did she sacrifice herself to save me? Was it simply for love? I failed to honor her sacrifice when I attempted suicide. It's another layer of my immeasurable guilt that I must bear.

People say Syann will return, that the light can never be extinguished. I wish I could believe them, but I can't. The darkness Uxaar left behind is too great, and without her, there's no light in life.

    -Oren Silvius

I could have kept writing in this journal Athena gave me. Instead, I only scratched the surface of my feelings. It's progress, I guess. It's all the time alone I'm allotted before Elouise returns to her uncle's living room with some mint tea for me. As soon as she enters, I turn to the next page and see myself in it—blank. A completely blank canvas that succumbs to whoever is around me. The numbed-out facade is the least hurtful to be around.

Elouise asks if I want to go horseback riding once everyone returns from work. Most people have been assigned to help with the town's rebuilding. With my injury, I've been excluded until I recover. I don't want to be in bed the rest of the day, so I opt to go.

Jace and Gene join us. Our uncle only has two horses, so we decide that Elouise and I will share one while Jace and Gene share the other.

"These creatures are so small!" Gene exclaims as he climbs onto it.

"What do you mean?" Jace asks.

"Right, only Oren would understand."

I can concur with Gene. After riding a harjin, even a dragon, a horse feels small in the best way possible.

Jace glances at me as my horse gains on theirs. "Care to explain, O?"

"Um—th-the Dawn has these—um, these b-big creatures like—called harjins. They make m—a-a-a moose look small."

"What's a moose?" Gene shouts with a snicker.

"It has large horns and a similar frame to a deer, but much larger," Elouise says. "You don't know what a deer is, either?"

"Nope!" Gene busts out laughing. "I still have much to learn about this realm, but I hope you can all come to the Dawn one day. It's so different." I'm surprised Gene seems so happy only days after losing Kip. Maybe he believes he will reunite with him again, after all the time he's spent with Athena and Elouise.

He describes the Dawn for Elouise, who's curious about it.

"Well, the grass is blue, the sky looks like when the sun rises here, but there's no sun or clouds. Day and night are new concepts to me! Oh, and rain! We don't have that, either! We have these large plants that hydrate the air with mist."

"The trees th-th-th-there are alive, too," I add.

Alive?" Elouise stares at Gene, shocked.

"Yeah! Trees are regarded as creatures where I'm from instead of plants. They're sentient, with branches that behave like arms. It's honestly freaky. Especially the hostile ones," Gene explains. "They've killed many people."

"Mm-hmm. One of them almost killed me. So, I-I-I prefer the trees here."

"You say that as if you didn't nearly get yourself killed by falling from one of our trees," Jace responds to me, and I swing my head toward him, startled by his statement. Elouise scolds him severely for it, while Gene awkwardly smiles. "I'm sorry. All I meant was you should keep your distance from trees. It rarely ends well."

Maybe I should. After all, I had every intention of using a tree to end my life yesterday. Is that what Jace meant by saying I should keep my distance? If so, did everyone else notice that? My chest gets heavy thinking about it.

Elouise scoffs. "Anyways, Gene, what's your favorite thing here so far?"

"The sun. It's so warm!" Gene replies. "The sunset is one of the best things I've ever seen. It doesn't ever get old, does it?"

I shake my head. Elouise and Jace agree with me. As the sun sinks ahead of us, it paints the sky with a breathtaking spectacle—one of the most magnificent sunsets I've ever seen. The gradient evolves from deep blue to rich orange, creating a harmonious blend of colors. Not a single cloud dares to obstruct the radiant orb of light. Instead, a fluffy mass carelessly floats high above, reflecting the sun's lavish hues. This breathtaking scene has the power to melt away my worries, which is priceless.

Maybe the Light isn't all gone. The same power that made the sun is the same power that Syann had. She shines on me.

"I know a good spot. We can watch it from there, Gene." Jace turns his head toward Elouise and me. "Follow us."

Dandelion Hill. I haven't been here since—I don't know how long precisely. Bittersweet memories flood my mind as I gaze upon the radiant golden hill saturated by the sun's golden glow.

This is one of my favorite places in the farmlands, yet somehow, I had nearly forgotten it. Since it's one of the farthest landmarks here, I didn't visit it often. I was only permitted to go if an adult accompanied me, and I rarely asked. Before my accident, I got away with taking Syann a few times.

Dandelion Hill was where I learned to make flower crowns, and our favorite place to play the Find Shapes in the Clouds game. What shapes would Syann find in the clouds now? The one high above could look like a songbird or a budding flower to her. She'd concoct the most preposterous interpretation of a cloud that resembled nothing.

Watching the sunset will be my new favorite thing to do here. This could be my and Syann's new thing. Here, I feel her presence blanket me. She's here, yet so far out of reach. Like the sun that traverses past the horizon.

These thoughts melt me into a vulnerable state as we sit and watch the sunset. The intense emotions become difficult to manage. I claw at the grass to try calming myself and uproot a dandelion in the process. I observe the vibrant yellow petals, Syann's favorite color.

My storming emotions can't be calmed—in fact, I'm raining now. Maybe no one will notice my tears, yet Elouise glimpses me at the wrong time. She asks if I'm all right with that worried gaze that jabs me. I wipe my tears away, hoping I can compose myself. However, Elouise draws closer, expressing her worry. There I break down.

"What's wrong?" Jace's voice and the thudding of his

footsteps resound. I curl into a ball, weeping into my knees while Elouise caresses my good shoulder. Gene asks what happened. No one knows how to answer him, including myself.

"It's all right, it's all right! We're here!" Elouise assures me. "Whatever you're feeling, you're not alone."

I raise my head, rubbing my slowed tears until they're gone. "I—I felt her so strong. It was like Syann was here."

"She is here. She's always here with the Light. That was her saying she loves you and to stay strong," Elouise whispers to me. I'm unsure if Gene or Jace could hear her, but her words mark me.

I twist the flower in my fingers. "But she feels s-s-so far. Like how the s—I-I-I feel the sun's rays, but it's a horizon a-a-a-away. I wish she could b-b-b-be here with us."

Elouise smiles bittersweetly and turns away briefly. She reaches in front of Gene to grab a puffy white dandelion. "Is that an official wish?"

I chuckle and sob simultaneously as I reach out to the flower. It's a childish gesture, one I usually wouldn't indulge in. However, here, in this golden sanctuary of my childhood, it feels different. Perhaps my life could be golden again, as Athena implied. That feels impossible, like this wish.

I hold the dandelion inches from my lips as I wish the impossible—

Please come back, Syann.

The breeze carries the feather-topped seeds far past the hill and out of sight. The sunset leaves the same way.

***

The metallic taste of blood wakes me. The tang of it nearly convinces me I'm still in my nightmare, where Uxaar and I storm in and level the farm village. I slayed multitudes with my sword or the clobbering of fists. Elouise, Athena, Gene, and Jace were all victims. Only Syann came to stop me. She rescued everyone by taking them to Secreth and left me behind with Uxaar. She sentenced me to dwell with Uxaar forever in the broken world we made.

I trace my lips with my fingertips. My hazy, tired eyes examine my fingers for blood. Rusted red glazes them as I expected, but the shimmering blue light frightens me more than the blood does. I must have gotten so restless that I bit my lip bloody in my sleep. As for my eyes, I try to forget they are marked like this forever, but I know that's impossible. Uxaar made it to where I'll never forget.

Miraculously, I woke no one up. So, there's no one to talk to in my restlessness. To pass the time, I doodle in my journal for a bit, but I grow tired of depending on my eyes for light. My hands are too shaky to draw anything well, too. I need fresh air.

My family would be upset if I left again, but the window shows me that sunrise is near. I know exactly where I hope to watch it from. This time, I ensure no one follows me.

I've never hiked to Dandelion Hill before. The journey is mere minutes on horseback. I discover it's an hour's walk.

It's dim out, while sounds of bugs, owls, and leaves rustling in the wind overtake the atmosphere. Elouise would be frightened to stroll at this hour, but I find it peaceful. There are much worse things to be afraid of than owls.

The soft grass is a suitable place to recline my tired legs after the walk. I don't care that it's damp from the morning dew.

Who knows how long I'll sit here? Hopefully not long enough for anyone to think I'm dead somewhere. If anyone concluded that I attempted suicide again, I wouldn't be surprised. After all, I denied promising Elouise that I wouldn't scare her again. After the sun rises, I need to see myself home right away. Until then, I will watch the east side of the sky.

"It's been three days," I mumble to myself sorrowfully, picking another fluffy flower. This time, I let the seeds blow off with the air's gust. They are countless. As for the days passing, it could be five thousand and twelve days since Syann left, and I would still remember the count. She's stuck with me.

Now I'm praying, hoping she'll hear me, and that somehow it will have meaning. "Three days…How many b-b-before I break? I needed you and the hope you gave me. Without you, there is n-n-no hope, only hurt and darkness. Yesterday on-n-n this hill, I felt your Light strongly, but it set l-l-like the sun! I need to f-f-feel you again if I'm to keep going, Syann!"

The edge of the sun peeks above the hills. Sunbeams bring a golden haze to the fields below me. Maybe the sunlight is trying to tell me she's listening.

"B-b-b-because without you, it's all darkness. That's all I was before you came…You c-c-came to save everyone from the darkness. Please save me!"

Unlike last evening, there's peace in being open with my tears. I'm finally alone and can shamelessly release the nastiest of sobs.

"Pl-pl-please! I can't do it on my own. I can't get past th-th-the guilt or forgive myself. When y-y-you already forgave me, and everyone h-h-has."

Blades of grass brush through my curling fingers, and my nails dig deep into the dirt as I close my eyes. The rays are warm, while the breeze is cool. Soon enough, the sun will warm all in contact with it, and the air itself.

Light changes the atmosphere, visually and physically.

I hope it can change me.

26 *Syann*

After death, the spirit must go somewhere, for it is eternal. Since the fall of Secreth, any spirit has ended up where I am now, the Underealm. The curse sealed Secreth away, and not even souls who belong to the Light can reach it. So, they slumber peacefully here, while those who cast their lot with the Darkness endure the torment dealt to them.

"Is this what you wanted?" Uxaar sneers at me. "Doom us all to this wretched place! Who's going to save the people you sacrificed yourself for now that you're stuck here! They'll perish and end up right here to suffer!"

"You've forgotten something, Uxaar. Light consumes the Darkness! You and the Geron that had a hold of me couldn't destroy my Light! Instead, it stripped you of your freedom! Here in the Underealm, you and the Geron are condemned to spend the rest of your days here! Nothing can free you from such a sentence!

"You're acting as if the Geron haven't sentenced you and your people to an eternity of damnation here! No one will ever step foot in Secreth again!"

"That's where you're wrong. Pure Light cannot dwell in this realm. Like the spirits that the Light has called good have rested peacefully in this realm, I have been deemed innocent. The moment I say the Incantations of Light over myself, I will be restored to Secreth, but that won't be done until every spirit you've held captive here is given the opportunity to join me." Pure rage builds on Uxaar's face. I won't let him revel in the torment of these souls any longer. I will demonstrate my power to him. "Now be gone, Uxaar!" I command him. "Never show your face to me again!"

Uxaar is forced to succumb to me, scurrying away in fear as the other Geron around me do. Only Roe remains. My heart sags, knowing there's nothing I can do to save them. "Roe."

"I knew what I signed up for," he says bitterly. "Leave me be. The spirits here need saving. Many have waited a millennium for this day."

"Roe, you have my gratitude. I wish it didn't have to be this way, but you can have the peace of knowing that your fall had a purpose. Without you, Brenda wouldn't have had anyone to turn to. You kept your oath and helped me whenever I needed it. Your sacrifice will never be forgotten."

"Nor will I ever forget you. Goodbye, my goddess." Roe bows.

"Goodbye, my friend."

Roe turns from me, fading away into the abyss. My chest feels heavy, as tears brim my eyes. This place is dreadful, and nearly everyone I grew up with in Seren is in it. Their screams ring in my head, piercing me. It won't be easy to stop this. It will likely take several days to free each person here using the Incantations of Light.

An unexpected noise of beauty rings in the air, music that sounds like home. It's powerful enough to stop my tears. "Stella?" I pivot sharply, finding the two-winged blue bird in the air. She's a spirit, with both wings! I lift my arm out to her. "Baby, come here!" She perches on my hand, and I bring her toward my face. "I was worried I'd never see you again, yet here you are, an angel in this dark place." I shake my head. "But you are not meant to be here. Secreth will be your new home, and I promise I will meet you again there."

The bird's beady eyes are expectant. I breathe deeply, preparing myself to say the Incantations of Light. I have no doubt this will work.

Accept the Light's call
By surrendering all
A new life awaits you
Leave the lost behind
Light renew your mind
A new life embraces you

***

Three days have passed, and I've been saving souls by dispelling the Darkness within them and sending them to Secreth. I recognize many of the spirits—people I grew up with in Seren, even my family who raised me. I also encountered Philip, Ebony, and Kipper.

I send myself home last, leaving the Underealm behind forever.

Arriving home is a comforting sensation that consumes me with warmth and love, like a cherished hug from the one I love most.

I approach my throne, surrounded by illuminated crystal walls. The space between me and the walls is filled by the sounds of the guardians' voices in the room. The loyal Geron have taken notice of my presence.

The sound of a horn blast overwhelms any noise. It summons tens and tens of the angelic creatures at my disposal.

"The Goddess of Light has returned!" the one with the horn announces. The creatures all bow, repeating the message.

I smile at the sight of each of them, remembering their names and all they've done for me in the past. They faithfully defended this realm during the war and guarded it in my absence for the past thousand years. I didn't realize how much I missed them until now. If only Roe could be here, too.

I observe myself clearly in my reflection in the floor. I am clothed in a gown as radiant as the sun, its yellow hue shimmering like stars. The sleeves of the gown flow effortlessly from my arms, creating a gentle breeze. My hair, adorned with eternal flowers, cascades loosely behind me.

The last time I was in this room, I was internally divided. I was in a form of Darkness that couldn't detect the spirit of Light calling desperately within it. Now, I'm *almost* complete.

"You may rise," I permit the creatures as I rise myself. "The war is over, the traitors are sentenced, and the borders of Secreth are open. The cost of this outcome marked the Dusk realm by destruction, with only less than half of the population surviving. One last time, we will set out to the ends of the Earth, bringing the survivors who are willing to come here. Those who refuse shall be left in the Dusk realm that will set into the Underealm."

They don't hesitate to venture into the newly opened borders of Secreth. I will pursue them in a different manner. The greatest source of light on Earth is the sun. Without it, life on Earth would not exist. With its power, I am connected to the Earth and its inhabitants. Currently, it rises over Seren. A young man sits in its light, seeking solace and praying to me from a state of despair.

"Oren." I utter his name. He's been waiting for me, and I don't plan on disappointing him. I manifest myself through the purest form of Light on Earth, in the beams of sunlight that shine on the one I love.

Oren sees me taking shape in them, gazing at me as if he's in a dream. He must believe he is dreaming. The Darkness placed so much doubt and hurt in his sweet but broken heart. I repeat his name as a smile spreads across my face. Yellow and fuzzy dandelions surround us. They're rooted within blades of dew-kissed grass that glisten in my Light.

"Syann?" he barely whispers, scooting back. His cheeks are tearstained. Though he isn't crying now, his blue eyes gloss over.

I set my hand on his cheek, lifting his chin gently. The shimmer in his eyes forms into falling tears. "I'm here. I heard you." I choke up.

"I-I-I watched you die!" he laments softly, looking to the ground.

"You're right. Brenda, the form you knew me to be, she died, yet she was reborn in this form with me. She's not gone, she's here with me."

A gleam of hope shimmers within him. "I don't—so you're—you're still you—do you r-r-r-r-remember?"

"Everything. The Darkness, the worries, and the memories with you and the people I love. Those memories cling close to my heart, along with the ones from this place, Dandelion Hill. You came here because you missed those times, too. I wish I could have come sooner. It took me days to save the souls in the Underealm before I could escape. With the sun's light, I felt you and your hurt. So, I came."

Conflict contorts his face, and he's lost in it. He eventually peeks at me with teary eyes. I embrace him, healing the wound Uxaar left on him. I picture the clash of Oren and his father that left his shoulder marred. The heartbreak he experienced weighs on me as his wounds mend.

Oren only cries harder after he's healed. He can no longer deny I'm not a daydream. I ask him what's wrong, but he's unable to form eligible words. He offers me a leather-bound book.

I take the journal in my hands, seeing the neatly written paragraph jotted on the first page. The words become increasingly discouraging.

Syann's death is the most unforgivable sin of mine. When I had her as a companion, my journal entries were filled with happiness. The stories we shared were treasures worth cherishing forever. But now, like when she left the first time, there's nothing joyful to write about. I didn't deserve her goodness or love, yet she gave it to me unconditionally. I try to comprehend how it works by convincing myself that if I were in her shoes and she were in mine, I would do the same for her without hesitation. However, when the roles are reversed back to how they played out, I don't understand because I'm not worthy. Syann was. She was worth everything. So why did she sacrifice herself to save me? Was it simply for love? I failed to honor her sacrifice when I attempted suicide. It's another layer of my unmeasurable guilt that I must bear. People say Syann will return, that the light can never be extinguished. I wish I could believe them, but I can't. The darkness Uxaar left behind feels overwhelming, and without her, there's no light in life.

I know Oren well enough to understand he would want to give up. Knowing he *tried,* though, is a pain that brings me to tears.

"I-I-I didn't believe you, a-a-and you still came. Athena said you-you would return." He cries inconsolably. "You died b-b-because of me. After you, I had nothing! Nothing but g-g-g-guilt I couldn't live with!"

I bring him into my arms, which he sobs heavily into. "Don't listen to the lies Uxaar put in your head. I defeated him, so don't let him win you over. You don't need to feel guilty about anything. Tell me what you ruined that hasn't been restored now? It's not me. I'm here. I'm better than I could ever be. Your parents are alive in Secreth, and so is Kipper. You will be, too! Everything will be restored!"

"I-I-I ruined their l-l-l-lives! The past eight'n—"

"The past, Oren! The past is gone along with Uxaar! You're here now! None of our lives are ruined. None of us are deceased. Yes, we all went through grim times. Ones we surely won't ever forget, but none of us lack a chance at restoration and a happy life ahead. We can all start over. Nothing is ruined or beyond hope."

"What if I-I-I don't know how to start over?"

"You don't have to know how, you just live! Keep going, and don't give up. As long as we live, we never run out of opportunities to start over. Every day is a new day, a new hour, a new minute, a new second, a new breath, a new chance to begin. We must learn to not let our pasts define us and focus on the Light ahead of us. If we can accomplish that, we can do anything!" Despite my words, fear still is rampant in his eyes. "What scares you now?"

"I'm scared I don't know who I-I-I am anymore—" he admits. "M-m-my whole life, Uxaar was in my head. Now that he's gone, I feel it, his absence. There's so many feelings, I-I-I don't know whose they are now. It's like—it's like my eyes, they're mine, but they're—they are also Uxaar's likeness. The-the mark isn't only on-n-n my eyes, it-it-it's in all of me, too—I don't know, I c-c-can't sort the thoughts. Which are mine, or not. I-I don't think I'll ever know."

"It doesn't have to stay that way. You can come with me to Secreth. The Darkness will leave you, and you will have peace. You'll know who you really are like I do."

"Who d-d-d-do you think I am?" he sniffles.

"You're my light."

Oren shakes his head. "There's n-n-n-no light without you, Sy—If th-there's any light in me, it-t-t-t comes from you. It's l-like I'm th-th-the moon, and you're th-th-the sun. I only h-h-h-have light when I s-s-see you."

"If you choose to come with me, you will be dead to this Earth and can never return. Darkness is no place for Secreth. You will be like me. Light will refine your soul and spirit into an immortal form. You'd be with me forever."

He nods; to him, death isn't a steep price. Part of him craves it, but all he really wants is peace. That I long to give him. "I-I can't be without y-y-you! I can't! I-I-I tried so hard! I can't st-st-stay here! I-I-I don't belong!"

"None of us belong here, Oren. Darkness was not meant for

any of us, which is why I'm here to bring everyone to the Light. We will be together, love." I withdraw from his embrace, taking one last glance at him before I send him away. I rest my hand on his face, wiping his tears away with my thumb. He's beautifully broken this way.

He cries out softly, leaning his head down. I tip my forehead against him affectionately. We stay that way for a moment, breathing each other in. "Thank you," he whispers.

I immerse myself in his sharp blue eyes, the eyes of a victor, fighter, and overcomer—not of a slave or monster. I keep them in lock as the Incantations of Light leave my lips. He doesn't understand them, only I can, but I know the words bring him peace.

His hand lingers in mine as the sun's light transforms his form into radiant rays. Oren's form rises, until he vanishes into sunlight. He has left this life, and I will follow him into the next. I'm certain that the Geron entering the farmlands will bring his family and others with him.

A horse carrying two riders, Athena and Elouise, approaches me. I assume they're searching for Oren, as he was the only one here. They're both amazed by my presence. Athena's face lights up with a tearful, vibrant smile. She dismounts from the horse and walks toward me. Elouise hesitates but follows behind Athena.

"Syann! I knew you'd return! I knew it!" Athena exclaims. Her voice is a mix of laughing and crying. I hold my arms out, letting her embrace me. "After all that time, I never doubted you."

I beam. Unlike Oren, I sense so much Light within her. "Athena, you believed in me when I didn't believe in myself. I couldn't be prouder of you or more honored to call you my friend."

Elouise is crying, too. Not driven from the same emotion as Athena's tears. Elouise is worried.

"Elouise. You won't find who you're searching for here." I smile.

Elouise sobs. "You found Oren, didn't you? That's his journal." She points to the book on the ground. I nod in response. "I woke up, and he was gone! I was terrified!" She breaks down. "I thought he might have been here." She smiles as she approaches me. "I knew you'd be the one to save him! I always knew!"

"It was you who kept him going through the Darkness, Elouise. You were his light while I was sleeping. You are such a light." I smile at her. "I want you both to come with me."

They both nod. "That's all I've ever wanted!" Athena exclaims.

We go together into the realm of Light. The two girls leave their darkness behind. They never doubt what they're leaving behind for a moment.

27 Oren

Is this for me? I find myself in the most luxurious bedroom I've ever seen. The crystal floors reflect my image, and the walls are a soothing mint green, my favorite color. The high-rise ceiling is graced with a magnificent chandelier, its jewels casting a dazzling glow across the room. Sitting by the window is a large desk, made from fragrant dark wood. It's adorned with jars packed with pens, quills, vibrant paints, and a journal. Across from it is a large bed framed with matching wood. The white blankets disperse enticingly across the mattress, like the three lush pillows on it. Why, I've never seen such nice furniture.

"Hello?"

Hmm. I suppose I have no choice but to explore.

I'm drawn to the journal on the desk, and the bright colors sprouting from the pages. I open the journal and inside lies a chain of luminescent flowers. On the page reads this message—

Welcome home, Oren. Use this journal to treasure all the memories we'll make here.

-Syann

I can't help but grin ear to ear as I trace the letters of her name with my index finger. The longing for Syann's presence overwhelms me. If only I knew her whereabouts. How much time has elapsed since my arrival here?

"Syann? Can you hear me?" I wait, but the silence verifies my loneliness.

Now I know this place is mine and I'm free to explore deeper.

There are three dark brown doors with crystal doorknobs. I draw near the closet, which is as large as my old bedroom. Inside are more clothes than in a market in Seren, I'd imagine.

What catches my eye before any specific outfit does is my reflection in the mirror straight ahead.

I'm naked, not a stitch of clothing on.

Typically, I'd be embarrassed and even revolted, but instead, I'm lured closer to the reflection. I hardly recognize the one before me. I'm glowing, like Syann was when I last saw her. My frame isn't gaunt. Instead, I'm healthy, even strong. My mouth forms a smile of disbelief as I do a double take. I'm—handsome, yet still me. How?

I eagerly search through the clothes, arousing a desire for fashion that I never knew existed. My past life was too tough on me to realize it, and I didn't have these resources.

I test several different vests and jackets but go with an attractive embroidered one. It's as red as a rose petal, soft and fragrant like one, too. I wear a white mid-sleeve shirt underneath, along with gray trousers and black boots. The only thing about my appearance I would like to fix now is my hair. In the next room, I find the resources for that. The bathroom has all the grooming tools that I could ever need. As a result of their use, my jaw is clean-shaven. While the hair that was shaggy at my shoulders before now swoops right below my ears. My bangs, I keep long enough to remain parted on the side. Instead of sticking out, they transition nicely into my waves.

I briskly observe the rest of the house, which has a roomy

kitchen with all the pans and dishes I could ever need. If only I knew how to cook.

A stunning living space with lush sofas and a dining table is right across from the kitchen. It is suitable for company to come over, something I never got to have in my teenage years.

Speaking of guests, I need to find the others. I hope my family will be here, and Syann, too! Where would I even begin to search for them? The only door I've failed to open in this house is the front door.

The view past it is beauty far beyond what Seren or even the Dawn ever could bestow. The exterior of the houses is built with sparkling stones, like precious gems. The walkways are paved with glass that reflects the beauty of this world so perfectly. Beyond the neighborhood is a still lake, reflecting the high mountains beyond it. Surrounding the lake is the greenest grass my eyes have met. Rainbow colors of glowing wildflowers sway in the green.

I could easily absorb this view for hours while trying my best to replicate it in my journal. However, that endeavor will be for another day.

On the opposite side of the horizon from the mountains is a castle. The best I can describe it is as if the most careful architects meticulously carved this palace out of a mountain of diamond. While also detailing the roof and windowsills with gold floral trim. The windows are like stained glass.

If Syann is here, she'll be there.

Like when I was with Gene and Kip, running on my own two feet brings me laughter. The sensation is rejuvenating. Unlike before, running doesn't leave me exhausted. I could run indefinitely. My joy quickly turns into anticipation as I approach the palace entrance. The gates are wide open, suggesting my welcome, but who's inside? Has Syann returned from Earth? Are my parents here? The uncertainty brings me to a stop.

"Greetings," a Geron says to me. He has golden hair and eyes, like the sun, and shiny armor that reflects my own image. The sight of the creature startles me, despite knowing I'm safe. None of the Geron will harm me. Uxaar is gone, yet this creature slightly resembles the fallen Geron I was accustomed to—only much more refined and even beautiful.

"Me?" I point to myself.

The creature chuckles. "Yes, no need to be alarmed. I mean you no harm, nor does anyone here. Your days of Darkness are over."

I grin slightly. "Um, do you—know if Syann is here?"

"Not yet. She has traversed to the Dusk realm to save the remaining souls there. I predict she shall return very soon. You are welcome inside. The celebration of the goddess Syann's return has already commenced."

I discover that the castle is truly as beautiful inside as it is on the outside, just like the one who rules it. I'm ecstatic to see her again. This time, we won't be separated from each other.

I follow the crowd to a grand ballroom, filled with laughter and cheers from those within. The room is bathed in light, and people and creatures dance carefree. A moat of deep water surrounds the ballroom, home to various marine life, including fish, crustaceans, and aquinnes. Each corner of the moat is marked by a grand three-tiered fountain, whose mist creates glittering rainbows.

I've never felt like I belonged in such a vibrant and enchanting atmosphere, amidst a vast and delightful crowd. The lively music draws families and couples together, creating a mesmerizing spectacle of swaying and twirling in circular motions across the ballroom.

A couple, different in size, catches my eye. A towering man with cleanly cut red curls, dancing with a small woman with long black hair. My parents! They are so infatuated with each other that they could be the only two people in the room. As the music fades out, the two share an affectionate kiss. How desperately they must have hungered for each other.

I ponder leaving them alone, to not disrupt their moment. The thought of confronting them is the first scenario here that genuinely rattles me. My past self wouldn't even have the courage to do it. Our past is tainted and shattered. Without the Light, we'd never have the second chance we have now. How dare I even consider letting our new beginning slip away?

Philip makes eye contact with me and directs Ebony to look at me. Every trace of emotion fades from her face, leaving only surprise. I timidly raise my hand, wiggling my fingers. It's a subtle gesture, but more movement than the rest of my body can muster. My legs are frozen in place, so I allow them to approach me.

Neither of them smiles anymore. They're as uneasy as I am. Ebony's hooded eyes are alert, and her breaths are heavy. She gradually brings her trembling hand toward my face, as if she's not sure I'll let her touch me.

My frozen frame allows her hand to rest on my cheek; my mother releases the tension that had been building up in her through a sigh. Her thin lips form a wavering smile as tears stream down her face. Unlike her previous behavior, her hug is sudden and unexpected. She wails into my chest, holding me tightly, and I embrace her back, feeling a sense of forgiveness wash over me. This forgiveness is not only toward her, but also myself. The conflict that had been plaguing us is finally over, dead and gone like our pasts. Now, we are home, truly alive.

Philip sets a firm hand on my shoulder, wearing a smile that's nearly as bright as his eyes. The guilt weighing his face down before is no more. Additionally, he was able to freshen up as well. His beard is trimmed cleanly, and the appearance of his prime has been restored. "I didn't know this was possible!" He breaks down without composure. "Thank the Light!"

I didn't know this was possible, either. Philip bled out before my eyes and haunted me, but now he's here, and happier than he's ever been. These thoughts bring tears to my eyes, but I restrain them.

He joins in the embrace, and I'm practically smothered between them. The air becomes thin, but for once it's all right. I have a family, and no one can tear it apart again.

I won't lie, I'm relieved when they let me go. I'm not entirely used to hugging others yet. My parents wipe their tears as they withdraw from me.

"You're all grown up," my mother says, smiling. Until it turns into sorrow. She gazes into my scarred eyes, a reminder of all that Uxaar's done to me. "Oren, I'm so sorry," she sobs.

A sense of grief-ridden thoughts washes over me, that we lost so much time. I can never be a child again, though I feel like one. I'm in a new place, with a new mindset, but in an adult's body. I'll never experience growing up with them. I wish we could have always been here and never known the Darkness that distorted us. At least we never have to be acquainted with it again. "It's over," I express my thoughts. "So—I want us to start over. Syann told me—um, it was never too late to. M-my childhood is gone, but there's eternity ahead of us. It isn't too late to be a family, right?"

"Of course, it's not!" my dad exclaims. "This is only the beginning."

"I'm so happy Syann found you! From the moment I lost you, Oren, I prayed that she would save you. She didn't let us down!"

I smile at the thought of her. The moment she returns will be when everything comes together. It can't come soon enough.

"Ebony!" Athena shouts. She and Elouise run toward us.

Relief floods me, as her name escapes me. My arms stretch wide out for her. She rushes straight into them, laughing into my chest.

"You made it!" Elouise laughs. "I was so worried! I woke up and you were gone! I thought I would be too late!"

"No! I found her! I found Syann!"

Elouise nods. "I know! She told me! I'm so delighted!"

Behind us, Athena reunites with my parents through weepy embraces. The sight warms my heart, and Elouise's.

"Was Athena with you when Syann found you?" I ask.

Elouise nods. "We both were looking for you."

I smile at her. "Well, I—I'm ready to make that promise to you, th-that I'll never scare you like that again."

Athena spins toward me, not hesitating to squeeze me in her arms. "Freckles, oh what a miracle!" She lets me go, meeting my eyes. "You and your family are all here!"

I smile at Athena a bit clumsily. It is a miracle, one I will never take for granted. I shift my gaze toward Elouise. "Elly, I want you to meet my parents—Mum, Dad, this is your niece, Elouise. We grew up together. She's like my sister."

"It's wonderful to meet you!" Elouise smiles, holding out her hand.

Mum shakes her head before reeling Elouise into her embrace. "Thank you for being there for my son when we couldn't. That means everything to me."

"He was always there for me. He's the best brother anyone could ask for," Elouise replies, before exchanging an embrace with my dad.

A fanfare from above plays a melody throughout the room, bewitching everyone's attention. This could only mean one thing, right?

"Lend your ears! Feast your eyes!" a Geron on the balcony announces. "The Goddess of Light has claimed victory over the Darkness that once threatened this realm and the ones beyond it. Now that this threat has been vanquished, our goddess has made her absolute return to Secreth. Behold, our goddess, Syann!"

She gracefully enters the balcony in all her glory and splendor, commanding the attention of every gaze in the palace. Her radiance is far beyond what the sun could ever dream of possessing. In fact, the sun only shines on her authority. A lavish ballgown of golden rays drapes from her elegant curves, while a crown of glistening flowers adorns her spiraling locks. Her eyes are a pair of rainbows, each and every color commemorating her valor and the sacrifice of burdening herself with the Incantations in my place. Why, she's easily the most breathtaking scenery this realm has to offer. Compare the rest next to her, and it's all trifle. She's everything perfect exemplified in a figure of magnificent beauty.

Everyone in the crowd agilely melts into a bow, but the moment I lay eyes on her, my knees became jelly. I'm flat on the ground, paying homage to the one who gave me and everyone here another chance at life.

Cheers and praises rise as the people around me stand, but I can't get myself up or say a word. I'm fortunate that I'm even breathing—my heartbeat is so boisterous it drowns out all the cheering.

"Oren?" Elouise pats my shoulder. "You can stand now."

"Can I?"

Elouise giggles and pulls me up by my arm. I didn't notice Stella was on Syann's shoulder at first, not until a rush of blue feathers flutters toward me. *"Oren!"*

"Stella?" I question, as the bird lands on my shoulders. I could have sworn she said my name, but in a way I've never experienced. It sounded like her typical singsong calls—but I understood it.

"Did you hear that?" Elouise questioned. "Stella said your name! I understood her!"

So, it isn't just me.

I nod before glancing back to Stella. "Look at you! You can fly!"

Stella suffered without a wing as long as I did with my leg. Syann healing us connects us. As Stella always connected me and Syann while I was away.

"And you can walk!"

"It's all thanks to her." I glance over to Syann. She descends on a helical staircase from the balcony, directly toward me.

"She's coming to see you! Syann's coming!" Stella squawks.

The Light among the Shadows

28 *Syann*

The ballroom has my attention, from humans, pixies, aquinnes, Geron, and various creatures in the crowd. I know each one of their names, their stories, and how they came to be here. I love and care for each of them, but one holds my special affection. The one the enemy tried to take me out with but failed. Oren Silvius is here, and he is mine.

I traverse down the staircase until I'm on the ballroom floor. All the bystanders below it reverently create a path for me, until I stop at my destination. Elouise, Oren, and his parents stand before me.

Oren Silvius is no longer brittle or broken. He's whole, healed, and ravishing. He's the same boy I knew and loved, but he's also not. The man I gaze at is who Oren was always meant to be, a companion of Light.

Oren's frame is strong instead of frail. His hair waves gracefully above his jaw. Best of all, he's joyful. The Darkness that was plaguing him is now a distant memory.

At the sight of me, he crumbles to the ground as Stella returns to me. "Oren." I offer out my hand for him to stand up. Meekly he gazes at my arm, before reaching out for me. I reel him into a tight embrace.

"Welcome home," I whisper against his shoulder.

"Thank you," he whispers back, a tearful sound in his tone. "Thank you," he repeats a little louder as he lets go. He utters my name through a sob. I raise my hand to his cheek, admiring the indisputable joy that shines from him—also, how handsome his form is here. I always thought Oren was lovely, but now he's even more so. He holds my hand against his face affectionately. I want more, to dance with him, to kiss him. The latter I don't hesitate to do. I lean in slow enough not to catch him off guard. He smiles, blushing a little. "In front of everybody? Again?" he muses as he rolls his eyes playfully. His distance from me grows thin.

"Yes!"

He chortles breathily before he snatches my waist and reels me through the mere gap between us. His lips plant themselves onto mine, and he singlehandedly isolates me in a moment of undiluted ecstasy. Oh, how long I could dwell in this kiss alone, while his arms encompass my waist, and my fingers get lost in his dark locks. However, I withdraw my lips as Elouise calls Oren's name, shocked. I know Oren and I have infinite chances to explore every thread of our beings together, intimately. There's no hurry—in fact, I will savor every moment with him.

Ebony's jaw hangs open, while her fiancé grins proudly. Athena's reaction to our kiss is the most amusing. She giggles while bouncing in place.

"You two are together?"

I hold Oren's hand, locking my eyes with his. "Yes," I respond to Ebony, then shift my gaze to Philip. "I told you he was wonderful."

Philip smiles, setting his hand on Oren's shoulder. "He is. He was worth waiting for, and all the suffering we went through."

"Do you all believe that this outcome was worth all of the pain the Dusk realm brought you?"

"Absolutely," Ebony answers me. "And that's saying a lot."

"Yes, without a doubt," Athena agrees. Elouise nods.

Oren contemplates his answer longer than anyone else does. He's the last one to respond. "Before um—coming here, my answer would've differed. Honestly—I wanted to die, but Syann showed—you showed me a hope that never—I never could've conceived on my own. B-Because of that, I can move on. We all can because of hope, no matter how dark our paths were."

"Well said, freckles." Athena smiles. Oren amusingly cringes at the use of that nickname.

"There are others you've lost long ago who are on their way here. Elouise, this includes your father and your mother's parents. Your family should be here soon. I'd keep an eye out for them."

"Our grandparents?" Oren's eyes sparkle.

"Every creature has a spirit, which is immortal. It has no choice but to dwell either in Darkness or Light. The reason I entered the Underealm was to restore the souls who rested there."

Athena laughs, surely remembering the family she lost long ago. The others smile expectantly as they chat among themselves.

I grab Oren's hand, taking him by surprise. "I have other people who I need to see, but I'll see you soon. I'd like my first dance to be with you."

Oren grins. "Who am I to deny my goddess's wishes? I'll be waiting for you."

I leave Athena, Philip, and Ebony to catch up with each other.

Floria enters the room alone, her clothing a stark contrast to her usual soldierly attire. Instead, she wears an orange blouse embroidered with delicate blossoms, dangling crystal earrings, and flowing brown pants. The overwhelming sights around her seem to captivate her, and when our eyes meet, she gracefully bows on one knee.

I offer my hand out, smiling. "How are the colors this time?"

Floria darts her head toward me, her hand outstretched

toward mine. "More breathtaking than I possibly could have imagined."

As soon as she's on her feet, I take her in my arms.

She squeezes me back. "My people are finally safe, even the ones who lost their lives on the previous side."

"Back when I was on the other side, when my perspective was limited, I hoped deeply that I could get you here, Floria. At the time, I wasn't sure I could. There was a point I didn't believe in any of this. The Darkness had completely disconnected me from my spirit, but now we don't have to live in a world that's so dark that it makes us doubt what the Light can do."

Floria nods. "I experienced Uxaar's Darkness firsthand. I was one of the two he created the Incantations with. I was on the side of the one who made this realm fall in the first place. For the longest time, I didn't believe anything could redeem me from such a crime, but I wanted to try. I tried leading my people toward you the best that I could." Tears glimmer in her eyes.

"And that you did, Floria, and I'm so proud of you. But please know, I loved you even at your darkest points. You were a child when Uxaar took you, no one expected you to not cave in when he abused you. When I was human, I said the Incantations too when he threatened my family. Anyone else would have done the same. I don't condemn you. I never did. I want you to be at peace here. You don't have to worry about leading your people anymore. I will take care of them and you. Just be."

Floria absorbs the crowd around her, as slow tears fall from her eyes. "Just be—I like the way that sounds. Thank you, Syann."

"You're welcome. I trust that I will see you soon."

I watch Floria walk away, keeping my focus on the crowds around me. Soon, Jace, Valerie, Gene, the Eleven, my earthly family, and the survivors of Secreth begin to arrive here. I know there won't be a dull moment uniting with each one of them.

How was I once so clueless? When I lived as Brenda, I longed for a steady, long life with a family of my own. That was what I always dreamed of. In her perspective, I thought when I lay on that altar, it was all over. I thought I would have no one to love, that I was doomed as a distant omniscient being who was feared. I couldn't have been more wrong. So many wonderful beings surround me, and we all are full of love and Light.

Life here couldn't be steadier. The Light not only kept Secreth alive but also nurtured it while I slept. The land is vast and suitable for many humans and creatures, including me, to thrive here. I have eternity to live my life and love and care for countless people, my friends from Earth or here—the trees, aquinnes, Geron, harjins, dragons, or fairies. I will never be alone, bored, or unloved—instead, I will experience the opposite. Secreth is a loving environment, and everyone here contributes to it. However, I must admit that one person stands out for me.

It's been several hours since I left Oren to be with his family. The sun is setting. Outside, nature takes on a bioluminescent glow, providing a new twist to the beauty of this realm. Many will stay at the celebration overnight—fatigue or sleep won't overcome us anymore.

I approach the castle garden, one of my favorite places in Secreth before the fall. It embodies a harmonious blend of the Dusk and Dawn realms. The vibrant green foliage is illuminated with flowers. Their petals shimmer like stellar jewels. Butterflies and fairies flit gracefully among the blooms, while fountains cascade crystal-clear water. The air is filled with the sweetest and most delicate floral scent, and hovering lights like fireflies.

Deep in the garden, by a fountain, sits Oren. I knew he'd be here. He's not alone, either—Kip is by his side. They both notice my approach.

"Syann!" Oren waves at me with a grin.

"Hi, Oren. Hello again, Kipper! Where's Gene?"

"He's catching up with his dad!" Kipper replies.

"I see."

"I overheard there was a garden, and the last thing Oren and

I did together at the Dawn was tour the garden there, so I thought it was appropriate."

"We were talking about how our rooms had gifts in them. How I had a new journal, and he had crocheting supplies."

"Yes, thank you! I'm definitely going to invite Oren over sometime and teach him how to crochet!"

"You're welcome, Kip. Oren is quite the artist, so I'm sure crocheting will come naturally to him."

"Well, you always told me when we were kids that you weren't an artist, but you technically designed all of this, right?"

"Yeah! This is the most beautiful garden I've ever seen," Kipper adds.

"The Light I possess created this place, which was before my form was created. Drawing is still not a skill of mine. I may be a goddess, but I'm still human. I don't excel at everything."

Oren chuckles at my response. I take a seat beside him.

Kipper smirks at Oren. "I'll leave you two lovebirds alone."

"Kipper!" Oren whispers bashfully. The interaction gives me the impression they were talking about me previously.

"I'll be at the banquet tables. I look forward to seeing you both in the ballroom!" Kip practically sings.

"All right, Kip!" Oren laughs, then directs his attention to me.

I smile. "I'm happy to see you both are getting along."

Oren nods hard. "I was—nervous with how things were left off between us. Thankfully, Gene had already explained the situation to Kip before we even bumped into each other."

"Yeah! Did you ever see your family, too?"

Oren nods, then laughs. "I never thought I'd see Grandma and Grandpa again. I always told myself I'd never get my childhood days back, that they were gone, my health was gone, my joy—yet then you changed everything. It was remarkable to see them again!"

I smile. "I'm so glad to hear that. How long did you all talk?"

"A good bit of the time you were away. They had a lot of

questions they asked me and my family. They eventually asked about my eyes…So, they learned that I'm not their biological grandson, which I was nervous for them to find out. Thankfully, they took it well. They were honestly surprised I was so involved with your return."

"Why were you nervous?"

"I didn't want it to put a wedge between us. I was there when Elouise's dad reunited with her and her family. Elouise introduced us and he clearly was disinterested in me. He was civil but—disinterested. I was involved with his death, so it makes sense. I was worried it would be the same with them."

"Give it time with your uncle. He spent years waiting to see his wife and kids again."

Oren nods. "I'm just happy Elouise finally got to meet him, and that they're all happy. Even if none of them wanted anything to do with me, I have you. That's all I need." He holds my hands. "Though I'm grateful for the family and friends I have, truly."

He rises, only keeping one of my hands in his grasp. My eyes pursue him. "Syann, my Goddess of Light, may I have this garden-lit dance with you?"

The music from the ballroom rings ever so faintly here. It's less crowded, but it couldn't be more perfect. "Yes," I stand up.

He brings my arm to his side while gripping my waist with the other. "I will warn you—I could use some practice."

"With dancing?"

Oren nods as we sway. "I stepped on Elly's toes a few times."

I laugh. "That's all right. After all I've been through, my toes can take it! Besides, we're not here to impress anyone."

"There are not many people to impress out here anyway."

"Kipper will be so disappointed." I smirk at Oren.

Oren shakes his head. "We have all eternity to dance in front of him. He'll be fine. I prefer dancing here anyway." He maneuvers his arms to twirl me. I giggle softly as I return to a waltzing stance.

"I'm sure all the crowds have been a big change for you."

Oren chuckles. "I've conversed with more people today than I have in my whole life. It was fun. A bit adventurous, but fun."

"I'm glad."

Oren nods. "But it's nice to have a break from it. I think this will be my favorite moment of today."

"Yeah?"

"And for once—" He leans close, smirking flirtatiously. "We're not in front of anybody."

"Then kiss me." I articulate the words slowly.

"You didn't have to ask."

His mouth crashes into mine, pressing into me in a way he never dared to kiss me before. This kiss obliterates my awareness of time and space transpiring around us. There's only us, no limitations, no injuries, and no bystanders. Our adoration harmonizes in this intimate beat, luring my mind into a state of euphoria. His fingers that cradle my face are warm like sunlight, the taste of him is chilling and invigorating like mint, and his scent is soothing, like the pages of a book you've read a million times to memorize every individual word by heart.

I yearn to memorize every fiber, every freckle of him by heart, because Oren Silvius, you are the most exquisite one of humankind, and I'll never get enough of you. My desire will never be satisfied, nor do I want it to be, because I want to relish you for all ages. And that I will. To think, this is just one moment of infinite elation I'll share with him. This sheer instant scratches the surface of the bliss ahead of us.

Who knows how long we've been kissing at this point, it doesn't matter. I'm too intoxicated by him to stand straight, so I lean into his shoulder. In that posture, we clutch each other tightly as our bodies rock back and forth.

"Oren—"

"Hmm?"

"I'd love music for us to dance to, and it's been far too long since I heard you sing. What do you think?"

Oren grins softly. "You know, there was this song about Secreth Elly used to sing to me. Back at the time, I didn't believe in this place, but something about the song always carried this peace I couldn't explain. I always looked forward to it when Elly sang it for me."

We sway to and fro, as his melodic voice ascends into tune. He sings so softly, yet with striking clarity and intent, like this song was meant exclusively for me.

A fragment of what our world used to be,
In secret, waits for you and me,
A haven without sorrows,
Or fear of tomorrow,
This realm is full of Light,

So, at night,
Look up to the stars
And remember Secreth isn't far
This is the hope we will cling to,
Until Syann returns for me and you.

One day our time will finally come
Where Secreth is where we call home
A haven without tears,
With nothing to fear,
Cause here, all is set right,

So, at night,
Look up to the stars
And remember Secreth isn't far
This is the hope we will cling to,
Until Syann returns for me and you.
Until Syann returns for me and you.

Epilogue *Oren*

The celebration of Syann's return will last seven days, but the only moment on my mind is this one—my hands rest on her waist while her hands wrap around my shoulders. Her radiant eyes, like rainbow flecks in diamonds, have my complete attention. Her pleasant humming resounds in the air. Our breaths mingle, so close we are as we dance in the garden.

I'm with her. This morning, I didn't think it was possible. Uxaar had blinded me with ideas of being worthless, weak, and undeserving of life. Thanks to Syann, I know that none of that is true. Her truth is my truth, that I'm loved, that I matter, and that I'm worth fighting for.

I finally belong. The days of being an outcast are over after eighteen years of struggles. At the time, I thought they'd never cease. Now I realize I was a hopeless fool. Thank the Light for second chances. I have a family, friends, a home, all one could ask for. It's been quite the adjustment. It's all new compared to the life I lived before. I'm like a child who needs a lot of guidance. Thankfully, this time, I don't lack it.

In the ballroom, a month later, we find ourselves lost in the dance again in a grand celebration, a long-awaited one at that. My parents are finally married after eighteen years of separation spent longing for each other.

I got to be my father's best man, while Athena was my mother's maid of honor. Arranging the wedding between us both, with much help from Elouise and Syann, was one of the most joyful projects I've participated in. Gene and Kip even helped me with a speech. I was uneasy about it at first; speaking was never my strong suit on the other side. Here it's easier, though I'm still a bit clumsy with words. That might never change.

Anyway, after the ceremony traditionally is the dance. Between Syann and me, it's slow and natural. Uxaar isn't there with any agenda. It's no trap or game played in my head. It's simply devotion, and I never have to question her love again for all my days. Thanks to Syann, I'm able to differentiate Light and Dark, neither are confused or muddled into a muddy gray. I know who I am. I know the sun will never set on the hope inside me. My Light will shine for eternity, while the shadow it casts will forever be behind me.

The end

Acknowledgments

I firstly want to thank my dear mom, for being my first fan—seriously the long explosive text you sent me after reading Oren's plot twist is still one of my favorite memories from my journey with this book. I deeply appreciate you listening to my rambles of my early concepts of this novel and waiting years to *actually* read it.

To my sister Sophie, thank you for being my only sibling who read this novel, and for being my roommate for a time. Without the solitude of our apartment, I'm unsure this novel would have seen the light of day. You've always inspired me, especially being so strong throughout the hardships you've gone through.

To my editors, Abigail Thompson and Shawna Hampton, thank you for polishing this story and helping bring it to life. I was nervous to say the least to go through the editing process the first time, but you both made the process easy for me. I deeply appreciate you both.

Thank you to my beta readers, Toria, A.C., and Kayley, for your insights and encouragement you gave me.

To my ARC reader team from book club, I love all of you and the community we have together. I can't thank y'all enough for your kindness and support.

And thank you, to the person who is reading this now, for embarking on this journey. I hope you enjoyed reading this story as much as I enjoyed writing it. If you take anything from this novel, let it be this:

"Keep going, and don't give up. As long as we live, we never run out of opportunities to start over. Every day is a new day, a new hour, a new minute, a new second, a new breath, a new chance to begin. We must learn to not let our pasts define us and focus on the Light ahead of us. If we can accomplish that, we can do anything!" -Syann

Don't give up dear reader, no matter the atrocities you've faced, there is always hope.

Lastly and most importantly, I want to thank the one I dedicated this novel too, my light among the shadows, my God. Thank you for giving me this story to tell, and these people listed who helped pave the way for this story to be printed. I owe all the thanks to you, the one who continuously pulls me out of my shadows and helping me see the light, even the times I turn my back from you.

Meet the Author

Lily B. Art debuts her first novel, full of her illustrations that inspired her love and passion for fantasy storytelling. She was born and raised in Kennesaw, Georgia, with her family: her parents, and three sisters and five little brothers.

Fiction (Fantasy especially) is practically Lily's love language. Diagnosed with Autism spectrum disorder and ADHD, she always struggled to connect with reality and the struggles that come with it. However, fiction is like the key that unlocks the passion within her, which she loves to share with others.

Her love for animation helped her find her knack for art, and since the age of fourteen she has drawn non-stop. From then on, she always knew she wanted to tell stories through her art, whether it be through novelizations, art, or animation.